D1241143

Roanoke Renegade

The Novels of Don Tracy

CHESAPEAKE CAVALIER

CRIMSON IS THE EASTERN SHORE

Roanoke Renegade

by DON TRACY

Dial Press · New York · 1954

Library of Congress Catalog Card Number: 54-10534

MANUFACTURED IN THE UNITED STATES OF AMERICA BY
THE HADDON CRAFTSMEN, INC., SCRANTON, PA.

FOR

Bill Sharpe
Lucille Purser
Aycock Brown

Part 1

1

THE TWO BARKS, *Tyger* and *Admiral*, clawed their way to the southwest, reaching for the Canary Islands and the Trade Winds they hoped would take them across the Western sea to the West Indies and, finally, to the coast of the New World, with all its boundless riches.

Tyger's captain, round-bellied Philip Amadas, dipped his quill in the inkpot and scratched a date at the top of a fresh page of the ship's journal.

MAY the 16th, 1584, and the 28th year of the Reign of Our Souvereign Queen, Elizabeth.

"God save the Queen," Amadas murmured piously, "and send perdition to all Spanish dogs."

This day, the twentieth since we sailed from Plymouth, he wrote in a phonetic hand that would be almost undecipherable to later generations, *our vessels are beset by winds and high waves.* Admiral *bespoke us at dawn and Captain Barlowe said the leak his vessel sprang and which was patched is holding fast, praise be to God. And yet I believe it would be wiser to put in to Grand Canary for a complete overhaul but our pilot, Ferdinando, will not hear of this. And we must follow Ferdinando's advice according to the commandments given us by Sir Walter Raleigh when we left London. Still, I cannot give my entire trust to the man, though he be the best pilot of the Western Sea to be found in—*

He looked up from his writing as the door of the tiny cabin

banged open. The man Amadas could not trust, Simon Ferdinando, the Portuguese (although many suspected he was really Spanish and an agent of Spain's Philip), handsome swaggerer and master pilot, entered.

Amadas frowned as he bent his head in a grudging nod. This hulking blackbeard was pilot of this expedition, the man who, through his experience in sailing the Western Sea, the knowledge of these waters gained in previous voyages, took command even over the masters of the two vessels. Granted that he held the fate of the whole venture in his hands, by his understanding of shoals and reefs, currents and wind, in unfamiliar waters, it was only mannerly, Amadas told himself peevishly, for a person to knock and await an invitation to come into the quarters of a ship's captain.

"Ho, my good Capitan," Ferdinando grinned, his teeth a white blaze against his jet spade beard, "this weather makes it sure we'll not run short of provisions, eh? Half—nay—most of the men aboard this bark are so sick at this little blow they turn green at the thought of food. And this but a gentle breeze against some winds I've seen."

"They're new at this," Amadas said curtly. "Few of them have sailed on anything but a lake or gentle river before this."

"Aye," Ferdinando chuckled, "they show that, plain enough. I had a bit of sport just now, waving a chop 'neath the noses of a few of those jelly-legged coxcombs and watching them clutch their bellies and run for the rail. Hah, I thought a couple of 'em would keep right on into the sea!"

"Now, Pilot Ferdinando," the Captain snapped, his frown deepening, "I'll not have ye makin' sport of the gentlemen aboard my vessel. Sir Walter charged me with making them as comfortable as this poor bark affords and—"

"Ah, a spot of hazing won't harm 'em mortally," the Portuguese shrugged. He crossed the cabin, balancing himself expertly against the pitch and roll of the deck, and dropped unbidden on a chest set against the further bulkhead. "Nay, it'd be a good thing to toughen 'em some before they meet what's waiting for them on the other side of the Western Sea. If they blanch at a bit of pickled pork now, what will they when they meet a howling savage?"

Amadas kept his eyes on the journal as he sanded the unfinished entry and slapped shut the well-worn leather covers.

"Methinks you have two stories to tell about the New World, sir," he said carefully. "One time you speak of a fair, gentle country with peaceful natives. The next you warn of a wild place peopled by shrieking devils. I was there, remember, when you told Sir Walter that you had visited lands so rich in furs and fruit and such that no Englishmen could believe it, with the natives so amiable that they burdened every visitor with gifts."

"And that is true," Ferdinando said. His smile stiffened as he kept his heavy-browed stare on the Captain. "And sir, I don't like the suggestion that I'm a liar in aught I say."

Amadas met the other's eyes squarely. He was undersized, and mild-mannered for a sea captain, but he was not a man to be intimidated by this arrogant adventurer or anyone else.

"I meant no slur," he said quietly. "I'm only pointing out that you said all this. Now you say we're due to meet howling savages when we touch the shore we're bound for. How do you fit one story with the other, Pilot Ferdinando?"

The black-bearded man held his glare for a long moment and then relaxed against the bulkhead with a light laugh. He fixed his eyes on the leather lanthorn that swung from the low beamed ceiling and hooked his thumbs in his wide belt, thrust out his rough-booted legs in a careless sprawl. The sword he was never without clacked against the chest with his movement; his salt-stained canvas breeches rasped as he shifted on the chest.

"I'll tell ye, Capitan," he boomed, with self-assurance that just missed contempt. "The land we sail to, that I'll take ye to, has all the riches I've spoken of and peaceful natives, too. But this is no England ye sail for. 'Tis a land as untouched as England was a thousand-score years ago, mayhap. The natives are full of whims. They worship strange gods. They see omens in a rain squall, a flight of birds, a tree struck by lightning."

He reached a long-fingered, black-nailed hand out to slosh half a mug of ale from the captain's own small cask, lashed to a cradle set in the bulkhead.

"By y'r gracious leave," Ferdinando grinned and drank. Amadas's features tightened and he choked back the words that struggled to be said. *Sir Walter bade us on no account to anger this fellow,* he reminded himself, *though I know he could not dream how hard a duty he gave us!* He forced himself to nod the ignored invitation. The spade-bearded man wiped the back of his hand across his mouth and sank back in his lounging sprawl.

"And so, Capitan," he went on, "I spoke truth when I told Raleigh the natives were friendly gift-bearers and I speak truth now when I say they're howling savages—it depends on their whim of the moment, y'see. Aye, the Spanish have learned that lesson well enough! When I was last in Florida, I heard of many a proud gentleman who scorned the natives as cowardly fools because they seemed so spineless. So, when the savages' whim changed, he lost his haughty life, nor did his blade or armor or matchlock harquebus save him."

The pilot rose from the chest and stretched, yawning cavernously.

"Aye, Capitan," he said, " 'twill be best to be careful with the natives—exceeding careful—when we reach those strange shores." His smile twisted as he added: "And best, too, that all your company heed what I say to do. I'm no courtier, I confess, and mayhap lack pretty manners, but, c'ld be that my rude advice will save y'r necks, no matter that I'm no knight or baron or even a ship's captain, but just a mere pilot."

" 'Tis not that we—" Amadas began uncomfortably.

"I know, I know," Ferdinando interrupted with a wave of his hand. "And now I'd best to the deck and oversee my duties, earn my pay. We should raise the peaks of Tenerife today, by my reckoning, and I'd not sail too close to Philip's war carracks."

He bowed—was it mockingly?—and left the cabin. Philip Amadas heard the pilot's boots clump across the deck to the ladder leading to the poop and clatter astern toward the helm. His brow was creased as he looked at the door.

Was he getting old and touchy, he asked himself, that he let a man's lack of manners outweigh his proven excellence as a pilot? When Sir Walter had engaged him and Captain Barlowe for this voyage, he had half considered refusing the commission until

Raleigh had told him that the best pilot to be found, Simon Ferdinando, would be along. Arthur Barlowe, Amadas knew, shared none of the distrust of the Portuguese that he, Amadas, held but maybe that was because Ferdinando did not sail with Barlowe but aboard the *Tyger*.

Amadas murmured, "Aye, two days of bearing him and even that cold fish Barlowe would be touchy."

The close quarters of a bark of a hundred and twenty tons burthen perforce rubbed men together overmuch and it was too easy for an irritation to become a festering sore. As Master of the lead vessel, Amadas had never been far out of the sound of Ferdinando's vexing voice or his smile that was wide enough, God knew, but which never seemed far from a snarl.

"And still," the little captain nodded, "what Ferdinando said was true—all too true."

Ferdinando, alone of all the company had ever seen the New World, he alone knew what to expect there and—pray God—how to deal with it. Even Raleigh had never been there; he had tried for New Found Land with his half-brother, Sir Humphrey Gilbert, but had been turned back by raging storms. Yes, Ferdinando was right when he said his rude advice might save all their necks.

"And so," the shipmaster murmured aloud, " 'tis my duty to Sir Walter, to my passengers, to myself—aye, even the Queen—to make my peace with the hairy bastard, gripe my guts though it might. And I'd best get a start at sweetening him now, with a smile and a friendly clap on the shoulder to show him Philip Amadas loves him like a brother—hah!"

He pushed aside the journal with a sigh of relief at the excuse to get away from the labor of quill and inkpot that he hated (but Raleigh had charged him with keeping an exact record of the voyage and Amadas, like a good many Englishmen in the year 1584, would have leapt into the sea if Sir Walter had ordered it). Amadas wedged himself out from behind the tiny table, bolted to the deck. His stubby legs carried him out of the cabin and up the ladder to the poopdeck, the captain bracing himself against the vessel's motion.

At the top of the ladder he grunted a curse as he heard a wind-tattered flurry of harsh words, raised in furious argument, the scuffle of feet, the screep and scrape of tempered steel.

Amadas flung himself across the deck, bawling frantic orders. "Now hold, sirs—hold I say! You, Pilot—you, Master Harvie! Put up y'r blades!"

The heavily bearded Portuguese and the red-hosed young man who faced Ferdinando ignored the shipmaster. Cat-footed, the big pilot and the gorgeously clothed gentleman circled, their swords flickering, touching, testing.

"Hold!" Amadas cried. "*I command it!* By the Christ, I'll charge ye both with mutiny do ye not hold!"

He flung himself between the pair with reckless disregard of the two-edged blades that were crossed between Ferdinando and the young gentleman. Amadas shoved violently at the slighter swordsman, a lurch of the bark aided him, and the man called Harvie staggered back against the rail, the point of his rapier dropping as he clutched for support.

Ferdinando, his lips tight over his white teeth, made a half step in Harvie's direction and then stopped, lowering his sword slowly, his hot eyes staring beyond the fuming Amadas at the man who had drawn against him.

"Hold Ferdinando," the captain panted again. "By Heav'n, I'll—"

"Let him come on!" grated the young man against the rail. "It'd please me to trim his beard for him, the mangy—"

"Aye, stand aside, Captain," Ferdinando said, his voice easy, almost pleasant. "We'll soon find out if this cockerel can use a blade half so nimbly as he uses his tongue." As Amadas spluttered, the Portuguese summoned a clipped laugh and returned his blade to its ring on the wide leather belt. "Oh, quiet yourself, sir," the black-bearded pilot smiled. "I'll not harm this twig, I pledge you. But let him stay out of my way—and tell his fuzz-cheeked lordship I'm not to be treated like one of his scullions back in England."

He laughed again and turned on his heel to stalk toward the helmsman, who had been gawking at the scene with popped eyes. Amadas whirled to clutch the arm of Harvie as the young man started after Ferdinando, his lean face livid, his tongue twisted by his rage, his slight frame trembling.

"Fuzz-cheeked—cockerel—by God, I'll show him—"

"Ye'll put up y'r weapon, Master Dion Harvie," Captain Amadas snapped, "or I'll have ye thrown in chains! I mean this! Aye, I'd let you rot in the hold rather than have you ruin this expedition!"

"That bastard—"

"I care not what he did! Ye're aboard my vessel only 'cause Sir Walter ordered it, and at the last minute, too—I had no commandment from Raleigh or anybody else that ye be let brawl and riot here, sir! You were to obey orders, like everybody else, and my orders are to put up y'r blade—*and now*—and go below!"

Dion Harvie cast one last glare at Simon Ferdinando, standing by the helmsman, and then slowly, grudgingly, returned his rapier to its ring. He looked down at the shorter Amadas and shook his head, the dark curls brushing his blue cloak at the shoulders.

"Captain," he said, his voice quieted, "y'r pardon, I beg you. I—I had resolved to hold my devil's temper in check, in keeping with what I promised Sir Walter, but he provoked me past the bearing of it, I vow! He—"

"Go below, Master Dion," Amadas said again. "I'll speak with ye later about this. And till I do, ye'll stay off the deck."

Harvie grimaced as he nodded.

"Aye," he sighed, "but there's a powerful stink down there and vermin that'll chew y'r boots off, if ye're not on guard every minute. Not"—he hastened to add—"that y'r vessel's not a fine ship, Captain Amadas—the finest I've ever sailed the Western Sea in, I can truly say."

The rotund Captain put up a hand to brush his moustaches and hide his smile. This young man's compliment of the *Tyger* he told himself, would be worth more if Dion Harvie had ever sailed on anything beyond some Thames River pleasure barge but —well, the lad was a handsome, friendly young man, eager to do what he was bidden, not forever complaining as some of the gentlemen did, a pleasant man to have aboard, saving this one brush with the pilot.

And, he added silently, Simon Ferdinando *was* a—

"Land, ho!"

The cry floated down from the masthead and as all eyes swung up to the lookout the man pointed a hand to the southwest. Captain Amadas left Dion Harvie and hurried to the side of the spade-bearded Portuguese. Ferdinando lowered the hand shading his eyes and nodded with a smile that edged a smirk.

" 'Tis the peaks of Tenerife," he told Amadas, "as I calculated and at the time I calculated. Few men alive could make so nice a reckoning—ye'll give me that?"

"Aye," Captain Amadas said, with sincere admiration. "To make a landfall on the hip in such weather, with these winds and seas, is fair wondrous, Pilot Ferdinando."

"Even though I be no gentleman?" the Portuguese asked, with smiling malice. "Even though y'r young friend, Harvie, calls me mangy?"

He widened his smile in the face of the Captain's confusion and Amadas lost his admiration abruptly.

"Our course is to be changed at once?" he asked curtly. Ferdinando cast him another heavy-lidded glance before he turned to study the dot on the horizon that marked the most westerly island of the Canaries.

"Another turn of the hour glass will be time enough," he said, at length. "There's a current further inshore that'll swing us into the Trade Winds, our fortune holding, and in this weather Philip's carracks will be huddled in Santa Cruz de Tenerife. The Spanish won't spy us out from that far south—also, our fortune holding."

He turned back to Captain Amadas.

"That young coxcomb I had words with a moment back," he said, nodding toward the waist of the bark. "I heard you call him Harvie but I do not remember the name being on the sailing lists Raleigh went over with you and Barlowe and me."

Amadas looked down at the waist deck, crowded now with sailors and gentlemen, all straining for a glimpse of the land cried by the lookout. As the captain watched, he saw Dion Harvie glance up at the poop, meet his eye, shrug apologetically and head for the hatch that led to the foul-smelling hold.

"He joined the company late, at Plymouth," Amadas told Ferdinando, briefly.

"These strange ones who scramble aboard a vessel a minute before it sails," the Portuguese said thoughtfully, "are often interesting. Mayhap this dauncey Master Harvie had pressing need to take sudden leave of England, eh?"

"No," Captain Amadas said stoutly. "No, he is a dear friend of Sir Walter and had plagued Raleigh for weeks to be let join the expedition. But because he was so young, Sir Walter hesitated until, at the last clock-tick, he gave in. So you see there was no midnight alarums to do with any of this."

Simon Ferdinando's teeth gleamed in his beard.

"I see," he grinned, and the words might well have been: *You lie!*

2

HARDLY HAD THE signal pennants reached the *Tyger's* masthead, bidding the following *Admiral* to change course, when a howling gale swept down out of the northwest, battering the two barks dangerously close to Tenerife and the Spaniards who, Ferdinando had warned, would give ships and men a warm welcome—too warm.

Drenched by the seas that broke over the taffrail, the big Portuguese and the pudgy Englishman, Philip Amadas, clung to the rudder whipstaff, squinting ahead into the rain curtain that was rent by the wind now and again to show the island looming larger. Both barks wallowed under bare sticks now; even the topsails had been chewed up when the storm clouds had boiled over the horizon. The few crewmen on deck huddled under the protection of the high bulwarks, soaked to the skin, shivering from cold and terror. The others, sailors and gentlemen, were below and hardly less wet than the men on deck; water sluiced through loosened caulkings with each pounding wave.

"We're sure to strike!" Amadas yelled, cupping his hand at Ferdinando's ear to be heard over the wail of the storm. "Unless we run for the passage to Santa Cruz, we're lost!"

The Portuguese shook his head violently. He brushed the water from his eyes and turned his white, savage grin on the Captain.

"I know these seas, Senhor," he roared back, "and I know these skies! I say this blow will end as quickly as it began. If we keep afloat, this will clear before we strike! The pumps, good Capitan—break their backs at the pumps!"

Below deck, gentlemen in bedraggled finery worked side by side with ragged seamen, manning the two wheezing, panting pumps that struggled against disheartening odds to keep the hold's water level from creeping too high. Others worked at moving the spoilable provisions to higher places, a dangerous task with the ship's tossing.

Among the men who labored at the pumps toiled Dion Harvie, son of Sir Clement Harvie, Lord Avronbeck, who ranked with Burghley and Walsingham in the counsels of Queen Elizabeth. He looked like no lord's son now. He had been one of the first of the gentlemen to leap to the rusty pump-shafts when the order had come screaming down from the deck: "Pump away, all, if ye'd live!" and he was still bending his wide-shouldered back to the muscle-wrenching, palm-blistering bar nearly two hours later, without more than a moment's respite.

He was past weariness; he was wrapped in a haze of agony. The pains in his legs, his arms, his back, had spread until they were joined in one mass of stabbing torture. Each breath was a sob and each sob bespoke a knifethrust in his side, his lungs, his groin. His long hair, grown lank with sweat and the spume of the gurgling pump, fell over his face as he bent, whipped back as he straightened, his head upthrust, straining for another gulp of air before he bent again.

Foul water sloshed about his shins, almost to his knees; bits of refuse nudged his legs. His hose had once been described by a lady as a second skin, so free of wrinkles as they always were; now the silken leg coverings drooped about his ankles and bagged at the knees; somehow the young man had ripped a great gash in the thigh of the left one and an ugly scratch leaked droplets of blood that persisted in oozing, no matter how often the wound was laved by the evil-smelling bilgewater.

The satin slashed galligaskins and the velvet doublet had made Dion Harvie a pretty picture when he had faced Simon Ferdinando on the poop deck a short time before. Now they had been reduced to stained and ripped rags. His cloak was gone, his hat was gone, and the rapier with the jeweled hilt was gone, all flung aside in his rush for the pump.

As wracked by pain as he was, as stunned by exhaustion, Dion Harvie still summoned an inner grin as he thought of what he must look like. Because he had been called a witless fop whose only concern was that his ruff be wider than the next man's and his perfume sweeter, he had lost his temper and had used his sword. And because of that—aye, and a few other things—he was where he was now, in the stinkingest hole, certainly, there was to be found on land or sea anywhere, fair killing himself at a task that looked more hopeless with every stroke of the worn and rusted pump.

He levered the bar once more and looked up as there was no answering push on the other side. The man who had been pumping with him for the past quarter hour, a broken-nosed, crop-eared crewman named Joseph, surely recruited from the shadow of the Tyburn gallows as most seamen were, staggered back from the pump, sloshing his way toward the ladder that led to the deck.

"We'll die like rats here!" Joseph growled. " 'Tis only folly to stay below! The vessel's sure to sink and here we'd perish without a chance! To the deck! There, we'll have a chance, at least, to cling to a spar if we're lucky. To the deck!"

"Hold!" Dion croaked. "By God's eyeballs, man, ye're tossing away y'r only chance! Keep at the pumps, I say!"

The flat-nosed man turned and spat a curse at Harvie, then made for the ladder again. The others in the hold, the terrified gentlemen and seamen, began wading after Joseph.

Dion's eyes searched for a weapon and found none. His glance fell to the rusty pump-bar his hands clenched in a paralyzed hold —aye, the thing fitted into a socket and could be pulled free! He heaved at it and as it came loose he raised it over an aching shoulder. He made for the ladder—Christ, this bilgewater was like thick mud!—and staggered up to Joseph just as the sailor was reaching for a rung to lift himself toward the streaming hatch.

"Get back, y'dog!" Harvie gasped. "Get back or I'll—"

The seaman flung a backhand blow with his free hand. Dion caught the knuckles over his eye and swayed. Then, as the bark lurched again, he pitched forward, bringing the heavy pump-bar down in a merciless sweep that caught Joseph across the nape of the neck. The crack could be heard over the torturous groaning of the ship's timbers. The sailor slumped lifelessly into the littered swamp of the bilge as Dion forced himself to turn and face the others who were fighting their way to the ladder.

"And any of you—aye, you too, Petman—who leave y'r duty here will get the same!" he panted. "Back to the pumps or I'll split y'r skulls as I split his! Back to the pumps!"

One of the gentlemen, Nicholas Petman, had kept his rapier at his waist through all this hurly-burly. It flashed free now—and went spinning as Dion swung the pump-bar to hammer it before it had made its first lunge.

"That for y'r blade!" Dion rasped. "The next will be for y'r neck! Back to the pumps, I say!"

They faced him, four gentlemen and half a dozen seamen, for the space of ten breathless seconds, urged by their panic to dare the murderous sweep of the iron bar, overruled by the wild glare of the drenched madman who guarded the ladder, the sight of the limp figure who floated face-down in the kneedeep water.

Slowly, sullenly, they turned and waded back to the two pumps.

One of the rust-coated, wornout machines began its creaky laboring. Dion staggered to the second pump and refitted the handle that had served him in this affair better than the finest Toledo blade he had ever worn. His teeth clenched over his lower lip, he resumed his wracking task.

Time passed—whether hours, minutes or seconds Dion would never know—and the pumps clanked on, the water crept higher, the bark heaved in spasms that surely would be death throes in the next moment—and then, as suddenly as it had come, the storm passed.

On deck, their hands clenched to the rudder whipstaff, Philip Amadas and Simon Ferdinando watched the miracle. The rain ceased as abruptly as though a pail had been emptied, finally; the black sky gave way to brilliant sunshine, the wind still squealed in the rigging and the waves still threw their white talons at *Tyger* but the fury of the gale and the vicious anger of the seas was spent. And the combers of the Tenerife shore still thundered more than three miles away.

The Portuguese smiled down at Amadas and said something in his native tongue, then translated it for the chubby captain.

"It was a near thing, that," he laughed. "For a moment, I confess I feared that Simon Ferdinando had been outwitted by this sea."

"God's blood," Amadas muttered. "A near thing, you say! Another minute and we'd—"

The black-bearded pilot chuckled. "But we're not, Senhor! Look you, the other bark's still afloat, we've not struck, the wind is turning as it always does behind one of these blows and in our favor. So, good Capitan, 'tis time to put on every rag we have, topsails, main course and sprits, and get us out of here before Philip's deerhounds catch our scent, eh?"

"Aye!" Amadas nodded. He cupped his hands to bellow at the seamen who clung to their places at the bulwarks.

"All hands!" he boomed. "All hands to sail, save eight f'r the pumps. All gentlemen to hale and draw. Be lively, now!"

The seamen reluctantly left their shelters and scrambled across the deck to the rigging. One of them lifted the hatch and yelled down into the hold. One by one, the sailors and gentlemen crawled up to the rain-slicked deck, blinking in the sunlight that was dazzling after the gloom of the hold.

"Boatswain!" Amadas shouted. "Send me Joseph to the rudder!"

The *Tyger's* boatswain, a crease-faced bull of a man who wore a red yarn stocking cap pulled down over his shaven poll, tilted his face toward the poopdeck as he shook his head.

"Be'ant he ain't wi' us!" he yelled. "Dead, he is."

"Dead?" Amadas asked. "Went overboard, ye mean?"

"Nay, Cap'n. Be'ant he got himself killed below by a young gentleman."

"Killed? By a—who killed Joseph, Boatswain?"

"For the love of the dear Christ," Simon Ferdinando gutteralled, "*let us make sail!* Y'think the Spaniards'll dally a fortnight before they set out to see what we're about?"

Amadas jerked himself back to his duties as master and began shouting orders. With the gentlemen "haling and drawing," which meant working at the side of the seamen again, the blue-grey canvas of the main course was unclewed and then the spritsails and topsails, yellow on the bark *Tyger,* green on the *Admiral,* were shaped as the two vessels' canvas gratefully took the Trade Winds that sped them away from the menacing coast of the Canary Islands.

"Aye," the spade-bearded pilot grunted, "I've done it." He put up a blunt-fingered hand to touch the pearl pendant that hung from his left earlobe and nodded. "Aye, Simon Ferdinando was called an ill-born mongrel by Ranuccio, the Duke of Palma, that man who loved his woman in strange ways. But this same Ferdinando has brought his vessels through a tempest that would have confounded Drake and Hawkins and all the other great mariners that live! Some day his name—"

He broke off, conscious of Amadas' stare, and gave his short laugh.

"And you, Capitan," he said, "you asked the boatswain what gentleman killed your man, Joseph, below decks? Here's my purse"—he dug beneath the broad belt to extract a heavy pouch—"that says it was my young friend of the scarlet hose and the pretty face, the cockerel you named Harvie—ah, a very good friend of Sir Walter, I know—who ran your man through with his blade, mayhap because the fellow vexed him by asking him to work a pump."

Amadas ran a hand over his scrubby beard and shook his head.

"Nay," he said, "I'm certain Master Harvie would never—" He walked to the rail of the poop and shouted down at the boatswain. "I asked ye who killed Joseph," he yelled. "Why didn't ye tell me?"

"Aye, sir," the man in the stocking cap replied, "I would've but ye ordered up the sheets and I—sir, 'twas the young gentleman that came aboard at Plymouth, Master Harvie."

Ferdinando tossed his coin pouch in the air, caught it on a wide palm and chuckled as he restored it to his belt.

"You see?" he asked. "Never wager with Simon Ferdinando."

Philip Amadas swung on his pilot with a furious gesture.

"Have done!" he grated. "I know the lad's no murderer! If he killed Joseph there must have been some good cause for it."

"Like saying only a popinjay would wear crimson hose aboard a ship?" Ferdinando asked idly. "That's what drew his blade on me."

"No—no, there must be more, I vow! Boatswain!"

"Aye, sir."

"Summon Master Harvie to the deck here."

The weatherbeaten officer tugged at his nose for a moment, started for the hatchway and turned back.

"Cap'n, sir, he's at the pumps," he offered.

"Summon him here!" Amadas repeated sharply.

"Aye, sir," the boatswain nodded, "but—the young gentleman—he saved us all, he did! He kept us at the pumps—ye see, Joseph—well, Joseph went mad along with all the rest of us, poor mariners and fine gentlemen alike, and when Joseph fled the pumps, screamin' we'd all perish, we rushed after him, each man willin' to kill the next to gain the ladder. And—and the young gentleman, Master Harvie, he—he snatched up a pump handle and he—"

The boatswain waggled his hands in his desperate groping for words, then looked up at the poopdeck again.

"If we'd followed Joseph, Cap'n, there'd been nobody at the pumps and we'd sunk, for certain. But Master Harvie dealt Joseph a blow that kilt him outright and the rest of us, we—we came to our senses, summat, and went back to our work."

His wrinkled face took on the look of a pleading hound.

"Pray Jesus," he added, "ye'll not charge him with murder f'r what he did."

Amadas shook his balding head, still bedewed by the rain and spray.

"Nay," he said. "I mean to commend the young gentleman for his excellence, if it's as you say."

"Aye, sir," bobbled the crease-faced man in the stocking cap. "Ye'll hear the same tale from all of us who were there, with naught added or taken away, I pledge ye."

He hastened to the hatch and disappeared down the ladder. Amadas turned to Simon Ferdinando. The pilot was lounging against the taffrail, using the dirk that balanced the sword in his belt to pare his grimy nails.

"You see?" the pudgy Englishman said. "I vowed Master Harvie would be right in this matter when it was explained, and so he is."

Ferdinando nodded, intent on his manicure, then looked up, a heavy eyebrow arching.

"Yes, good my Capitan," he smiled. "I accept my error in the affair of the pretty Master Harvie and the unfortunate Joseph. Aye, Master Harvie is a hero who saved us all from the sea serpents. But does that mean I lose my wager? Did he kill poor Joseph less dead because he slew him in saving this vessel?"

"We made no wager," Amadas said angrily. Ferdinando's eye fell to his knife and then rose again.

"So we did not," he said, tranquilly, "but mayhap we can make one now. What part of your purse will you risk, Senhor, in a bet that Master Dion Harvie, fourth son of Lord Avronbeck—ah, you see I know certain things—don't bring grief to this expedition?"

His voice hardened as the spade beard jutted.

"What will you risk, Captain Amadas, that this firebrand won't bring us trouble, as he's brought trouble to Milord Avronbeck and Milady and his sisters and his half-brothers—ah, especially his brother Charles who has a pretty wife—and to every man who's tried to call him friend? What do you wager on that, good Capitan?"

"Not a groat," rasped a voice from behind the two men. "Not half a groat—else he'd be a reckless gambler."

3

THE TWO MEN swung their heads to stare at the figure who wavered at the head of the ladder, clinging to the rail with either hand.

"Master Harvie!" Amadas exclaimed when he found his voice. "Pray sit ye down—ye look close to fainting! Here, sir, let me—"

"This'll do," Ferdinando said quietly. He gently lowered Dion to a coil of ship's line. Then, as though ashamed of this brief show of graciousness, the Portuguese straightened and laughed down at the drenched wretch who sat before him.

"And how do you like life at sea now, Senhor Harvie?" he jibed. "A bit at odds, I'll wager, with what you thought, eh? No mermaids with green teats, no great adventures falling one upon the other, no gold guineas to be scooped from each passing wave. Nay, 'stead of that, there's man's work to be done aboard a vessel, ye've learned! A pump must be worked, a sail must be clewed, a rudder must be tended, a ship must be gentled like one of the colts y'r father has at Avronbeck Hall."

Dion raised a blistered hand to push aside the dark hair that masked his haggard eyes. He looked up into the bronzed, hawk-beaked face of the pilot and twisted his bloodless lips in a grimace.

"Avronbeck Hall?" he asked huskily. "My half-brother Charles? My mother, my father—it seems, sir, that you know a deal more of me than I do of you."

Despite the sway of the deck, Ferdinando made an ironic leg, sweeping his right hand across his broad chest.

"Let us say," he offered pleasantly, "that no one who's been in England beyond a fortnight can have helped hearing of Master Dion Harvie and his gracious family."

Dion's bristled chin sank to his breast, then jerked up again. He made a brief struggle to get to his feet but sank back to the coil of rope, unable to stand.

"I've heard a bit of you, too, Ferdinando," he said in a measured voice. "I've heard—"

"And now ye'd best be abed!" Philip Amadas broke in. "Ye've worked y'r share and past it, Master Harvie, and nobody could say you weren't deserving of a bit of sleep. Your quarters are soaked, I'll warrant, but you can have my cabin till—"

"A moment, by y'r leave," Dion interrupted. His eyes stayed fixed on Ferdinando's.

"You knew me well, Sir Pilot," he said slowly. "Mayhap too well for the health of both of us."

The black-bearded man widened his smile still further as he nodded.

"Mayhap I do," he agreed calmly.

"Now, now sirs," Amadas broke in hurriedly. "We'll have no more of this cock o' hoop fencing betwixt the two of ye, I command! Pilot Ferdinando, you heard the boatswain say this young gentleman saved our vessel! Master Harvie, I'd have ye know—aye, I say it m'self—that what you did below decks by stopping the mutiny at the pumps was matched and more than matched by Pilot Ferdinando's work here above. So then, were it not for the both of ye, we'd be at the bottom of the sea at this minute. Ye're heroes both—without one, the other would have perished, without the other, the one would have drowned. So make y'r peace, I say, for many a long league is ahead of us and only the gentle Jesus knows what dangers lie in wait. The success of this expedition—aye, all our lives, I vow!—depend on harmony amongst us. So you, friend Simon, and you, friend Dion, do ye now have done with y'r dislike and be ye friends!"

He put a broad hand on Dion's shoulder and looked appealingly at the Portuguese.

"Come, sirs," he said earnestly, "won't ye both give y'r hand to it? If not for my sake, then for Sir Walter's—even for the Queen's? You both know what we have at stake, furtherance of the Queen's realm and confusion to the Spaniards—is your private quarrel worth risking the success of this?"

There was a taut silence on the poopdeck for a moment and then Ferdinando took a step closer to the young man who sat on the coil of the rope. The black-bearded pilot thrust out a hand, palm up, toward Dion Harvie.

"Our honorable captain's right," he said quietly. "My hand on it that I'd be y'r friend, will ye have me for one. If I've said aught to injure your feelings, sir, I withdraw the words and ask your pardon. I'm a seafarer, and too often given to rough words."

Dion hesitated and then laid his blistered, broken-nailed hand over the pilot's.

Philip Amadas let out his breath in a gusty sigh.

"Now there's the way two hale fellows be!" he exulted. "Handsomely said, Sir Pilot, and handsomely replied to, Master Harvie!" He clapped both men on the shoulder and laughed aloud in his relief. "Aye, now things are as they should be," he continued. "Fair winds and good friends give a vessel what she's meant to have." He glanced aloft, his honest, homely face alight. "Tight canvas and the storm over—so it's ho for the New World and the great good fortune that awaits us all there!"

4

That night, with the Trade Winds holding firm and with Tenerife dropping astern, Dion Harvie stood on the foredeck of the bark, his arms folded along the bulwark, his eyes fixed on the foam-laced darkness that lay ahead.

Above him, the sails boomed and the lines twanged, from beneath his feet came the never-ending protest of straining timbers as *Tyger* heaved and bucked her way onward. Dion did not hear the chantey sung by the sails and lines nor the complaint of the timbers; he did not feel the pitching of the deck. Dion Harvie was leagues away from Captain Amadas' stout little vessel. He was back in England—Avronbeck Hall, London, Hampton Court Palace, his father, his mother and his sisters, his three half-brothers, Charles and Blount and Adam, and Charles's wife, Helen—ah, sweet Helen of the tender lips and great round eyes!

Sweet, foolish Helen—but what woman wouldn't cast her wits to the winds when her sour-faced husband's well-favored half-brother whispered in her ear? Dion hunched his cape closer about his shoulders and grinned into the night.

Nay, he told himself, don't blame Helen for what had happened nor blame him for making it happen. If it had started out to be no more than a neat way of avenging himself on Charles for all the indignities, the humilities, that long-faced pizzleheaded eldest son had heaped on him, it had turned out to be a delightful dalliance. Aye, Helen had learned her lessons well—but then, she had been an eager scholar for his brand of teaching, doubly interesting after Charles's dusty rote.

That it was morally wrong that he should have coveted and

covered his half-brother's wife had never entered Dion Harvie's mind. In Elizabeth's England, a woman was a woman, wife or maid, and except she was in close family relationship she was something to be wooed, skillfully or bluntly as her station deserved, and, if possible, won. And the winning seldom was too arduous a task for any purposeful man.

No, Dion had no doubts about the moral aspects of his conquest of his half-brother's wife, if only because the morals of his day did not obtain in this instance. A gentleman did not steal; Dion had not stolen, unless claiming Helen's love from Charles could be called stealing and how could one be robbed of something he never had owned? A gentleman did not cheat at dice; no dice had been involved. A gentleman did not boast about his conquests; Dion had kept his lips tight shut. A gentleman did not relieve himself in the sight of ladies, he did not beat his servants without cause, he did not abscond with money entrusted to his keeping, he did not forge another's name, he did not let an insult go unanswered, he did not seduce the wife or daughter of his immediate host—Dion Harvie had done none of these things, *ergo*, he was still the Elizabethan gentleman.

In fact—and he felt quite smugly virtuous about this—he had proved himself strait-laced in at least one thing. There was Blount's wife, namby-pamby Caroline, who had seemed to be always underfoot every time he stayed at Avronbeck Hall, her eyes sidling at him, her tail switching provocatively, but he had kept hands off her. Blount was not much better than Charles—given the power vested in the eldest son he might prove worse—but Dion had felt no great need for revenge on the dough-faced Blount. And, besides, there was always the thought that having two of his sweetlings living in the same house would require a bit finer touch than even he possessed, lest they be at each other's throat and at him, bringing the whole house down about his ears.

So there were no regrets connected with his thoughts of the affair with Helen as he stared at the dark sea that stretched the many leagues toward the West Indies. He scowled now at the bad luck that had crossed his path with the man Groven's at the wrong time.

For Charles had found out, not definitely enough to bring Helen the torture only a man like Charles could think up for her but surely enough to send him squealing to his father, Sir Clement. It had been like Charles that he would go to Lord Avronbeck rather than seek out Dion himself, but Dion guessed his eldest half-brother had always been afraid of him, sneer at him though he might.

Sir Clement was an indulgent father where his youngest son was concerned. There was so much of Sir Clement in Dion and so much of Sir Clement's first wife—ah, she must have been a frozen bitch!—in his three other sons that he had spoiled Dion from the cradle.

"The lad has overmuch spirit," he was wont to say whenever the story of another of Dion's scrapes reached him, "but so did I, at his age. He'll quiet with the years, as I did."

Sir Clement's quieting could never be called a complete desertion of the lustier side of life for the staid precincts of the elders. At sixty-three he was a straight-backed, high-chinned, quick-bladed denial of the maxim of the day: "To be past fifty is to be but unburied." Handsome with his mane of white hair and his silvery pointed beard, as fashionable as the youngest courtier in his raiment, Sir Clement still had a ready pinch for the behind of any likely-looking serving wench. He had more than a pinch for a lady who might challenge him to prove he was as young in other things as he was in his speech, his manner, the way he rode a horse and drank and danced and dressed and fought.

If it had been possible, Dion knew, Sir Clement would have brushed this complaint of Charles's aside with some homily about youth deserving forbearance in its trifling errors, but even the indulgent father could not condone the cuckoldry of one son by another, no matter if the offender was his favorite.

While Charles had stood at one side, trembling in impotent rage, Dion's father had paced up and down in front of the huge stone fireplace in the great hall of Avronbeck, his hands clasped behind his back, his mouth pursed, his shaggy brows lowered thunderously. Dion had waited, his uneasiness growing. Now he had done it at last; his father's patience had reached its limits, finally, and woe betide him when Sir Clement unleashed the fury for which he was famous!

"I can't believe," Lord Avronbeck had said at last, in a voice that whipcracked through the high-ceilinged hall. "I can't believe that what I hear is true. Nay, 'tis idle gossip! There's a thousand whispers in Avronbeck Hall for every inch of the place—always have been! They have me laying with some peasant trull or scullion a dozen times a day!"

"Sire," Charles began, "I must—"

"Silence! I'm not done yet!" He had whirled on Dion. "I'll not ask ye the truth of this," he had continued. "As a gentleman ye'd lie about it even if 'twere true—which I know 'tis not! Some villain sees you exchange a smile, a word, with your brother's wife and then it's started. And I'll not have it!"

"No, sire," Dion had murmured, quietly.

"And so ye'll ride up to London in the morning," his father had ordered, "and there ye'll stay till I send for you. And ye'll attend me in this! *Ye'll stay out of trouble!* Another son would know his father holds whatever position I do in court on an exceeding thin thread, as do all who're close to the throne. I have my share of enemies—mayhap more than my share—and I'd not have them pointing their finger at me and crying: 'What's this, what's this? Milord Avronbeck advise Her Majesty and yet he can't control his rakehell son?' Aye, they've done it in the past and I've cried them down by saying you were a mere boy. Well, ye're eighteen now and a man and, by God's eyeballs, I'll not have ye ruining me with y'r excursions!"

He stood for a moment with his hands on his hips as he glared at his youngest son.

"Ye'll behave y'rself," he said, "and ye'll pick no quarrels with anyone. Ye'll mind that temper of yours if ye have to grind y'r teeth to do it! Ye'll watch y'r ways with the ladies and ye'll leave the dice and wine alone. If I hear one word of you being in any kind of trouble I'll haul ye back here to Avronbeck by the scruff of y'r neck and hand ye over to Charles as his clerk, I swear!"

Dion had shuddered briefly.

"Now bid ye farewell to y'r mother and y'r sisters and get ready to ride to London at the dawn," his father had ended abruptly.

"I must say, sire," Charles had put in whiningly, "you seem overgentle with this young knave. Is it all ye'd do to him, just send him—"

"And what would you?" Sir Clement had roared, wheeling on his eldest son. "Ye'd have me whip him out of Avronbeck Hall, mayhap, or string him up on a gibbet? Even if y'r story were true—and it's not—any man who can't so enchain his wife in love, as I have Milady, that she'd not look at another man almost deserves what he gets!" He had turned back to Dion. "And now begone," he had commanded.

So Dion had bade his goodbyes to his beautiful, gentle-voiced mother who had accepted his banishment calmly, having grown to expect such surprises in the son she had named Dionysus, after that merry god of wine. After that, he had said farewell to his two sisters, Elizabeth and Joan, who were as beautiful as their mother but given to tears on all occasions, sad or joyful, and on the next morning he had ridden up to London.

He had followed his father's orders, too, barely stirring from his lodgings except to dine two or three times with his closest friend, Sir Walter Raleigh, and, of course, to visit a tailor or two as was necessary to keep in the mode. He went to the Hampton Palace Court with Sir Walter and bent a knee before the horse-faced, enameled, red-wigged woman who was the Virgin Queen, Elizabeth, "Gloriana," the rasp-voiced vixen who held the fate of all England in her knob-knuckled hands.

"Young Harvie back with us," the Queen had gravelled, after the Lord Chamberlain had announced him. "We thought you were safe in the country for a time."

"The beauty of this court, Your Majesty," Dion had returned with something that came close to impudence, "entices me past enduring when I'm away from it."

A hoarse chuckle sounded deep in the Queen's stringy throat. "You learn well from y'r sponsor, Sir Walter," she nodded. "Though which of y'r pretty words are his and which y'r own would be hard to tell." She had turned to Raleigh. "And you, sir—I suppose you're hot for y'r patent, eh?"

"By Your Majesty's generosity," Raleigh had murmured with the bow that only he knew how to make.

Elizabeth squinted at him, one painted eyebrow arching as she examined her court favorite.

"And ye're hot to go on this expedition, too, I'll be bound," she added.

"By Your Majesty's gracious leave."

"Well, we won't have it," the Queen had said abruptly. "No, damme, no! 'Twas enough we lost y'r half-brother, Sir Humphrey Gilbert, in an exploration voyage—we could not spare you, Sir Walter. Y'r patent you shall have, but on condition that ye'll stay here in England, and only on that condition!"

As Dion watched his friend, he saw Raleigh's eyes cloud with disappointment, a chagrin so keen that it almost burst into speech. Harvie knew that Raleigh had been counting on a change of heart by the Queen, one of the reversals of edict for which "Gloriana" was noted, that would permit him to accompany the expedition which he had financed and outfitted.

Of Sir Humphrey Gilbert, Dion knew only that he had sailed to some land beyond the Western Sea and had been aboard a cockleshell named *Squirrel* on the return voyage. He knew too, as all England did, that when the escorting vessels had tried to reach the foundering *Squirrel,* a tiny vessel, Gilbert had cried, just before he sank: "We are as near to heaven by sea as by land." At the time, Dion had thought the words heroic but the whole venture a mad expedition—why toss oneself about on a sea full of serpents when one could take his ease at the most civilized court in the world?

Raleigh had bowed to the Queen's demand with a reluctance that had brought a frown from the woman who reigned.

"Milord Chamberlain," Elizabeth had commanded sharply, "ye'll read Sir Walter's patent to him, that he may hear the terms of it in our presence."

Then had followed the sonorous reading of what had seemed to Dion to be an endless scroll, something about Raleigh being given royal permission to explore and settle remote heathen and barbarous lands, countries and territories not actually possessed by any Christian prince or inhabited by Christian people. To young Harvie it had been a boring piece of business and he had trouble once or twice suppressing a yawn, but to his friend, Sir Walter, it had seemed the most wonderful document in the world.

That was one thing about Raleigh that Dion never had been able to understand. At thirty-two, Raleigh was the handsomest, most loved man in all Christendom. A favorite of the Queen, he had opportunities at every hand to make fortune upon fortune through the Queen's grants of franchises. Yet he chose to spend his every effort in reaching out into the unknown; he was intent on exploring the savage wilderness where everybody knew lurked great female giants named Amazons and God only guessed what other terrible creatures. He had a dream of an empire beyond the Western Sea and he clutched this dream to him as he would a beautiful woman—nay, his love of his dream was fiercer than the love any woman would ever receive from Raleigh.

The *Tyger* took the blow of a wave on her steerboard quarter as the helmsman let the bark yaw. Spray cascaded over the bulkhead and Dion bent his head as the icy shower drenched him. He swore quietly, monotonously, and huddled his soaked cloak about him. Would he ever be dry again? His fine clothes were gone, ripped to shreds, doublet and galligaskins, and now he was clad in a seaman's rough canvas breeches, a shirt that felt like it had been fashioned of woven thistles and a padded jerkin that did not fit half so fine as it stank. His beautiful leather hat with its sweeping plume had disappeared and now he wore a coarse wool cap that itched intolerably. On his feet were a pair of rough clogs that took the place of the fashionable heeled, cork-soled shoes, wonderfully embossed and—it had developed—made to fall to pieces when soaked in bilgewater.

"Aye, Dion," he sighed aloud, "you could go back to London tonight and walk the streets without a Queen's man recognizing you. I 'fackin's, you could saunter up to Avronbeck Hall and be ordered to the kitchen door as a beggar by the fair Helen herself."

He wondered about Avronbeck Hall's reception of the news of his latest trouble and his disappearance. His father, he guessed, would stoutly defend him before the Queen if she called him to

London; he hoped Gloriana would deflect none of the blame for this on his father but it was impossible to guess what she would do when she was angry—and she must be foaming. Raleigh? Sir Walter had taken a risk, certainly, in smuggling him aboard this tatterdemalion vessel but who in all the world would imagine Dion Harvie gone to sea in one of Raleigh's ships?

No, they would search for him the length and breadth of England, they would hunt through Scotland and Ireland for him, but unless one of the Queen's spies had seen him in Plymouth, no one would dream of his true whereabouts.

"True whereabouts," he murmured now, "and exceeding temporary, if today was any example. Before another sundown I'll likely be in Heaven or Hell. Sir Humphrey said we're as close to Heaven at sea as on land—he forgot to mention the direction I'd more likely take. Ah well, dear Brother Charles will be content, at least. But Mother and my sisters. . . ."

Gloom threatened to swamp him as he thought of his mother and the girls, Elizabeth and Joan, his father and Helen of the deceptively demure mouth. If he could have sent them a message—but Raleigh had forbidden it and he owed Sir Walter that much for what he had done to engineer his escape.

"Damn the heart of that man, that Captain Guy Groven," he cried over the squeal of the wind in the rigging. "Damn him to the deepest pit in Hell, the mouthy braggart!"

5

DION'S MEETING with Captain Guy Groven had occurred more than two weeks after Raleigh had been given his charter by Queen Elizabeth. The evening had begun ordinarily enough. Dion had eaten with Sir Walter and had pretended an interest he could not honestly summon in Raleigh's description of the outfitting of the two barks under Captains Barlowe and Amadas and their departure from the Thames for Plymouth.

"I tell you, Dion, that we're bound to succeed in this where poor Humphrey failed," Raleigh had enthused. "I feel it in my bones. Look you, we have the best pilot to be found, Simon Ferdinando, and two of the best sea captains ever to sail a bark. The vessels are sound" (Dion grimaced at his memory of that statement), "the company is stout, the winter storms are through" (another grimace) "and there's naught to stop us, I vow. Ah, would Her Majesty would let me sail with them to be present at the very moment her banner is planted in the New World and the land claimed for her!"

Dion clucked his tongue sympathetically while he wondered how he could escape this dry discourse without offending his friend.

"You see this chart?" Raleigh had asked, hauling out the scroll Dion had seen a hundred times, or so it seemed. "Look ye, the course will be down to the Canaries, here, and so. . . ."

And on and on, while Dion had fretted and shifted his butt on the hard bench and nodded and shook his head and sipped occasionally at his wine until, in desperation: "Y'r pardon, good Walt, but I must be off. There's a certain matter I must tend before it grows too late. Ye'll tell me more of this tomorrow when we meet. I hate to leave you, but the lady. . . ."

Raleigh rolled up the scroll, his teeth shining in a smile that split his sharp beard and long moustaches.

"Always a lady, eh, Dion?" he asked. "If you'd half the interest in exploring new lands that you have in exploring white flesh I'd make you one of my captains, 'stead of Amadas or Barlowe—aye, and you'd be a better pilot than Ferdinando, I'll be bound."

Dion had laughed. "Nay, Walt, count me not amongst the heroes who sail the seas for Raleigh. I feel queasy at the sight of a mill pond, I vow. Nay, I'll keep my exploring confined to silken territories, by y'r leave."

After he left Sir Walter, Dion had sauntered more or less aimlessly through the city, casting about for some relief from boredom. He had no appointment with a lady, although there were three or four on whom he could call with a reasonable certainty of welcome, and he was not particularly enlivened by thoughts in that direction. He could go over to Southwark to watch the bear-baiting or he could go see a play at Master Burbage's new theater. Or he could try his luck with the dice at half a dozen houses within walking distance.

He had been bidden by his father to leave the dice and wine alone but surely Sir Clement had not meant total abstinence from either! And, Dion told himself, he had been very careful with the cup and the cubes, so there could be no chance of trouble born of too much Sack or too little luck.

He chose a nearby house operated by a gentleman named Wenrick who had fallen on hard times by reason of the very games he now offered to recommended clients. He arrived to find the game room crowded, the rattle of the dice cups a continuous tattoo, the hum of voices swelling and lowering in a surflike rumble, the curses of the unlucky players and the shouts of the lucky ones occasionally spiking the heavy, indistinct undertone.

For a time, he contented himself with following the play at the various tables. Young Molerton was staggering, as usual, and losing, also as usual; Sir Peter Fenton had his long face cast in the grim lines that meant he was winning; here a man cast the dice with a determination that fairly willed them to roll right, there another tossed them carelessly, as though it did not really matter whether they rolled at all. There were the usual faces, flushed, pale, perspiring, panic-stricken, gay, languid, avaricious, brutish, supercilious, amused, bored. There were the hot eyes and the cold stares, the slitted eyes, the popeyes, the scowls, the arched brows, the spittle-leaking mouths and the lips so parched they must be continuously wet by a nervous tongue. Dion saw hands that trembled with hope, with despair, with triumph, and others that were so steady that they could lift a brimming beaker of wine without spilling a drop.

On an upholstered bench against the wall sat a young man with whom Dion had a bowing acquaintance, a stripling just come into a title and a vast estate by the death of an older brother. Now he slumped with his head in his hands, his fingers tangling in his long hair, staring at the floor, obviously close to weeping. Dion's lip curled as he glanced at the miserable figure; icod, if the fellow would gamble away his heritage so recklessly, the least he could do would be to accept his losses in the proper way, with a laugh if he could summon one or, if that was too great a task, with a curse and a shrug.

He had just turned away from the newmade bankrupt when his eye lit on a figure at the center table and he sniffed, not quite audibly.

"God's teeth," he muttered beneath his breath, "Wenrick must be hard put to it to let that person play here."

It was Captain Guy Groven and only this was known of him by Dion and his friends, even by Sir Walter Raleigh, even by Sir Clement Harvie: He was young, he was exceedingly handsome in a dark, Italian manner, he was apparently rich although no one knew by what means, he was an officer in the Army of the Queen and had served in Ireland. Most important of all, he was in Elizabeth's favor to a degree no other commoner of the time could boast.

It was this last fact that made him one of the most hated men in a court where envy, jealousy, suspicion, intrigue ruled. Walsingham, Burghley, Avronbeck, Raleigh, Essex, Leicester, Drake and the others plotted and schemed endlessly to get and keep the Queen's regard, for their own ends and, beyond that, for what they held to be the good of England. To have this nobody come out of nowhere and be handed the favor the others had struggled and sweated for galled every courtier within bowing distance of the throne.

Groven himself did nothing to temper this general aversion. Where high-born gentlemen walked and spoke carefully, fearful of Elizabeth's explosive temper and cruelty-streaked whims, Groven strutted so recklessly that at times it seemed almost that Elizabeth feared *him*. The captain was disrespectful to gentlemen who had served the court for more years than he could count his own; he was derisive in his open comments of some oldsters who, though they might be dodderers now, had served England and the throne well in their day; he was contemptuous of the honors amassed by families that had been great since the days of the Plantagenets.

Because he was the Queen's darling (the world had yet to discover that all Elizabeth's darlings were lovers in name only by reason of her odd deformities) Groven never had been challenged, although the provocations had been many. Hands had gone to rapier hilts more than once but the blade never had been drawn; the fear of the Queen's anger always had cooled the heat of the moment. Groven knew he was secure; he exploited his position to the fullest—and he was careful never to venture abroad at night without the company of two or three guards.

And there he was, that night that Dion Harvie had wandered into Wenrick's in search of an hour's diversion before going on to his own apartments and to bed. Dion knew that his sensible course would be to quit this place and visit another—there were several within easy reach of Wenrick's—but as he turned to go Groven looked up from the table and his dark eyes fixed themselves squarely on Harvie's.

"How now, Master Harvie?" he called. "Have you come to match your luck 'gainst mine?"

Heads turned as the call rang through the room, then swung back to Groven. There had been something in the man's tone which seemed to Dion to *dare* him to gamble. Yet there was Sir Clement's orders and surely this was the sort of thing Dion's father had wanted him to avoid at all costs. He clenched his teeth as he forced a smile and shook his head.

"Nay, Groven," he called back. "I was looking for a friend I thought might be here. I see he's not, so I must go on with my search."

Groven's smile became a distinct sneer.

He said, "Come come, Harvie, the man ye seek can wait. I'd match my skill at the dice with one of England's most fashionable gentlemen and it's not often that we meet at the tables."

Dion had forced himself to return a bow to the sarcastic compliment and shook his head again.

"Another time," he said. "I'm occupied this evening and, besides, I fear my purse is too flat to interest your wondrous skill with the dice."

There was a second's silence, a sharply inhaled breath here and there. Had Dion put a faint accent on the word "wondrous"; had he inferred Groven's skill was remarkable past honesty? Groven apparently thought so; his smile faded and his face darkened.

"I don't like y'r tone, Harvie," he said stiffly. "It bears the hint of malice."

Dion's reply had been accompanied by a shrug of his elegant shoulders.

"I'll bid my tongue watch itself then, sir," he said. "He's a rough fellow, that tongue, and not accustomed to dealing with words of high-born gentlemen."

Now the quiet of the room was deathly; the insult had come out from behind its mask of spurious badinage and lay there on the gaming table for all to see. In the parlance of the times, to call a man high-born when he obviously was not was to accuse him of being base-born. Walsingham might be the son of a common serjeant of London, Sir Francis Drake's father might have been a mere yeoman, others high in the Queen's council might have had modest lineages, but all such men were frank in admitting them—were even proud of them as contrast to what they had become. This Groven had carefully hidden his background and by doing so had laid himself open to the most scornful implication to be found in Dion's return.

Now the dark-browed Captain swung away from the table and advanced on Harvie, walking carefully, stiff-kneed, wary. Two paces away from Dion he stopped and deliberately raked the younger man's tall frame from shoes to plumed hat.

"Icod," he sneered, "'tis a shame y'r tongue don't match the pretty rest of you, Master Harvie. Tell me, do you young gentlemen of fashion think of aught save that y'r ruff be wider than the next and y'r perfume stink the sweeter?"

Dion's eyes had been hazed by a bloody mist as he had gone for the jewel-hilted rapier that hung at his side. Dimly he heard somebody—probably Wenrick—cry: "Hold, gentlemen, hold!" but it had been too late for that. There had been the screep of his blade against Groven's and the fight was on.

Another wave crashed against the steerboard planking of the *Tyger's* hull and again spray dashed over the lone figure at the forepeak bulkhead. Water sluiced along the deck and drained through the scuppers. Dion shivered and swore without conviction; he was back at Wenrick's, facing Captain Guy Groven.

At the first exchange, he had discovered that Groven had a

hard wrist, a soldier's attack, little or no finesse with his blade. It was apparent from the start that the Captain was more used to a heavier steel, a sword with which he could hack and slash; during the days he had swaggered about the court he had neglected to learn the nicer art of using a Toledo rapier so as to give himself all the advantages offered by that springy, near-human length of shining death.

Dion had been borne back by Groven's first onslaught, taking the Captain's heavy lunges near the hilt of his weapon, offering a *riposte* when Groven pressed in too close, and waiting, waiting. About the two swordsmen, the gamblers in Wenrick's watched silently, hopeful that Groven would get what nearly every one of them had wanted to mete out and had not dared, fearful of what would happen to young Harvie if he should kill this man, Elizabeth's darling of the day.

Snorting, grunting, snarling a savage curse each time his attack failed to break through Dion's guard, Groven pursued the retreating Harvie about the room. Every time he seemed about to pierce the younger man's defenses, Dion's *riposte* flicked out to force Groven to cover himself. And it was after one of these thrusts that a sigh, a joined exhalation, swept the room. Groven's cheek streamed blood from a shallow slice that marked the place where Dion's blade had found flesh.

The Captain, chest heaving, drew back a step and lowered his rapier with reckless contempt.

"Stand and fight," he panted. "Cease y'r running, gutter-born son of a mangy bitch!"

There was a swirl of the crimson mist before Dion's eyes, a mist that cleared as he turned from the defense over to the attack. Now his blade was a shimmering blur, now Groven found himself in retreat, desperately warding off the biting point that came at him from everywhere. He backed, slashed, backed again and his eyes that had been narrowed by his hate widened in his fear of the rapier that would not let him set himself for even the clumsiest stroke.

It was when he raised his shoulder to parry what he thought was a high *quinte* that Groven left his side unguarded and Dion's blade streaked in with a *seconde*. The Captain gave a shrill, thin cry as his sword dropped to the floor, he clutched at his side, staggered and doubled over a table, cried out again and slid to the floor. As he lay there, stared at by a silent room, a red trickle began coiling its way across the floor from beneath him.

There was a long, stark silence as Dion Harvie gazed down at the man he had felled—then pandemonium!

"God's gullet, boy!" somebody grated in Dion's ear as the tumult mounted. "Get out of here and flee! That's Her Majesty's pet ye've killed and she'll not rest till y'r head is on the block for this! Quick, Dion, rid y'rself of the town, the whole country! Flee, man, whilst ye've got the chance!"

He found himself fairly hurtled out of the room by the others, flung pell-mell into the street by his well-wishers who waited only until Dion had begun running before they themselves scattered, leaving poor Wenrick to summon a physician, dispose of the body or flee for his own life.

Dion had turned a corner, raced down a cobbled alleyway, found himself in a *cul de sac,* had turned and run back. Through the twisting streets he had fled, dropping his gallop to a lope and then to a long-paced walk as he made his way back to the chambers of the one man he could turn to in this calamity, Sir Walter Raleigh.

He had found Raleigh still up, still poring over his maps and charts, still dreaming his dreams of a wonderful land beyond the Western Sea where gold was to be found in great lumps and where the sun always shone, the crops burgeoned untended, the natives and the animals of the forest were as gentle as man and beast had been in Eden.

To Sir Walter Dion gasped out his sorry tale while Raleigh tugged at his beard, scowling. It was typical of the man that Raleigh had wasted no time in recriminations; he had been terse in his directions to Dion, given as he flung a crimson-hosed suit of his own at Harvie to replace Dion's blood-stained clothes.

"You'll ride for Plymouth," Raleigh barked, "and you'll spare neither the whip nor the spur till you get there. I'll write a letter to Barlowe—no, Amadas 'cause Barlowe has a long, suspicious nose—and ye'll board the *Tyger.* Aye, you'll be safe there, or as safe as you'll ever be, with Elizabeth crying for your head."

"You mean—you mean I'm to *sail* aboard your vessel?" Dion had faltered.

"Of course," Raleigh snapped impatiently. "It's your only chance. Think you that you can hide from the Queen's men with Gloriana herself whipping them on to find the one who's harmed her darling?"

"B-but I'm no adventurer, dear Walt," Dion protested. "I'm no—"

"You're a man with a price on his head," Raleigh broke in, "and it'll be a fair staggering one, I'll be bound, for all our gracious Queen's a pinch-penny in most things! 'Tis a stroke of fortune mayhap you don't deserve that my two vessels are ready to leave Plymouth. Ride, I say, as soon as I write you y'r letter and get you a horse!"

"My family—my father and my mother—would'st have me leave without a word to them?"

"I'll try to find a means to let them know where you are," Raleigh said, "but not at once, not while the hue and cry is up. The Queen will have her spies watching every man who even bids a good day to Avronbeck for some time to come." He laid a hand on Dion's shoulder and his voice was grave when he spoke again.

"Ah, Dion, Dion," he said, "ye've dealt y'r father and y'r family a mortal blow in this. Elizabeth's no more vengeful than any other monarch, I trow, but you must know that by stabbing that dog Groven ye've wreaked a deal of harm on those ye love and who love you. There's no justice in it, I know, but it's always been the way of monarchs, man or woman, to treat harshly with the whole family of a subject who enrages them, as you've enraged Gloriana."

Dion had stared numbly at the floor as his concern for himself was penetrated by the realization of the trouble he had brought Sir Clement, his soft-voiced mother, his two sisters. He saw his father kneeling before a Queen who scourged him with a vituperation of which only she was capable. He saw Sir Clement's honors stripped from him, even his title retracted. He saw his mother denied the court, his sisters' position brought so low that no worthy gentleman would seek them as wives.

"If I gave myself up?" he asked humbly. "If I handed myself over to the Queen's men and—"

Raleigh broke in harshly. "To what point? You'd still lose your head and, worse still, Her Majesty's pretty jailors would find means to have you confess to all manner of wild things; you'd wind up screaming that Groven's death was part of a plot against the Crown. Ah, don't say you wouldn't—I've some knowledge of what can be done to the stoutest heart, squeezed by the proper hand."

His tone had gentled as he gripped Dion's shoulder.

"But don't worry y'rself overmuch, dear Dion," he had said. "Your father, praise be to God, is a friend of Burghley—and my voice won't go unheard when we speak in his defense. Elizabeth's always treated him as a sort of elderly lover; mayhap she'll deal more kindly with him than we'd guess now. But we waste time, when hurry's the only word in all the language for you now!"

So he had galloped out of London, past the guards at Ludgate who had not tried to stop him and so gave him reassurance that the alarm had not yet been spread. He had worn out four horses, had slept in the saddle; he had reached Plymouth a gaunt, unshaven spectre, his doeskin boots muddied to the hips, reeling with weariness, but he had gained the seaport ahead of whatever pursuit Elizabeth had sped after him. Aboard the *Tyger* he had stayed below until, on the twenty-seventh day of April, 1584, the bark had weighed anchor and had pushed out into the Western Sea.

"And God wot what comes now," Dion Harvie murmured as he looked into the tossing darkness that lay ahead of the ship's stubby prow. "Whate'er it be, it could be no worse than what lies behind—disgrace to my family, an assassin's flight, exile from my England. Aye, 'twould be best, mayhap, that I find my death in this sea or in this New World they say lies beyond it."

6

And on the second of July, Philip Amadas wrote laboriously in his journal, *we found shoal water, where we smelled so sweet and so strong a smell as if we had been in the midst of some delicate garden abounding with all kinds of odoriferous flowers, by which we were assured that the land could not be far distant; and, keeping good watch and bearing but slack sail, the fourth of the same month we arrived upon a coast, which we supposed to be a continent and firm land, and we sailed along the same a hundred twenty English miles before we could find any entrance or river issuing into the sea.*

The first that appeared unto us we entered this day, though not without some difficulty, and cast about three harquebus-shot within the haven's mouth, on the left hand of the same; and, after thanks given to God for safe arrival thither, we manned our boats and went to view the land next adjoining and to take possession of the same in the right of the Queen's most excellent majesty as rightful Queen and. . . .

On deck above the Captain's tiny cabin, Simon Ferdinando stood beside Dion Harvie and grinned down at the slighter man, tugging at the pearl pendant that dangled from his ear.

"So, my good Master Harvie," he said, "what think you of this grand New World, eh?"

Dion's eyes roved over the sandy shore ahead of them, over the cedars that led back from shore line to the taller trees further inland and his eyes were bleak as he turned to the Portuguese.

"This—this is all?" he asked.

"And what did you expect, good sir?" Ferdinando chuckled.

"I—I don't know," Harvie stumbled, "but surely something more than this—this desert."

Part 2

1

IT WAS, in truth, almost a desert, that first land touched by Amadas and Barlowe, a land of stark dunes that heaved themselves skyward three hundred feet or more, a country of coarse sea grass and few trees, a place that baked under a relentless sun, offering little shade. Compared to the West Indies, where the two barks had paused to take on fresh water and supplies, this wonderland that Raleigh had dreamed of was a desolation.

Except for one thing—the grapes. Dion Harvie had seen the vineyards of France and Portugal but no carefully tended tracts could compare with the vast tangle of ground-hugging vines that covered great sections of this sandy shore. In places, these vines grew down to the water's edge, surrendering clusters of their fruit to each surge of a crashing comber, offering tribute to the sea gods.

Ashore with Ferdinando, Dion plucked a handful of grapes and put one to his mouth. He was conscious of the Portuguese eyeing him as he tasted the fruit and found it pleasantly bittersweet, wonderfully tangy after the flatness of the ship's water; he noticed later that the pilot kept slewing his eyes at him as he finished one bunch of grapes and reached for another.

"God's teeth," he finally said, irritably, "why do you watch me so? Am I poaching on some heathen king's preserves by helping myself to a few grapes?"

Ferdinando pointed his black beard at the sky in a bellow of a laugh.

"Nay, Master Harvie," he said when he recovered his breath. "I watched to see how this fruit sat in y'r belly. In Florida and further south I've seen fruit more beautiful than this that'd have a man writhing with the gripes before his second bite. And seeing that I'd relish some grapes myself, I thought I'd have you taste 'em for me."

"Now damn me!" Dion swore. "So ye'd have me die playing at king's taster for you, eh?"

Simon's grin was wide and unabashed.

"I would," he nodded. "Look you, Master Harvie, there's a rule you must always remember, here in this strange land. We're all of a company, aye, but out of the company the one who counts most to you is you—in my mind it's me. If there's the littlest doubt about what's safe and what's not, it's always wisest to have some other man find out for you, if you can. God knows there'll be plenty of times when nobody will be handy to set you your example and you'll have to take the risk alone. Aye, I've learned that more times than I've picked my teeth."

He gestured toward the base of the dune where Amadas stood talking to Arthur Barlowe, master of the *Admiral.* A tall, thin man who was perpetually suspicious of others' imagined attempts to rob him of authority and recognition, Barlowe presented a dour contrast to his colleague, Philip Amadas. He had hoped to rank Amadas on this expedition; when he had failed to convince Raleigh of his superiority and had lost the command of the flagship to Amadas, his naturally grim taciturnity had deepened into bleak gloom. Thin-lipped, never given to the faintest smile, he had seemed a weighty ponderer to Dion the few times Harvie had seen him; to Ferdinando, Barlowe was a fair-weather sailor who masked his inadequacies with an air of stern impressiveness.

"Come," the Portuguese said now, "let's join Sir Doloroso and Captain Amadas and the others and get a view from the top of that mountain of what lies to the west. Amadas swears this is the mainland but I've wagered it's a long island. What Amadas and Barlowe call a river, where we're anchored, is only a cut through this island, I think. I've bet four golden pounds that we'll find water to the west and land beyond that which'll be the real mainland."

The ascent of the dune was hot, tiring work. The wind-sifted sand lay so loosely on the surface that the explorers' feet plowed in to above the ankles; a step up the sloping side of the dune was really only half a step because the foot slid back half a stride each time. The two captains had ordered all those who had gone ashore to wear steel corselets and helmets—an order that Simon Ferdinando had blithely ignored—and Dion and the other gentlemen were further burdened by heavy, cumbersome harquebuses, those weighty matchlocks that were replacing the bow and the pike despite their complete undependability. With the sun seeming to bend down to focus all its strength on this little band of white men, perspiration began to trickle at the first few steps up the hill; it streamed, then torrented as Dion and the others toiled toward the top of the dune.

"Now I need never fear Hell," Dion gasped as he struggled through the tormenting sand.

He was so exhausted, so beaten by the heat when he reached the crest of the dune that he sank to the sand without even sparing a glance at the view he had fought his way to see. Gulping lungfuls of air so hot that it seemed to taste of brass, wiping at the sweat that blinded him, easing the cruel corselet that had chafed half a dozen raw spots on his hide, he was dimly aware of the exclamations of Barlowe and Amadas, a prideful remark by Ferdinando which, he supposed, meant that the pilot was right. They were on an island and not the mainland of the New World.

"Island or mainland, to hell with it," he muttered savagely. "Had I known we were sailing straight into a furnace I'd have let the Queen's men grab me back in London."

But at length, when he found his wind again and his heart slowed its jarring, when he roused himself to look about him, he was impressed by what he saw. To the east spread the vast expanse of the ocean, quiet now, a drowsy giant napping through the heat of the day. To the west lay another body of water, tawnier than the sea but sparkling under the sunlight, ruffled in places by desultory breezes that sprang alive and were snuffed out within the space of seconds. And beyond the water was land, real land, with tall trees and a bluff raising it from the water and birds, pigeons by the looks of them, clouding the sky over the tops of the trees in great flocks, and—and yes, by God, a boat, tiny at this distance but plain enough to know it for what it was, just pulling out of sight around a point!

" 'Tis as I wagered, gentlemen," Ferdinando was boasting. "We're on an island and yonder lies the mainland—though by the looks of it I'd not be surprised to find that *that's* a big island, too, with the real mainland a league or so behind it."

"Ye've been here before?" Amadas asked.

Dion saw the Portuguese hesitate and then hunch his shoulders, spread his hands.

"I cannot say, Senhors," he replied, smiling. "I've been so many places and there are some that look like others, down to the last speck of sand, the last blade of grass. Mayhap I've been here before, but I'd not swear to it."

Barlowe sniffed skeptically, "Aye, and when you browbeat us into betting this was an island and not the mainland, you had no idea your bet was safe, I vow."

"But no, Capitan," Simon grinned. "I merely trusted to my luck which is uncommon faithful, as you know."

Dion got to his feet, wincing at the rasp of the steel corselet's straps on his blistered shoulders and staggered through the sand to the others. Now he discovered it had been a mistake to let himself drop, as he had done; sand, he learned immediately, had a fiendish way of violating a man's privacy, even though he sat on it without moving. Dion had been off his feet only a few minutes, he had certainly done no tossing about while he had fought to get his breath back, and yet now there was sand down his neck, in his boots, between his teeth, in his hair, under his arms, decidedly in the most uncomfortable place of all.

"This cursed stuff can crawl," he told himself. "The island's bewitched."

"That boat we just spied," Barlowe was saying, "you said was a native craft, eh? You're sure it couldn't possibly have been a Spanish barge?"

"'Twas what they call a *canoa,*" Ferdinando said, "and it was a savage craft, for sure, no barge. I've seen many of them in Florida and the Indies; the natives fashion them out of tree trunks by halving the log and burning out its center with live coals. They push the *canoa* with their oars 'stead of rowing as we do and they can make better speed in even that clumsy boat than the stoutest rowman when they have three or four men to the paddles. Why, I've seen 'em—"

He broke off what he had been about to say and shook his head, the ear pendant swinging.

"Spanish barge?" he asked. "Nay, Captain Barlowe, ye'll find no Spaniards this far north. I've told you time and again that there are no Spaniards here—what is it, do you suspect me of plotting to lead you into some Spanish trap?"

"No, no. I only—"

"'Cause if that's your fear, I'd bid you remember I'm a Portuguese who refused to bend a knee to Philip when the Prior of Cato, Don Antonio, lost our throne to the Spanish dog. Ranuccio, Duke of Palma, made himself my enemy and hounded me out of my own country to England. And ye think I'd put my own head on the block by delivering myself over to the Spaniards?"

"Nay," Amadas said, as Barlowe scowled. "'Tis but that the good Captain is cautious, as is no more than right in this strange land."

"Aye, cautious," Ferdinando grunted, "to the point of suspicion." He shrugged again and his voice changed to a lighter tone. "But cautious or no, methinks we'd best move our anchorage from this inlet to beside that higher land there. Storms brew in an eyewink hereabouts and inside this island or reef or what it may be we'd be protected from a gale. Also, you'll want to explore that wooded land there, I suppose."

"D'you think the natives who were in that craft were friendly?" Amadas asked hesitantly.

The pilot flashed his teeth in one of his characteristic smiles, just skirting contempt.

"That we'll soon find out," he said. "Seeing it's summer with plenty of food at hand, I'd say they are. But as I've told you, their whims are past understanding. With all your armor and your harquebuses you're not afraid of them, are you?"

"That I'm not!" Amadas returned hotly. "I'm only thinking of the precautions to be taken to meet every possibility."

"Of course," Ferdinando nodded, gravely, "and be it to your credit, Captain. I'd suggest you do what the Spaniards do when they enter strange waters.They shoot off their weapons as they anchor to show the savages that they're armed, if the natives have seen guns before, or to frighten the savages into thinking they're gods if the benighted heathens have never heard a harquebus."

"An excellent idea," Amadas said and turning to the others: "Back to the ships, gentlemen, and we'll move into this bay to the west, close to the wooded land, for a look around."

The descent was much easier than the climb to the top of the dune. Dion Harvie and the others had only to keep their balance as they skidded down the slope like small boys sliding on an icy hill and there was a touch of carnival spirit as the company went slewing and lurching downward, whooping as one of their number, weighted by the armor and the heavy harquebus he carried, lost his footing and took a tumble. By the time they reached the bottom all except Simon Ferdinando were well covered with the viscid sand; on the decks of the *Tyger* and *Admiral* there was the clang and clatter of corselets and helmets tossed aside as the gentlemen stripped themselves to pour buckets of sea water over each other.

Anchors weighed and spritsails unclewed, the two barks moved with the tide more than the wind into the sound that stretched before them. Once through the inlet, the errant breezes that had dimpled the surface of the little landbound sea caught the flapping canvas and even gave the two vessels a slight "bone in the teeth," a curving wash at the bow. Steadily, although slowly, the wooded shore the men had seen from the dune drew closer.

Under Ferdinando's direction, Amadas put *Tyger* on a tack that carried the bark to the south of the nearest point, then brought the ship about again to follow the shore line to the southwest.

"And now the shots, Captain," the Portuguese suggested, "to show the savages we make magic with thunder and lightning."

Dion and two others, Nicholas Petman and John Wood, rested their harquebuses on their standards, their "hooks", poured powder and ball into the full-throated barrels, sprinkled coarse powder in the priming pan and then used flint and steel to light the slow-burning fuses attached to the hammers. At a signal from the captain, the three men pulled the triggers of their weapons. The hammer of Petman's harquebus refused to fall, Wood's powder, dampened by the sea air fizzed and spluttered and went out, but Dion's weapon produced a splendid *boom,* billowing out a cloud of thick, black smoke and sending the heavy shot arching almost thirty feet.

"God's gullet!" somebody yelped. *"What's that?"*

The echoing crash of the shot had produced wild confusion ashore. There was a hoarse scream wrenched from a thousand throats, a thunderous beating, the churning splash of water, and into the air burst a whirling mass of great white birds. Panicked, fighting each other for air space, they gyrated skyward, long necks outstretched, legs trailing, wide-spanned wings flopping in heavy, powerful strokes.

"Swans!" Amadas cried. "By the heavens, a great army of swans!"

"Not so, Capitan," the Portuguese corrected easily. "No swans, those, but what're called cranes or herons. Wild swans there are, too, in this region but not in the summertime."

"I've seen cranes in England," Amadas said, staring, "but never more than one or mayhap two together, never such a horde as this!"

"In this New World," Simon smiled, "all things are in profusion, birds, fish, furs, fruit—aye, and dangers, too."

"And gold and pearls?" Dion asked. "In England I heard it said that pearls are to be had for the picking up along any shore."

The Portuguese touched a finger to the pearl that dangled from his earlobe, his smile sardonic.

"If there be such places," he said bitterly, "it's never been my good fortune to visit them. This little bauble I wear was bought with good English coin, not picked up on a beach. As for gold, aye, the Spanish bastards have found plenty of that in Tenochtitlan and other places so who can say it is not here?"

Nicholas Petman said, "Then let us land and find us some."

Amadas turned a frown on the thin, long-legged Petman, a gentleman who was no favorite aboard the *Tyger* because of his aversion to work aboard the ship, his reluctance to "hale and draw" with the others of the expedition.

"No gold-hunting now, Master Petman," the captain said. "We must not forget our purpose here is to take possession of lands in the right of the Queen, to find a suitable place for Sir Walter's colony, mayhap to discover a passage to the Southern Sea, but not to seek our fortunes in gold. Before all else, we must survey the country, make maps, find out in what humor the natives will receive us and make friends with them if they'll have us for friends, conquer them if they won't."

Ferdinando said, "And to that end, I'd suggest we explore along the shore to find out for certain whether this be another island or in truth the mainland."

The two barks crept on their way, just offshore, while Dion and the others, seamen and gentlemen, lined the rail, straining their eyes for sight of the wild savages that their glimpse of the *canoa* had proved were somewhere about. *Tyger* and the trailing *Admiral* rounded another point and bore northwest, turned a third promontory and sailed due east.

"'Tis another island," Amadas muttered. "I size it at about twenty miles long and, say, six miles across. What say you, Sir Pilot?"

"I would say ten miles long and four miles across," Simon said and added, with a bow, "but I must be wrong, to be so far away from your estimate, Captain Amadas."

The short, pot-bellied captain sniffed as he turned away from Ferdinando.

"I'd not wager a groat that ye're half a mile off in y'r estimate," he said acidly. "If this voyage has taught me but one thing, 'tis that it's foolhardy to stake a coin against any judgment or prediction o' yours that concerns this country."

"We Portuguese," the spade-bearded pilot grinned at Amadas, "are lucky in all things save affairs of State. And now, I humbly suggest we anchor off this shore and wait for our hosts to show themselves."

"Wait for them?" the captain asked. "Why not land a party and seek them out?"

"Because, my good Captain, things are not done that way in this New World. No, 'twould be better to let the natives make the first advances—they'll feel safer and easier if we sit quiet till their whim tells them to wait on us. Besides, to go stumbling about this strange island would be to invite a trap that would delight the savages. No, my advice is to wait."

Amadas, and Captain Barlowe when he was informed of the idea, grumbled at the delay in landing and exploring the island. Amadas might be stern in reminding all the adventurers that the prime purpose of the expedition was to find a location for Sir Walter Raleigh's colony but his severest lectures did nothing to dim the thought in most minds that great stores of plate, huge lumps of raw gold, caches of pearls—perhaps even diamonds and rubies—were within a stone's throw, theirs for the taking.

Still, Raleigh had given Simon Ferdinando the final say in such matters so they waited. One day passed, and a second and then a third. The Portuguese lounged on the poopdeck of the *Tyger,* alternately dozing and rousing himself to seek out some hapless shipmate—usually Dion—to provide an audience for his endless and staggering stories of Simon Ferdinando. The greatest pilot in the world, the hottest lover, the most reckless gambler, the most fearless fighter—he was all of these. He littered the sun-baked deck with panting high-born ladies, with fortunes won and lost at the cast of a die, with puddles of blood and bashed-in skulls, with storms and sea serpents and green-skinned mermaids who somehow managed to stay alive out of water long enough to surrender to the charms of Simon Ferdinando.

Below, in his oven of a cabin, Philip Amadas worked over his charts with a finicky zeal that deserved a better result than the weird map he finally concocted. The passage where the two barks had first anchored he named Trinity Inlet, never knowing that in centuries to come topographers would argue themselves close to blows in trying to pin down its location. The island off which they were anchored he made three times as long and twice as wide as it actually was. The mainland he indented with rivers that did not exist. He made towering mountains of the sand dunes, fashioned a veritable ocean of the five miles of water between the island and the mainland. All this he tastefully decorated with a unicorn rampant, a fire-breathing sea serpent and a galleon that, in comparison with the shore line, certainly was the biggest vessel the world was ever to know.

It was close to noon of the fourth day and Dion Harvie was listening to the story of the Italian comtesse who resorted to curious practices to ensnare Ferdinando—and not bothering to smother yawns as the pilot's voice flowed on.

" . . . and so, forthwith, this great lady cast off her—*aha!*"

Dion, jerked out of his boredom by the pilot's exclamation, brought his word-glazed eyes back in focus to see Ferdinando staring past him at the water beyond the stern of the anchored bark. Turning, Harvie saw a rough log canoe paddled by three naked men, each wearing feathers bound to his shaven head, moving out of a shallow cove that lay south of the two vessels' anchorage.

"Quick," said Ferdinando in a quiet voice, "rouse Amadas and bid him come on deck. Don't beat up any great alarm. To have the whole ship's company come thundering topside would be to frighten those natives away—ah, they're a fearful lot save when they're in the mood to kill; then the Devil himself couldn't frighten them. Go quick!"

Harvie slipped down the ladder and hurried to the Captain's cabin. His word brought Amadas scrambling from behind his littered table and puffing up to the poop, full of a purposeful energy which included a certain trepidation.

On his return to the upper deck, Dion saw that the canoe was moving along the shore, between the barks and the beach, the three natives keeping their eyes fixed on the strange vessels that idled at their moorings. Despite Ferdinando's warnings, Dion told himself these savages did not seem fearful, only curious; they came within what Harvie estimated was the distance of four harquebus shots from the ship, then rested their paddles and drifted with the tide, eyeing the barks and jabbering among themselves.

"Think you," Amadas asked Ferdinando, "I'd best warn the men to put on their armor and stand to their weapons? These three may be only a foreguard of an army that'll—"

The pilot broke in impatiently. "No, no, they come in peace and to parade a force of armored and armed men now would but send them skittering back into the forest! Hail Barlowe on the *Admiral* and bid him keep his men quiet, too. This'll take another bit of waiting, till those savages decide the time's right to bid us welcome."

While Amadas shouted Ferdinando's instructions across the space between the two barks, Dion fixed his eyes on the canoe to bring the three Indians (for so they came to be named before the expedition's stay ended) closer. The three, he saw, owned faces that might have been cast in the same mould, with high-bridged noses, thin lips, square jaws, large dark eyes. Their skin was coppery and taut, showing no wrinkles, their heads were glistening-bald except for a narrow strip of hair that bristled from the nape to the forehead, exactly in the middle of the skull, their faces were clean-shaven. When they moved their arms in their gesticulations, muscles rippled under the skin that shone with oil—aye, these were powerful men, these savages!

He turned to Ferdinando who was watching him quizzically.

"Big, those fellows," he said, "and handsome to boot, in their rough way. I had in mind they'd be littler, more brutal, than they are."

"Aye, they're handsome, right enough," Ferdinando nodded, "and their women are fair beautiful, some of 'em, and not over-given to fashionable protests at the sign a man would enjoy a bit o' dalliance." He chuckled. "Nay, not those wenches—when they burn they're free to demand a quenching from the nearest man at hand.

"Or," he amended quickly, "that's the rule in some tribes I've seen. Yet in others, the men guard their women closer than any Turk. So best find out what's the mode here, friend Dion, before ye seek a toss."

"With a savage wench?" Dion asked, his lip curling. " 'Od's blood, Sir Pilot, you must think I'm hard put to constrain myself if you think I'd bed a heathen barbarian."

Ferdinando's laugh rolled out, loud in the stillness of the heat-shimmered morning.

"A wager?" the Portuguese asked. "Mayhap you'll bet a few coins on the strength of y'r continence?"

"No wagers with you, Sir Pilot," Dion grinned back, "for I've learned that to bet a shilling with you means to lose it, even if the loser has to change his way of life to do it."

Despite the orders of the two Captains to stay below, the crews and passengers of both barks found excuses to make their way to the decks and before long the bulkheads of both vessels were lined with staring Englishmen, filling their eyes with their first look at the savages of the New World. The Indians were not sent "skittering back into the forest;" indeed, they seemed doubly interested in the fact that these huge *canoas* could disgorge so many men from their insides. Their gesticulations grew more fervid and, at a signal from the man in the bow of the canoe, who wore three egret plumes where the other two wore single feathers, they dipped their paddles to bring their rough craft closer to the *Tyger* and the *Admiral*.

"A sign?" Amadas asked Ferdinando. "Some way of telling them we come as friends?"

The Portuguese replied, "No sign. They'd not understand it and, besides, it's up to them to make the first move."

A half hour passed, another, and still the natives neither came alongside the barks nor paddled away.

"It needs patience," the pilot observed quietly as Amadas muttered under his breath. "Now—aye, they've made up their minds at last."

The Indians, suddenly come alive, were racing their rude craft toward the beach, directly opposite the *Tyger*, digging in their paddles as though they were in some sort of race. As the canoe touched the sand, the foremost paddler leaped out. The canoe then backed off and scurried to a position about three hundred yards downshore, where the two remaining savages rested on their paddles and drifted.

The man left ashore faced the two English ships and raised his right hand high above his head.

"Ah," Ferdinando breathed, "he bids us welcome, Captain Amadas. Now we go ashore—and bring plenty of gifts for his shave-polled majesty if ye'd have any success in this venture."

Dion Harvie went with Ferdinando and Amadas, along with three other gentlemen from the *Tyger*. The morose Barlowe and four gentlemen came ashore in *Admiral's* smallboat that followed *Tyger's* to the beach.

The Indian waited, arms folded across his bronzed chest, as the white men grounded their boats and stepped onto the driftwood-littered shore. Dion saw that this savage was a good head taller than all the explorers except Ferdinando and himself; he towered over Philip Amadas as the ranking captain of the expedition stepped up to him.

Although he must have been burning with curiosity, perhaps awe, almost certainly apprehension, the Indian's face reflected not one visible emotion. Unless the Spaniards had visited this region—and Ferdinando had said that if they had the Indians surely would either hide or fight, never come in peace—these were the first white men these savages ever had seen. The two barks must have seemed terrifyingly enormous to men who never had glimpsed a craft longer than twenty feet. These strangers wore glittering vestments (for Ferdinando had agreed it would be best to don corselet and helmet for the landing) and carried objects such as the one that had blasted fire and smoke and sent the cranes whirling into the air (for Ferdinando had said that every move the expedition had made since entering Trinity Inlet had been watched by the Indians). Yet the savage met these supernatural beings with a dignified impassivity that would have done credit to a Burghley meeting a French ambassador at Hampton Palace Court.

"I'll do the talking, by y'r leave, Captain," the Portuguese pilot murmured as he stepped up to the side of Amadas and Barlowe. "I understand some of these savages' language if it be similar to what is used in Florida."

Without waiting for permission, he turned to face the Indian. He raised his hand over his head and said: "Ho." The Indian replied with his own raised hand and echoed Ferdinando's greeting gravely, then refolded his arms. The Portuguese tapped himself on the chest and said: "Ferd-in-and-o." He touched the rotund captain's shoulder and said: "Am-a-das"; he pointed to grim-faced Barlowe and pronounced his name in two widely separated syllables.

The Indian's jet eyes moved from one man to the next as Ferdinando made his introductions. There was a silence as the savage pondered and the Portuguese repeated the performance, deliberately, slowly. Then the Indian nodded and unfolded his muscled arms to point a long forefinger at his own bare chest.

"Gran-gan-im-eo," he announced. "Granganimeo . . ." He lapsed into a string of gutturals which Dion saw were puzzling to the self-appointed interpreter, Ferdinando. The Portuguese nodded confidently, then grunted a reply which brought another freshet of words. Frowning slightly, the pilot turned back to Amadas.

"It is a different language from what they speak in Florida," he said, "but near enough that I could pick out some of the words—I think. What I make of it is that this man is named Granganimeo and he is the brother of the chief of these savages, named Wingina, and the name of the tribe or clan is Roanoke and this is their hunting island. These savages live not here but on the mainland where there is a village. This I gathered from his words but I confess I may be wrong."

"And what is the name of this island?" Amadas asked. "I need the name for my map."

Ferdinando turned back to Granganimeo and swept a hand in a curve that encompassed the island, grumbling a question as he did so. He had to repeat this gesture half a dozen times before the Indian answered and then the reply was only the one word: "Wingandacoa!"

"Wingandacoa!" Amadas exclaimed delightedly. "A pretty name and one that'll look most weighty on my map. Wingandacoa! And what does that mean, Sir Pilot? You say all savage names for people and places have a meaning."

The Portuguese tried to get an explanation of the meaning of Wingandacoa but his limited knowledge of the language was not up to understanding the torrent of words that burst from Granganimeo. Amadas had to be satisfied with putting the island's name down as Wingandacoa, meaning unknown.

"The gifts now, Captain," Ferdinando directed. Amadas and Barlowe stepped forward and offered the tall Indian the presents they had brought from the ships, a flat cloth cap which sported a bedraggled plume (it had belonged to John Hewes of the *Tyger's* complement of gentlemen but had been ruined in the storm off the Canaries), a seaman's shirt of coarse sacking, a pair of breeches, slashed and diapered, a rope of glass beads, a cheapjack bracelet set with glass "jewels".

Granganimeo accepted the presents somberly, showing neither delight nor disappointment, then turned to signal the two Indians who had stayed in the canoe, beckoning them to the beach. The paddles winked in the sunlight as the pair bent into their strokes, pushing their craft through the water at a speed that surprised Dion, as blunt-prowed and unshaped as the log boat was. Granganimeo's companions proved as tall as the chief's brother, and as undemonstrative.

"Manteo," Granganimeo explained, pointing to the first one out of the canoe. "Wanchese," he added as the second Indian came up. Beyond a raised hand and a grave "Ho!" the two late arrivals remained silent, then and throughout the first meeting; Granganimeo, the chief's brother, was obviously the ranking man, it was his right, his duty, to speak any words that had to be said to these strangers.

Dion Harvie wondered at the calmness with which the Indians greeted the whites that first day. He had heard that the savages of Mexico had fallen to their knees, overwhelmed by a visitation of the gods, when the Spaniards had first set foot in that region. Here, Granganimeo, Wanchese and Manteo conducted themselves with all the aplomb of an English noble receiving the party of a neighboring lord, dropped by on a journey—aye, the Indians were more serene than any English host could be in those times; in Elizabeth's day no man could be certain that his neighbor was not buttocks-deep in some new intrigue and the visit not arranged for hidden reasons.

It could be, Harvie told himself, *that friend Simon knows this language a deal better than he makes out. By his uncommon luck in his predictions about this place it could be, too, that he has been here before. Mayhap we're no surprise to these tall savages.*

"And now they'll come aboard the barks," Ferdinando was saying to Barlowe and Amadas. "They're assured now we're friends and 'twould be best to feed 'em some meat and wine to bind the pledge. Once they've broken bread with us we'll have no cause to fear treachery—till they change what goes for minds in those cropped heads of theirs."

The three Indians followed the smallboats out to the barks and boarded first the *Admiral* and then the *Tyger,* where a meal of pickled beef, corned in brine, ship's biscuits and sweet Romeny wine was set out for the guests. Granganimeo and his companions ate ravenously and with a fine disregard of even the haphazard table manners of the times, using their long fingernails to tear shreds of beef from the joint, cramming their mouths so full that their chins were decorated with bits of meat and biscuit crumbs, draining the mugs in gulps that Dion thought surely must choke them before they'd finished. And as he ate, Granganimeo talked, incessantly, with flourishes, while Ferdinando nodded, as wisely as though the Indian spoke the Queen's English.

"He says," the Portuguese interpreted, "that there are many tribes in his region—besides his Roanokes there are the Hatorasks, the Croatoans, the Secotans, the Wokokons, the Pasquiwocs and others. I gather from his words that all are peaceful tribes for the most part, especially when there is plenty of food—these people seem to war against each other only when their bellies are empty. The name of their main village sounds like Dasamonquepeuc, and there are others on the mainland.

"He also says that his brother Wingina has had a leg broke in a fall and so could not come to greet us himself. He lies in a village at the northern end of this island but I do not understand the name—mayhap it has none, being no more than a hunting camp. He bids us visit his brother on the morrow."

Barlowe asked, "Do you trust him far enough to make such a visit?" Ferdinando shrugged.

"As far as I'd trust any man, white or savage," he said briefly.

The board cleaned to the last morsel, the three Indians made their way to the rail, still blank-faced and without a word of thanks or farewell, dropped nimbly down the rope ladder to their canoe and paddled off, not even glancing back over their shoulders at their hosts.

"Well," Dion grunted, "as ungrateful a set of trenchermen as ever I've seen. Ye'd think they'd at least make some motion to show us they liked their presents or their food."

Ferdinando swung his black beard toward Harvie, one eyebrow aloft.

"Dear friend Dion," he said, "you must remember ye're not in London now—these savages never had a French dancing master nor saw an Italian with manners to copy. No, these barbarians are little more than animals that walk erect and have a sort of language—though God knows swine speak clearer—to separate them from the wild beasts. What would you, that they'd make a dauncey bow and burden you with flatteries? Be thankful they didn't greet us with their arrows and clubs and stones. If they'd but seen what I've seen, the way their kinsmen have been treated by the Spanish, I warrant we'd get a different reception."

"But we'll never do what the Spanish have done," Amadas said stoutly. "Nay, Sir Walter's strongest recommendation was that we treat these savages kindly and win them as allies, half-animals though they be."

"Yes," said Ferdinando, his voice heavy with cynicism, "those were Raleigh's instructions, I know. But—well, how's for a wager, Captain Amadas, that 'ere too much time has passed the Indians will hear the harquebus, and not to frighten cranes, either?"

"Impossible!" Amadas scoffed. "I'll not bet with ye on such a—a brutal question but I know with all my heart no Englishman in

Sir Walter's service would ever mistreat a poor, miserable savage."

"God grant," Barlowe added, firmly.

"And look you," Dion broke in, "at what our friends do now."

The men aboard the *Tyger* followed Dion's pointed finger to see the three Indians standing in their canoe, plunging long, thin spears into the water, boating fish with each strike, or so it seemed. Silently, methodically, Granganimeo, Manteo and Wanchese loaded their craft until its gunwale sank to within an inch or two of the water, then, still standing because there was no place to squat in that burdened boat, they paddled back to the two barks.

The chief's brother hailed Ferdinando, pointing to the flapping, glistening cargo his canoe carried, held up a finger and crossed it with the forefinger of his other hand, then pointed at the *Tyger* and then at the *Admiral.*

"Ho, Master Harvie," Ferdinando laughed, "there's y'r ungrateful trencherman for you. These savage dogs who made no sign of thanks have merely spent a good hour gathering fish they now want divided between this vessel and Barlowe's as repayment for what we gave them."

Dion stared down at the stone-faced Indians below.

"By my word," he murmured beneath his breath, "these savages truly have some sense of honor. They'd not take all and give nothing—like many a fine English gentleman I've met in Elizabeth's court."

2

Dion had glimpsed generosity before—not too much of it, to be sure, because free-handedness was not a cardinal virtue of Elizabeth's England. But he never had seen, he never had dreamed existed, such complete unselfishness as was the rule in the Indian village the white men visited the day after they met Granganimeo, Manteo and Wanchese.

The village itself was a small group of thatched huts surrounded by a stockade of sharpened logs. It was situated near the northern shore of the island but screened from the water by a thick growth of the red cedars in which the island abounded. The place was reached by a tortuous, well-masked path which the whites never would have found had not a guide been waiting for them on the north shore beach when the barks were moved at dawn.

There were about twenty-five men at the village and a dozen women. To the Englishmen, starved for sight of a woman for more than two months, these were tawny goddesses, copper-skinned Aphrodites. They merited the savoring stares that were pinned on them although if they knew what hunger they aroused they did not show it. Their returning gaze was calmly acceptive to the devouring eyes that roved their supple loveliness.

They were all statuesque, from the youngest to the most matronly, and they wore only brief aprons of deerhide that swayed with unconscious invitation as they walked. Except for two old women, their breasts were firm, high, unbearably provocative.

"What think ye now, Friend Dion?" Ferdinando laughed as he nudged Harvie, jostling his inspection. "You said you'd never bed a heathen barbarian—d'ye still say it?"

"I—uh—that one by the carved wooden post," Dion managed. "She—do these women have names, like the men?"

Ferdinando peered at the girl Dion had indicated and made a juicy noise with his full lips.

"Icod, if she hasn't I'll soon give her one," he snickered. He turned to the guide and asked a question; the native returned a stream of gutturals.

"As near as I can understand," the pilot told Dion, "her name's Rycko and she's kin—a granddaughter, mayhap—to the chief. She'll tell you more, no doubt, when you teach her what an Englishman's made of."

Harvie recovered himself with a start and turned a frown toward the grinning Portuguese.

"Have done," he said roughly. "You called these people animals y'rself—d'ye think I'd have anything to do with beasts?"

"Aye, they may be near animals," Ferdinando nodded, "but that one would be sweetly close to human in a tumble, I trow."

Dion snorted and walked away. Still, as he inspected the village, he found himself switching his eyes back to the girl, Rycko. She was, he told himself, outstanding even in this group of smooth-skinned beauties.

He idly compared her with a lady of Elizabeth's court. Rycko was straight-backed, with a posture that thrust out her firm breasts to their best advantage; she walked with an easy swing of her hips, she was flat-bellied and small-crouped, as instinctively graceful as a doe. Her features were a bit sharper than the other women's, her mouth not so wide and her lips not so dark. Her eyes were enormous, velvety.

And a woman of the court? First, she would wear so much enamel on her face as to make it a lifeless mask. There would be glaring red spots on each cheek; her eyebrows would be painted on because she would have plucked out her own to make way for the artificial streaks—the Queen, you see, had no eyebrows. Her chief concern would be that she grow too healthily rounded; Elizabeth was skinny, angular, and it would be dangerously disloyal for one of her ladies-in-waiting to look unseemly healthy.

Her hair would be inevitably red and as inevitably false, piled in a frizzed mass high above that frozen face and decorated with loops of precious stones. Elizabeth herself was bald, *ergo*, false hair was demanded.

Her lace ruff would be almost, not quite, as high in back as the Queen's, reaching to a point just below the top of that mass of hair. Her bodice would be cut so low that it would seem she was out to prove she could suckle children, if forced to the unwelcome duty.

Here in this Indian village, certainly, there was more nudity and yet, to Dion at least, there seemed more modesty, too. For while the ladies of the court covered their skin with yards of silk and satin, their gowns were designed to give men glimpses of their charms that were more salacious than this nakedness which these Indian women bore so unselfconsciously.

The whites' inspection of the village was broken off by the arrival of a litter carried by Granganimeo, Wanchese, Manteo and another Roanoke. Reclining on the makeshift couch was the most impressive man among this tribe of imposing men. Before his name was spoken Dion knew he must be the ailing chief of the Roanokes, Wingina.

He was older than the others and his face was that of an eagle, cruelly beaked and owning a pair of blazing eyes, harsh-mouthed and gaunt, with a hollow-eyed haggardness not born of hunger or illness but of a zealot's inner fire. Wingina was the first Indian Dion saw who seemed to Harvie capable of the murder and torture Simon Ferdinando had called the common practice of the natives of Florida.

Yet Wingina proved friendly enough, although with a certain reserve, when he spoke. Dion Harvie and the others, of course, understood nothing of what he said and Ferdinando admitted that he could only fasten on a word here, another there, but the chief's gestures, his tone of voice, reassured even those who heard nothing but a stream of grunts and growls.

Wingina's welcome, given through Ferdinando, told Amadas and Barlowe that this village and everything in it was theirs, the huts, the furs, the fires and the cookpots and the food.

"And," the Portuguese ended, "he invites us to a feast."

"Where?" asked Barlowe sourly, looking about him. "I see not a table or a bench in this whole place."

"Mayhap because ye've been too busy lookin' at the wenches," Ferdinando grinned, then held up a hand. "Now, now, y'r pardon, Capitan—no offense meant. As for the tables and benches, the savages do not use 'em. Sit ye on the ground and ye'll get y'r belly filled, I promise."

Filled they were, with dripping venison that was more delicious than any these men ever had tasted, coming as it did after weeks of a diet of pickled meat and ship's biscuits. There were baskets of corn, roasted in the husk, fish wrapped in clay and baked so that scales and skin came away from the flesh when the clay envelope was broken. There were thick chunks of bear steak, crackle-skinned geese and ducks, dozens of broiled pigeons, countless cornmeal cakes smeared with wild honey. There were wooden trenchers of frogs' legs, great heaps of oysters, crabs and crayfish steamed in seaweed, eels boiled in some herb-tanged sauce, a stew with ingredients best not inquired into.

The Englishmen gorged themselves, belched, groaned with surfeit, and ate again. Because there were no eating implements, they soon rivalled their hosts in the coating of grease with which they bedecked their hands and faces. And as they ate, as they chewed and gulped and reached for more, their eyes stayed fastened on the warm-skinned women who served them.

Wingina, eating sparingly, shifted his piercing eyes from one guest to the other, then addressed Ferdinando at his side. The Portuguese listened, smiled and nodded before he called across the circle to Philip Amadas.

"His Lordship says that those of us who'd use a woman are welcome to pick our choice from amongst those here and others at Dasamonquepeuc. And unless I heard him wrong, these include his own wives."

"Damned heathen!" Nicholas Petman jerked out. "Think of a man offering to bed his own wife with a stranger!"

"Now, now, Master Petman," the Portuguese protested, "don't be too hard on the chief, sir! Why, 'tis certain he makes this offer only to be a good host—he's not like many a fine gentleman I c'ld name who's done the same with his wife in hopes that he'd gain favor and position from the one he let cuckold him."

"But—but there's a *delicacy* to be observed in such things," Petman explained. "A gentleman who'd use his lady for his own advantage would surely turn his head and shut his eyes, not stand ready with refreshments at the foot of the bed."

"Ah well," Ferdinando said with heavy gentleness, "these are benighted savages after all, Master Petman—they cannot be expected to know the niceties as you Englishmen do."

Philip Amadas lowered a venison chop from his mouth and spoke through his food.

"What think ye, Sir Pilot?" he asked. "Would it be best to order all our company, gentlemen and mariners, to avoid the women? Wouldn't it bring trouble to deal familiarly with these wenches?"

"I think 'twould be more likely to bring trouble if we didn't accept the offer," Ferdinando replied. "They're touchy, these people, and if we said no to Wingina's invitation he might think we hold his women unworthy—which, God knows, they're not.

"Besides," he added with a chuckle, "I doubt y'r sternest order would be obeyed past the first time one of us got alone with one of these fair charmers."

Amadas gave his dubious permission for the acceptance of the chief's generosity and Barlowe was quick to protest, glimpsing a stand that might profit him in Walter Raleigh's opinion.

"Ye may do as ye see fit, Captain Amadas," the gloomy ship-master said, "but *I* do order all those under *my* command to leave these wenches alone! Sir Walter will not hear it said of me that I let my charges lower themselves to bed savage women."

Simon Ferdinando raised a hand to hide the smile that parted his beard. He said nothing but Dion, watching him, saw that his eyes mocked the dour captain's idea that his order was more than so much wind.

As for Dion, he was determined that, regardless of Amadas' permission, he would shun these Indian women. He was a Harvie, son of Lord Avronbeck, a gentleman born and bred, and while his code allowed him to make love to his brother's wife, it certainly would not permit a coupling with a dirty savage.

Well, not dirty, certainly, because the Roanokes, men and women, were forever bathing, splashing about in the water in mixed groups, as unconcerned as children that men were made differently than women. Further, they made a fetish of their depilations, painfully plucking all their body hair out by the roots and, in the men's case, submitting to what must have been a minor torture to tweak each hair except that mid-skull ruff from their pates.

In the days that followed, the Englishmen came to be amazed at the abundance of fish and game to be found on and about the island that, for lack of an understanding of the Indian name, the explorers called Roanoke Island. Amadas wrote enthusiastically in his journal of the deer, hares, conies and water rats as well as what he described as "a great abundance of the goodliest and best of fish in the world" which the Roanokes killed with their arrows or netted and speared in the waters. The white men ate well; the first days on the island brought one feast after another until, seeing their men bogged down by swollen bellies, stuffed to stupidity by the endless meals, Amadas and Barlowe ordered all hands to join in an exploration of the mainland.

Carried in canoes paddled by Wingina's braves, Dion and the other white men made the short trip to the Roanokes' biggest village, Dasamonquepeuc. It proved to be a stockaded town four times the size of the hunting camp on Roanoke Island but almost identical in its circle of open-ended, thatch-roofed huts, its storage sheds at one end of the elliptical stockade, its common cooking and council fire. Beyond the walls of Dasamonquepeuc were fields under cultivation, with maize standing eight feet high and low vines, carefully tended, covering many acres. These vines, the explorers soon learned, carried bulbous roots which were edible when boiled—and so Dion Harvie was one of the first Englishmen to ever taste a white potato.

He was one of the first, too, to see tobacco smoked. The Roanokes had not used the weed on the island; the smoking of the rank leaves was reserved for ceremonies held at Dasamonquepeuc and even the imperturbable Simon Ferdinando was startled the first time he saw Wingina and the other Indians puffing at their clay pipes.

"Now, by The Book," he exclaimed, "here's something I never saw them do in Florida or other places! What madness is this, that they'd poison themselves with these fumes?"

The tall Portuguese fingered his beard and then added, with a shrug: "But I'd try it, I vow. It's my intention to be able to boast I've tried everything I've seen another man do."

The other members of the expedition gathered around Ferdinando while he placed the pipe handed to him by Wanchese between his lips and sucked at the reed stem. Then erupted a storm of coughing that left the pilot black in the face and gasping for air.

" 'Tis a deadly drug!" the Portuguese spluttered when he could speak. "Don't touch it, on y'r lives!" He saw Dion grinning at him and almost let himself look sheepish; he knew that Harvie was remembering his advice, to always let another man test something that might be dangerous. He squared his broad shoulders and defiantly placed the pipestem to his mouth again, sipped a tiny puff and quickly blew it free. "I'fackin's 'tis not so bad as I first thought," he added brazenly. "In truth, I'd call it exceeding pleasant—it's all in not swallowing the smoke, but keeping it in the mouth, I see." He puffed and blew, puffed and blew, obviously refusing to let the hot bitterness in his mouth change his expression of satisfaction.

Following Ferdinando's lead, the others in the party tried the pipe, Dion Harvie last of all. He drew only one puff of the acrid smoke, expelled it with a gasp and spat in disgust.

"God's gullet," he snorted, "there's one heathen custom they can keep! Thank heaven civilized folk have better sense than to suck such foul stuff into their mouths."

The visit to Dasamonquepeuc was followed by trips to other villages, Hatorask, Secotan, Pomeiok, Aquascogok, and journeys up the rivers that entered the sound in which Roanoke Island lay, excursions further inland. Everywhere they went, the white men found game in abundance, waters full of fish, skies clouded by pigeons, marshes teeming with ducks, although Wanchese told Dion that winter brought a thousand times more wildfowl to this region.

The woods, Amadas wrote, *are not such as you find in Bohemia or Moscovia, barren and fruitless, but the highest and reddest cedars of the world, far bettering the cedars of the Azores or the Indies; pines, cypress, sassafras, the gum tree, the tree that bears the rind of black cinnamon and many others of excellent smell and quality.*

Of gold or pearls, Amadas wrote not a word and for the reason that nowhere in their travels did the whites see a scrap of gold, a single pearl. During one of the ceremonies at Dasamonquepeuc, Wingina donned a wide arm bracelet that, for a moment, brought tight-throated excitement to Petman and the others who hoped to find gold but closer examination proved that the bangle was no more than crude copper, inexpertly smelted and hammered. And this, Ferdinando was able to learn from the chief, had been a present from a tribe living far to the west, a people who had passed through this country years before and had not returned.

"Poor Sir Walt," Dion told Amadas. "He's dreamed of a land where gold and jewels had to be kicked out of the way for easy walking and now we find there's not a bit of treasure to be had."

"Not so," Amadas countered. "Sir Walter did not send out this expedition to find gold, sir, but to locate a place for the settlement of a colony for the Queen. Let Drake and Hawkins rob the Spanish dogs of their gold plate and jewels—we're part of a plan to gain far more enduring riches for Her Majesty, an empire on this side of the sea."

"Oh aye," Dion said, his mouth quirked, "but I'll warrant friend Walt and Gloriana herself would not be downcast to have us sail back with some tons of gold in the holds of our vessels or a cask or so of jewels."

The expedition scouted down the coast as far south as a cape that marked the southernmost tip of Secotan, and north to the Chesapeake Bay, Amadas diligently working on his fantastic map and scrawling in his bulky journal. Everything that he saw, thought he saw or heard that someone else had seen went into the report to Raleigh. When Nicholas Petman returned to Roanoke Island from a fishing trip with the word that he had glimpsed a band of horses on the mainland close to the great river north of the island, down on the pages of the journal went the account. The fact that nobody else saw the horses, that the Indians themselves were bewildered by Ferdinando's efforts to describe a horse, obviously never having seen one, did not touch Amadas' gullibility in the slightest.

The days flowed past smoothly. The sun toasted the white men to a deep tan as the corselets and helmets were cast aside and the Englishmen went naked to the waist. Thunderstorms came out of the west, flickered and boomed and grumbled their way out to sea. Petman and a few others kept up their relentless search for gold. Ferdinando held Wingina spellbound with stories of which the Roanoke chief could not have understood a half. Amadas and Barlowe bustled about on their explorations. Dion Harvie, if only to fend off lethargy, studied the language and the ways of the Indians.

His teacher was the girl Rycko and Ferdinando loosed a howl of delighted laughter when he discovered this.

"Now here's a pretty picture," the Portuguese chortled. "Our chaste Master Harvie who'd never, never fall so low as to bed a savage wench picks for his tutor the choicest maid of all of them! No wonder she was the only girl who refused Petman and the others who approached her!"

"She did that?"

"Oh aye, and 'cause she's Wingina's pet granddaughter the warning was given that she must pick her own partner. And so it's you, Master Never-Touch!"

"Only to learn the talk and these people's manners," Dion explained virtuously. "She's teaching me the words and how to cast a net for fish and—"

"And ye show her the manners of great ladies in the grip whilst she gives you lessons in how a barbarian woman engages in the lists."

"Arrgh, it's not that at all," Dion snarled. "I'd ha' picked a man —Wanchese is friendly enough to me—as my teacher but you know Amadas and Barlowe keep them busy every day as guides. I chose Rycko only 'cause she looks a bit more intelligent than the others."

"Intelligent?" Ferdinando sniggered. "What does the word mean—cunningly fashioned? For she is that, and lively as a. . . ."

Dion fled, ears burning. For it was true that Wanchese, his closest friend among the Roanokes, would certainly have been relieved from his duties as guide by Wingina if Dion had asked the tall young brave to be his teacher. Rycko did have an air of superior intellect compared with the other women but Dion did not dare ask himself whether it had been that or the sleek beauty of her lithe body that had made him choose her for a don.

Still, having made the choice, he was glad he had. She was good to be with, nice to have close to him. Her every movement was a delight, her warm presence was a comfort and yet an urgent disquietude.

During those first lessons in the Roanoke language, Dion held himself rigidly apart from Rycko, reassuring himself that Ferdinando was a satyr who could see a fleshly purpose in the most impersonal things. The girl, shy as the doe her grace resembled, kept her own distance. Thick-lashed eyes downcast, knees clasped tight, hands crossed over her copper-skinned middle, she sat at the far end of the log on the cove beach Dion had found for a classroom.

The lessons went slowly. The Roanokes, it developed, used only a limited number of words whose meaning changed with the slightest shift of one vowel's inflection. A single word meant a rabbit, a gull, the bank of a river, the act of going on a short journey, a raincloud, a forked stick, depending on the position of the accent, the depth of a vowel tone, the sign that accompanied it.

Still, Dion made progress and as he learned enough to carry on a sort of conversation, as Rycko picked up enough English to speak haltingly in an hilarious accent, the space between the two on the log grew narrower until they were sitting side by side, their shoulders touching.

Her skin was warm but it could not have been as burning as it felt to Dion when it pressed against his bare arm. Her breasts were soft, rising and falling with her breathing, but they could not actually have begged to be stroked, as Dion thought. Her eyes were deep when she gazed up at him they could not have been beseeching, as he saw them. Her taut-skinned middle, her dimpled belly, her straight thighs forking down from the scrap of deerskin —all these could not have been reaching for him as he imagined.

Even with these thoughts, Dion might have held to his old resolve of impersonality if he had heeded the warning that night lessons could prove dangerous.

The nights—ah, they were fashioned to be the undoing of far stronger men than Dion, with the sky draped in purple velvet, the stars a scattering of blue-white diamonds broadcast by a profligate Somnus, the winds drenched by the perfume of grapes. And Dion was eighteen years old. His first experience with a woman had come at the age of thirteen; he had been neither more nor less dissolute than the average young gentleman of the age, which meant that to him chastity was a thing that ranked with the unicorn, doubtless extant but seldom encountered, at least in England.

For close onto four months—it was now mid-August—he had been living in self-enforced celibacy and living a life calculated to quicken the hot blood of youth, not temper it. The girl beside him might be a heathen savage but her breath carried the same scent of grapes as the wind and her skin glowed in the gold dust of starlight. The posing puppet-ladies of England always wore a sour smell beneath their heavy perfumes; this Indian girl exuded a cleanliness that was at once refreshing and seductive.

She had long since lost her shyness and now, as she looked at him her eyes were enormous, luminous, her teeth shone white in her dark face. Was it in subtlety or in innocence that she turned toward him, laughing at some ludicrous mistake he had made in pronouncing a word, and pressed a hard-nippled breast against his arm, leaned against him so that the cool fire of her body flowed into him?

Innocence or subtlety, the result was the same. He stared down at her as his arm came up to encircle her shoulder, his hand held her in a clutch that would have been painful at another time. Her eyes widened, then their lids half shut, her lips parted, her body went limp in immediate and frank surrender.

He plunged his face down to hers and the Roanoke girl, Rycko, tasted the first kiss she ever had been given, probably the first kiss a woman of her people ever had been given, and gloried in it, shared it, took command of it instinctively. Her hands stroked him, plucked at him, soothed him and aroused him with an art that was more compelling because it was not studied.

Savage wench, savage wench, savage wench! Dion's brain hammered, and another part gasped, *Ah God, how sweet, how sweet!*

The world heaved and bucked, the heavens spun and the soft breezes lashed themselves into whirlwinds, the seas resolved in a waterspout that thrust higher, higher, higher until there was the blinding flash of lightning, the deafening crash of thunder, the cloudburst of molten sleet and the slow, gentle swing back to the beach at Roanoke Island, the soft pressure of Rycko's panting bosom, the whisper of the wavelets along the shore.

She did not speak before she left him to wade into the water, a slender, straight silhouette, a naiad of the New World, replete with love. Nor did he say a word to her before he strode down the beach toward the huts the Indians had built for their white guests.

A simple tumble with a heathen woman who's scarce human, he kept telling himself as he walked, *and nothing more, so why do you feel so distressed about this, fool?*

3

REVULSION CAME with the morning and with it came a loathing for Rycko, for all Indians, for this island and this country, this New World with its dull peace, its spineless, simpering brotherhood, its cloying abundance and its total lack of such spices as anger and envy, intrigue and conspiracy, great ambition and ruthless reaching, high success and depthless failure.

"God's sake," he complained to Simon Ferdinando, "when do we quit this place? Amadas and Barlowe must have seen every tree in this country by now and still we dally, wasting the days."

The Portuguese peered at him curiously, his thick brows updrawn.

"How now, friend Dion?" he asked. "Why are you so suddenly hot to go back to England? 'Twas my thought you'd welcome a lengthier stay here, what with certain persons wanting so much to put their hands on you back there—and with another certain person having all she can do to keep from putting her hands on you in front of everybody here."

"Ye're wrong about me bein' wanted in England," Dion lied recklessly, "and as for the other certain person, I suppose y'mean Rycko. Well, I'd not touch her with your finger and ye know it!"

"Ah, Dion, Dion," the Portuguese murmured with a sad shake of his heavy head, "the truth is not in you this morning, for certain. Know you that these people think no more of recounting the story of a tussle of love—and down to the last detail, mind—than they do of saying their name? What happened betwixt you and Rycko last night was a common story in the village before it had been finished two minutes, I trow. Aye, she was most happy that you'd been generous enough to give her your embrace."

"Damned heathen bitch," Dion muttered.

"So?" Ferdinando asked, his eyebrows up again. "Damn me, but ye're an ungrateful fellow, Dion Harvie! Roanoke she may be but still she entertained ye and—"

"An Indian entertained *me?*"

Ferdinando sighed. "There speaks y'r English gentleman. What did they teach you at y'r Oxford—to be a self-minded prig, only? Here's a wench who pleasured you and now you—ah, never mind. Ye called her a bitch, eh? Well, then, if you feel thus, I'll take steps to have her wag her tail at me." He preened his beard. "Aye, on thinking of it, I've seen her cast a glance my way of late—mayhap last night's was not the first toss, after all, and she's in need of more than Sir Fuzzface has to give her."

"Touch her," Dion grated, "and I'll show you that a buggy beard's worth nothing in a fight."

Ferdinando's face stiffened and his eyes narrowed.

"Do I hear threats," he asked, "or was some sparrow cheeping in a tree? Fight, you say? With words or black looks or with good steel?"

"With this!" Dion's rapier came out of its ring with a sweep and went *en garde* to be met by Ferdinando's blurring blade. The two men poised, bowstring tight, their eyes locked across their swords. They glared at each other for the space of a dozen heartbeats and then Simon Ferdinando stepped back, lowered the point of his blade and uttered a sheepish laugh.

"We both must be moonstruck, Dion," he said, "when we draw 'gainst each other over a wench neither of us wants." His sword went back into its ring and his smile widened. "For know you I could've had Rycko from the start had I not picked a lustier playmate."

"A crone," Dion jeered, "who's a granny ten times over. I've seen her."

"A woman with experience that fits her to engage a champion," the Portuguese said loftily. "Not some wide-eyed maid who must have it explained to her what this is for and that."

"Now, damn me—"

"Ah, ah, Dion," Ferdinando interrupted soothingly, "let's not get full of bile again. Why your black mood today?"

" 'Tis this damned place! I'm sick to death of this wilderness! I'd change it all for the smoke and stink of London at this minute."

Simon Ferdinando looked about him, at the burdened grapevines, the cool forests, the sparkling water, the untainted sky, and shrugged, grimacing.

"Each to his liking, then," he nodded. "And as f'r sailing back to England, it won't be so long as you might think. Amadas and Barlowe plan to start back within the fortnight or as soon as they can coax Wingina to go with them."

"Wingina!" Harvie exclaimed. "Y'mean they hope to take the chief back to England with them?"

"Certainly," Ferdinando said, spreading his spatulate hands. "Think on it, friend Dion, and you'll see why Amadas needs must take a savage back with him. For what else can he bring Raleigh to prove he's been here—a salted fish, a strip of smoked venison, mayhap, or a bunch of grapes? No, aside from the potatoes and the tobacco, he has nothing to offer, no gold, no pearls, no precious stones, to show he landed here and explored this place. But to furnish a live savage—ah, there'd be proof enough to satisfy even the Queen, and so the two captains hope to convince Wingina he needs a sea voyage for his health."

"He'll never go," Dion said. " 'Twould mean handing his kingship over to Granganimeo and he'd never do that. Aye, the undercover mistrust between those two marks the only sign of civilization on this island."

Ferdinando chuckled as he nodded.

"No more he will," he agreed, "but when our two doughty captains finish their stumble-tongued arguments and fail, mayhap Simon Ferdinando can furnish them with two live and lusty savages to take back to England with them—at a price. Manteo and Wanchese."

"Those two? Ye think they'd go?"

"I know they will," the Portuguese said calmly. "I've filled them with so many stories of the wonders of England that they're all but ready to swim there. For though they do not show it, both of them have lofty ambitions in their heart; they'd follow Wingina as chief, each of them, and throw Granganimeo to the sharks, if need be. It was a simple matter to cozen Manteo—harder with

Wanchese—with the hint that if they went to England with us, they could not help but be the wisest men of all the Roanokes and so rule the tribe when they came back. Of course I spoke to each one alone and each thinks he steals a march on the other and licks his lips at the thought of his triumph."

"But if they both go—"

"Ah, what happens then will have to be seen. Enough that Amadas and Barlowe will have some genuine savages to give Raleigh and the Queen."

A week passed while the two captains argued fruitlessly with the dour Wingina, a week in which Dion Harvie first refused to go close to or speak to or even look at Rycko and then, relenting, comforted her with a smile, a word and a pat on the shoulder and finally returned to the log on the beach with her.

" 'Tis all a matter of safeguarding my health," he told himself firmly. "A man needs must cool his blood at regular times or risk the worst of vapours."

During the last few nights the expedition spent at Roanoke Island, Dion Harvie armored himself against a plague, a scourge, an epidemic of vapours and found each preventive treatment sweeter than the last.

When it came to sail it was as Ferdinando had predicted; Wingina was adamant in his refusal to leave his people, Wanchese and Manteo elbowed each other in their haste to get aboard the barks. Wanchese was given a berth aboard *Tyger* while Manteo joined the *Admiral's* company; the braves glowered at each other across the stretch of water that separated the two ships before the anchors were weighed, the sails raised and the vessels stood down to Trinity Inlet.

The farewells between the whites and the Roanokes were long and fervent. Wingina pledged eternal friendship with the tribe of Amadas and Barlowe, gave the white men bundles of tobacco leaves and deerhide sacks of potatoes. A banquet given for the departing guests stretched on and on as Dion, acting at Amadas's and Barlowe's interpreter, expressed the Englishmen's thanks for the Indian's generous hospitality and promised to return with more fine presents.

Then, when Harvie had begun to think these ceremonies would

never end, the goodbyes were suddenly over. Wingina got to his feet, raised his hand, barked a few words and disappeared into his hut. The other Indians scattered to their various duties, long unattended because of their services to the explorers.

None of the squaws showed interest in the departure except Rycko. When Dion Harvie obeyed an urge to turn and look back, he saw her standing at the stockade gate, shoulders braced, head upraised, hands at her sides. When she saw him turn, the girl raised her hand in a gesture that was nearly a civilized woman's wave.

Dion turned back without replying. All that, he told himself, was over and done with. He was going back to England and he'd best forget he ever yielded to his flesh so much as to couch a dirty, heathen wench.

Part 3

1

IT WAS September eleventh, 1584, when the two barks cleared Roanoke Island for the voyage back to England. It was November fourth before *Tyger* and *Admiral* crept up the Thames and came to anchor off Queenhithe, beyond London Bridge and opposite the frowning bulk of square-steepled Saint Paul's Church.

Dion Harvie stood at the rail of *Tyger,* feasting his eyes on the spires, the towers, the houses and public buildings, guild halls and warehouses of his beloved London. Gratefully he sniffed the turgid breeze that brought him the thousand blended smells, none of them fragrant, of the great city; to his ears came the subdued roar of England's biggest town, a place that was rapidly gaining on Paris in size and importance. Indeed, the city was growing so fast that it seemed a lad whose clothes would never fit; it had burst out of its old walls years before and pushed back from the Thames into the low-lying hills to the north, it had spilled over the river to make Southwark a bustling city itself. The Thames was jammed with shipping, new quays were being built to relieve the congestion at the two original ports of entry, Queenhithe and Billingsgate, but even these quays and wharves, Three Cranes, The Stilliards, Botolph's Wharf, Galley Quay, Tower Wharf and Paul's Wharf, were already overcrowded. Vessels had to wait days, sometimes more than a week, for docking space to discharge or take on cargo.

There she lay, Dion's beloved city, and as he gazed at the

teeming waterfront he swore silently that come what might he never again would leave England. Dirty, dangerous and despicable in many things she might be, but London was Dion's true love and he would not desert her a second time.

Yet—well, he could confess it to his inner self—there had been certain things about Roanoke Island that he wished he could have brought home with him, though he had scorned them in the last days of his stay there. True, the life had been too effortless, replete to the point of surfeit, but there had been something more than bodily comfort; there had been a peace, a spirit of brotherhood, that could not endure longer than a spark from a blacksmith's anvil in London, or all England, for that matter.

Dion recalled that on the island the common seaman and the high-born gentleman had both forgotten the vast differences in their positions and had worked together, eaten together, hunted together, fished together, even indulged in horseplay together. The *Tyger's* boatswain had proved to be the ablest man in picking up the proper handling of the Indian bow and arrow and had given instruction in the use of the weapon, stubbier and stiffer than the English bow, to such gentlemen as Petman and Wood, never sparing in his wrath at their clumsiness.

"Naah, naah," he had bellowed, "ye must have the nock at the level of y'r eyes, ye ninny, not down by y'r shoulders! God's teeth, ye couldna hit yon stockade usin' that kind of stance!"

And when he had praised one of his pupils for a good shot, the gentlemen beamed—where they would have been insulted by any fraternal word or gesture from such an underling back home.

It was not right, Dion realized; it had bordered on lunacy for him and the other betters to have hob-nobbed with the scum, the seamen snatched from the shadows of the gallows of "Deadly Never Green" on the banks of the Tyburn, and yet it had not been shocking at the time; indeed, it had seemed somehow right that a man be judged by what he could do, not by the name he carried. Nicholas Petman, for instance, had been looked down upon because he had not pulled his weight with the others and yet Petman was but one step away from knighthood, his family's fortune was enormous.

Ah Roanoke, Dion asked silently, *what magic did you make to bemuse us all so completely?*

The spell of fellowship had not lasted beyond one full day at sea. The dunes of Hatorask had not dropped below the horizon before the boatswain was bowing, almost cringing, each time he spoke to one of the gentry; the gentlemen were cloaked again in their proper pride; the void between the thoroughbred and the common stock gaped as widely as it ever had.

"And all that happened over there had best be kept silent," Dion murmured under his breath, "else I'll be sneered at by everyone I know. I'd bring shame to my family to add to the trouble I've already brought."

As soon as he went ashore, he vowed, he would get a horse—Raleigh would doubtless lend him one—and ride to Avronbeck Hall and an accounting with his father. Enough time had passed, he was sure, for the Queen's anger over Groven's stabbing to have cooled; Elizabeth was such a many-mooded woman that she probably had forgotten her darling Captain in a fortnight and doubtless some new favorite was enjoying her curious affection now.

Yes, it would be safe to go home; his father's hurt would be healed; he would be given the same reception by his mother and sisters that he had enjoyed so many times before, the Prodigal Son come back to feast on the fatted calf.

So hurry, Captain Amadas, and finish your inquiry to learn my standing. Bring back your report that all is well and let me hie myself to Avronbeck Hall and my family. And I promise that Charles's wife, big-eyed Helen, will be safe from my attention from now on.

He swung his gaze toward the Queenhithe dock again, searching for the round-bellied shipmaster and the black-bearded pilot, Ferdinando, who had gone to Raleigh's apartments to notify him of their return. They had taken with them the potatoes and the tobacco; their two human specimens of life in the New World, Manteo and Wanchese, had been left aboard to await a more propitious time to land, properly heralded and with a crowd to gape.

Dion turned as there was the soft scrape of a moccasined footstep behind him. It was Wanchese, topside at last after the miserable weeks he had spent below, retching in seasickness. Now he was grey beneath his bronze skin, shadow-eyed and slump-shouldered, a poor caricature of the man he had been on Roanoke Island.

The Indian cast his flat gaze at the bustling waterfront, shifted it to stare at the steeple of Saint Paul's Church and the spires of Bow Church and Saint Lawrence Poultney, beyond, and returned his eyes to Harvie's.

"Big," he grunted. "Too big. A man would not have enough room to draw a bow there."

"You need no bow in this place," Dion replied in his faulty Roanoke. "This is a place where there are no deer left to be killed for meat, no enemies to be slain for blood."

"So?" Wanchese asked with a hunch of his shoulders. "But Amadas and the one with the black beard wore long knives when they went into this great village. Aye, the man Ferdinando was most careful to test the edge of his long knife before he put it on his hip."

" 'Tis but a manner of dress," Harvie explained, "like the feather you wear. A sword's less a weapon these days than an ornament as necessary as a doublet, to be in fashion."

"And never used to kill?"

The vision of Captain Guy Groven lying in his blood rose before Dion's eyes and he grimaced.

"At times," he admitted. "A blade's a handy thing to have about in case the need for it comes upon a man without warning."

"In our country," Wanchese said simply, "we do not need to carry bows or knives or clubs unless we hunt or go to war. Here, you white men wear your long knives as a part of you. Why do you not make peace with each other, as we have done?"

"We are at peace," Dion said stoutly, and lapsed into English. "Of course there are times when a man must defend his honor and—"

"Honor?" the Roanoke asked. "What does that word mean?"

Dion Harvie groped through his meagre stock of Indian

phrases to explain the theory of honor and came up with this explanation:

He said, "Some men are born to high position and a name they defend against all insult. If a man slurs me, by word or deed, I must be quick to wash out the stain against my name with my sword, my long knife. It is demanded of me as a gentleman."

Wanchese pondered on this, his brow wrinkled, his eyes puzzled, then slowly shook his head.

"I do not understand this," he said, "but I will believe it because you are my friend and cared for me while I was sick, crossing the sea. But if another man said Wanchese was a thief and a liar, it would either be true or untrue. If it were true, I would hide my face in shame. If it were untrue I would spit on this man, not try to kill him, for he would be so false no tribe would let him sit at a council fire."

He moved his eyes back to the wharves and docks.

"Tell me," he said slowly, "something of this woman, this Queen, who rules you and of the man Raleigh, who Amadas tells me is my chief in this strange land. Why do you white men allow a She to command you? Is she so wise, so all-seeing, that no man in this land can equal her and so you made her your queen?"

"No," Harvie said, " 'twas not because of her wisdom that she is queen—though she's exceeding wise. 'Twas because she is the daughter of a king we called Henry the Eighth, born of Henry's second queen, Anne—Anne Boleyn, that is, not Anne of Cleves. You see, of Henry's first wife, Catherine of Aragon, he had another daughter, Mary, who took the throne when Edward the Sixth died and when Mary died—they named her 'Bloody Mary' for her slaughters—Elizabeth sought and won the crown, though Mary, Queen of Scots, daughter of James the Fifth, would take it from her if she could and—"

"Enough!" Wanchese said brusquely. "To keep account of your rulers is like numbering the bees around a honey tree. But you can tell me something of this man, Raleigh, that is more simple?"

"Ah, Raleigh," Dion said, his blue eyes alight, his young face wreathed in a smile. "He is my closest friend and ever will be, I hope. He's—how shall I say it to you? He's as tall as you are and his very greatness makes him seem still bigger. He has a sharp wit and a high temper—many's the time I've seen him fly into a rage at nothing and quiet himself as quickly. He's the handsomest man in all England and the most deserving. He's been one of the Queen's knights since Spring and I vow he'll end as the Queen's First Minister, so closely does she heed his advice. His age is thirty-two but he seems no older than you or me. His youthful face has so distressed him that he wears a beard and full moustaches to look his age; shaven, he is a boy who could scarce command the Queen's attention."

"And what has he done to be a knight?"

"Done—done? What has he not done, friend Wanchese? When he was but a lad he went with his cousin, Henry Camperdown, to fight with the French Hugenots at Jarnac and acquitted himself well. Five years ago, or so, he went with his half brother, Sir Humphrey Gilbert, in command of a vessel, the *Falcon,* in a raid on the treasure ships of the Spanish Main. 'Twas then he got the eye of Her Majesty, the Queen, and he's held it since. He is a proud man—aye, three times he's been put under arrest for duelling and there's a hundred times no warder knew about. He's gained a great fortune by the Queen's favor, yet he's ever in debt because he throws his gold away on expeditions such as the one that brought a meeting 'twixt you and me."

"He has a woman?"

"He has a hundred of them, and no wife. 'Tis said he has a burning love for one of the Queen's ladies-in-waiting, Elizabeth Throgmorton, but Her Majesty won't give the permission to marry that all her attendants must have. Gloriana is fair cruel in keeping her gentlemen from marrying those they love. 'Tis said that—ah, but I'd be disloyal if I repeated the gossip."

Wanchese followed the course of a smallboat that was edging out of Queenhithe and making for the two barks that swung at anchor in midstream, and grunted again.

" 'Tis the captain and Bright-Ear, the big, black-bearded one," he told Dion long before Harvie could identify the wherry's occupants, "and with them is a third who must be your good friend, Raleigh, by your description."

"Aye, aye, 'tis he!" Dion said excitedly. "Mark how straight he sits, how handsomely he holds himself. God's blood, he puts to shame every companion's appearance, even though he need not half try! I vow, in rags he'd outshine all the gaudiest gentlemen in the court—though pray God he's never reduced to rags."

Wanchese glanced curiously at the young man standing beside him and half shrugged in something close to embarrassment. Such extravagance as Dion used in his praise of Sir Walter Raleigh was so foreign to Indian manners as to be grotesque; the tribes of the Roanoke area might respect their chiefs and outstanding braves but they never showed their high regard too openly. Wingina commanded a strict obedience, his word was a law from which there was no appeal, and yet except for a headdress that was a bit more elaborate than the others', a hut that was a trifle larger, a robe of multicolored feathers that he donned on occasions of state, there was little difference in his life from that of a stripling just come to manhood.

Now the smallboat drew alongside the *Tyger* (and Dion leaned so far out over the rail in his greetings to Raleigh that Wanchese felt constrained to clutch his wide leather belt lest he fall) and Sir Walter, teeth flashing in a wide smile, cloak and hat plume tossed by the November wind, reached for the rope ladder and scrambled nimbly to the deck.

"Dion, Dion!" he cried as his hands came out to grasp Harvie's shoulders. "It's good to see you, man, back from the New World and never looking better, I vow! Exploration agrees with you, 'tis easy to see, and I have it from Captain Amadas that you were one of the most valuable men of the expedition, I'll be bound!"

Dion's lips twisted in a wry grin.

"Well, then, ye'd best find another valuable man for the next trip," he told his friend, " 'cause I'm done exploring for a century or two. Nay, let some other worthy win the captain's praise on the next voyage, for I'll be content to stay in Merrie England."

Raleigh's smile faded as he tugged at one of his long moustaches, shaking his head.

"On that," he said slowly, "we'll have to talk, friend Dion. Things are still not so smooth for you here as I had hoped they'd be. We'll—but that can wait a bit." He turned toward the unsmiling Wanchese and held out a hand. "Ho, Wanchese," he said and, although the Roanoke could not have understood more than a word here and there, added: "Welcome to England, my good friend, and may your stay here be as pleasant as the captain and Master Simon tell me their sojourn in your land has been."

The Indian looked down at Raleigh's outstretched hand, then hesitantly met the handclasp, his face still expressionless, his natural aloofness held rigid. The time would come when Manteo would lose his reserve, even learn to smile in the white man's fashion and curry favor from the English with an artificial deference, but never Wanchese. Manteo would go on to greater honors and a high-sounding title, Lord of Roanoke and Dasamonquepeuc, but he would make his sacrifice to attain these things and the price he would pay would not be low. To the end, Wanchese would scorn every suggestion of opportunism and, in Dion's eyes at least, be the better man of the two for it.

"You speak the language, Captain Amadas, Ferdinando?" Raleigh asked. "I've an audience with the Queen tomorrow morning and I'd fain to have an interpreter who'll present these men's words to Gloriana in the proper fashion."

"Dion's the best versed in their talk," Ferdinando laughed. "You see, Sir Walter, he had a most skilled teacher and he attended his lesson so closely he scarce did eat or sleep, eh, Master Harvie?"

"Now hold," Dion began furiously. "'Twas not like that at all, friend Walt. I but—"

"It matters little," Raleigh broke in impatiently, "'cause you can't serve as interpreter before Elizabeth in any case. Nay, we'd best keep you well out of sight of Gloriana's men."

"You mean that damned Groven affair still rankles Her Majesty? I thought by now—"

Raleigh cocked a significant eyebrow and Dion left his sentence hanging. Throughout the voyage to the New World, the stay in the Roanoke country, the fiction had been preserved that

Simon Ferdinando did not know Dion had boarded the *Tyger* as a fugitive. Harvie was almost sure the Portuguese knew the true story down to the last detail, certainly he was well-informed about the near-scandal that had banished Dion from Avronbeck Hall to London, but if Sir Walter thought different, and his glance showed that plainly, Dion would keep his mouth shut in front of the big pilot. Ferdinando had been closer to him than any other member of the expedition, he had proved himself a good friend on more than one occasion—but Dion had never been able to convince himself that the Portuguese could be trusted past the point where it would mean one more gold coin in his pocket to betray that friendship.

So, impatient to talk to Raleigh alone, Dion fretted and fumed while his friend made an inspection of the *Tyger,* then had himself ferried to the *Admiral* to meet Manteo and confer with Barlowe. It was nearly dusk when Sir Walter returned to the larger bark and signalled Harvie to join him in the captain's cabin.

There, with the door and the single leaded window to the stern gallery tightly shut, Raleigh spoke rapidly, in a hushed voice.

"Ye'll not interrupt me, friend Dion, till I'm finished, by y'r leave, and I'll acquaint ye with all that's happened since you rode for Plymouth, a jump and a half ahead of the headsman's certain attentions. First, Groven did not die of the wound you dealt him."

"Did not die? Then—"

"Damnation, must ye break in? Nay, he did not die though for a time it was thought sure he would. Gloriana was in a most wondrous rage, as we knew she would be. She swore to find you if she had to turn all England and France and Spain and Italy topsy-turvy to do it. She called your father to court and all his friends trembled in their boots for him, so sure we were that she meant to have his head, could she not have yours. But Sir Clement being the man he is faced her without the slightest show of fear, though Gloriana was fair foaming. He said truthfully that he knew naught of y'r whereabouts; he even dared to say that if it was truly you who wounded Groven, the hound deserved it—God's gullet, I thought the Queen would blow up with apoplexy at that!"

He waggled his sharp-pointed beard, clucking his tongue at the remembrance of that scene.

"Milord Burghley," he went on, "was hard put to calm Her Majesty but he did noble work—aye, and Leicester put in a good word and I can say without boasting that my own efforts were not wholly wasted. It ended by Elizabeth cooling, especially after 'twas known that Groven would live—she cooled where y'r father was concerned, that is, but not in your case."

"You mean she still hates me 'cause I pinked her pretty boy?" Dion asked. "Why, it was a fair fight, forced upon me."

"Oh, aye, we all know that but the Queen refuses to admit to herself that her favorite is the skulking dog he is. And there's another thing—"

Raleigh's beringed hand went to his beard to tug at it fretfully.

"Aye," he said after a pause, "I've placed myself in a poor position in y'r behalf, Dion Harvie. For Gloriana suspicioned that there was a connection twixt y'r complete disappearance and the sailing of my ships from Plymouth. She called me to court and asked me straight out if I'd helped you escape her and I—I lied in my teeth when I told her no."

"How can I ever thank you, friend Walt, for—"

"Ah, 'twas as much f'r my own neck as f'r yours," Raleigh scoffed. "Think you the Queen would have spared me if I'd confessed I went against her will to hide you? But so you see, Dion, that you must stay out of her sight—and her men's sight, too—and go back to the New World when Amadas and Barlowe sail again. This much you owe me, I believe."

Dion Harvie looked down at the deck, biting his lip. He had vowed there would be no more leaving England and now it was plain that what Raleigh said was true. His friend had risked everything, his wealth, his court position, his very life, to save him—could he do less than meet his request now? And, to look at the situation selfishly, what would his life be worth in England so long as Elizabeth still was angry with him?

"I see," he said gravely and then, as anger swept him: "Curse the luck and curse that bastard Groven! Why did I have to walk into Wenrick's gaming rooms when there were a dozen others to choose from? Why didn't I stay at your place and listen to your plans for the expedition; why was I so ungenerously wearied by your talk? Another time, I'd—but what's the sense in wishing that the past could be changed?"

"There's none," Raleigh agreed, as gravely.

"But I can ride to Avronbeck and see my family, Walt? Certainly the chase has died down by now!"

"I counsel 'gainst it," Raleigh said regretfully. "You know how things stand twixt your half-brothers and you—they say Charles was overjoyed at your troubles though fearful the Avronbeck fortunes would be ruined by the Queen's anger. If you were to go home I'd wager my purse that Charles would betray you. Nay, Dion, best hide till my next expedition is ready to sail again."

"Aboard this damned vessel?" Harvie asked gloomily. "I'll go raving mad unless I get my feet on good solid ground soon."

"No, not the bark," Raleigh replied. "Both vessels needs must be careened before they set out again and you couldn't stay aboard, even if it were safe, which it wouldn't be; Elizabeth's curiosity concerning who's aboard my ships is likely to be still unsatisfied. Nay, I'll arrange for you to stay in a snug hideaway where they'll never think to look for you—a friend of mine by the name of Burnie, not quality but of the best of heart and exceeding close-mouthed when needs be. 'Twill be no mansion you'll be staying in but it will suit our purpose well. As soon as it gets properly dark we'll move you thence."

"Where is this Burnie's place, in the country?"

"No, no; the heart of London Town is best for you. My friend Burnie has a house—I warned you 'twas no mansion—in Lime Street and though 'tis not the most fashionable part of the city you'll be properly lost there."

When he saw the place on Lime Street, Dion agreed that he would be properly lost, but his heart sank at the cost of ignominy. To call Burnie's home no mansion was the depths of understatement; it was a ramshackle building, a rabbit warren that housed a score or more of families, all of them, Dion suspected sourly, intent on keeping out of the eye of authority.

"In God's name," he groaned as he walked into the hallway of the building, "how did you find a good friend in this place? I'd never think you'd seen this stinking street, much less found an ally here."

"In my position," Raleigh said simply, " 'tis best to have friends in as many walks of life as possible. A man never knows when he may use the most humble supporter—as witness your case. But you'll like Burnie. He's a good man for all his station and his heart is as big as the holes in his hose. His quarters are at the end of this hall; watch sharp you don't stumble over one of these leather pails that smell so fragrant."

"I thought the *Tyger's* hold smelled worse than Hell's sulphur," Dion muttered, "but 'twas sweet perfume compared to this. God damn that Groven again, that he sends me here instead of to the comforts of Avronbeck."

The man Burnie (in all the time Dion stayed in Lime Street he never learned his landlord's first name if, indeed, he owned one) turned out to be a tiny fellow with a hump on his back and a ferocious squint, a frog's voice and an ever-present grin. He was clad in doublet and hose to match his dwelling. All the things he wore obviously had been cast off a dozen times before they reached him and, apparently, he was too busy with his host's chores to do any mending or cleaning of his garments—or to bathe.

But it was evident to Dion, even in the uncertain light of the cluttered room at the end of the hall, that the man revered Sir Walter Raleigh. This was shown by no bowing or scraping—Burnie, Dion was to learn, would be grudging in a bow to the Queen, herself—but by his tone of voice, the light in Burnie's narrow eyes as he looked at Raleigh, in a hundred half-discernible things that told Harvie his newfound landlord idolized the tall, handsome gentleman who was not only one of Elizabeth's favorites but also the favorite of all England in those times.

"Aye, Sir Walter," Burnie chirruped, "we'll make your young friend all tight and comfortable in our palace here. He'll have the finest rooms I can offer and if they do not suit him, why then I'll boot every devil's son and daughter out of here till we find rooms that do. And they'll not bother him, I pledge you that—I'll pass the word that the young sir is sufferin' from the plague and can't be touched or even looked at without horrid results."

"Nay, Burnie," Raleigh laughed, "ye'd better not be so forceful as all that or ye'll have the dead cart at the door, lookin' for trade."

"That ye'll never see at this place, Sir Walter," the humpback said. "The driver of the dead cart for this part of London lived here a spell and nipped away owin' me rent. Nay, I c'ld pile corpses six deep in front of the house and he'd never come after 'em. But let's to the rooms and get y'r young friend settled, eh?"

The rooms were on the third floor, in the rear of the house, and Dion gaped in astonishment when the door opened onto them.

The hall door led directly into a bedchamber, larger and more comfortable than Harvie's own at Avronbeck Hall. Incredibly, the floor was covered by "Turkey-work" carpeting, dark green with a bright, multi-colored design—a rich duke's ornament, certainly. In one corner of the room was a bed with a panelled front, or footboard, that reached to the ceiling, making of it a sort of huge cupboard, open on one side. Heavy draperies of embroidered silk curtained the opening but not so completely that Dion did not glimpse a thick mattress and enormous pillows, waiting to give ease in sleep or dalliance.

Two elaborately carved chests were set at the foot of the bed. These, Burnie demonstrated to disclose hinged doors that gave entry to the chests without the necessity of raising the lids. Revealed inside were nests of drawers capable—as Dion told himself—of holding a wardrobe a thousand times as plentiful as his, at the moment.

Set in the wall opposite the bed was a fireplace with a hooded chimney that captured most of the smoke curling from the fire on the hearth. Close to the fire was a small "credence table," its top crowded with bottles, flagons, glasses and silver cups. In the center of the room and vying with the bed for domination was a heavy table, richly carved, surrounded by stools and two folding

X-shaped armchairs, both inlaid with ivory and colored woods and obviously of Spanish make.

Set against the doorway wall was a writing desk (the first Dion Harvie had ever seen) faced by a third armchair. Beside the desk was another small table, as handsomely turned as the larger one.

Three-candle sconces were fixed on each wall and from the ceiling over the table was suspended a hanging lamp with a floating wick, the aggregate fixtures providing what to Dion was dazzling illumination.

Off the main room—and promptly examined by Harvie—was a smaller wardrobe with deep presses, cupboards and lockers lining its walls. This room, too, had its rug, a luxury exceeded only by the great mirror that hung over an exquisitely fashioned dressing table.

Dion turned to Raleigh and the landlord, his face disbelieving. Raleigh smiled over his wide ruff and jerked his head at Burnie.

"Surprised at the comforts Burnie offers?" he asked. "Think ye you're the first gentleman to take advantage of his hospitality? If you but knew who's rested here on occasion ye'd be fair amazed, wouldn't he Burnie?"

"Ah, we've had our share of the great ones," the little man chortled. "Methinks the balmy air of Lime Street has been good for the health of half the noblemen of England, at one time or another. I vow, I expected to see Mary of the Scots come runnin' in before the misguided lady placed herself under Elizabeth's protection."

"Now, now," Raleigh warned, "no politics, Burnie, if ye please, and not a word 'gainst the Queen. We've troubles enough without adding disloyalty to 'em. Nay, just keep my good friend, Master Harvie, comfortable for a time and guard his true name from all ears, see that he's well fed and bedded and"—his eyebrow quirked as he glanced at Dion—"if he has need for a woman's companionship, make sure the lady is tight-lipped."

"That would be Margery," Burnie sniggered. "A tasty wench but never given to blabbing. Nay, she knows what'd happen to her if she so much as squeaked. And now I'll leave you two gentlemen to your own affairs. Master Harvie, if ye want me, yon pull-rope will summon me in a trice, f'r food or drink or any other need. Sir Walter, would you favor me by droppin' by my throne room as ye leave?"

He was gone, a chuckling gnome, pander and protector, a misshapen mite of merriment, a scraping of scum that feared no law, bent no knee, held no allegiance to any but his oddly assorted friends. Torture could not wrench one word from him if the word meant the least harm to such as Sir Walter Raleigh; he would betray any man or woman to the block for a silver groat or merely for the pleasure it would give him if the one betrayed did not command his good will.

It was said, and likely could be true, that the twisted little man of Lime Street had amassed a huge fortune by his devious favors to some of the biggest men in Elizabeth's England; there were others, Dion was to learn, who insisted that Burnie was of fine family, himself, and maintained a vast estate in the country where a wife, two sons and a daughter travelled in the best of circles under their real name. Later, Dion heard a hundred stories about Burnie but which were cut from whole cloth and which may have had a smattering of truth, he was never to find out.

Now, as the door closed behind the frowsy landlord, Raleigh turned to Harvie, his hand reaching for a leather pouch tucked under his belt.

"Here, Dion," he said, "ye'll need this for y'r creature comforts. Trust Burnie in all things and no one else save Burnie tells ye to. Keep to your rooms here until I say 'tis safe for you to leave—mayhap I can fix a way for you to see y'r father, at least."

He clapped a hand to Dion's shoulder and raised his voice.

"Come, come, Dion, be not so glum as all that," he said cheerily. "This is not forever, mind, and even were it so 'twould be better than the axe or the noose. I'll visit you often and keep you informed of what's what—though if you can stand his ripe smell in close conversation I doubt not that Burnie could tell you as much and as quick as I can of what goes on at court. The friendly little fiend must have as many spies as Elizabeth herself."

He hesitated, frowning, as his hand went to his beard.

"I'd counsel you 'gainst too much wine," he went on, "and if there needs be a woman it must be this Margery that Burnie spoke of—she'll have a close mouth, for one thing, and no pox, f'r the second."

"There'll be no need for a woman," Dion said emphatically. "Think you I'd dally with a wench who no doubt outstinks Burnie?"

"Well-ll—she won't if Burnie says she won't; ye may be sure of that. But I must fly. I've been too long in this place as it is and Burnie wants to see me on some other matter." He laid a hand on Dion's shoulder again, gripped it hard. "Courage, Dion. This thing we can work out together, do ye heed my counsel now."

"I will," Dion promised. "And—and I'd not have ye think me ungrateful for all you've done, Walt. If I wear a glum face, 'tis only because on the long voyage home I dreamed of coming back to all I knew before Groven and whetted my appetite till it's a sore disappointment to find that all that must wait."

"I know. But again, courage. And farewell for a time."

2

THE DAYS at Burnie's on Lime Street dragged by on shackled feet. As far as his bodily comfort was concerned, Dion Harvie could ask for nothing more. The food that Burnie supplied him with was excellent (and where in this part of London could there have been so splendid a kitchen?), the Malmsey and Sack and other wines were good, the bed had a minimum of bugs—so few, in fact, that Dion almost hated to squash one between his fingernails, afraid he was exhausting the source of even this diversion. The rooms were as warm as any rooms of the times, heated by fireplaces that burned smoky sea coal from Newcastle. Raleigh brought him books by Chaucer, poems by Spenser, the plays of Udall, the fiery tracts of Bishop Bale, and Burnie entertained him by the hour with conversation that unwound stories of noblemen and nobodies, high-born ladies and harlots, pimps and princes.

Aside from Raleigh and Burnie, Dion had no visitors, unless the slattern who cleaned his rooms could be called such. Harvie became so desperately put to relieve his boredom that he tried to strike up talk with the cleaning woman; he soon learned that she was a deaf mute and therefore accredited by Burnie as safe to know that a gentleman was housed in relatively sumptuous apartments in the third floor rear. Burnie, in fact, told Dion that if blindness had not been too insurmountable a handicap, he would have found a blind mute for the work.

And so, despite the efforts Raleigh and Burnie made to relieve the torture of his strange imprisonment, Dion Harvie paced his rooms with all the amiability of a baited bear. Nor did the news Raleigh and the landlord supplied him with do much to soothe him. While it was all good, as far as Sir Walter's ambitions for a colony in the New World were concerned, Dion still was a hunted outlaw with a fat price on his head.

"No, Gloriana has not changed in that," Burnie chuckled, "nor does it seem she will till some fine fellow finally kills that whoreson Captain Groven. He's still the Queen's pretty darling—aye, if the Queen was different from what she is I'd say he was possessed of the most wondrous engine the world has ever known. While he's at Elizabeth's elbow he can make certain she don't forget you. But take heart, young sir—Groven has more enemies in court than a herring has scales and one of these days somebody will rid your world of him."

But although the reascendance of Dion's star seemed indefinitely postponed, Sir Walter Raleigh's was never higher than in that winter of 1584 and 1585. Unpredictable Elizabeth had proved delighted with the results from the Amadas-Barlowe expedition to Roanoke Island; the tobacco and the potatoes had interested her as much as the gold and jewels dumped into her treasury by John Hawkins and Francis Drake, and the two Indians, Manteo and Wanchese, she found fascinating.

"Indeed," Raleigh reported to Dion, "she's making a courtier out of Manteo, complete with satin breeches, Italian silk hose and a cartwheel ruff. Wanchese still wears his mangy savage robe and his feather for all I do persuade him to don something warmer. Aye, he's a granite man to try to coax but for all that I feel the Queen looks on him with perhaps more favor than she does on Manteo, in her heart."

"He's worth a dozen Manteo's," Dion growled. "I thought Manteo would turn into a lickspittle, given the chance, and I see I was right. But Gloriana exclaimed over the tobacco, eh?"

"Exclaimed, man? Nothing must do but that she try the stuff herself, and at once. Manteo showed her how to cram the pipe and she fair filled the privy closet with clouds of smoke. Though her eyes watered and she near coughed her borrowed hair off her head she claimed she liked the taste of tobacco."

"Now, by God's eyeballs," Dion grunted, "we'll see a country of chimney pots! What Gloriana likes or says she likes becomes the law in England forthwith. And once I thanked Heaven we were too civilized in this country to ever take up that savage pastime."

"And the potatoes!" Raleigh went on. "She barely touched the dish before she proclaimed it the tastiest thing she'd ever eaten. I've a command to fill one of my ships with nothing but tobacco and potatoes when I return from my next expedition."

"Ah?" Dion asked, eyebrows arched. "She's given you permission for another voyage, then?"

"Next Spring," Raleigh exulted, "and I'm sure to be allowed to go this time. I think I cinched that when I proposed the name Virginia for the new land in honor of her, the Virgin Queen. And this will be a far bigger venture, Dion!"

"With Philip Amadas and Arthur Barlowe in command again?"

"Not Barlowe, no. He feels he has been slighted by my treatment of him since his return but what would you? Amadas worked hard to bring me true reports and maps while Barlowe, as far as I can learn, did nothing. Simon Ferdinando will pilot the expedition again, of course—we could never do without him—and sharing with me in command of the entire company will be my cousin, Sir Richard Grenville. Aye, Dick has already consented to go with us."

Even the antipathetic Dion was impressed by this. Grenville had fast been approaching the stature of Drake and Hawkins, Sir William Winter and Martin Frobisher, the Queen's doughtiest admirals; if he were to be released by Gloriana from home waters and the naval guard against the threat of Philip's Spain, then Elizabeth must certainly be more than ordinarily enthused about this colony in "Virginia."

"Then we'll have Captain Ralph Lane as governor of the colony when it's established," Raleigh was rattling on, "and—"

"Captain Ralph Lane? I don't know him."

"A soldier, Dion, and a good one with experience in government. He has a name for excellence in the building of forts and—"

"Forts? And why forts, in God's name?" Harvie broke in. "You think the Roanokes are going to begrudge your settling in their land? You do not know them then, friend Walt, for I tell you that they're the most peaceful folk in all the world. I cannot think what would make them go to war—though Ferdinando did say once that they sometimes fought each other in times of famine."

"But these forts," the sharp-bearded gentleman explained, "won't be raised 'gainst the savages but 'gainst the Spaniards. There's always the danger—though I did not mention this to the Queen—that the Spaniards in Florida might try to oust us from our Virginia, most particularly if we should find gold."

"Ah, gold," Dion sighed. "The hope of finding it is in your mind, then, for all Captain Amadas claimed you were only interested in building an empire for England by setting up colonies."

"That's the main intent," Raleigh said, "but if we find gold there, surely we shall pick it up. And if the Spaniards hear we have found gold, those greedy dogs will likely be on our necks, trying to take it away from us. Therefore, Captain Lane and his forts."

Dion nodded, his eyes brightening. If that did happen, he told himself, Roanoke Island would not be as dull as it had been that past summer. It might be a good thing, after all, that he was bound to go back to the New World; a fight with Spain could restore his honor with Elizabeth and—well, yes—there always was the chance that there *was* gold there and a fortune to be pocketed.

"And who else sails with you, Walt?" he asked. "How many ships?"

"Four or five vessels, besides *Tyger* and *Admiral,* and at least a hundred men, all told. Already signed are Thomas Cavendish, who has more salt water in his veins than blood, I vow, and John Arundell, half-brother of Grenville and my cousin, as is John Stukely, Dick's brother-in-law. The most favored artist in the realm, John White—and an excellent judge of things politic, too, besides being a painter—is hot to go. And Thomas Hariot, the scientist, and—ah, Dion, we'll have a company that'll be the best that ever sailed!"

"And when do you sail?" Dion asked. "I would to God it were tonight, to get me out of this place!"

"As soon as we can be outfitted and the winter gales subside," Raleigh said. "I'm determined to start before something happens 'twixt Spain and England that'll change Elizabeth's temper. This is late January—we should be ready to leave by the first of April, at the latest."

"Two months," Dion groaned. "You'll have to chain me in the hold of the ship that carries me; they'll want no madman raving on deck."

"Patience, friend," Raleigh smiled. "I'm all but certain I can arrange a safe way for you to journey to Avronbeck before another fortnight's out. No promises but—well, I'll hold my tongue lest I raise false hopes and cast you deeper into gloom. Meantime, why don't you pleasure y'rself with the wench Burnie spoke of when first you came here? Methinks a woman would speed the hours till you can leave here."

"I've thought of it," Dion admitted, "and more than once. But there's always the thought that she'd turn out to be as high-smelling as her sponsor and so turn me against all women. On Roanoke there was a—but here I hold you in idle prattle, Walt."

"On Roanoke," Raleigh echoed, "there was an Indian maid, so Ferdinando tells me, and she—"

"You know that windy braggart couldn't tell a straight story if his neck depended on it!"

"Well, all he said was in praise of this girl, Dion. He said she was as sweetly made as any he ever saw and soft as velvet."

"How could he know how soft she was?" Harvie grunted. "She'd have naught to do with him."

"But she was pleased to treat you more kindly, eh?" Raleigh pursued.

"Aye, Walt, she—she was most gentle with me, was Rycko. Ye'd be fair confounded by the kindness that is in those people, truly, and Rycko was—oh, 'tis but this dull life, I suppose, that makes her seem like a goddess in my memory. Still, she was a tender piece that I'll have trouble forgetting, I confess."

Forget Rycko—when the restless nights brought her to the chamber on Lime Street, when Dion's dreams summoned her to his bed so many times? Harvie's self-imposed celibacy adorned his image of the Roanoke girl with a seductive allure that heated his blood, roused his desire, until he suffered virtual physical pain.

It was when he awakened from a nap and Rycko's nude loveliness vanished that he yanked the pull-rope that brought Burnie as promptly as though the humpback landlord had been waiting outside the door, spying on his dreams.

"That wench you spoke of," Dion said, his voice harsh with his urgency, "is she still at hand?"

"Y'mean Margery?" Burnie giggled. "Oh aye, and fair pantin' to be called to you. I told her I expected you'd want her and she's been wonderin' why so long a time has passed. Were you ill, she's asked me a hundred times, or did you prefer men to women, as some Italians do? I told her no on both counts and—aye, I'll fetch her immediate."

"After all," Dion told himself as he waited for the girl, "if she be too ill-favored I can shut my eyes and think of Rycko. But it won't be as good—and how could it be with any other woman?"

3

THE GIRL Burnie sent was tall, as the women of Elizabeth's day went, and because she was not of the quality her hair was her own, not borrowed, frizzed and dyed an Elizabethan red but warmly brown and neatly coiled. Harlot she might be but the first impression she gave Dion was of a cleanliness that was all too seldom found anywhere in England and doubly amazing in this multi-tiered sty on Lime Street. Her teeth were white, her green-gray eyes were clear, her unpainted face was smooth-skinned, her slender throat showed no shadows such as were worn by some of the highest ladies of Elizabeth's court.

She was thin without being scrawny, except in the hips and bosom which were admirably fashioned for her trade. Her wrists and ankles were neat, her feet were small considering her height, and her voice—lo, it was quiet, perfectly modulated!

"Milord Frisbie?" she asked with a smile that did not seem wholly artificial. "Burnie said you might be lonesome and so welcome a bit of my poor company. I'm Margery Hollis, sir, and at your service."

Dion caught himself just before he bowed and forced his face to show no surprise. Totally unprepared for such a woman, he found himself uncertain as to how this Margery Hollis should be treated. He had dealt bluntly, brutally, with doxies, he had treated high-born ladies scarcely less directly or, when the occasion had demanded, with a certain delicacy which had delayed the business at hand with farcical hesitancy—with this girl neither manner seemed quite proper.

"Pray have a chair," he said in a tone that mixed courtesy with contempt. "A glass of wine?"

"If you would be so kind." She nodded as she crossed the room to the chair Dion's curt gesture had indicated. She moved gracefully but with none of the mincing of the whore trying to play the lady. When she accepted the glass of Sack from Dion he noticed that her hands were long-fingered and her nails unrimmed with grime.

She sipped daintily, sat back and waited for him to speak if he wished, to make the next move. The impression crossed his mind that she would be quietly, yet whole-heartedly, receptive to anything he proposed, from the idlest by-play to the most involved convolution of love-making. He had the idea, also, that if he wished he could carry on an intelligent, interesting conversation with this woman and enjoy it.

A conversation—hah! Did he propose to waste time in chit-chat with her in the room, the swell of her round, high breasts straining the cloth of her dress, the deep cleft showing above her low-cut bodice, her whole lithe body offered for other things than talk?

Burnie had called Margery a tasty wench and for a change he had not been boasting. To a young man who had just passed his nineteenth birthday (in this strange confinement and without even a visit from Raleigh to help him celebrate the day) and who had been shut up in these rooms without having seen a woman except the old and dumb slavey in something like four months, the presence of this girl with the quiet voice, the clean skin, the gentle smile, the thighs made for love, was bound to send the blood thudding through the veins.

"I—I had not thought to see so fine a lady in such a place as this," he managed. Her eyebrows arched as her smile widened.

"Lady, milord?" she asked. "Surely you make mock of me. I've been called many things but never before a fine lady."

"But you—I mean, how is it that you—"

"That I am a strumpet, milord? You mean you want a long story of misfortunes and disasters that brought me to this poor estate? I can recount one that I vow will keep you spellbound but it would be false, all of it." She sipped her wine again. "Nay, Mag Hollis was not plunged into this bawdy life by some great stroke of ill fortune. She chose to be what she is with never a regret."

"But surely you could have done better by yourself than this!"

"I could? You think I should've chosen to be a peasant's wife in a village by the moors and break my back birthing children and hauling on a plough rope an hour after the child was born? My mother did that, milord, and her mother before her and *her* mother, back to the days of Penda and Athelstan, I vow." The smile that had faded widened again as she added: "They were ancient kings, milord."

"You need not explain," Dion said haughtily. "I'm not wholly unlettered."

"Y'r pardon," Margery murmured. "But as I said, I vowed I'd never live the life my grandmothers did and so, when the time came, I ran away. I knew there was but one way for an eight-year-old girl to get along and so I paid my passage to London with the oldest coin that's known, albeit this coinage was barely minted and exceeding painful, at times.

"An eight-year-old girl!" Dion exclaimed.

"Oh yes," the woman said calmly. "Think you that's too tender an age to make use of the only worthwhile thing God gave a woman? Why, in my home village I've known fathers to—but why speak of things you might find unpleasant. Let's leave it that I made my way to London and soon found out there was a slavery here worse than even the peasant woman's bondage. So I once again paid my way in a manner I learned excellently to do, though I'd not boast. And here I am, milord, to serve you."

Dion poured another brimming cup of Sack and drank a swallow.

"You speak like a schooled person," he said and then *did* bow. "Y'r pardon, Mistress Margery; I do not mean to pry."

"Oh, come, sir," she scoffed. "What pardon do you need for looking into a doxy's secrets any more than you'd need for putting y'r hand on her knee? As for the way I talk, I had a protector once who was a bookish man, and very kind. His age forbade him lustier pleasures save on great occasion and so he took delight in teaching me my letters, in making me what he thought was a lady." She laughed in a murmuring chuckle. "He had a most rare idea, for a gentleman—some amiable madness brought on by age made him think a body must scrub herself from head to foot once every blessed day. To humor him I did it—I think it was his greatest pleasure to watch me sluice myself—and when he died, God rest his soul, I found myself afflicted with the habit."

She eyed Dion over the lip of the cup.

"I trust it does not offend you, Milord Frisbie," she added. "I know there's some who prefer the gamy flavor."

"Not me," Dion said fervently. *No, after Rycko with never the taint of stale sweat on her, 'twould be hard to overlook the least offensive smell, even in the clutch of love.*

"I have another fault, milord," the girl went on. "This oldster who I speak of could not abide perfumes or sachets. Again, I fell into the bad habit of not bedecking myself with beautiful scents but I can douse myself if it be y'r wish and—"

"No, no," Dion broke in. " 'Twill be refreshing to—but I must say this ancient protector of yours was an odd one. Who was he? Mayhap I knew him."

Margery's eyes stared straight into his but now their light was dimmed almost imperceptibly by a translucent veil. Her smile was as wide, but with the suggestion of a set at the corners; the woman's pliant body seemed indiscernibly tautened by an instinctive wariness. Yet when she spoke, her voice was as easy, as friendly, as it had been.

"Let us say he was Lord Greyhair," she suggested, "or Sir Bentback. What does it matter who he was, milord, now that he's dead and no doubt trying to teach the poor souls in Hell to speak gently and to wash themselves once a day?"

"Burnie said you were never given to blabbing," Dion nodded.

"And he told you, too, that I know well what'd happen to me if I did blab," she smiled.

"He—he said something of the kind," Harvie admitted, "but Burnie spouts such tales on all occasions that I paid no mind to what it was." He looked down at his cup, revolving it between his fingers. "I suppose he was but being his windy self, as always," he suggested.

There was a silence from the other side of the room. Dion waited for an answer, then looked up to see the girl smiling at him quizzically. Anger rose in his throat as he gulped his wine. What manner of whore could treat him so? He had been too kind to this doxy; he should have commanded her at the start to strip and ply her trade and get out! Hedgerow bitch, strumpet in the meanest stinkpot in all London, spreadleg to any man Burnie would send to her—she dared to mock Dion Harvie, son of Sir Clement Harvie, Lord Avronbeck?

"Though on second thought," he gravelled, "I do not think friend Burnie lied when he said he had your neck between his greasy fingers. What was it, Mag—murder or treachery or mere common thievery, the lifting of a man's purse whilst your other hand kept him clutched to your skinny charms?"

Her smile did not falter, her eyes did not waver.

"Why not all three, milord?" she drawled. "Why not that I first stole the man's gold, then coaxed him to be disloyal to the Queen while he was fair fainting at the excellence of my skinny charms, then murdered him when he threatened to uncover me as a Spanish spy?"

Dion flung his silver cup at the fireplace, the spilled wine painting a purple parabola across the room before the goblet clanged against the brick and rattled along the floor.

"Begone, witch!" he shouted. "Get ye to some gutter swine who'll relish y'r playing at the great lady! I'd not touch ye with Burnie's finger—that no doubt has explored all of you!"

Margery Hollis finished her wine, placed her glass on the small table and arose, smoothing her skirt.

"As you will, Milord Frisbie," she said quietly, and moved toward the door. Her hand was on the knob when Dion spoke again.

"Hold—hold, Mistress Margery," he said. "I am a bit undone and did not mean to screech like a jackdaw. Pray come back; I pledge you better manners."

"Manners?" she asked lightly. "Why sir, you did not strike me or kick me."

"I called you witch," Dion said. "I did not mean it. It was only that you angered me—y'see, I'm all edgy with this being bound by these walls and not let walk the streets or see a play or a bear-baiting or talk to my friends or even know if my family's in good health or—"

"They are," Margery said placidly. "Milady Avronbeck and Milord and Lady Joan and Lady Elizabeth are all in the best of health but worried, a bit, at the circumstances that keep you from them, Master Frisbie."

Dion stared at her as she folded her hands and looked down at them demurely.

"Why then—why then—" he stuttered, "you knew who I was all along! This Master Frisbie was but a laugh in y'r gullet, then! Who told you—Raleigh—Burnie?" His hand swept to the hilt of the sword he carried. *"What is this, woman?"*

She raised her deep eyes to his and her voice softened.

"Remember, I'm Mag Hollis who never blabs 'cause it would mean her own neck if she should even whisper in her sleep. Who you are, ye know, and what ye've done to bring you here is twixt you and those you hide from. Who told me who you were?" She leaned forward until Dion's nostrils widened to her warm ripeness. "Mayhap I dreamed you were Dion Harvie and mayhap I dreamed you stuck your sword in one of the Queen's favorites and mayhap it was all part of a fancy that a great black-bearded man with a pearl in his ear has been walking this part of London for the past weeks, describing you down to your last toenail and asking if any has seen you."

"Ferdinando!"

"Aye, that's the bravo's name. A handsome brute, with his bright teeth and his halloo that'd drown out the imps shrieking in Hell. I questioned this Spaniard and—"

"He says he's a Portuguese," Dion interrupted.

"Ah? Aye, he's a Portuguese, then. But I say I questioned him, when he was all limp and suspicionless, and—"

"You lay with Simon Ferdinando?"

Her chin lifted for an instant and then sank as she shrugged.

"I am a whore, milord," she said simply. "Does a chemist refuse to sell his powders to a man with gold because he does not like the pimple on his nose? Besides, this sea captain sprinkles money like a March wind sprinkles snow and, when all is said and done, a doxy cares for nothing save money. But I spoke of questioning this Ferdinando. He asked after a certain man I did not know and he described him down to the last freckle, though"—and she peered closer—"I see no freckles on you, milord."

"Have done! What did he want?"

"Why, he offered a wondrous purse to the man or woman who could tell him where this Master Dion Harvie could be found. Twenty golden pounds, and all for saying that this man was at such-and-such a place."

"Twenty golden pounds! Icod, I knew Gloriana was enraged but not to such a length she'd offer so much that Simon would pay twenty pounds to a spy!"

"He never said he was seeking this man to hand him over to the Queen's soldiers," Margery said carefully. "He said he had great news for this Dion Harvie—he said he was his good friend. He bade me tell this Master Harvie, an I should meet him, that he would be each night, at the stroke of eight o' the clock, at a tavern called The Boar and The Plume, near here."

Dion walked to the window and looked out at the unkempt skies that hovered over the spired and towered horizon of smoke-blanketed London. He clasped his hands behind his back as he stared unseeingly at the murk.

"You do not blather," he said in a harsh voice, "but do you sometimes take the coin and whisper, Mistress Margery?"

"You fear me as a traitor, milord?" the girl asked evenly.

"I fear you as a woman," Dion replied, "and no woman was ever born who couldn't have her conscience buried by a weight of gold."

"Why then, tell Burnie that I'm false—I promise he'd rid you of any danger I might have for you quick enough."

"I'll not tell Burnie," Harvie said gruffly. "I may be a fool for doing it, but I trust you, Margery Hollis."

"For which," she almost whispered, "I'll thank you in the best way I know how."

He turned and saw her walking toward the curtained bed. She gave him one brief, inviting smile over her shoulder before she put her hands to the few garments she wore and then stepped out of them. He stared at her thin-stemmed back, her rounded croup, as she bent to strip the stockings from her legs. The heat of his desire mounted to his throat, his appetite welled in a flood that swamped his anger, his suspicion, his clamoring sense of danger.

She turned toward him, a nymph sprung, alive and fresh and sweet from the squalor of the poorest part of London Town, a tall, placid-eyed goddess come to one of the filthiest parts of man's earth, a woman who held promise of the realization of all the dreams a man could dream within the arms she half held out toward Dion.

She was majestic. She was Athena, Diana, Venus, as she stood there, the claret-colored bed drapes making her a background. The prostitute, the creature of Burnie, stood there, her bosom rising and falling, flanks narrowed, eyes wide, hair touched with a nimbus by the setting sun that struggled through the smoky fog curtain outside to slant through the window—she stood there and smiled at Dion Harvie.

"By God!" Dion burst out.

"You find me comely, milord?" she asked.

"Comely? God's blood, you're beautiful!"

"Then shall we have done with all this talk and get to the reason we're met?"

He half ran across the room to her, his sword thudding to the floor as he cast it aside with his belt. He joined her unarmed, defenseless, all the caution Sir Walter Raleigh had warned him to preserve abandoned to the flame that consumed him.

Margery Hollis had said she had learned excellence in her calling; now she proved she had. When conventional love-making was outdistanced, adroit invention served.

She was the palpitating corolla of an orchid, the sinuous panther that purred and screamed, the moth's wing that fluttered against every tortured nerve, the whip that goaded and the balm that soothed, the urgent guide to the very brink of ecstasy and the restraint that held Dion gasping there until his hoarse plaints cried his agony and she enveloped him to hurtle into rapture with him.

Later, when their shuddering, their sobs, had eased, she brushed her hair back from her eyes and smiled down at him.

"How now, milord?" she asked softly. "Do'st find Mag Hollis's skinny charms acceptable?"

"Sweet Mag," he grinned, "what kind of fool was I to put off finding you so long?"

"Better than pondering that," she murmured, "let us try to make amends for the lost time."

4

A WEEK PASSED, another, with Margery Hollis a constant visitor to Dion's rooms, always at a call from him, never venturing to knock on his bolted door but appearing a minute after Harvie notified Burnie he wanted to see her. He had told Burnie, speaking with a generosity born of Raleigh's fat purse, that he was buying the girl for the duration of his stay on Lime Street and, consequently, her time was his.

"And a better bargain ye won't get in all London," Burnie had chortled when he mentioned the price for these exclusive services. "I pride m'self I furnish the best bawds in England and Margery's the best o' the best."

"She seems gently reared," Dion ventured. "Is it true she was a farm girl, run away to London at eight years old?"

The little hunchback had peered up at Harvie, his eyes slitted, his lizard's mouth twisted in its ever-present grin.

"Now, young sir," he had said, "ye have y'r own secrets and so do I and so does Mag. Why stir up questions that're best left layin' still, eh? What Margery's been may turn the Devil's face black just by thinkin' on it but so long as it's what she *was* it's no concern today, I say. No, Master Harvie content y'rself with enjoyin' what she has to give ye and let all matters of her luck or lack of it fly out the window with y'r chamber pot."

About Simon Ferdinando and his questions dealing with Dion Harvie, Burnie had wrinkled his forehead in a heavy frown.

"I heard he was about," he had told Dion, "before Mag came to me with the story he was askin' for you. But Ferdinando is a man almost as clever as me. I've known him or of him for the past five years or more and even I can't rightly say whether he's a Spaniard or a Portuguese, as he claims to be. He's Walsingham's man, that I know, but who else pays for his services? No use to tell Raleigh that the man's dangerous—Sir Walter swears by him and always has ever since Ferdinando captained the *Falcon* on the voyage to New Found Land in Sir Humphrey Gilbert's luckless expedition. As to why he's seeking y'r whereabouts, I'll ask a question here and another there and if the Spanish bastard has evil designs on you, I'll have him dealt with."

"Nay," Dion protested, "I don't want him murdered!"

"Ah, just a cloak over his head and a twine about his neck and —zzzrrrkk!"

"No, I say, Burnie! The man was a friend to me and perchance he seeks me now in a friendly cause."

Burnie had put his arms akimbo, tiny bent legs spread wide under the chicken-breasted bulk of his heavy-shouldered torso, and had leaned closer to Dion.

"He'd do a friendly thing?" he asked. "Let me tell you, young sir, the last friendly thing Simon Ferdinando did in all his life was quit his mother's womb so she'd be rid of him."

"He's not that bad, Burnie! Why, on Roanoke Island he—"

"That island in the New World wilderness? He befriended you there? I tell you why he did. He saw you for what you were, a man fleeing from the Queen's axe, and to have more proof on which to base his treachery, he made himself a friendly fellow, a man you'd tell the secrets that'd be worth two hundred golden pounds to him when he collected the Queen's reward."

"Two hundred golden pounds she's put on my neck?" Dion gasped.

"Aye. Are ye flattered?" The little man turned and spat decorously into a corner of the room. "Don't be," he said, turning back and lifting a log-thick forearm to wipe his mouth. "I had more'n three hundred pounds on my head in Bloody Bitch Mary's reign, before you were born. I hid Bishop Hooper of Gloucester when he was being hunted and when Mary's men came to take us we both ran for a cave he had marked. I got inside, unseen, but the Bishop, being a more fulsome man than me"—he looked down at his dwarfed body—"could not stuff himself in and so was caught. And so was burnt at the stake. They say that when the fire reached him he—" He rubbed a grime-blackened hand across his grinning lips and added, absently: "Ah lackaday, he was a good man, for all he was a priest. I'll send Margery to take y'r mind off such things as the stake and the axe and the rope."

After the first few days and nights of heady transport, however, Margery became more of a companion, a conversational respondency, to Dion than just a bedmate. He told her of Roanoke Island and Wingina and the grapes, the cranes and the sand dunes, the cedar forests thick with game and the waters with their boundless schools of fish, the clean, clean wind and the different sort of sun that was on the other side of the Western Sea, a sun that was brighter, warmer, closer than the tarnished disk that hung over London Town.

He even taught her a few sentences in Roanoke talk—and laughed at her efforts as Rycko had laughed at his. Raleigh had brought him a potato; he had Margery boil it and watched as she ate it and laughed delightedly when she murmured, "It must be a taste only the quality can savour, knowing that the Queen is so enthused, but I do confess, milord, that I don't find this so excellent."

"No more do I," Dion agreed. " 'Tis only 'cause it's something new that Elizabeth went into raptures over it, I vow!"

So, as the days passed, there grew between Dion Harvie, the nobleman's son, and Margery Hollis, the bawd, a companionship that never could have been imagined under any circumstances except as odd as these. And though he might say wild, intimate words in the dark, though she might draw fervent cries from him in their enfevered grappling, there was never a thought in his mind that the bottomless chasm that stretched between their two lives could ever be bridged. He was in this Lime Street hideaway because the Queen's axe glistened outside; he would be gone as soon as Raleigh told him it was safe to go and he never would see this place or this woman again, nor even think of her except as an amazingly clean trull, wonderfully versed in arousing, titillating and then satisfying a man's appetite.

And Margery—what thoughts might she have entertained? Was she so hardened a whore that never once did the thought of love for this handsome, gay, charming young Dion Harvie invade her secret self? Did she never dream of a miracle that could raise her to Dion's level or lower him to hers—no, not lower him because he was too fine, too worthy, to be. . . .

"I thank you for the fine garters you had Sir Walter get for me," she said now to wrench her thoughts away from the impossible. "I vow no lady at court has so fine a pair, all worked with seed pearls and spelling out something in French that I can't read—my protector knew no French."

" 'Tis a weighty truth some wise man struggled to think up," Dion laughed. "One garter says: *'Si jeunesse savait!'* The other says: *'Si viellesse pouvait!'*."

"Which means, milord?"

"If youth but knew; if age but could! Clever, eh? But enough of the garters; Sir Walter was here today and gave me good news! He's arranged to have me visit my family at Avronbeck, at last. I leave here tonight at dark and walk to Queenhithe where there'll be a man waiting for me with a horse. I'm to ride straight to Avronbeck and see my father and my mother and my sisters—and in the kitchen, of all places! My beloved half-brothers are to be kept away from the house on some excuse and so dear Charles won't get the chance to betray me to the Queen."

"You—you think it wise to take this risk?" Margery asked hesitantly.

"Wise? Wise? By God's eyeballs, I've listened to naught but caution since last November and I'm sick to death of this hiding! Even if Sir Walter hadn't fixed this plan I think I'd have broken out of here from plain boredom! It will be good to ride again—how long has it been since I was on a horse?—even though I must go skulking through the streets to Queenhithe like a common thief in the night."

"And is my company such a tiring thing, then?" the girl asked.

"No, no, Margery; you know it's not. But even the sweetest wine cloys the appetite unless it's spiced now and then. Danger? I welcome it—I'd even relish a bit of swordplay to shake the rust from my right arm, if I didn't fear it would bring harm to my family and Raleigh. As it is, I'll be as good as gold and avoid all hurly-burly as I would the plague."

Margery gnawed at her lower lip, shaking her head slightly. She murmured, "I cannot help but feel that it is a mistake for you to venture forth. But—well, Sir Walter must know better than Mag Hollis what's right and what's not."

Her mood of preoccupation held the girl in its grip throughout the day, although Dion laughed at her doubts and scoffed at her fears. As for the young man, he found the waiting for full night intolerable; the streets were not as dark as Raleigh had advised when he slipped out of the Lime Street house, swathed in a voluminous cloak, and began picking his way toward Queenhithe. The twisting, turning alleys, a few just recently cobbled as part of Elizabeth's program of making London a finer city, were lit only by an occasional lanthorn hung outside a tavern but the fog and murk had lifted and there was a moon that made the streets uncomfortably bright.

He was only three squares away from Burnie's when he turned a corner and ran full tilt into the towering figure of Simon Ferdinando.

Dion's cloak had been held high to mask the lower part of his face but the impact of the collision forced him to drop his hand to keep his balance and Ferdinando's delighted crow of recognition boomed out at once.

"My friend, Dion!" the Portuguese cried. "*Por Dios,* if you but knew how I've turned all London upside down to find you—where in God's name have you been keeping yourself?"

"I've been away," Harvie said briefly, "and I'm in a great hurry now, friend Simon. By y'r leave I'll—"

"Now, now, is that a way to greet a friend you haven't seen in months?" the black-bearded man protested. "Come, there's a tavern close by where we can share a tankard and live over again those days on Roanoke Island. That savage wench, Rycko, do you pine for her overmuch? And—"

"Nay, Simon," Dion interrupted, "I've not the time to spare tonight. Another day, mayhap, we'll get together and renew old friendships, but now I'm late for an appointment that will not keep. And so goodnight."

"A moment," the Portuguese said, and the rollicking gayety faded from his voice, giving way to the hint of an ominous note. "I said I had been seeking you, Dion, and that I have and for your own welfare. I know you don't put too much trust in me, despite that I did what I could to show myself a friend, once we had cleared the air with our—er—disagreement over the fitness of crimson hose aboard ship." He waved a blunt hand as Dion started an angry reply. "Nay, nay, don't raise your hackles so, I beg of ye—I'll confess I was wrong in that affair. But as I said, the dispute cleared the air and later I was favorably struck by the way you handled those dogs who'd leave the pumps and so sink us all."

"God's teeth, man," Dion burst out impatiently, "what's this lead up to? It grows late."

"Then I'll be blunt in saying it," Ferdinando shrugged. " 'Tis this; don't put the trust you withhold from me in certain others who are false friends. I hunted you to warn you of this—I even offered a price I could ill afford for information of your whereabouts."

"And who are these false friends?" Dion demanded. "Name them or confess they are but creatures of your fancy."

"Nay, Dion," the big pilot said with a shake of his head, "I'll name no names, thankee. But suppose I needed the Queen's full favor for the very life of a venture I held above all else. And suppose her Majesty would be as grateful to the man who betrayed a person she wants to lay hands on as she would be wrathful at a man who might hide that person. Would I not be tempted to assure myself of the Queen's lasting favor by causing a—shall we say slip-up?—that would deliver the wanted man to Gloriana?"

"Now, by my soul," Harvie gritted, "I do believe you mean to cast doubt on Sir Walter's loyalty to me!"

Ferdinando shrugged again, spreading his hands.

"I named no names," he smiled.

"Nor needed to—the story's plain enough without! And I do a disservice to Sir Walter by troubling to deny your suspicions, but I will. Know ye, Ferdinando, that Raleigh has had every chance to betray me if such a base thing could cross his thoughts! He's risked everything to keep me safe, he has ever been as close as a brother to me—aye, much closer than my half-brothers, by a league's length. You say he'd turn me over to the Queen? If you but knew how close he's guarded me!"

"By letting you roam the streets of Queenhithe without an escort?" the Portuguese asked bluntly. "Is this the way Raleigh protects you?"

"Hah, letting me roam the streets—know you 'tis the first time in close onto a year he's let me free of—but of what concern is that to you?"

"Of great concern, Dion," Ferdinando said soberly. "You walked into me—why could you not stumble on a patrol of the Queen's men as simply, strolling about London Town as boldly as a beggar?"

"I don't stroll about London Town! I'm on my way—hah, ye'd trick me into telling, wouldn't you?"

Ferdinando's face was bland as he hunched his shoulders again.

"No need to trick you, Dion," he said, " 'cause you have a boy's lack of guile for all y'r fierce talk. If I would, I c'ld puzzle out why ye're abroad and where ye're going, but I won't be bothered. Still, I bid you to take care."

"You and y'r warnings—you and y'r talk of Raleigh's plots! I know not whether you be knave or fool to hold such evil thoughts of such a man!"

"Now hold, Master Dion Harvie," Ferdinando scowled. "Not many men have given me the insult and been let walk away, as I'll let you—because I thought myself your friend. Go to wherever it is you're going; I'll not press you with my warnings 'gainst y'r will. But ye cannot say I didn't try to caution you!"

The Portuguese gave a brief nod, turned his back and strode off into the darkness, leaving Dion to stare after him bleakly.

"The dog," Harvie muttered. "Walt puts such great faith in him and he serves him in this way, with lies as black as his beard. I'll tell Raleigh about this; if Ferdinando slanders him so in my affair, what does he not do in other matters?"

He huddled his cloak about his face again and hurried toward Queenhithe, grumbling his rage at the perfidy of Simon Ferdinando.

"Raleigh betray me? As well say my own father would, or my mother! Nay, Walt's one man in all England who'd never let the promise of Elizabeth's warmest regard, her fullest support of his beloved colony, change him."

Or (and the thought was there, coiled in his mind like an adder) would he? Raleigh's dream of a colony in the New World certainly surpassed the love he had for any woman; would it outweigh his loyalty to Dion Harvie? Suppose that Raleigh had found out the chase after him was getting too close? He knew the Queen would ruin him if she ever learned he had protected the man whose head she wanted, so might Raleigh not have arranged this ride to Avronbeck so as to. . . .

"Never!" he jerked out. "Not Walter Raleigh! The Portuguese dog lied in his teeth!"

The horse was waiting at Queenhithe, tended by one of Raleigh's servants who stood thumping first one foot and then the other against a warehouse wall in his efforts to relieve the numbing cold.

"Ah, young sir," he greeted Dion, " 'tis good you're come, not only 'cause I'm close to freezing but, too, I feared something had gone amiss."

"I was delayed," Dion said briefly and swung up into the saddle. The servant came closer and spoke in a low tone.

"My master bade me tell you to ride straight to where you're going," he murmured, "and back to where you were as soon as ever possible. He further said he would be here but was summoned by the Queen not two hours past. He tells you to use caution and if the leastest thing seems not right to go back to—where you were, at once."

"Oh aye," Dion nodded. "This horse, where do I leave it?"

"In the yard of the Bell Inn on Gracechurch Street, young sir, where 'twill be expected. Or if there be trouble, desert the stallion anywhere at your thought that ye'd be best without him. 'Twill cause my master no harm; 'tis not one of his animals and so cannot be traced to him. And now, Godspeed—ye'd best not tarry here too long else ye'll not make it back afore dawn."

Dion dug his heels into the chestnut's flanks and clattered away toward Avronbeck Hall. To walk abroad even in London Town after dark was dangerous; to ride the highway at night was still riskier, yet it was a chance that had to be taken if Dion would see his family again after all these months. This, he was determined to do; there was no telling if there would be another opportunity before Raleigh's second expedition sailed for Roanoke Island with him.

Besides, he told himself grimly, any highwayman who might be prowling about on a night like this would be too stiff with cold to give much of an account of himself. The wind had freshened since dusk and now it cut through Dion's thick cloak as though the garment had been left behind; young Harvie's toes were numb in his boots before he had been astride the horse five minutes and his nose felt as though it would snap off like an icicle at a twist.

The stallion Raleigh had gotten for him proved a fast and willing animal. Once outside the city walls and with the moon providing ample light, the beast made good speed along Fleet Street and The Strand, through Charing Cross and on down King's Street past Westminster. Beyond Whitehall, Dion shook out the big horse and let him gallop over the frozen road toward Avronbeck Hall, hooves ringing on the icy ground as though they were thumping across a ship's deck. Two or three houses in the hamlets he passed through showed a light. The farm cottages were dark; the people of this neighborhood went to bed with the sun and bolted their doors strongly against witches and warlocks as well as against the wanderers of the night, wretches who were only a shade more miserable than the peasants but that shade enough to lend them murderous desperation.

The journey down from London took nearly four hours and Dion Harvie was chilled to the marrow when he saw the lighted hulk of Avronbeck Hall on its gently sloping hill, surrounded by the gaunt skeletons of the leafless oaks. It was an enormous manor house, one of the biggest buildings in all England, surpassed in size and splendor only by the royal palaces, and yet it had a warmth, a beauty, that so many of the great estates lacked. Sir Clement's father, the second Lord Avronbeck, had built the place in Henry the Seventh's reign and Sir Clement had added to it with an eye for architectural excellence that had joined the old parts with the new to present an anomalous picture of hospitable grandeur.

Now, on this wintry night, the sight of Avronbeck Hall never had been more welcome to tooth-chattering Dion. He swung his lathered horse up a side lane that circled the rear of the great house and led to the door Sir Walter had directed him to use, the one that opened on the kitchen. He would have preferred to ride to the stables, there to have his nag cared for, but Raleigh's instructions had been to keep close to his horse every minute he was at Avronbeck.

"I *think* the plan's well laid without a chance of a mishap," his friend had told him, "but there's no such thing as over-caution in as touchy a position as this. It's enough of a hazard that you'll be abroad and risking a meeting with somebody who'd recognize you and raise the hue and cry again. I *think* the Queen's convinced you're in Italy or even Germany, that dismal land of dismal people, and it would not do to have her know you're in England; 'twould spur her to a new search I doubt even Burnie could confound."

So, with a muttered curse at the necessity of leaving his horse outside and not rubbed down, inviting a cough that could ruin the sturdy animal, he looped the reins through a ringbolt set in the side of the house. Then he moved cautiously to the wide-planked door, tested it and found it unbarred, and opened it inch by inch, one hand at the hilt of his sword.

The kitchen was lit only by the subdued flicker of the massive fireplace, laid with thick, unseasoned logs to last the night, and the shadows were so deep that Dion thought at first the room was empty. Then, as he tiptoed over the flagstone floor toward the fire and the warmth it offered, he tensed, whirled at the scrape of a footstep.

"Nay, my son," Sir Clement said softly. "No need to bare your blade here unless you mean to use it against me, your mother or your sisters."

"Dion!" It was a muted cry and Lady Avronbeck stepped into the light, her arms outstretched. Young Harvie crossed the room in long strides to clasp the woman who had borne him, the woman to whom he had brought so many heartaches and this, his condemnation by the Queen, surely the worst. Wordlessly, the two clung to each other before he bent to kiss her lips, then turned to receive the welcome of his sisters, Elizabeth and Joan, both as weepy over his homecoming as they had been at his departure, almost a year before.

That done, Dion faced his father, Sir Clement. The two men eyed each other silently, almost warily, before Lord Avronbeck reached out to grasp his son by both shoulders with a sound that was the mingling of a chuckle and a groan.

"As hale and hearty, I see, as though ye'd but been up to London for a fortnight of romps and merriment," the older man nodded, "and still as sure of y'rself as always, by the look of ye. No matter that the Queen—"

"Ah, milord," Dion's mother broke in, "we have so little time to spend with our son, must we waste part of it reproaching Dion for irking that ugly old woman?"

"Milady!" Sir Clement said sharply. "We'll have no disloyal talk in this house, no matter what our grievance! And this jackanapes of ours has sorely angered Gloriana, and after I warned him to behave himself, so—oh, let it go, let it go! Sit ye down, Dion, and you, Elizabeth, bring your brother a bite and some hot wine; he must be frozen to the liver after his ride. Sit ye down, my son, and tell us what's befallen you in all these many months. Raleigh has told me some but I'd hear it from you, y'rself. You're well?"

"Never better," Dion nodded as he crossed to a rough bench set at a table used by the scullions, "save for the longing to see you and my chafing at having to hide. This hiding—certainly the Queen has forgot me by now, 'spite of what friend Walt says!"

Lord Avronbeck shook his head slowly as he ran a hand over his silvery hair.

"I would she had," he sighed, "but Elizabeth never was one to forget and forgive too easily. She's never forgotten that your mother's brother, James, was for Mary of Scots, for instance, and that was close to twenty years ago. And this cursed Groven still basks in Gloriana's smile and never loses a chance to remind her 'twas your blade that stabbed him—in a villainous attack, he says."

"Why, the dog!" Dion flared. "He brought the fight upon himself and—"

"I know, I know," Sir Clement said, with upraised hand. "All who know this Captain Groven can say he's false as a wooden shilling but you know the Queen has—er—a strong will in such matters as protecting her favorites. But enough of that; Raleigh tells me you're to sail back to the New World with him on his next expedition."

"If I must," Dion Harvie said dolefully. "I do not have to tell you that I'd like it a thousand times better to stay here, where I belong."

"And you must go," Lord Avronbeck said sternly. "Your being in England is a danger to your mother, your sisters, and me—aye, and your half-brothers, too, though I doubt you'd consider them. Give Her Majesty more time—Groven must make a misstep and so fall out of favor some fine day. Sail with Raleigh and keep out of harm's way in the New World till that day comes and you can return."

"Ah, Dion," Lady Avronbeck sighed, "I dread to think of you in that wilderness, fighting those fierce savages at every turn."

"Why, as to that, Mother," Dion laughed, "the savages of Roanoke Island are misnamed—we call them Indians, by the by. They are not so savage as a London dock porter, I'll be bound, and all the fighting of them was to stave them off from feeding us so much we'd split our breeches with fat. Nay, have never a fear on that score; 'tis the unending idleness that rankles, not war with the Indians."

"And do you tell us about the New World," Joan said eagerly. "I've heard 'tis a place where pearls lie thick as pebbles along the shore."

"Not pearls, grapes," Dion said, and spent the next hour describing Roanoke Island, the natives and their strange customs, answering endless questions, breaking down the ridiculous fancies about this newly-named Virginia that prevailed throughout England. He did not mention Rycko nor, when the talk swung back to his hiding place in London, did he say the name of Margery Hollis.

"'Tis a spot as safe as any church," he said, "and safer than most, by the way the Queen's men have grabbed some poor wretches at the very altars they fled to for sanctuary. Do not concern yourselves that I'll be found there; 'tis only when I stray outside that I'm in any danger and, God wot, that's been never, save on this one occasion."

"And 'tis best to end this occasion now," Lord Avronbeck put in regretfully. "I sent your half-brothers away for the night, to look after some affairs of mine in another part of the county, but there's no telling when one of them, especially Charles, might come galloping back. He—er—has a somewhat suspicious mind and though I believe I impressed on him the need for the three of them to spend the night away, it was an unusual thing and Charles just might—but I'm getting to be a fearful old man. Still, it's best you ride now, Dion, so's there'll be no scraping the edge of the time you should be back in your hideaway."

Dion Harvie bade his farewells, promised his mother he would be careful in his dealings with the Indians, comforted his weeping sisters, exchanged a bone-cracking handclasp with his father and left the kitchen. Outside, the wind seemed more cruelly cold than ever but his horse, he was glad to note, seemed to have suffered no ill effects from its stand in the icy night. Scattered clouds dimmed the moon fitfully as he jogged down the curving lane to the highway but it was never too dark to pick out the road and Dion spurred his mount into a canter as he turned the animal's head back toward London and Lime Street.

He was tired, he was busy with his thoughts, he was not as alert on the ride back as he had been during the journey to Avronbeck Hall; thus it was that he nearly missed the instant's gleam the capricious moonlight struck from the deep shadows of a roadside grove.

It was an upswung sword the moon had caught and Dion Harvie was ambushed. He knew that before the bellowing cry rang out:

"Stand, in the Queen's name!"

5

DION'S FIRST IMPULSE as he went rigid in the saddle was to wheel his horse and gallop for Avronbeck Hall. He spurned that thought at once; to dash for home would bring certain disaster to his family. There was a chance, a bare chance, that these men did not know who he was; it could just possibly be that they were hunting some highwayman and challenged every night rider to give an account of himself.

If that were so—he scanned the road ahead. There were only four horsemen in sight, distinct now as they rode out of the shadows, their burgonet helmets catching the moonlight. They were astride heavy cobs that looked little better than sumter horses, pack animals, and Dion silently blessed Elizabeth's close-fistedness that kept her from outfitting her troops with anything but the cheapest. If he could win through these four men and if they were not merely an advance guard of a large patrol, he would have a chance to leave them in the lurch in a run for London. Of course, if the alarm had been sounded, his whereabouts discovered, he stood no chance of getting back to Lime Street; all the gates of London Town would be guarded against him and even this stout stallion could never jump the forty-foot City Wall.

But, he told himself grimly, he had no choice but to try to break through the horsemen ahead. If he surrendered this close to Avronbeck Hall he would point the Queen's accusing finger at Sir Clement; if he lost his fight to beat his way through the roadblock and was killed in the trying—well, a dead man couldn't be forced to confess to anything by Elizabeth's accomplished "questioners."

All these thoughts, as detailed as they were, took less than a second to reach a decision. Dion's blade flashed up as he flung back his cloak to free his sword arm while shielding his face with his left hand, which gripped the reins.

"Aside, ye murdering highwaymen!" he yelled. "Aside, before I run you through!"

"Queen's men!" the leader of the little band warned him.

"Aye, many a cutthroat has used the ruse before!" Dion snarled. "Aside, I say!"

He hammered his horse's ribs with his heels and streaked forward, his sword rising to slash at the leading horseman. The blinding suddenness of his attack, the horsemen's uncertainty engendered by Dion's cry of cutthroat, the speed of the stallion Raleigh had furnished and Harvie's skill with the blade all combined to give the first advantage to Dion.

The leading Queen's man clumsily tried to parry Harvie's slash and cried out as the blade sliced into his shoulder. He clutched at his wounded arm and lost his balance in the saddle to go sprawling over the side of his bulky mount onto the frozen highway. By the time he hit the ground, Dion was hacking at the two men directly behind the leader.

There was neither the time nor the space for even the rudimentary niceties of mounted swordplay now. Dion hacked as blindly as the others parried but the fury of his attack forced the ambushers to pull their heavy cobs aside. One of Dion's maddened slashes bit into horseflesh, there was a squeal and the animal reared, sending its rider sliding backward over its rump. Harvie wrenched the stallion's reins to send the powerful brute past the third confused Queen's man (if that they truly were) and headed straight for the fourth soldier.

This man was ready for him. While his companions had bunched to take the impact of Harvie's charge, the fourth helmeted horseman had lain back; now he had room to meet Dion's avalanching assault.

Fierce exultation bubbled up in Harvie. He had told Margery he would relish a bit of swordplay—he had it now, and more than a bit from the looks of the man ahead. This was no crude foot-soldier-on-horseback by the way he sat his saddle; this man obviously knew what to expect and how to meet it.

"Ho!" Dion yelled. "At you!"

"Die, then!" the other shouted back.

They came together with Dion trying for an overhanded chop and with the helmeted man striking the cut aside with a practiced parry. Dion hauled hard on the stallion's reins, bringing his mount's forefeet off the ground as he twisted in the saddle and backhanded a sweeping slash.

The blade struck the other's saddle, jarring against the high wooden cantle and glancing off. Harvie spurred the stallion ahead in time to avoid the soldier's whistling slash by a fraction of an inch. The chestnut turned under the pull of the reins and Dion got his blade up in time to block the other man's recovering slash. Harvie came in behind the helmeted rider's cut and sliced hard at the soldier's belly.

It was the other's cob that saved his life. The untrained animal, wall-eyed and snorting, curvetted out of reach of Dion's slash, then lurched forward again. Bringing his sword back frantically, Harvie sent the thick, dull top of his single-edged blade thudding into his opponent's ribs.

It was an abrupt, almost comical, end of the fight. The two men had been out to kill—now Dion's man was knocked out of his saddle, gagging for wind, by a blow that could have been delivered with a stick, not a razor-edged sword. The soldier landed on his back, arms and legs straddled and helmet bowling over the frozen road, while Dion swung his mount around again and rattled over the highway toward London.

"Hah, that was good—*good!*" he cried aloud. "So even if 'twas a freakish thing by which I unhorsed him—I would've nipped his head off in another stroke, I vow! Go, good steed, pretty steed, and show them you can run as invincibly as I can fight!"

Behind him faded the yells of his ambushers, bitter now in their rage and shame at having let their man escape, although outnumbered four to one. Dion howled back a jeering curse and told himself those four would be wise to report they had met no night rider in their search. Of course the first man he had met, the one whose shoulder he had wounded, would have some explaining to do but—and Dion laughed aloud again—he might convince his superiors that he had cut himself with his own blade; he was clumsy enough to make the story sound true.

As the stallion thudded along the highway, Dion spoke his thoughts aloud, talking into the cruel wind that whistled about him.

"And now," he asked the night, "who set the trap if trap it truly was? Or did I but blunder into a patrol that was hunting someone else, or even just moving from one station to the next? At this time o' this kind of night? Nay, they were abroad on orders of some kind, those four.

"And it must have been me they sought and hence somebody who knew my plan to visit Avronbeck betrayed me. But why, if the Queen was told, did she send only four men to catch me—surely I deserve a troop, if she's so angered at me that she'd post a price of two hundred golden pounds on me. Aye, there's the question.

"Then, too, why was I waylaid on the road when I could have been taken at Avronbeck Hall? Is it that mayhap the one who betrayed me still holds my father in regard and so planned it that I'd be caught away from my home? But, curse all, that points to Raleigh and I'll not believe it!"

For if Raleigh was indeed a false friend, he reasoned further, why had he not sent the Queen's men to the Lime Street hideout? And, unbidden, a possible answer came to him. Burnie's spies were as clever as the Queen's own; the little hunchback would know immediately if Raleigh plotted anything that would get *him* in trouble. But if Sir Walter's treachery took place away from Lime Street and Burnie, the dwarfed landlord would giggle at the plan or, at the most, merely shrug his shoulders at the betrayal.

"But no, I'll not believe it of friend Walt," Dion spat out. " 'Twas—why, am I blind? *It was that bastard Ferdinando, for certain!* Curse him for the foul cozener he is—he and his sly way of casting suspicion on my true friend, Walt! When next I meet the Portuguese hound I'll make sure he never plays the traitor again. I'll—but first I'd best make certain I do see him again and not fall afoul of more of the Queen's men at the gate."

The flaring brazier that marked the guard post at Ludgate showed down the road and Dion's throat tightened as he slowed the stallion. This was the risk that outweighed them all; if the alarm had been sounded he was sure to be caught here; it was suicide, perhaps, to ride straight into the arms of the men who would start him on his way to the noose or the block—but what other course was there to take? He couldn't wander about the countryside, rousing suspicion everywhere; he couldn't go back to Avronbeck Hall for a multitude of reasons; Lime Street offered his only sanctuary.

And there was that question of why only four horsemen had been sent to take him when the Queen might have sent a troop, a company. Elizabeth's stinginess was a by-word but in this case it would not have cost her a penny more to have sent an adequate party to seize or kill him.

"Aye," he murmured under his breath, "it's 'cause it was passing strange that only four were sent for me that I dare believe the alarum has not been sounded—and why it hasn't been I'll have to think upon if God takes me through that gate safely."

He trotted the stallion up to Ludgate, every nerve afire, his heart thumping, his breath caught in his throat. At every second he expected to hear the command to halt, the clatter of pikemen springing out at him; instead there was a silence broken only by the crackling of the brazier's flames. He walked his horse past the guard hut and relaxed at the ripping purr of a resounding snore.

"Asleep, by God!" he muttered. He raised a hand to the brim of his hat and tipped an ironic salute. "My thanks, good and watchful pikemen," he said. "Heav'n grant ye dreams as beautiful as y'r snores sound to these ears."

He walked the stallion past the guard hut, then sent the animal into a trot. The first warning streaks of light showed in the east. He would be cutting it fine to get to the Bell Inn to leave the horse—and the stallion had proved himself too worthy to be abandoned now—and walk to Lime Street before full dawn. Even though he knew now that no widespread alarm had been sent out for him, there was still the danger that even in the Lime Street district he might be recognized if he sauntered along in daylight and he had promised Raleigh and Burnie that if he were discovered within the city he would lead any chase that might develop away from the ramshackle house with its hidden luxuries.

A sleepy hostler accepted the horse at the Bell Inn on Gracechurch Street without a word and Dion Harvie gave the tired beast an affectionate slap on the flank as he was being led away.

"Take the best care of him," Harvie told the yawning hostler. "He's done me a great service. And to make certain ye don't forget—" He tossed a coin at the groom, who caught it without more than half opening his red-rimmed eyes.

He met no one who gave him anything but the stupid glance of the recently awakened in the trip from the Bell Inn to Lime Street and his hand was just raised to knock on the door of the looming ruin when it opened.

"Inside, young sir," Burnie chuckled, "and be quick! God's toenails, ye had me worried, comin' back so close to daylight." He closed and barred the door, then used flint and steel to scratch a light for a taper, peering at Dion over the flame. "All went well?" he asked, grinning. "It must ha', for ye're back, albeit ruinous late."

"And no thanks to—" Dion began and then held his tongue. He would discuss this night's strange happenings with Sir Walter Raleigh before he'd say a word to Burnie or Margery. Raleigh would counsel him on whether to talk or keep silent and he would follow Raleigh's advice, as he always had. "No thanks to the horse," he told Burnie lamely. "The beast dawdled on the way, no matter how I'd spur him. That's why I'm so late."

"Aye," Burnie said and nodded, with a snirt of laughter. "And I'll wait to hear all of it from Sir Walter. Ye'll tell him what ye'd not tell me, I'll be bound, and Raleigh tells me everything. Ye must be fair famished f'r sleep, so I'll not hold ye longer. And I'll get word to Sir Walter that ye're back and want to see him, eh?"

"Aye," Dion said wearily. "I doubt not I can sleep for a week without so much as rolling over in bed once."

"Ye'll not be wantin' Margery then," Burnie sniggered, "though sometimes a full night of ridin'—and, mayhap, fightin'—makes a man so edgy he can't sleep without a wench to calm his temper."

"Not me," Dion said, yawning hugely. "I'd but fall asleep if all the fairest maids of Elysium were to clamber into bed with me.

I bid you goodnight, Burnie, and do you please get word to Sir Walter that I'm back, as you said you would."

It was only four hours later when Sir Walter Raleigh's hand shook Dion awake and the knight's anxious face bent over Harvie.

"I'd let you sleep," Raleigh said, "but Burnie sent word to me that something went amiss with last night's adventure. What was it?"

"And how does Burnie know aught of what happened?" Dion grumbled. "I made sure to tell him nothing till I'd talked to you."

"Ah, Burnie sniffs such things as a dog sniffs out a bone," Raleigh explained. "I sometimes think the man has eyes that can see into a person's head, leastwise it's as useless to try to cozen him. But what happened?"

"All went as it was planned," Dion said, rubbing his eyes awake, "save for two things. I happened to meet Simon Ferdinando on my way to Queenhithe—"

"Ferdinando! I thought he was at Plymouth!"

"Nay, he was here in London last night and full of questions where I had been."

"He's a curious hound, that one. It fair drove him mad when he asked me about you, using his clever roundabouts in a try to get me to let slip where you were, and I evading everyone. It made me laugh—"

"Then ye'll not laugh when ye hear further," Dion broke in grimly. "Aye, he told me he'd been seeking me and he told me why. 'Twas to warn me 'gainst a certain man he called a false friend, a man who'd betray me to the Queen to ensure Her Majesty's full support of his next expedition to Virginia."

"Son of a whore!" Raleigh cursed. "Were he not the best pilot to be had anywhere I'd make him answer to me with his sword on that! Named me traitor, did he? Icod, I'll roast his ears with what I tell him when next I see him."

"And that's all you'll do, Walt?" Dion asked in amazement. "Ye'll let him go unspitted after he said this of you?"

Raleigh paced the room, stroking his moustaches in fierce sweeps. As he strode back and forth, he hurled his answer to the man on the bed over his shoulder.

"I do not wonder at your surprise, dear Dion," he said, "but you can't fully see the true situation. You know all my dreams have been wrapped up in the colony I plan, the place we've named Virginia. For the success of that, I'll risk everything, suffer everything, even an insult from such a dog as Simon Ferdinando. Now look you; this lying Portuguese is the ablest pilot I can find, the one man amongst them all who can come close to guaranteeing the safe arrival of my ships in the New World. And if I do what I ought, call out the bastard and run him through, who would I get in his stead?"

"Amadas—"

"Would not sail for Virginia without Ferdinando as pilot. No more would Dick Grenville or Tom Cavendish or Captain Lane or the artist, John White, nor any of the others. You see the position I'm in? So, for the time, I must swallow his base slanders till my need for him is ended. And then the reckoning, I pledge you."

Dion stared at his friend from where he lay. It was possible, he realized, that his drive for the success of his colony could make a man as proud as Sir Walter Raleigh endure lying insult but—was it likely? Could any man, and especially the touchiest gentleman in all England, suffer himself to be called a treacherous friend and do no more than promise a reckoning in some hazy future?

"Aye," Harvie said slowly, "I can see your position, friend Walt, but ye've not heard all my story. After I'd seen my family and when I was riding back to London, all bemused and half frozen, I was waylaid by four horsemen."

"*Waylaid?*"

"As neatly as though they knew I was travelling that road, as they must have. They bade me stand in the Queen's name but I proved myself a poor subject of the gracious Gloriana and charged 'em. One, I managed to carve up a bit, the second I unhorsed, the third I slipped past and the fourth I fought down. They were miserably mounted and I had no trouble running away from them."

"They recognized you? They spoke y'r name?"

"No, they didn't call me by name and I doubt they saw my

face for more than a glimpse on a road lit only by the moon. I cursed 'em as highwaymen before I made at them but I don't think they were fooled, Walt—I think they knew who I was and that I must come that road on my way back to London."

Raleigh's face was black as he flung himself into a chair, his long legs stretched out in front of him.

"Now here's all Hell broke loose!" he crackled. "The Queen knows ye're in England and she'll spare nothing to hunt you down!"

"But does she?" Dion asked. His friend flung out an impatient hand.

"Why ask ye that? Of course she must, else why were you waylaid?"

"And if she knows, why were only four men sent to take me? And why were the guards at Ludgate fast asleep when I rode past them?"

Raleigh scowled, twisting a heavy ring on a long finger.

"Aye," he said slowly. "Those four might have been cutthroats, using the Queen's name."

"And mounted and wearing burgonets and carrying broadswords? Strange highwaymen these, don't ye think?"

Sir Walter ran his hand over his long, black mane, muttering.

"And I believe they knew 'twas Dion Harvie they hailed," the young man on the bed pursued ruthlessly, "and so I'd know who betrayed me into this strange ambush. 'Twas Ferdinando, I'm convinced."

"I'll not believe it," Raleigh returned. "Villain he might be but not that black. He's served me for many a year, first aboard the old *Falcon* and then with—"

"And shows his loyalty to you by calling you my false friend," Harvie put in idly.

"Ah, 'tis but his strange way. No doubt you irked him in some way when you met him at Queenhithe and he is a touchy man—for one who's no gentleman."

"He asked me to have a dram with him and spend some time in talk about Roanoke Island but of course I could not tarry and so dismissed him."

"That was it, then. When he fancies himself slighted, he's likely to speak the wildest words that mean nothing. I remember the time—"

"Y'r pardon, Walt," Dion cut in again, "but if it was not Ferdinando, who was it—Burnie?"

Raleigh snorted his ridicule of that idea.

"Never Burnie," he said. "The fellow'd suffer the rack and never peep a word that'd harm me. That, I know." His voice grew thoughtful. "There's the wench, of course," he said slowly. "The doxy ye've spent so much time with."

"Margery? And I'll never believe *that*."

Sir Walter cast a sharp glance at Harvie, his mouth twisted in a grimace that was almost a sneer.

"I see," he rapped out. "Ye'd blame the worthy pilot who took you safely to the New World and brought ye back and who befriended ye whilst ye were on Roanoke Island; ye'd blame Burnie, who runs a mighty risk to shelter ye, and yet this whore's above suspicion, eh? And if you know she is so blameless, and I know Simon and Burnie are, who do you next suspect—mayhap the man you call friend Walt?"

Dion tried to meet Raleigh's bleak stare and dropped his eyes to the coverlet.

"N-no," he hesitated and then strengthened his voice. "No, I'd never believe you'd turn against me, Walt. Believe me when I say that 'cause I mean it with all my heart!"

Raleigh grunted and fell to stroking his moustaches again. A lump of sea coal crumbled in the fireplace and belched a puff of soot into the room. From beyond the windows came the muted roar of the great city. Then, with a curse, Sir Walter jerked himself out of his chair and stalked to the side of the bed, his hands planted on his hips.

"We're dolts," he cried, "both of us! Here we be, twisting our brains to unravel this snarl and the traitor's right before our eyes for us to see. 'Twas your half-brother Charles, o'course! Oh, Simpleton Raleigh and Nincompoop Harvie, that they did not know that on the instant!"

"But—"

"It explains all," Raleigh said as he plumped himself down on the bed. "Our dear Charles somehow learned of your coming to Avronbeck Hall and he left where he'd been sent by your father and rode for home. Somewhere he hired four bravos and somehow he outfitted 'em to resemble soldiers—the armory at Avronbeck has old burgonets and broadswords, don't it?"

"A-plenty," Dion nodded, "but—"

"Don't you see, man? Charles himself can't kill you, first because he fears you and second because his father'd never forgive him. But he can have you killed on the road back to London and never bear a moment's blame. He'd avenge himself of y'r cuckolding him, he'd rid himself of his father's favorite, and all the time he'd be furnished with a perfect plea of innocence—he was miles away from the scene at his father's orders."

He got up from the side of the bed and began his pacing again. "Everything fits," he exulted. "Charles can't betray you to the Queen 'cause it'd mean that Gloriana would deal mercilessly with the whole family, especially since you had visited 'em. Charles feared to lose what he'll inherit and so he forged this scheme. That's why there were only four men—Elizabeth would have sent a hundred. That's why the guards at Ludgate slept. The Queen doesn't know you're in England and Charles can't tell her you are—ye're safe, Dion, and all our fears were for naught."

Dion sank back on the pillows and stared at the bed canopy above him.

"Aye," he said slowly, "everything fits and cunningly, too. And all our fears were for naught—if it were truly Charles."

6

ALTHOUGH HE could not wholly accept the idea that it had been Charles who had made a spur-of-the-moment attempt to have him killed, Dion had to admit that it was the most likely theory after days passed and no move was made to follow up the first failure with another attempt to take him or murder him. Life for Harvie went back to its even course of confinement to his rooms at Burnie's, dalliance with Margery and visits from Raleigh, whose spirits never were higher, now that his second expedition to Roanoke Island was almost ready to clear.

"I can't wait to see the place," he said, over and over, "and explore the lands that Amadas and Barlowe didn't visit. 'Twill be my happiest day when I set foot in Virginia. 'Twill be doubly—a thousand times—worth all the disappointments, all the setbacks, I've suffered and the fortunes that I've spent to get there."

"The Queen, then, has consented to your going?" Dion asked.

"Ah, she's in fine spirits now," Raleigh nodded, "with her dear cousin, Philip of Spain, so well-behaved, scarce murmuring about the raids that Drake and Hawkins make on his treasure ships." He laughed in his delight at the levelling of all the obstacles that had kept him from realizing his most overwhelming passion. "Icod, I ask God's blessings on Philip for being such a fool each time I say my prayers. What other king in all the world would stand still for such nose-tweaking as Elizabeth and her knighted pirates give poor Philip?"

"Why does he abide such things?" Dion asked. "Not that he don't warrant them, the Spanish dog, but how can he call himself a king and still wink at the great losses he has suffered in the Spanish Main without taking some sort of revenge?"

"Oh, some think he is but biding his time until Mary of Scots leads a rebellion 'gainst Elizabeth, at which time he can invade us. There are others who guess that Philip still hopes to win Gloriana's hand in marriage—which is a far-fetched idea, at best. She might have led him on with such a half promise once but now nobody but a fool—and mayhap Philip really is a fool, though I doubt it—would think she'd marry now, the Spanish king or anybody else. But what care we why Philip takes one hurt after another without striking back? Whilst he's meek, Gloriana is most gracious and pray God he stays as spiritless as he is now till we clear Plymouth for Virginia."

The date for the sailing of part of Raleigh's little flotilla from London—the other ships were being fitted out at Plymouth—had been set for March twenty-third, 1585, and it was on March twentieth that Walter Raleigh burst into Dion's rooms at Burnie, in a foaming rage.

"The whore, the strumpet!" he frothed. "The lying bitch! The stinking pot of false promises! Aye, take me to the Tower—I'll shout it from my cell there! Elizabeth cannot be trusted past the wink of a gnat's eye—she takes delight in diddling all those who'd serve her well!"

"God's sake, man!" Dion exclaimed. "Dost want all London to hear you clamor treason?"

"I care not who hears me!" Raleigh raged. He stumped across the room, clenched hands shaking in the air. "Let all the world hear me! She pledged me her word, I tell ye! A dozen times, a hundred, she pledged it! And now she smirks and shows her yellow fangs in a lying smile and tells me a monarch has the birth-born right to take back her pledges at her will or deny she made them and they were never made!"

"You mean the Queen has stopped y'r expedition?" Dion gasped.

"No, no, she'll let my vessels leave," Sir Walter grated, "but I must stay! Aye, she simpered, England has need of every man of your kidney, dear Sir Walter, now that the Spanish are aroused over our friendships with the Dutch since William the Silent was murdered. And with their new Portuguese marine, they may strike at any time—those were her words."

He flung himself down on the bed and glowered at the floor.

"Ah, how Raleigh pleaded then," he went on in a quieter voice. "No craven churl ever begged harder for his neck than Raleigh did for the Queen to honor her own sacred pledge. I carried it so far that she went into a royal rage and threatened to hold the whole expedition here, so then I had to turn about and grovel at her feet with my promise to stay in England."

He spat out a curse and shook his head savagely.

"I'll never see my poor colony," he muttered. "That—Her Majesty will always find a means to keep me away from it, through her royal perversity."

"Walt, Walt," Dion said soothingly, "I know this thing's a hard blow to you but don't let it unsettle you entirely. Of course ye'll see your Virginia—we'll be together on Roanoke Island and together we'll explore rivers that reach to the Indies, I vow! You know Gloriana is a creature of whims; it could well be that before a month is out after our sailing she'll be demanding to know what ye're doing in England and why ye're not in Virginia, where you belong."

"Nay, Dion," Sir Walter said gloomily. "I have a feeling in my heart that whatever happens, no matter what success my colony might enjoy, I'll die before I set eyes on it."

It required all Harvie's efforts to rouse Raleigh from the slough of despond Elizabeth's last-minute staying order had cast him into. In the end, Sir Walter forced himself to don at least a semblance of his old self when Dion warned him that his despair might infect the whole expedition.

"God's sake, Walt," young Harvie implored, "put on a smile, even though it pains you! What will the men's spirits be like if they see the leader of this whole plan moping like a mother who's lost a babe? This is no pleasure jaunt they embark on, no matter what your wondrous Simon Ferdinando can do as pilot, and I'll wager my leg that half of them expect to be greeted by fierce savages when they reach Virginia. They need your confidence now, Walt, and if you can't be with them, why the next best thing's to bid them godspeed with a show of stout spirit."

"They'll think I fear to face what I've coaxed them to brave," Raleigh grumbled. "They'll say I chose to stay snug in London rather than—"

"They'll think and say nothing like that, Walt!" Dion interrupted. "Christ's thorns, man, they know you! There's not a man in all England who don't know ye've been at Gloriana f'r months, years, to let you sail to the New World. Nay, not a man of them will ever have a thought that you'd acted the unworthy part in any way."

So, on March twenty-third, Sir Walter Raleigh stood on the poopdeck of his little fleet's flagship, the hundred-and-forty-ton *Tyger* (not Philip Amadas' bark, which had been renamed *Roanoke*) and held a farewell counsel with the men he had hoped to lead on this expedition. With him were Sir Richard Grenville, very handsome in an embossed corselet, popeyed and heavy-browed; the fiercely bearded Captain Ralph Lane, a fire-eater by the very look of him; Thomas Cavendish, a quiet young man who would have laughed if he had been told that one day he would be the third man in history to circumnavigate the globe; Captain George Stafford, the dark-skinned, taciturn soldier who was Lane's aide; Philip Amadas; the artist, John White; the scientist, Thomas Hariot; Raleigh's cousins, John Stukely and John Arundell.

"I have not much to say, gentlemen," Raleigh said quietly. "You know you have my prayers for your safety and success. Ferdinando waits with the others at Plymouth and he has my complete trust, Sir Richard, once you've landed these men and gotten the colony started, ye'll return here for the supplies you find you need and whilst you're gone Captain Lane will act as governor. But all this ye all know. Take you good care of the two savages, Manteo and Wanchese, so their safe delivery home to Roanoke Island will assure the natives we are friendly in our intentions."

He paused and looked down at the deck's planking.

"I'd not deafen you with my entreaties to win success in this excursion for the Queen's sake, for England's," he went on slowly. "I know y'r hearts are set on it as much as mine. So now I'll bid ye all godspeed. Farewell."

He turned abruptly and walked to the ladder that dropped to the smallboat waiting to take him back to shore. But before he turned, those assembled on the poopdeck saw the tears that glistened in his eyes. They saw and understood; Raleigh had hoped to go at least to Plymouth with this part of the expedition to watch the little fleet make sail into the Western Sea but the Queen's command had forbidden even this; though he had spent his adult life proving his loyalty to her, Elizabeth would not trust him from under her thumb.

Below decks aboard the newly-christened *Roanoke,* Dion Harvie heard the rattle of lines, the thump of feet on the deck above, the groaning of the anchor windlass and then felt the stir of life through the hull of the old bark, felt the vessel take the wind and move away from her anchorage. He lay back in his bunk, his hands behind his head, staring at the planks above him.

He had been smuggled aboard the *Roanoke* the night before

and had been kept below ever since, with only Amadas knowing his identity. Time enough, when the fleet was safely out to sea, for Grenville and the others to learn they had aided the escape of a man wanted by the Queen; Raleigh had been sure that they would accept his presence in the right manner, all of them having as high regard for Lord Avronbeck as they had low regard for Captain Guy Groven.

The two friends had said their farewells in the chamber at Burnie's before the humpbacked landlord had taken Dion to the boat. The Queen's eye was fixed on Raleigh to make sure he did not leave London and for Sir Walter to go with Harvie aboard the *Roanoke* had been obviously much too dangerous..

"Grenville's coming back for supplies," Raleigh had told Dion, "and if the situation's better for you here I'll have the supply ships return you to England—if that indeed be your wish. I would ye'd make up your mind to settle in Virginia. Just think, Dion; ye could be an important man in the new colony, knowing the language of the natives and their ways, and—"

"Nay, Walt," Harvie had interrupted firmly. "I love you like a brother, on my soul, but to exile myself forever in that land of one dull day after another—nay, I couldn't do that, even for you."

"Well—I'd never keep a man there 'gainst his will," Raleigh had said ruefully, "and so we'll work to smoothe the way for your return here. God's teeth, here's Raleigh who'd give his soul to go, and can't, while you, who has the chance to stay in Viriginia, won't." He exhaled a deep sigh. "Ah, that's the way the world's made, I suppose, so why try to change it? Farewell, Dion, and good fortune."

"And good fortune to you and an early turnabout of the Queen's will."

After Raleigh had left, it had come time to say goodbye to Margery Hollis. It should have been a matter-of-fact affair (was she not a doxy hired to relieve boredom?) but it was not.

Dion wondered at its not being a casual leave-taking—for how could he, a son of Sir Clement Harvie, Lord Avronbeck, suffer any sadness at parting from a strumpet? Ah, she might be beautiful, and clean above all things; she might be nimble-witted and as accomplished in conversation as in love, but she was still a harlot who would lose no time in getting another protector once he was out of sight—or perhaps not fasten herself to one man but serve all comers.

And why should she not? Why should Dion expect any faithfulness to him? Or want such continence in a whore any more than he could have wished that Rycko would keep her knees closed to the Indians of Roanoke Island after he had left her?

But—it could not be called love because that was denied Mag Hollis, harlot—but there was a *gratitude* (he fastened on that word) owed her that made the parting more than an idle farewell. And this sense of "gratitude" was disconcerting; he fought against the realization that it might foreshadow another emotion, utterly impossible of acceptance.

Therefore, that he remember Margery with "gratitude" and no more, Dion resolved to end this relationship with his departure. There would be no loose ends left trailing for him to trip over, possibly, when he returned to England.

"And so, sweet Mag, I'm away at last," he had cried as she had entered his room. "Our fine friendship's at an end and happy you must be that there'll be another head beside you on the pillow tomorrow."

"Not so, milord," the girl had replied in a low voice. "I'm everything but happy that you're leaving, though I know you've chafed at this confinement—and, mayhap, y'r poor company."

"And I say not so to that. You've been all that saved me from the chains of a madhouse and I'm grateful. Ye've been a wondrous fair bedmate and a pleasant wench to talk with. What more could a man ask?"

"And when you return to England, mayhap we can renew our—arrangement?"

"Ah well, as to that—no plans, no promises from either of us, eh? Instead, let's make this parting one we'll remember so long as we're alive to kiss and clip. Here, Mag—right here—and with this—and—so—ah, now. . . ."

She had been arduous enough, Dion thought now as he stared at the timbers over him, but in the most frantic of their joined writhing there had seemed in her a sort of desperation; it had been as though she were trying to clutch him in an embrace that would hold him to her forever.

"Ah, Dion, Dion! There'll never be! There can't! Ah, ah! Sweet Dion! This is more! More than I ever knew! Not end! Oh God, you must come back to me and never leave!"

And as the paroxysm wrenched them both she choked, "Eh-yee! Sweet! Come ye—ah, ah—come back to me, Dion! Again and forever!"

When he was able, he had touched her tear-dampened cheek, softly, tenderly, and had told her his lie.

"No, sweet Mag," he had said, "I cannot come back to you. Y'see—y'see, there's a lady who is love itself to me and—and when this need for hiding's past we'll be married and—"

Her fingertips stopped his lips.

"No more, I beg of you, Dion," she murmured. "I should have known. I leave you now and mark my smile—see it here on my mouth? Farewell, Dion, and know you that I'll be here if you should ever want me."

Head bent, shoulders shaking, she had half run out of the room.

Part 4

1

RALEIGH'S SECOND EXPEDITION to Roanoke Island, a fleet of seven ships, a company of a hundred and eight men, all under the command of Sir Richard Grenville, left Plymouth on April ninth, 1585. The flotilla was at sea two days before Philip Amadas, captain of the *Roanoke,* let Dion Harvie go above decks.

"Aye," the rotund captain grunted, " 'tis best ye show y'rself before Simon Ferdinando so forgets his piloting duties that he wrecks us all. The man has been keeping his eyeglass trained always on this vessel from the *Tyger* ever since we hove to at Plymouth, after our journey from London, and I know of no other interest than you he ought to have in this bark. So go above and make y'rself known to the Portuguese somehow and relieve his burning curiosity."

On deck, Dion paused to blow the stale reek of the forecastle from his lungs with deep breaths of the fresh sea air before he made his way to the tossing bowsprit and clambered up onto the prow of the *Roanoke.* The *Tyger* held her position three vessels ahead and four lengths aport the smaller bark and as Dion squinted in the flagship's direction he caught the wink of the sun's reflection on a pearl ear pendant.

He laughed aloud as he swept off his hat and waved it above his head in sweeping circles. Let the Portuguese big-beard look his fill. There was no way now that Ferdinando could send word to the Queen of his whereabouts even if he would.

He roared words into the wind that snatched them from his lips; he whooped, he hallooed.

"Here I am, you black-maned bastard who'd call Raleigh my false friend and then plot an ambush for the taking of me! Look well, Simon Ferdinando, 'cause the day will yet come, God send, when I'll prove ye the treacherous hound I know ye must be and even all the scores! Look till y'r eyeballs drop out and wonder why y'r schemes all went awry!"

He kept his eyes on the pendant's bright twinkle, then laughed again as he saw the tiny figure on the leading ship's quarterdeck raise his own hat in an answering wave.

"I hear you now, Ferdinando," Dion said bitterly. " 'Ah, good friend Dion, I have been fretted to distraction about y'r safety, y'r fine health! Where was it that ye hid y'rself in London? Try as I might I c'ld find no trace of you after that one meeting near Queenhithe. I am y'r friend, dear Dion, I swear it!' "

He settled his hat on his head and climbed back down to the foredeck.

"And when we touch our first land," he told himself, "that lying spy will fair smother me with his greeting, depend on that. And I, curse all, have not a jot of proof that he's a knave who'd sell his mother to a Moorish slaver if the price was right. But proof I'll find some day and then we'll settle it all, and not with words."

The first land touched by Grenville's fleet was a spot promptly dubbed Mosquito Bay on the Island of St. Johns, later to be known as Puerto Rico. That was on May twelfth, 1585, and Dion's predictions that Simon Ferdinando would descend on him with protestations of friendship proved true when the two men first met ashore.

"Friend Dion!" the pilot exclaimed. "Ah, I was sure you'd come with us on this expedition, though Raleigh swore he did not know your whereabouts, and—"

"And did he blister your ears for telling me he was my false friend?" Dion broke in.

"False friend? Sir Walter?" Ferdinando asked with a puzzled frown. "Y'r pardon, but I do not understand."

"Y'mean to stand there and say you didn't accuse Walt of plotting to turn me over to the Queen so's this expedition would be sure of her support?" Dion demanded.

The Portuguese shook his heavy head slowly, his eyes wide, his lips pursed thoughtfully.

"Good friend," he asked after a long pause, "was there a fever aboard your bark, *Roanoke,* or has this gentle sea trip proved harder to bear than that stormy voyage we first made together? 'Tis often the case, friend Dion; a man who does not stir a hair in a gale is bedazed by the idle motion of a peaceful sea."

"Now hold, by God's gullet!" Harvie barked. "I'll not be called a madman for facing you with the truth. That night in Queenhithe when we met in that dark street and I refused y'r offer of a dram at a tavern close by and you—"

"Dion, Dion," Simon Ferdinando said gently, "I was in Plymouth all but a few days between the time we reached London and the time we sailed again. And those few days were passed in Northumberland, where I have cousins. It must have been another man you met—and you say he slandered the good Sir Walter? Tsk, tsk—what villains walk abroad these times!"

"Now—now—" Dion choked. "I vow I'll—"

"Master Dion Harvie?" asked a clipped voice behind him. He spun about in the beach sand to face the helmeted, corseleted figure of Sir Richard Grenville.

Dion had met Grenville several times at Hampton Court Palace, had even dined with him at Raleigh's apartments, and yet the stern-visaged fleet commander addressed him now as a complete stranger. And that, Harvie told himself, must be because he never had been able to bring himself to like the man, Raleigh's cousin though he might be and one obviously destined to do great things at sea in the Queen's name—and Grenville's protuberant eyes had seen his dislike.

He was a haughty man, Grenville, entirely unlike Sir Walter Raleigh and never to be a hundredth part as much revered as was his cousin though he might become one of Elizabeth's greatest admirals. His manner was reserved to the point of icy formidability; he was brusque with his equals, contemptuous of his underlings. Grenville's men sailed and fought for him because they feared him; the men of Drake and Hawkins and Raleigh and Frobisher sailed and fought because they loved their commanders.

"Master Harvie?" the helmeted man asked again, coldly. Dion bowed with heavy irony.

"A great honor to meet you, Sir Richard," he said. "I've long awaited this day."

A chill gleam showed in Grenville's eyes for a moment and then disappeared.

"I'd have you know, Master Harvie," he said, "that if my cousin, Sir Walter, had seen fit to inform me that you were hiding aboard one of my vessels I'd have had you put ashore instanter and given over to the Queen."

"Why then," Dion said pleasantly, " 'tis easy to see why friend Walt did not see fit to inform you, sir. And as for my hiding aboard one of *your* vessels, Sir Walter somehow misled me—he gave me to understand these ships were his."

"Have done, sir!" Grenville blared. "I'll stand for no insolence in my command! The lowest dog of a seaman or the highest-born gentleman goes into chains if he makes mock of my authority! And you, sir—"

"Y'r pardon, Sir Richard," Simon Ferdinando interjected smoothly. The expedition's leader turned with a scowl to be met by the bearded man's easy, white-toothed smile. "This Master Harvie," the Portuguese went on unbidden, "is my dear friend, my companion on our first visit to Roanoke Island, a man much respected by the savages there."

"I—" Dion began, and stopped at a sharp gesture from Ferdinando.

"I would not see my friend mistreated by anyone, even your honored self, Sir Richard," Simon went on. "For were we to return to Roanoke without three men, Wanchese, Manteo and Dion Harvie, we could no more make peace with the natives than we could grow wings and fly from here to Virginia."

"I need no boy to help me teach the savages to keep peace," Grenville grated.

"Why then, good my Admiral," Simon Ferdinando smiled, "mayhap you do not need me to get you to Roanoke Island."

The armored commander stared at the spade-bearded pilot, his jaw dropping in his amazement.

"Ye mean ye'd desert us if this cockerel were disciplined?" he asked. Ferdinando shrugged and spread his big hands.

"Let us put it this way, Sir Richard," he suggested. "I would not feel easy on Roanoke Island if my friend were out of sorts over our treatment of him. For though I know and admire your great skills, still Dion Harvie is a power 'mongst the people where ye'd found y'r settlement. He has one special friend, one named Rycko, who makes strange magic 'gainst the white man and if this Rycko felt Dion had been mistreated"—he snapped his fingers loudly—"we are all lost."

"I do not hold with witches, wizards or magic," Grenville said, but with his voice strangely lacking its usual iron.

"I vow ye've never heard of one like this Rycko," Ferdinando said solemnly. "With my own eyes I've seen Rycko reduce a hale and hearty white man into a ruined wreck, and all in the space of an hour or so and with the use of no torture machines. They say this Rycko can—"

"I don't want to hear any more about this magic," Grenville snapped. "And if you say Master Harvie is so much your friend ye'll not go on with us unless he's pardoned for his impudence, why then I pardon him—but only 'cause we needs must have a pilot to get us to Virginia."

Without a glance in Dion's direction, the man in the helmet and corselet wheeled and stalked away. Ferdinando watched him go and then turned to the purple-faced Harvie who was choking again, this time on suppressed laughter.

"Oh, Simon, Simon," he gasped when he could speak, "they have a special lively bed of coals waiting f'r you and y'r lies in Hell! Rycko making ruined wrecks of white men with her magic—I trow, when Grenville sees the wench he'll have you strung up by y'r thumbs."

"Lies?" asked the Portuguese in a wounded voice. "What lies did I say? You think Rycko can't make a wreck of a white man in an hour? Ho, I've seen you strut down the beach with her and stagger back within half of that time, a frazzled wretch who scarce could put one foot before the other."

"And that's a base untruth again!" Harvie said hotly. "I—oh, have done! I—I thank ye for coming twixt Sir Richard and me. I confess I did speak insolently to him but his arrogance irked me."

"Aye," the Portuguese nodded seriously, "and God send that proud bearing of his don't bring worse trouble than this small by-play. On the flagship I've heard him talk about what he means to do to teach the savages their manners. God's teeth, ye'd think he was readying himself to storm a Spanish bastion by the plans he makes."

"He thinks like all Englishmen that the Indians are fierce wild men," Dion said philosophically. "When he meets them and sees how different they are from what he thought, he'll change his views."

Ferdinando fingered the pearl pendant in his ear, frowning.

"Ye'll mind," he said after a pause, "that once I said—or no, 'twas Amadas I told this to—I said that your savage is two people, in truth. One's a peaceful, loving simpleton and him we met and lived with on Roanoke Island last year. The other's a howling, shrieking daemon with cruelty that'd make a Spaniard blanch, with a madness that makes a harquebus or pike or cutlass mean nothing. And these wild daemons are the same persons as Wanchese and Wingina and Granganimeo—I'll leave out Manteo because that simpering bastard has fair turned my stomach with his airy ways."

He dropped his hand to his beard and combed its luxuriant growth with his long fingers.

"What I mean to say," he went on, "is that if our good Grenville's wise he'll tread softly when he reaches Virginia. But as I know men, he'd no more treat gently with these savages he regards as sand under his bootheel than he'd clap a ragged mariner on the back in praise of a task well done. And that, I vow who have seen it happen in Florida and in Mexico, will bring us all a deal of woe before we're through."

There was a silence and then Dion asked: "Tell me, Simon;

did you mean it when you said you'd quit the expedition if I was flung in chains or was that more of y'r high-sounding talk?"

The Portuguese grinned at him. "There's no need for me to swear I meant it or didn't, is there?" he asked. " 'Twas enough to send Sir Richard on his way, his head filled with wondering about this awful magic of Rycko's and the end was served, so leave it there."

"And—and why did you befriend me when, a heartbeat before that, you were lying in y'r teeth about meeting me at Queenhithe that night and saying—"

"Ah, Dion," Ferdinando laughed as he reached a hand to Harvie's shoulder, "I am an unscholared Portuguese mariner, mind, and I have no talent for understanding jests. No doubt this is some riddle you'd confuse me with and another time I'll provide ye with y'r sport, but now I've things to do and must be about them."

He swaggered away, sword rasping against his canvas-clad hip, legs encased in turned-down sea boots, pearl pendant gleaming in the hot sun of the West Indies. He left Dion spluttering ineffectually in his rage.

He had little time to wonder at the maze of personalities that made up Simon Ferdinando. Hardly had the bearded Portuguese left Dion before the youngest son of Lord Avronbeck was confronted by the crimson-faced, fierce-eyed Captain Ralph Lane, Grenville's immediate lieutenant and commander of the forces when they were ashore.

If a search had been made for two direct opposites, a better pair of examples could not have been found than Captain Lane and Sir Richard Grenville. Where Grenville was cold, clear-headed, capable, Lane was choleric, loud-voiced, with an impetuosity that, in the past, had plunged him into disastrous error. If the two men had one thing in common it was their innate cruelty but whereas Grenville's was a calm, scalpeling pitilessness, Lane's was a brash brutality.

This was young Harvie's first meeting with Captain Lane but he had heard stories of the soldier Raleigh had chosen Governor of Virginia. None of these accounts had been flattering;

indeed, the popular question had been how Raleigh possibly could have picked Lane for the post.

"Perhaps," Amadas had said dubiously, "all army captains must brag and bluster to impress their troops but Lane does both overmuch to my liking. 'Tis as though he were unsure of himself at all times and seeks to cover his shortcomings with an overlusty manner. And if that's so, I wonder at his worth as governor of Sir Walter's colony."

Said Ferdinando, briefly, "The man's a windbag who's lost entirely without an enemy to fight. Brave enough—aye, but thick-headed past belief."

"Master Harvie," Lane said now, "ye've been attached to my company by Sir Richard and ye're under my orders, sir."

"Aye," Dion nodded. "Yours to command, Captain Lane."

The red-faced soldier glared at Harvie, swallowing the chagrin that came with the younger man's easy acceptance of his subordination. Lane obviously had been told by Grenville that this Dion Harvie was a youngster who would need taking down, and who better to do the taking-down than Ralph Lane?

"Well then," the captain blustered, "let's be about our work! There's a fort to be built, a hundred things to do before the Spanish bastards come down upon us."

"About forts," Dion said, "I confess I know little—although I hear you are fair wondrous at the work of building 'em."

Lane just repressed a smirk. "Ah well, I've builded my share of them and all were good enough to win generous praise from my superiors. There was one I put up at—but we waste time, Master Harvie. Follow me."

Dion trooped off behind Captain Lane to join a work party that had been gathered on the beach, at a point north of the expedition's landing place. And for the rest of that day and the next day and four days after that, Harvie sweated with the others under the merciless sun at the job of throwing up an earthworks under the sharp eye and the blaring voice of Captain Ralph Lane. After the months of soft living at Burnie's and with no toughening exercise since the previous November (the voyage across to St. Johns had been such a fair-weather journey that he had not once been called on to pull a line or man a pump) Dion found the work a hand-blistering torture.

Completed at last, the fort turned out to be a curiously designed affair, hard for Amadas to describe in his journal. The round-bellied ship's master puzzled over his inkpot for a long time before he finally drove his spluttering quill across the salt-stained page.

On this day, he wrote, *Captain Lane proclaimed the fort completed, praise God, and now we are ready for any attack by the Spanish villains although we have not seen a sign of them. The fort is a marvelous affair, being builded of logs covered by sand and with a moat ten feet deep surrounding all. In shape it is like unto a four-pointed star with the lowest point clipped off. Each of the three points is a strong redoubt which is connected to the main enclosure by a narrow passage easily defended by a few men should the redoubt be carried by the enemy. The water side of the fort is the side where the star's point has been sheared off. This side has inward curving walls to an opening through which all enter and leave the fort. In the main enclosure is space for several huts used as storage places and a forge. The whole thing is proof that Sir Walter chose wisely when he placed Captain Lane in charge of our defenses.*

This last statement was one to which Captain Lane, at least, subscribed heartily. The captain preened himself under the compliments of Grenville and the others until Dion Harvie's stomach churned; nothing must do but that the artist, John White, bring out his water colors and splash off an impressive picture of the fort at Mosquito Bay.

Simon Ferdinando watched the congratulatory proceedings with a curl to his lip.

"God's sake," he told Dion, "these gentlemen are fine ones at bussing each other's buttocks over something that ought to be scorned! Think ye that fort will stand the puniest savage raid?"

Harvie asked, "Y'think the Indians can take it?"

"Not with any massed charge, mayhap," the Portuguese said, "but the savages are not given to massed charges. Nay, they'd stand outside the range of our guns and loft arrows over the walls, and stones. We c'ld bang away till our powder and shot were gone whilst they dropped their little love messages in our midst and killed us all. What'd better serve us would be trenches, covered save for embrasures so's we'd be protected from above."

"You should tell the captain that," Harvie suggested.

"I did," Ferdinando replied briefly, with a quirked eyebrow. "Mayhap ye'd like to try the same."

"Not me," Dion said, with a decisive shake of his head. "And anyway, this fort's for use against the Spaniards."

"Best send a message to the Indians, then," laughed Ferdinando, "and tell them that it's intended to fight white men only."

Neither Spaniards nor natives came near the stronghold at Mosquito Bay, to the visible disappointment of Captain Ralph Lane. Despite the isolation of the strip of sand and the fact that neither a ship nor a man on foot could slip up on the fort unseen, Lane kept Harvie and his other men on constant guard duty, four hours at post and four hours off, clad in full armor and wearing helmets that became cauldrons after minutes in the sun.

"If there be cannibals about," Dion told Ferdinando, "they'd welcome this treat—their meat already stewed for them."

As the soldiers stood their sweltering watches, staring at the blinding sand and the impossibly blue sea, other men working under John Arundell, Raleigh's cousin, set up a forge and began making nails to be used on the buildings at Roanoke Island. Others, under Sir Richard Grenville himself, began putting together a pinnace to replace the one which had sprung too many leaks on its tow from England to be profitably patched. It was a forty-foot, single sail boat, little more than a skiff, with a single sail and a shallow draught that would permit it to run up streams the larger vessels could not navigate.

On May twentieth, Dion was standing guard, deep in a heat-burdened stupor, when he was jerked on guard by the yell of "*Sail ho!*" blaring from the northern redoubt. He swung his head in that direction and saw two sails, dangerously close (meaning that sentry must have been as stupefied as Harvie) and bearing down on the island under full canvas. Atop their mainmasts streamed the crimson and gold pennants of Philip's Spain.

There was an eruption of excitement that edged panic within the fort. Lane yelled orders to man the ramparts; Grenville bawled commands to board the English vessels and prepare to engage; Ferdinando howled loudest of all:

"Let 'em come in!" he shouted. "They think this is a Spanish fort! Let 'em come in and we'll have 'em on the hip before they can find out they're wrong!"

The pilot's advice carried the day but not because anybody listened to it; while the Englishmen were scurrying about, trying to follow half a dozen conflicting orders, the two Spanish frigates came up just outside the easy rollers, dropped anchor and lowered their sails. As the defenders of Mosquito Bay watched breathlessly, the two vessels put out their longboats and the Spaniards rowed leisurely in to the beach.

This was Ralph Lane's finest hour. As the two boats touched the sand the captain led a scrambling charge through the gate and the astonished Spaniards—there were twenty-three of them—found themselves encircled by a wall of English harquebuses.

"Surrender!" Lane thundered with a flourish of his sword. "Surrender or, by God's blood, we'll cut you down without mercy!"

The Spaniards did not understand Lane's words but they understood the staring belled muzzles of the harquebuses, the flickering gleam of Lane's blade. To a man they dropped to their knees, their arms outstretched as they begged reprieve from an unshriven end. Dion stared at them as they grovelled on the beach; were these the Spanish cutthroats who roasted young babes and tortured English women after raping them? They looked, he told himself, more like Cornish fishermen than fiends from the deepest pit and the biggest of them would not have fared too well in a children's rough-and-tumble.

His "enemy" crushed, their anchored ships surrendered, Lane strutted up to Sir Richard Grenville and saluted with a flourish.

"Beg leave to report," he puffed, "the capture of two Spanish frigates and twenty-three men. We suffered no losses and the fort was not breached."

"God's sake," Dion muttered, "Sir Richard saw the whole thing—why that curious ceremony?"

"Ye'll find," Ferdinando snickered, "that our Captain Lane needs must make the most of what little he has to bolster his name as a brave commander. And Sir Dick, ye'll see, will go along with the farce to make this a great victory."

Dion smothered another exclamation as he saw Grenville nod gravely at Lane's news.

"Exceeding well done, Captain," the expedition's leader said seriously. "A trap well set—by *both* of us—has brought another triumph for the Queen."

This, then, was the first clash—if it could be so termed—between Spain and "Virginia" in the New World. Although they could not realize it, the comedy at Mosquito Bay should have told Grenville and the others that the power that once was Spain's had weakened to the point of collapse, especially in America. That King Philip's generals and admirals would let the English invade Spain's rich domains beyond the Western Sea and set up a colony close enough to Florida to threaten all Spain's holdings on the mainland without opposing the move vigorously spelled indolence, uncertainty, even indifference, where every Spanish interest called for swift, harsh action.

Now that the "trap" had closed, both Grenville and Lane for some reason were hot to get out of Mosquito Bay. The pinnace was left unfinished—did not the Englishmen have two fine Spanish frigates?—the forge was dismantled, the torch was put to the fort that had cost so much agonizing labor. The fleet raised sail and headed for Roxo Bay, further along the northern coast of St. Johns Island.

The twenty-three Spanish captives were treated generously; instead of being put to the sword, as Lane suggested, they were left at Mosquito Bay. That they had no provisions and less than a long chance of making their way to food was, as Grenville piously put it, "in the hands of the vengeful God who sent them to this predicament."

At Roxo Bay, Grenville and Lane landed men from two vessels and raided a salt deposit, scattering a handful of scrawny native slaves and a Spanish overseer with two volleys from the harquebuses and a shot from a culverin. Harvie was one of the landing party, rejoicing at what he hoped would be a fight, then cursing the luck that had included him in a company ordered to load salt aboard smallboats.

He had helped fill the last one and was straightening with a groan and a hand pressed to his aching back, when Lane's bull's voice came booming across the salt flat to him.

"And here," the captain was saying, "we will build another fort."

"Oh God," Dion Harvie moaned. "The man is mad!"

The second fort was not nearly as splendid a place as the Mosquito Bay defenses. It might have been except for the fact that Sir Richard Grenville, it appeared, was tired of fort-building for the moment; he was anxious to be on his way and he was brusque with Lane when the captain outlined his plans for a second great stronghold on Roxo Bay.

"—and commanding the inlet," Lane enthused, "we'll raise a mighty—"

"Have done, Captain," Grenville broke in, waspishly. "I see no need to build us a Cartagena at this lonely place since we'll not return here."

"But 'tis a handy thing to own, a fort," Lane protested. "Who knows but we shall meet reverses further north and have to repair to a stronghold here? The greatest military scholars all say—"

"Oh, build your fort, then," Grenville said impatiently, "but I can't spare more than a day in its construction."

Lane grumbled beneath his breath but he built his fort, if a rude sandbanked enclosure could be called a fort. The captain was still sulky when the little fleet sailed out of Roxo Bay and headed northwestward toward Hispaniola and the great Spanish city of San Domingo.

"Sir Richard," Philip Amadas complained to Dion, "is a wise and weighty gentleman and must be right in what he does, but why does he so entreat disaster by walking into that hellhole?

Likely we'll all be murdered, our ships sunk, the moment those Spanish dogs see the Cross of Saint George at our masthead."

"We could always crack a spar and so be forced to drop behind the others," Dion suggested. "Simon Ferdinando once said 'twas usually best to have another sample a strange dish—mayhap 'twould be better to have Grenville and our bloodthirsty Lane taste this dangerous stew before we dine or shun the plate."

"And desert our comrades?" Amadas asked, aghast. "Nay, friend Dion, you know you could'st not do a thing like that!"

"I suppose not," Harvie said moodily, "but if Captain Lane breathes one breath about building one of his damned forts at San Domingo, this expedition will have a deserter, and without a second's waiting, I vow."

Historians were to wonder in future centuries just why Sir Richard Grenville was so confident in putting his head in the lion's mouth by sailing boldly into San Domingo harbor and paying his respects to the Royal Governor of Hispaniola. Despite their learned calculations they never found a reasonable answer. Some held with the theory advanced by Simon Ferdinando when the Portuguese pilot answered Dion Harvie's questions.

"'Tis easy to see," the big, bearded man said, "that our Sir Richard knows something we do not; 'tis not past believing that the Governor has given word to Raleigh that his expedition won't be harmed if it visits him."

"But why take the risk?" Harvie persisted. "The whole world knows a Spaniard's word is not worth the breath it's given in."

"This company," Simon explained, "needs many things the Governor of Hispaniola has to sell—sheep, swine, sugar. And these Spanish officers, I know, would sell their sisters for enough gold. Rich as they are, they're all still penny-fathers. This Governor could see a chance to load his money chest still heavier by trading with you Englishmen, enemies of his King though you may be, and forgetting to tell Philip about it. In any case, I have no fear this visit will fail, else I'd not pilot the expedition hither and, God knows, nobody else in this company could find the mainland, much less Hispaniola."

Ferdinando's confidence proved well-founded. No cannon fire

greeted the expedition as the ships sailed into San Domingo harbor; the Governor's barge was quick to come out with greetings to Sir Richard Grenville and his companions; His Excellency was flowery in his acceptance of Grenville's invitation to attend a banquet to be given on the flagship *Tyger*.

Dion was not included among those who gathered about the banquet board nor had he expected to be, considering Grenville's cold disdain, but he got a full account of the affair from Philip Amadas.

"Never had those Spanish whoresons seen a more splendid feast," the *Roanoke's* little captain said. "All the officers and other persons of distinction were served on silver plate, chased and gilt. The meal was a sumptuous thing with nineteen dishes—God's teeth, Sir Dick must've robbed his stores of all that could be spared, and more—and whilst we ate musicians made fair music. 'Twas as polite a gathering as though 'twas London and all about the table were dear friends. The Governor has invited us to dine tomorrow in his palace—aye, 'tis wondrous how friendly these bastards be to us."

"I hope they're friendly enough to give us stores to fill the holds Grenville emptied for his feast," Dion gloomed. "Whilst you ate y'r bellies full, we who were not there had only a morsel of tough pickled beef to gnaw on."

"There'll be a-plenty tomorrow," Amadas nodded. "Already, Sir Dick has arranged to buy a fill of stores."

His Spanish Excellency proved a man of his word or, as Ferdinando would have it, a man with an eager eye for a gold piece. The following day was spent in loading pigs, sheep and goats, together with sugar, ginger, salt fish and great quantities of fruit. Dion Harvie labored from sun-up until past dark, calling on his whole considerable store of profanity to express some of his feelings as he wrestled with the baaing, lowing, whinnying livestock and trundled casks and kegs, barrels and bales, aboard the vessels.

"And when I meet that dung-souled blasphemy, Captain Guy Groven," he swore fervently, "I'll make him pay for every minute of this, I vow!"

His muscles were still aching, his hands were still blistered, when Sir Richard Grenville's fleet weighed anchor in San Domingo Bay and headed for the mainland. He had not completely eased the soreness of his big frame when, on the twenty-sixth of June, 1585, the *Roanoke* and the other vessels furled their sails off an island just south of the Cape of Hatorask. The place was a bleak, narrow strip of land marked on Philip Amadas' weird map as Pasquiwoc and there Grenville called a council aboard the *Tyger*. This time, Dion Harvie was asked to attend.

"I told him," Simon Ferdinando explained *sotto voce* as he accompanied Harvie to the poopdeck, "that bein' a favorite of the Indians as you are by your close familiarity with the great Rycko, we'd best have your advice on how to go further."

"Ye're cooking up a hot pudding for the two of us," Dion growled, "with all this talk about the great Rycko! When Sir Richard sees that big-eyed wench he'll have y'r beard for cozening him."

"We shall see," the pilot grinned. "I don't think Grenville will rant and rave overmuch—he still needs me to get him back to England, you know."

The expedition's leader was curt, but no more than ordinarily so, when he greeted Dion. Lane scowled and tugged at his beard; the captain had no love for Harvie and never had bothered to conceal his dislike. Since that first day in Mosquito Bay, when Dion had robbed Lane of the chance to be the stern disciplinarian by cheerfully accepting menial duty, the captain had regarded the tall, blue-eyed young man with loathing. Dion's ill-guarded remarks about Lane's precious forts had done nothing to endear him to the soldier.

"Now, Master Harvie," Grenville said without preliminaries, "our pilot, Ferdinando, seems to think you the best informed on whether 'twould be safe to land our people here without an attack first. By your connections with the savages, he says, you can tell us whether they are friendly or warlike on this island."

"Warlike, Sir Richard?" Dion asked. "I've said a hundred times, to Sir Walter and to anybody else who'd listen, that these Indians are the most peaceful men in the world! I don't know why you'd hesitate to land here on Pasquiwoc when ye sailed into San Domingo as though 'twere Plymouth, sir."

"And I didn't summon you here to listen to y'r disapproval of my course at San Domingo," Grenville lashed back. "'Tis this island I'm concerned about, Master Harvie."

"Why then I say land here, if ye be so minded," Harvie said, frigidly. "Ye'll find the natives friendly—aye, so friendly Captain Lane won't even have to build himself another fort."

Sir Richard asked, "Ye think we do not need a scouting party to test these people's temper?"

"I think 'twould be a grievous mistake, sir. Guns and armor might plant uneasiness in even these poor simple savages' minds but if we come in peace they'll welcome us more heartily than did the Governor of Hispaniola."

Lane broke in. "I say the risk's too great! This lad's—"

"Master Dion Harvie, Captain," Dion interrupted. "I do not like the word 'lad' as though I were a snot-nosed boy."

"Now, now," Grenville said impatiently, "we'll have no hackles raised here! Captain, Master Harvie has lived with these savages and knows them, so Ferdinando says, better than any of us save Manteo and Wanchese. Those Indians will not land here—they have some objection about asking shelter from this tribe that I confess I do not understand—so we needs must employ Master Harvie as our guide and spokesman."

"But we lay ourselves open to treachery," Lane gravelled.

"A chance we must take, Captain," Grenville said, "and since Master Harvie himself will be in the van of the party, surely he will not lead us into any danger that threatens his own neck."

"You make it sound as though I planned trickery, Sir Richard," said the tall young gentleman with the shoulder-length dark hair.

"I did not mean to, truly," the heavy-browed leader said hastily. "What I meant was that if your first inclinations after landing were that the savages had changed their temper since you saw them last, ye'd recognize the signs and so make good a retreat in time."

Grenville's sincerity shone through his explanation and Dion

Harvie bowed his acceptance of it. He was in the leading boat that pushed off from the *Tyger* and he was the first to step out on the sand that stretched up to the silent fringe of yaupon bush, scraggy pine and live oak that faced the sea.

"There's not a sign of life," Grenville muttered. "Mayhap the savages have deserted this island for some reason."

"Oh, they're here," Dion said. "I'd wager that a hundred eyes are watching us this minute."

"And a hundred spears and knives are ready for us, I doubt not," Lane grumbled.

"Probably," Harvie nodded lightly. "What would you? How would you prepare y'rself if a fleet of galleons, a hundred times bigger than England's biggest, were to anchor off Billingsgate and discharge a company of green men carrying forked lightning? For something such as that this great company must seem to them." He turned away from Lane and shouted toward the silent woods in the Roanoke dialect.

"We come in peace!" he yelled. "We are friends! When the hot moon was in the sky we were here—now we come again with more friends! We bring presents!"

There was quiet in the bush beyond the beach. Dion motioned toward the chest that had been brought ashore and a seaman flung back its lid. Harvie reached inside to pick up a handful of gewgaws, glass beads, a looking glass, a length of bright cloth, and held it over his head.

"Presents!" he shouted. "Presents for our friends of Pasquiwoc!"

There was a stirring of the yaupon bushes, a waving of the high beach grass, and into view stepped a score or more of naked Indians, hands held aloft. Their spokesman, a thickset brave who wore a cluster of egret feathers in his topknot, advanced to within three paces of Dion.

"Ho," he said gutturally. "Is it you who lived at Roanoke so many moons ago?"

"We are those men," Dion answered. "There are others with us now but all of us are friends." He turned to Sir Richard. "Gren-ville," he explained. "Lane. Ar-run-dell, White. You know Ferdinando."

The brave nodded vigorously, smiling. Yes, he remembered Simon Ferdinando and, quite obviously, thought well of the bulky Portuguese pilot.

"Ho, Bright-Ear," he said genially, with a finger reaching up to touch the lobe of his right ear, where Ferdinando wore his pearl pendant. "You have come back from over the sea."

"As we said we would," Dion nodded. "What are you called?"

"Tolepuec," the brave replied. "I am chief of these people. I will take the presents and give them to those who deserve them."

"At a great feast," Dion said. "Where is your village and what is it called? We must know this so we can bring fine food to the feast."

The squat Indian pointed to the south.

"The village lies there and is called Aquascogok," he said. "It is a mighty place, far better than"—he spat into the sand—"the water rat hole they call Dasamonquepeuc."

"What does he say, man?" Grenville asked impatiently. "Are these people friendly?"

"Entirely, Sir Richard," Harvie said. "This chief is Tolepuec and he bids us repair to his village, Aquascogok, and bring food for a feast."

"Now, need we waste provisions on these black dogs?" Ralph Lane asked. " 'Tis they who'd better set a table if they'd keep from feeling our whip."

Dion Harvie turned to the red-faced captain, his eyes glacial, his lips thinned, his brows lowered.

"Before ye make a misstep," he cautioned, "ye'd best know that these people are not too friendly with those further north, the Roanokes. They've ready to welcome us, yes, but if they are not treated right, they'll blame their woes on the Roanokes we'll be living amongst and there'll be war for certain."

"And think ye I'd tremble at such a prospect?" Lane asked.

"Ah nay, good Captain," Dion said acidly, "but Sir Walter would hardly be pleased to know his expedition spent its time fighting Indians instead of setting up the colony he ordered."

"Master Harvie's right," Grenville said abruptly. "Tell this Tolepuec we will come to his village with presents and food."

Lane muttered, "I never thought to see the day I'd be party to the coddling of a pack of heathen savages."

Sir Richard Grenville whirled on his captain, underlip thrust out, face taut with anger, popeyes blazing.

"By God, Captain Lane," he barked, "that sounds too like an uncivil remark f'r me to let it pass! If ye doubt my leadership, return to y'r ship and spend y'r time sharpening y'r blade. I'm in command here till I sail back to England and only then do you take over authority!"

"Y'r pardon, Sir Richard," Lane hastened to say. "I offer my apologies for a thoughtless speech." And, as Grenville bowed coldly, the captain shot the grinning Harvie a black glare.

On his way to Aquascogok, Dion pondered the difference between this landing and the arrival of the two vessels at Roanoke Island a year before. Then, Amadas and Barlowe had been eager to cultivate the Indians' friendship; now, the man who would be governor of the colony when Grenville went home was straining at the leash to show his authority in the only way he knew, by the musket and sword. Ferdinando had said at Mosquito Bay that the leaders of this second expedition would bring trouble to them all before they were through and now it seemed that the Portuguese had known what he was talking about. Grenville might be irked now by Lane's near insubordination but under his cold reserve Sir Richard, like Lane, believed that only a stern hand could control ignorant savages. It was not impossible, Dion knew, that the two men would forget their personal differences and join forces to demonstrate their civilized superiority by the blade and the bullet before they were finished.

If only the Spanish would attack—he laughed at himself for the thought. If the demonstration at Mosquito Bay when the two Spanish frigates had sailed into the muzzles of the English guns was any indication, the smallest Spanish force could massacre this hydra-headed company of Englishmen. For while Grenville had roared one command, Lane had yelped another; there had been muddled confusion without a shot fired or even a culverin brought to bear as the two frigates had delivered themselves over to the English. If a Spanish company had come down on Lane's fort in an attack—Dion winced at the thought.

Still, if Lane and Grenville could work off some of their fire in a fight with the Spanish, there would be less danger of an incident that would make enemies of the Indians and bring slaughter to this slumbering Eden. Not, Dion hastened to assure himself, that he was afraid of a war with the savages—aye, he'd relish any kind of excitement after the monotony of the past months—but these simple people had befriended him the year before and it was less than gentlemanly that they be repaid for their hospitality with lead and steel.

"And that," he chided himself, "is a sure sign that you are getting soft, Dion Harvie. The son of Lord Avronbeck worrying about what might happen to a pack of witless Indians—'tis past imagining."

As though to salt the wounds Lane had suffered by his rebuke, Grenville made the Indians' feast a lavish banquet. The silver plate that had been displayed to the Spanish governor was brought out again and the trestle tables set up on shore were loaded with pickled beef as well as fresh pork and lamb and tropical fruits from Hispaniola, ship's biscuits and gallons of wine.

All these things the Pasquiwocs devoured and gulped ravenously and with typical taciturnity. Nor did they give a word of thanks or even a smile of appreciation when Grenville and Lane grandly distributed their gifts of cloth, beads, knives (quite rusty but still serviceable) and slightly mouldy sweetmeats. Dion's experience had proved that because they gave no indication of gratitude did not mean the Indians were the thankless churls they seemed; he knew that Tolepuec and his tribesmen would repay their visitors a hundred times over in hospitality—when it suited their convenience. To Lane and Grenville, as to Dion on his first visit, the savages' ingrate attitude was maddening.

"By God's teeth," the captain huffed, "I knew all these supplies and presents would be wasted! Look you, that chief, Tolepuec, even has the gall to ask if this is all we brought!"

" 'Tis their custom," Harvie explained once again. "Tolepuec but asks if our part of the feast is finished before he orders his men to do their part in this ceremony."

"You mean they'll set a feast for us now?" Grenville asked. "And give us presents in return?"

"Not at once, mayhap," Dion said, "but it is mannerly amongst the Indians for them to wait until their guests finish their greeting complete before responding."

The Indians of Pasquiwoc, however, had customs that proved more leisurely than those observed by the natives of Roanoke. Whereas Granganimeo, Wanchese and Manteo had delivered a boatload of fish to the *Tyger* and the *Admiral* within an hour after they had finished their feast that first day off Roanoke, Tolepuec and his braves let three days pass without making the slightest gesture of hospitable return and each sundown found Ralph Lane burning hotter, Richard Grenville deeper in an ominous chill.

"God's sake," Philip Amadas begged Dion, "go to Tolepuec and ask him to do something—anything—to ward off Lane's anger! The leastest present from the Indians would serve them well right now; I fear that sword-rattler will blow up in rage if another day passes."

"You know it wouldn't do," Harvie replied with a shake of his dark head. "For us to ask for presents would belittle us in their eyes. They can call for gifts, aye, but because we never asked for a thing at Roanoke was the reason they fair swamped us with all we needed and more. Had we asked, we'd not have gotten an ear of maize—Rycko told me that."

"Pray the good God, then, that they're moved to pay us back today, else there'll be no holding Captain Lane!"

But the Indians of Pasquiwoc did not consider that day the one to welcome their visitors, or if they did they had no chance to announce it. For it was barely noon when Sir Richard Grenville and Captain Ralph Lane strode up to Dion Harvie on the beach and spiked the young man with a stormy glare.

"How now, Master Harvie?" Grenville rapped out. "Y'think these heathen savages are such friends of ours when they steal our valuables?"

"Aye," Lane bellowed. "Ought we spread another feast to thank these dogs for their thievery?"

"Thievery?" Harvie asked wonderingly. "Nay, Sir Richard, these Indians don't know the meaning of the word, I vow!"

Grenville said icily, "Mayhap they don't know the word but they know the deed well enough."

"You mean—"

"I mean some black hound has stole my silver cup!" Lane cried. "My precious silver cup that was given me by my father and which I've carried through a hundred campaigns! Let me get my hands on the bastard that stole my cup and ye'll see how an Englishman treats a savage thief he's not afraid of—as some seem to be!"

Dion's hand dropped to the hilt of his rapier as his lean face went white.

"Ye'll take back that slur," he told Lane in a flat voice, "or try to prove I fear any man, Englishman or savage!"

"Put up y'r blade, Master Harvie," Grenville rasped, "or I'll clap you in chains, Ferdinando or no Ferdinando—and I mean this!"

"But this man said—"

"I care not what he said, Harvie! I'm done with coddling these graceless savages! Ye'll arrange to have these people return Captain Lane his silver cup and at once or I'll make reprisal that they'll remember for awhile, I swear!"

"I tell ye, sir," Dion said earnestly, "that these people do not steal! At Roanoke—"

"Aye, at Roanoke," Grenville broke in. "At Roanoke they treated you well, as Captain Amadas and Ferdinando have said to support you, but this is not Roanoke; this is Pasquiwoc! And I do not intend to be diddled by a lot of heathens who're probably laughing at our meekness now while they rifle our goods."

"My cup," Lane lamented, "was of the finest silver and worth two golden pounds, at least, besides the memories it held for me! Let me find the—"

"When did you last see this cup?" Dion asked.

"What matters it?" Lane blustered. "I had the cup and now I've not. Think you a member of my own company stole it?"

"Thievery," Harvie returned boldly, "is known to Englishmen but never to an Indian."

"Y'see?" Lane cried, whirling toward Grenville. "Our Master Harvie takes these savages' part against his own kind! By God's gullet, we have a strange kind of Englishman here! No wonder that Her Majesty—"

"Enough!" Sir Richard said with a curt gesture. His popeyes pinned themselves on Dion. "To prove I am a generous man," he continued, "I'll give ye leave to ask Tolepuec to give back the cup instanter, before I have our men make a search for it. "A search," he added grimly, "that will not be gentle."

"But sir—"

"Ye'd rather have us search at once?" Grenville blared. "Then tell me, and I'll order it!"

"Nay, Sir Richard, I—I'll talk to Tolepuec. But I know—ahh, I'll speak with him now."

He knew it was a useless visit as he knew that any search of the village of Aquascogok would be futile, but Dion Harvie trudged through the deep sand to the chief's thatched hut, gave a greeting and walked inside to squat beside Tolepuec. The leader of the Pasquiwoc tribe was sorting a collection of shells (one of his duties as chief was to grade the shells that would be used as body ornaments and apportion them to his braves, the finest going to the sub-chiefs, the next best to his strongest men, the more common shells to the old men and boys) and he responded to Dion's "ho" with a curt grunt.

"Great chief," Dion said, "there has been a bad thing happen to the Captain Lane."

Tolepuec grunted again, not raising his eyes from the pile of shells.

"Aye, the Captain Lane has lost a cup, a silver cup, and he is sore grieved. The cup was his father's and he wants it back."

"Then let him hunt for it," Tolepuec said indifferently. "I cannot have my men leave off their work to search. The women are all busy. The Captain Lane has plenty of men—let them find the cup."

"But the Captain Lane thinks the cup was taken," Dion Harvie forced himself to say. "He wants the man who took it to give it back."

The Indian raised his eyes then in a wondering stare. His brown hand stirred the shells absently as he held his puzzled gaze on Dion.

"The cup was taken?" he asked slowly. "The Captain Lane thinks one of us took his cup?"

Harvie nodded silently. It was impossible that an Englishman of noble birth should be shamed by the look in a savage's eye but Dion could find no other word for what he felt under Tolepuec's stare.

"But why would we take his cup?" the Indian asked. "Are we not friends? Did you not eat with us and give us presents?"

"Aye, but—the cup is gone and the Captain Lane believes one of you took it."

"You think this, too?" the chief asked quietly.

"Nay, I know 'twas not—" He stopped short. *Our Master Harvie takes these savages' part against his own kind!* "If one of you did take it," he went on, hardening his voice, "you'd best have it given back now, else our chief, Sir Richard, will have the village searched, and more."

Tolepuec got to his feet in one lithe motion, for all his squatty bulk. As Dion rose, the chief faced him, his arms folded across his barrel chest, his features a mask, his voice a level drone.

"Tell your chief he does not need to search Aquascogok," he said. "I will have my people empty their houses that he may see we did not take the cup." He strode to the open end of his hut and barked a command. The Pasquiwocs in the village, men and women, cast their chief one disbelieving glance and then hurried to their houses in bewildered obedience. Within five minutes, all the few belongings of every hut were arranged in front of the doorways.

"Look at them," Tolepuec told Harvie, his voice tinged with contempt, "and see there is no cup."

"And would the thief be fool enough not to hide it?" Ralph Lane snarled as he came forward with Grenville, backed by a troop of men clad in breastplates and burgonets and carrying pikes and harquebuses. "Does this dog think we're simpletons?" He strutted up in front of the impassive Tolepuec and pushed his short beard forward at the chief. "Give over the thief who stole my cup," he demanded in English, "or I'll find ways to make the pilfering rat squeal loud enough."

"What does this man say?" Tolepuec asked.

"He says—he says the one who took his cup has hidden it. He bids you find the man and have him give it back."

"But there is no man," Tolepuec said patiently. "How can I make a man—out of sand, out of water, out of air? Am I the Great One that I can build a man to give the captain his cup?"

"He says his braves didn't take the cup," Dion said helplessly, turning to Sir Richard. "He asks how he can hand over a thief when there is no thief in his tribe?"

"Curse him for a liar!" Lane stormed. To Grenville, he said: "Dost mean to let these villains go unpunished, Sir Richard? For if you do, ye'll have y'r troubles with the others, and a-plenty! They'll know they can steal and think they can murder, without a jot of punishment."

"Now sir," Simon Ferdinando put in, "I counsel 'gainst hasty action here. I do not think—"

Grenville's agate eyes swung to the black-bearded Portuguese as he held up a gauntleted hand.

"I'm in command here, sir," he said, hard-voiced. "And my thought is that Captain Lane is right. These animals must be taught never to trifle with Englishmen." He turned back to Dion. "Tell Tolepuec," he snapped, "that unless the cup is given back and now, the village will be burned, and the storehouses."

"Sir," Dion asked, "has Captain Lane looked high and low for his cup? It may be but misplaced and—"

"Tell him!" Sir Richard Grenville barked. Dion opened his mouth to make another protest, closed it again, shrugged and turned back to Tolepuec.

"Our chief, Sir Richard, says that unless the one who took the cup gives it back now your village will be burned," he said.

Tolepuec looked long into Dion's eyes and it was the young Englishman who dropped his gaze to study the ground. Then, wordlessly, the Pasquiwoc chief turned his back on Harvie, Grenville and Lane and stalked in dignity to the council fire that smouldered in the middle of the circle of huts. There, he raised his face and addressed the sky.

"Tell me, O Great One," he asked, "why do you punish us so? Why do you set these white men against us who were their friends? Why do you let them say we did this thing we did not do? What evil have we been guilty of that you frown upon us?"

When he finished and stood there, face upthrust as though waiting for an answer from the Great One, a low wailing broke out among the men and women who stood by their huts; they did not know what was to befall them but they knew some catastrophe hovered.

"I was sure," Dion heard Lane tell Grenville, "that a show of force would make these scurvy dogs whimper. See, they have no spine even to defend their own homes!"

"These are not warlike men," Dion protested. "I've told you a thousand times they're peaceful folk."

"Aye, and ye said they were an honest people," Lane sneered.

"And so they are! I know they didn't steal your cup!"

"Enough," Grenville snapped. "They'll not return what they stole, eh, Master Harvie?"

"They did not—"

"Captain Lane," Grenville broke in ruthlessly, "show these savages that we're not to be idly dealt with."

Prodded by pikes, the Indians were herded out of Aquascogok through the stockade's gate and onto the beach. They were obedient enough after a few words snapped by Tolepuec hushed their first protests. Dion could not catch what the chief said but his brief command brought a change to the Pasquiwocs. Where they had been confused, fearful, now they were mantled by a sort of proud dignity that almost seemed to make *them* the masters, the Englishmen the losers in their own outrage.

Silently, their faces set in unyielding impassivity, they watched Lane's soldiers put the torch to their village, saw the flames race from one hut to another, witnessed the burning of the town of which they had been so proud. One of the women started to wail but stopped her cries at a terse grunt from the chief; the children stared wide-eyed as the smoke writhed up, the tinder-dry wood and thatching crackled and vomited sparks, the fire leapt high, dwindled and then bloomed again as another building caught.

Captain Ralph Lane watched with the air of a commander

seeing his troops carry a well-defended height, a general watching his soldiers sweep an important battlefield against great odds. Feet apart, arms akimbo, he strutted without moving, he preened himself without lifting a hand.

Sir Richard Grenville watched with the frigid detachment of a cold-souled man who would never let his handsome face betray his delight in cruelty.

Simon Ferdinando watched with a troubled frown creasing his forehead, his lower lip caught between his teeth.

Philip Amadas watched with dismay, John White, the artist, with pleasure at the play of colors in the conflagration; Thomas Hariot, the scientist, with a curiosity at the Indians' strange dignity.

Dion Harvie watched with a nausea born of guilty horror. He had heard stories of what the Spaniards had done in Mexico, in Hispaniola, in Peru, and he had been proud in his assurance that no Englishman could ever be a party to such massacres of the savages. True, no blood had been spilled here on this sandy island but the fact there had been no slaughter did little to leaven the crime of the burning of Aquascogok. Lane, the soldier who must prove his worth by manufacturing violence where none was at hand, had had his way; Grenville, the gentleman who must always keep telling himself that inner warmth was a weakness, had backed him—and these two men would govern Roanoke Island when they reached the beach where Dion had lain with Rycko on the warm sands, under the bright stars, covered by a blanket of the sweet grape-scent.

2

DION HAD EXPECTED Grenville to lead his expedition north from Pasquiwoc after the burning of Aquascogok but Sir Richard and Captain Lane had no idea of giving the Indians the impression that they had fled after the levelling of the village. The flotilla stayed at anchor off the island for almost a month while Tolepuec's people laboriously rebuilt their town. During that month Grenville peremptorily called on the natives to provide the expedition with fish and maize, wildfowl and oysters.

"Else," he told the stolid chief through Dion Harvie, "worse will befall you than the burning of a few shabby huts."

Tolepuec listened to the threat without a ripple of emotion. When Harvie was finished he nodded briefly and spoke to a sub-chief who stood scowling at his side. The other Indian hesitated and opened his mouth to voice a protest but a sharp word from Tolepuec stilled him and he left the group of whites.

"Tell him," Grenville ordered Dion, "that if he plans trickery we'll be well ready for him, and more. Any harm to us will bring swift vengeance to the women and children, first, and then to him and all the other men of his tribe."

"I know," Tolepuec said when Harvie relayed this message. "I know the white men will war on our women and children. Else why have I bowed my head?"

"Know you," Harvie said in the Pasquiwoc tongue—and damn Lane and his taunt, "I am not a chief—I give no orders—I but hand the talk between you and my people."

There was a glimmer deep in Tolepuec's eyes as he looked at Dion.

"You are a white man," he said tonelessly. "You share their great victories—and what may come after."

"Come after? What do you mean?"

Tolepuec swept a stubby-fingered hand in a gesture that encompassed the island, the bay that lay beyond the sandy reef and the country where lay Roanoke.

"You plan to seize all this world from us," he said, "and in the war to seize it you must surely win, for the gods have given you stronger weapons. But before we all are dead, some of you too will die, for our surrender here does not mean we do not know how to hate and fight."

"Nay, Tolepuec," Harvie protested. "The chief of this party is a man who would never have let your town be burned, a man named Raleigh. And he is for peace, not war. He is an"—he sought the Indian word for "honorable" and could find none—"he is a man such as you who would not wrong another."

"Where is this Ral-eigh?" Tolepuec asked, contemptously. "Why did he not stop the burning of our village?"

"He is far across the sea," Harvie explained weakly. "He does not know what his sub-chiefs do."

Tolepuec said, "I could send my sub-chiefs to the moon and know they would never do a thing I had forbidden them to do. Your great chief must be a feeble man if his sub-chiefs disobey him so. I spit on your great chief as I spit on all you white men."

"What does he say?" Grenville asked, irascibly. "You two have been gabbling like so many geese and I caught Raleigh's name in your jabber."

"He does not understand," Harvie said in a white voice, "why you have burned his town when Sir Walter, our leader, would not have countenanced it."

"Now, damn me!" Lane exploded. "Here's another bit of dauncey insolence, Sir Richard! Our young stowaway here—"

"Stowaway, is it?" Harvie gritted. "By God, Lane ye'll pull my blade from its scabbard yet with y'r tongue! Know you I'm Lord Avronbeck's son, no scum of a soldier ye're used to dealing with! Know you, too, that Sir Walter is my great and good friend and will listen to what I have to report when I see him again!"

Lane's face, always ruddy, flamed bright crimson and flecks of spittle bubbled at the corners of his mouth as he roared back at Harvie.

"Think you I care what you report to Raleigh?" he demanded. "I'll furnish you with pages for y'r report before I'm through. I was named governor of this colony of Virginia, to take office when Sir Richard departs, and I was given full authority to—"

"To set up a colony," Harvie broke in, "not to bedevil friendly Indians and burn their villages—make bitter enemies of them!"

"To do my duty as I see it!" Lane raged. "And if I see it needed, I'll burn every black whoreson's hut and he inside it!"

"Aye," Dion rasped, "that's work you have a kidney for, I trow! I do not wonder now that Her Majesty could spare you for this expedition instead of keeping you at home to deal with the Spaniards!"

Lane's sword came up with a thin shriek of steel against the silver ring and Dion's blade blinked free in the sunlight. Sir Richard Grenville and Captain Amadas flung themselves between the two men recklessly.

"Now hold, in the Queen's name!" Grenville cried. "Before God, I'll clap ye both in chains—aye, you, too, Captain Lane if you do not put up y'r weapon! Captain Amadas, take young Harvie to your ship and keep him there! Captain Lane, I bid you repair to the *Tyger* and await me. This expedition's ruined if we fight amongst ourselves before we even reach Roanoke Island."

"That cockerel—"

"Is Raleigh's dear friend, as he said," Grenville put in, coldly, "and as such merits some distinction. And, aye, ye did treat him as though he were some common soldier and not Lord Avronbeck's son."

Lane stared at his superior, stunned by Grenville's abrupt turnabout. He had counted on Grenville to back him in any clash with this insolent stripling who dared criticize his way of dealing with the Indians; now he saw Grenville's cold eye turned upon *him,* as though *he* were the one at fault.

"Sir Richard," he said uncertainly, "I but meant to discipline the lad, as ye told me to, y'rself."

"And by disciplining Master Harvie," Grenville said frigidly, "I meant to curb his brash ways with thoughtful training, not to harangue him as ye would a drunken recruit dragged from a London stew."

"I—"

"So here's an end to it," Grenville went on. "Master Harvie, ye'll stay aboard the *Roanoke* till I summon you. Captain Lane, ye'll command an exploring party that'll survey these islands that lie south of us and to the north as far as Trinity Inlet. That'll keep you two apart and so serve all our purposes best."

He walked away as Lane's reproachful eyes and Dion's thoughtful ones followed him. Harvie had heard that Grenville was nothing if not a cold-minded strategist who prepared for every eventuality; here was proof of it. He might despise Dion but he would never forget that Dion Harvie was Walter Raleigh's good friend, Lord Avronbeck's favorite son, while Captain Lane was a nobody in court circles, a professional soldier who had been chosen governor of Virginia because Raleigh had for some reason been carried away by Lane's enthusiastic accounts of his own abilities as a builder of forts. Dion knew what Grenville was thinking; Harvie's position as Raleigh's friend was as solid as any position could be in those times; Lane's was shaky, bolstered by no bonds of personal regard. If Lane was booted out of his command—and Dion could not believe that Sir Richard did not see that possibility—Grenville could not afford to be too closely linked with the captain. If Harvie was elevated to a higher place in this situation—and, again, Dion thought Grenville foresaw that chance—it would not do for Grenville to find himself on the wrong side of the fence.

Dion was well acquainted with the thinking processes of Elizabeth's courtiers; Lane was not. Therefore, while the captain fumbled through his bewilderment at the sudden desertion of his ally, an unsurprised Harvie weighed Grenville's mind and made his own calculations.

Aboard the *Roanoke,* Dion went to Amadas' cabin and joined the round-bellied captain in a cup of wine.

Harvie mourned, "It seems I'm forever bein' banished to this vessel! Not that I don't appreciate y'r hospitality, Captain Amadas, but whenever there's a puff of wind to ruffle the sea, somebody orders me aboard this old tub—y'r pardon for speaking so harshly of y'r bark.

"When I ran afoul the Queen a year ago, Walt hustled me into hiding on the *Roanoke*—the *Tyger* then—and when we sailed back to London c'ld I disembark with the others? Nay, I had to keep myself aboard till Raleigh found a place for me. Then I had to hide on this vessel when we cleared London in April. Now I'm y'r ungrateful guest again."

"Old tub my ship may be, Dion," Amadas smiled, "but more comfortable, I think, than being wrapped about Captain Lane's sword, as you were too close to being just now."

"That windy stink?" Harvie grunted. "Think you he could have come close to stabbing me? Hah, I'd soon show him he wasn't treating with a peaceful Indian if he'd tried to lay on me!"

"Make up y'r differences with Captain Lane, Dion," Amadas begged. "Ah, I know the burning of the village was a foul thing but—well, he's to be governor when Grenville's gone back and he c'ld make it hot for you, as such."

"The Roanokes," Harvie said, "will make it hot for all of us if Lane tries such treatment on them. Mind you Wingina's death's-head face, his eyes like a fish-hawk's? Rycko told me that there is no chief in all this land so talented in war and 'twas no idle boasting, that I know. Rycko never bragged to me."

"Nay," Amadas said with a quirked mouth, "I believe she was honest with you, friend Dion, with all the great love she had for you."

"Love, Captain? What do these Indians know of love?"

"Well, what do we, then?" the little shipmaster asked quietly. "I am not nobly born, I know, but I have eyes and ears and I have seen and heard enough about the great ladies who move in high places to know true love has deserted our England complete, or nearly so. And the lower classes ape the higher, so virtue and chastity are outmoded. Marriage is too often but a means to better a couple's position, with true affection of no importance. Many a gentleman uses his wife as a pimp would use a whore, to gain favor and gold, and whilst she plays the beast wi' two backs in one room, he cuddles his cuckolder's lady in the next. Love, Master Harvie? Ah, I fear ye'll find honest love amongst these simple people where ye won't in all England—always excepting y'r own fair lady, of course."

"My own fair lady?" Dion laughed. "She's yet to let me cast my eyes on her, Captain. Nay, before my affair with that craven Groven—God's sake, I could make a rhyme there, eh?—before I had the bad luck to anger the Queen, I dallied with my share of tender ladies and toughened wenches but none interested me past the end of the sweet play."

"Not one?"

"Well-ll—there was one far choicer than the rest, in bed and out, but she—hah, Captain Amadas, ye'll know how serious it was bewixt us when I tell you she was a doxy, skilled at her trade beyond any other I ever met and well-versed in polite manners and conversation, but still a bawd."

"And Rycko?"

Dion cast the little captain a startled glance and saw that Amadas was not joking. He felt a surge of anger at the question, then swallowed it and forced himself to answer in an even tone of voice.

"Now, Captain," he said, "you speak of an Indian wench—how could I feel for her with any civilized emotion? Sweet, clean, good, honest—aye, she's all of that, or was, but my father has greyhound bitches that are all those things. I love the hounds, surely, but as hounds. Anything I felt for Rycko was the same—almost."

Amadas drained his goblet and poured more wine into his cup and Dion's.

"I see y'r point," he said gravely, "or at least I think I see y'r way of reasoning. As f'r me"—he heaved a sigh—"well, I'm not nobly born, as I said, and have none of y'r learning in the arts and manners, but were it not f'r my own family in England I vow I'd settle here with the rest of you and—and find myself an Indian maid to be my wife."

"Y'r bedmate, you mean? Well, they are good companions in—"

"Nay, Dion," Amadas broke in, "my wife. I'd give her what small honor there'd be in my name in return for the love and honesty she'd give me."

"Now this," Dion said, "is curious talk, Captain Amadas."

"Aye," the shipmaster said, lifting his cup again, "and I'll not tire ye with it much further. Enough to say I've—certain troubles at home. A man who follows the sea must put too much trust in his wife, mayhap, and women have forever yearned for gaiety and luxury and used what means they had to get them." He finished his wine and pushed his bench back from the table. "And horns," he added, almost wistfully, "are almighty uncomfortable to wear, even though I've no real proof they've sprouted."

After the captain had left the cabin, Dion sat at the drop

table, his thoughtful eyes looking down into his cup, pondering Amadas' strange words. To marry an Indian wench—the man must be crazy to even give the idea a thought; it was as foolish as for him to think of marrying Margery! It must be that Amadas' wife was a flighty woman, spending her husband's time away from home by welcoming lovers who could give her ribbons and laughter and dancing, and the captain entertained this wild dream of wedding an Indian girl as some sort of revenge, never to be really tasted but to be rolled about on the mind's tongue in a vain endeavor to sweeten the sourness of the wife's deceit.

Amadas might be all wrong in this, Dion told himself, but he might be almost right in saying there was more true love and honesty among the Roanoke men and women than in all England. But was this not merely a mark of these savages' simple minds; did it not merely prove they lacked the intelligence to enjoy the full flavor of life?

And why, Dion asked himself, *am I so resolved to prove this to myself? Why give the good captain's blathering importance by debating it in my own mind?*

3

On july twenty-seventh, 1585, Sir Walter Raleigh's second expedition anchored off the shoals of Hatorask, opposite Trinity Inlet, the break in the outer sand banks that Amadas and Barlowe had used to get through to Roanoke Island the year before.

Soundings proved the channel that had floated the *Tyger* and *Admiral* had filled enough to keep out the new *Tyger* and other vessels of the flagship's draught. The lighter craft, the pinnaces and flyboats, therefore, were called on to ferry supplies and men through the cut into the sound from "Port Ferdinando," as Simon grandly named the anchorage off Hatorask and as John White, official mapmaker in Amadas' stead, marked it on his chart.

By the time the fleet reached Trinity Inlet, Dion Harvie had been accepted back into Sir Richard Grenville's councils, in spite of Ralph Lane's scowling and muttering. And it was to Dion that the sharp-bearded leader of the expedition admitted his first doubts of the wisdom of burning Aquascogok.

"Think you," he asked Dion, "that what we did at Pasquiwoc Island heated the savages at Roanoke against us?"

"That'll be answered, sir," the young man shrugged, "as soon as we try to land on the island. I doubt not they'll tell us aye or nay soon enough."

"I say we cowed 'em all proper," Lane put in, "and if these savages have got word of Aquascogok it only told 'em we're not to be cozened by the likes o' them!"

"And certainly they'll know your silver cup must be left alone," Simon Ferdinando added smoothly.

"Aye, that they will!" the captain nodded. There was a stark silence; then Lane swung his head toward the Portuguese, glaring at the pilot, silently damning Simon for having tricked him into a mistake.

"Your cup?" Grenville asked to end the pregnant pause. "You mean ye've got your cup back?"

"Oh aye, Sir Richard," Ferdinando said easily. "I thought you had been told. It seems the good captain but mislaid the cup—it was not stolen, after all." His thick frame shook in a chuckle. "Which is," he added, "a merry jest on the witless savages, eh?"

Grenville's mouth tightened as he kept his eyes on Lane. The captain tried to meet the other's stare, failed and shifted his eyes back to the grinning Portuguese.

"The cup," he said, "was put in my chest the day after the village was burned. I doubt not that some savage dog was scared into returning it."

"Oh, for sure, captain," Ferdinando nodded pleasantly. "I mind the deck of the *Tyger* was fair crawling with Indians that day and any one of them could've brought a silver cup aboard hid in the flowing robes they wear in Summer's heat."

A ripple of suppressed laughter ran about the council table, set on the *Tyger's* poopdeck. The chuckle empurpled the captain's face and brought a snarl to his mouth.

"You call me a liar, sir?" he rasped.

"Why no, Captain Lane," the pilot replied in a shocked voice. "You said an Indian put back the cup—I but agreed with you, as everyone here can swear."

"But," Grenville crackled, "the Indians skulked in the woods all the day after the fire, never venturing forth, and to hide a cup in the single scrap they wear about their middles would take some doing. How now, Captain?"

The man who was to be governor of Virginia squirmed under the inquiring gaze of a dozen pairs of eyes and Dion Harvie smiled inwardly in satisfaction.

"Why—why, Sir Richard," Lane said, "it must ha' been some savage swam out to the *Tyger* that night and—and crept into my cabin—"

"Which you share with me," Grenville interrupted. "And I am a sleeper who's awakened by a rat's squeak, no matter how weary I may be. Think you a savage could evade the watch, get into our quarters, put a silver cup in your chest—which you keep locked, Captain Lane—and make his escape again without rousing a soul?"

If Ralph Lane had been anybody else, Dion Harvie might have felt a twinge of compassion for the man. Poor Lane; he had embarked on this expedition with the assurance that he was the second in command, the one who would take the top position when Grenville returned to England for stores, and now he was the fumble-tongued schoolboy caught in a garbled explanation of a broken windowpane. Lane might roar his commands to his soldiers but all his bluff authority went out of him under Richard Grenville's cold and disapproving eye.

He stammered incoherently and then flung out his hand. "Well, God's sake," he cried, "mayhap I was mistaken, then! Mayhap one of the seamen aboard the *Tyger* stole the cup—the lock's a poor one—and put it back when he was frightened! Aye, I admit I was too hasty in blaming the savages but—well, what harm's done, in any case? The heathen dogs needed a lesson and we taught it to them, without harming a hair of their mangy heads."

"Twenty-six huts and four storehouses," Dion Harvie murmured quietly, "put to the torch because Tolepuec didn't spread a feast instanter. And what harm's done?"

"And you," Lane cried, turning on the lean-faced young man, "will be to blame for any trouble that might follow this mistake!"

"*I'll* be to blame!"

"Aye, for you've all but wept and wrung y'r hands at the poor savages' mistreatment," Lane said. "If it hadn't been for you, they'd ha' taken it all as rightful punishment dealt them by the white gods who came out of the sea."

"Now, I—"

"Enough!" Grenville said abruptly. "Captain Lane, I fear you've erred in a direction that may cost us dear and you, Master Harvie, have erred in the opposite way, by being too friendly with the savages we mean to rule. A peasant can't be treated as an equal without trouble—what advantages d'ye think these savages would take over us if we didn't keep them in their place?" He turned to Ferdinando. "What is your opinion of the Indians' temper after what happened at Aquascogok, Sir Pilot?" he asked. "You have the oldest acquaintance with the Indians and their ways."

The Portuguese hesitated, his hand at his ear pendant, and then turned to spit over the side.

"Whilst all this talk and pother has been going on," he said, "I took the time to speak with Manteo and Wanchese. Manteo was fair delighted by the burning of the village—he said the Pasquiwocs are but lice, worthy only to be squashed. But Wanchese was not half so merry about the fire. I got the thought that Wanchese, though he has no love for Pasquiwocs, fears that what happened at Aquascogok could happen at Roanoke and Dasamonquepeuc.

"And a word of caution to you all," he went on. "A word that can be vouchsafed by Captain Amadas and Master Harvie. Never put dependence on the thought that these Indians believe you white gods come up out of the sea, as Captain Lane has said.

Mayhap that was once their belief but that was long ago, when the Spaniards first reached these shores. Now they know we are but mortal men. They found out in Florida that a white man could bleed and die and scream in the dying, and the word travelled faster than a bolt of lightning, I swear."

"What's your advice, then, on what to do—Master Harvie—Pilot Ferdinando?" Grenville asked.

"Well, first," Dion said before Ferdinando could speak, "I'd order every man in the company to bend every effort to prove our friendliness with the Indians. I'd tell the men, seamen and gentlemen alike, that any untoward actions 'gainst the natives will be sternly dealt with. I'd make it plain that any grievances we might have must be taken to our commanders, you, Sir Richard, and"—he added with an effort—"Captain Lane. And also, I'd be doubly careful in guarding 'gainst a mistake such as the one at Aquascogok."

Grenville nodded grudgingly and looked inquiringly at Ferdinando. The black-bearded pilot grimaced in Dion's direction and spread his hands.

"Friend Dion has robbed me of my words," he complained. "He's said all I would except, mayhap, that we must not forget the Spanish bastards in our concern over the Indians. This port must be protected at all times 'gainst a Spanish sweep. The governor of Hispaniola must have told his King about our visit and perchance Philip is not overjoyed at our being here."

"The fleet will be prepared," Grenville said in his clipped voice. "And we sail to the island of Roanoke on the morrow."

The following morning, the flotilla of light boats crossed the sound and cruised to the northeast shore of the island where Amadas and Barlowe had anchored the previous Spring. Their welcome was different from the empty silence that had greeted the first expedition; the beach was crowded with Indians and as the pinnaces lowered their sails a dozen canoes shot out from the shore toward them.

"And not a spear or club amongst them," Simon Ferdinando said, "so either the Roanokes have not heard of Aquascogok or they approve of what we did, thank God!"

Wanchese and Manteo mounted the rails of their respective vessels (it was still thought wiser to keep the two Roanokes apart as much as possible) and gutturalled their greetings to the first canoes that reached the boats. Manteo was a splashy picture in yellow hose, padded trunks of green and gold satin, green velvet doublet and wide ruff, a plumed hat and doeskin half-boots, with a jewel-hilted rapier hanging at his side. The tall, grim-faced Wanchese wore a grey wool blanket that had succeeded the robe he had left Roanoke in, and his only ornaments were the osprey feather he had always worn in England and a wide copper bracelet that Raleigh had given him.

Dion watched the faces of the Indians in the canoes as they shifted their eyes between Manteo and Wanchese. His months spent on Roanoke Island the year before had taught him that while an Indian's face was as mobile as a white man's in joy or deep sorrow, usually only his eyes reflected his thoughts when he was making a first appraisal of a situation or a person. And the paddlers' eyes, as far as Dion could make out, all hinted at the same reaction as they scanned the changed Manteo and the unchanged Wanchese—a sort of mocking contempt for the transformed Manteo, a relieved approval of the second Roanoke who had returned from across the sea.

Wingina was still chief, Dion saw, and standing in the prow of the lead canoe, the first Roanoke to mount the ladder of the *Tyger*. Granganimeo, then, had not succeeded in taking over; he still was second in command, carried to the ladder by the second canoe and with his scalplock still lacking the feathered crown that distinguished his brother.

"Ho, Wingina," Dion said as the Roanoke chief slipped over the rail to the deck.

"I am Pemispan," the chief replied, with dignity. "The gods have told me to take the name Pemispan and cast off the old name, Wingina. This will bring the gods' smile to my people."

"Now here's an odd thing," Harvie laughed, turning to Grenville and Lane. "The gods have tired of our friend's old name, Wingina, and have picked another for him, Pemispan. A convenient custom we could use in England. F'rinstance, if a man found himself crowded by debts under one name he'd need but listen to the gods and take a new one and let his creditors weep for the vanishing of their debtor."

"To me," Lane grumbled, "it smacks of trickery."

"Have done, captain," Ferdinando laughed. "Ye'll find stranger customs than the mere changing of a name before ye're finished here."

Aside from his new name, Wingina was the same Roanoke chief with the same hawk's eyes, lit by a glimmering flame that Dion never had seen blaze forth but which he somehow knew would be deadly when it leapt. Pemispan seemed genuinely glad to greet the white men; the canoes that trailed the welcoming flotilla were filled to the gunwales with venison and fish, grapes and corn, which were brought aboard Grenville's pinnace and joined with meat, bread and wine, to provide a feast. Manteo and Wanchese were ferried to Grenville's vessel to join the banquet and while Manteo struggled to keep a balance between due deference to his chief and his London-born self-esteem, Wanchese spoke in monosyllables and only then in answer to Pemispan's questions.

Yes, he had been kindly treated by the Englishmen and no, he had not wanted to stay across the sea and yes, the Great Queen was a powerful woman chief with big houses and fine clothes and many braves to fight for her and no, he would never leave Roanoke Island and Dasamonquepeuc again and, yes, he had been offered shining robes like Manteo's but he had preferred to dress as he always had.

And Manteo: "Aye, the white men gave me many gifts—these are rags besides what I have on my ship. I was called to the Great Queen's court many times—and Wanchese was called but three times—and she gave me everything I asked for and the women there smiled on me and the men all bowed their heads. And I—"

Wanchese grunted and Manteo hesitated long enough to shoot him a venomous glance.

"And I ate at the table with the white men," he went on, "but Wanchese did not, and I—"

"You did many things," Pemispan broke in bluntly, "while Wanchese did none of these, or only a few. Yet Wanchese is your elder and he was a sub-chief before you were. How is this?"

"O Chief," Wanchese explained, casually, "Manteo would have stayed across the sea and changed his skin to white, if it could have been done, while I am content to be a brave under your wisdom."

Score one for Wanchese, Harvie chuckled inwardly. *A few more remarks like that and he'll elbow Granganimeo right out of the line of succession whilst Manteo ends up with haughty memories and naught else.*

"Master Harvie," Sir Richard Grenville called from the head of the table, "is the great magician, Rycko, in this company of savages?"

At the word "Rycko", Pemispan's face and the eyes of all the other Roanokes present swung toward Grenville and then moved to Harvie. Dion felt his cheeks grow hot and his flush was not cooled by the sound of Simon Ferdinando's choked snort of laughter from across the table. Damn the Portuguese! Granted that he'd first used the myth of Rycko the Magician to turn Grenville's anger at Mosquito Bay, he had not needed to embroider on the falsehood as he had!

"Ah—no, Sir Richard," Harvie managed. "I hear from Pemispan and his brother that the great Rycko is dead—passed on during the winter of a croup."

"Rycko," Pemispan said eagerly in the Roanoke tongue, "awaits your landing with the impatience of a maid never covered but about to be." He smiled broadly and clapped a hand to Dion's shoulder with damnable geniality. "Yes, young friend, she has not forgotten you while you have been across the sea."

"What does he say?" Grenville pressed. "His manner shows no sorrow at his wizard's death, for certain!"

"Er—why, he tells me," Dion said desperately, "that Rycko's dying has brought great fortune to his tribe in some way. Also"—and the perspiration bedewed his upper lip as he struggled with his lie—"the magician's daughter, who was named—uh—something different when we were here before, has taken her father's name now. So there is still a Rycko, but a mere maid."

He slumped back on the bench, half expecting the grinning Ferdinando and the anxious Amadas to break into applause at his neat explanation. He met Grenville's calculating eyes squarely, candidly, and expelled a smothered sigh of relief as the leader of the expedition nodded.

"A pity the wizard died," he said ponderously. "I'd fain ha' seen him make his magic—though I put no faith in such things. And did Pemispan or the others speak of—what happened down the coast?"

"Nay, and I feel 'twould be better not to mention it. Let Wanchese and Manteo tell them what happened, I'd say."

"But we could—er—explain the error," Captain Lane suggested. "The way that sour-faced Wanchese would tell it, we'd seem all to blame."

"And were we not, Captain?" Harvie asked quietly, and added as Lane scowled: "But blameless or no, 'twould be best to have Pemispan hear the story from his own men—and they'll tell it straight, I promise you. If we tried to soften the tale and Pemispan heard it a different way from Wanchese or Manteo, he'd lose his trust in us—and keep his trust we must at all costs if we're to succeed here."

Grenville considered the question, tugging at his beard, and finally spoke to his second in command, Lane.

"I hold with Master Harvie," he said, "although I understand your reasoning, Captain, and welcome your suggestion. Manteo, at least, approves the burning of the village, as Pilot Ferdinando has told us, and if Wanchese puts us in a worse light, 'twill but balance Manteo's story. Aye, we'll follow Master Harvie's counsel in this."

"Aye, Sir Richard," Lane said grudgingly, and made no effort to hide the fact that he had totted up another item on his account with Dion Harvie.

"Now let us to the island," Grenville said, rising from the bench and surveying the wreckage of the feast. "God wot these people have filled themselves to the last scrap and our ending this banquet now can't be rude, eh, Master Harvie? I want a look at this wondrous land you reported at such great length in your journal, Captain Amadas."

The round-bellied shipmaster bowed. "I hope my admiration of this place and these people didn't blind me to the faults, Sir Richard. Whatever errors you find in my descriptions charge to my enthusiasm and to no intent to deceive Sir Walter."

Amadas was nervous and, Dion said silently, he had reason to be. The little captain had been vying with Arthur Barlowe for Raleigh's favor and patronage on that first voyage and Amadas had used his journal as a weapon in the struggle; he had dragged up every high-sounding adjective at his command in describing Roanoke Island because he had known that Raleigh wanted Roanoke to be a paradise. Though he had beaten Barlowe, who was a less imaginative man, now Grenville's chill eyes were going to see, not read about, the place Amadas had called "the goodliest and the best in the world in many things."

It was apparent the minute Grenville set foot on Roanoke Island that he had thought there would be much more than what there was. Like most Englishmen, Grenville may have expected an Indian town in "Virginia" to offer at least a semblance to a town in England, with streets and brick houses and shops and markets and crowds; his dismay at seeing the rude stockade that enclosed a dozen shabby thatched huts was clearly stamped on his chiseled features. True, he had seen—and burned—Aquascogok but Philip Amadas had not written any glowing passages about the Pasquiwoc village; the little shipmaster had let his determination to win Raleigh's approval catapult him into flights of exaggeration that now made his precious journal's description of Roanoke ridiculous.

Grenville's frown deepened as he went through the hunting village, peering into the dirty hovels that presented such a contrast to the Roanokes' personal cleanliness, sniffing the sour, spoiled stink of the stew that bubbled scummily in the community pot over the common fire; poking his sharp nose into the dank storehouses where corn and meat and fish mouldered in the shadows. As for Lane, the corseleted captain muttered and grumbled as he inspected the place; it was plain that he, too, had thought there would be more than this to take over and govern at the start.

"So this is great Roanoke," Grenville sniffed when he had finished his tour. He shot a dark glance at Philip Amadas, his lip curled. " 'Tis far different than you described it, sir!"

" 'Tis but a hunting camp, Sir Richard," the chubby captain explained, hopefully. " 'Tis not the Roanokes' main town."

"And is this Dasamonquepeuc a grander place than Aquascogok, then?"

"Well-ll—in many ways it is," Amadas lied, desperately. "Leastwise Wingina—Pemispan—has more people than did Tolepuec and—and there are more houses and—"

"Ye call these houses?" Lane demanded. "God's teeth, these huts would insult an English pig! Methinks Sir Walter has been diddled in this whole affair—he has spent a fortune to lay claim to a parcel of tumbledown jakes."

"But—but the countryside hereabouts is so rich in so many things," Amadas protested, "that Sir Walter and all the rest can't help but get their money back a hundred times over. And with your colony built, Captain Lane, ye can show these poor heathens how a man was meant to live."

"Aye, Captain," Grenville added. "Y'cannot say ye haven't a full field for displaying all y'r talents here. Ye start from nothing so there'll be no question of whose will be the credit for what ye make of it."

Lane's eyes swept the palisaded enclosure before the stocky captain walked to the gate in the fence and surveyed the beach and the woods that crowded down to the sand. There was a smile of satisfaction on his face as he turned back to Grenville.

"Put that way," he nodded, "I see that I've been given a fine opportunity. I'll build me a town fronting on that cove to the northwest, by that creek. There I'll raise my fort and in good time we'll have a great city the likes of which have ne'er been seen in this New World."

4

Pemispan had told Dion that Rycko awaited his return with all the impatience of a bride listening for her husband's step outside the bedchamber door but if she did, Harvie told himself liverishly, she had restrained her fervor well. She was nowhere to be found in the village when the white men got there and neither was she among the women who were ferried over from Dasamonquepeuc that evening to provide for the comfort and entertainment of the new arrivals.

Three times, Dion started to approach the Roanoke chief with his question of where Rycko was hiding herself and three times he left the chief with the query unasked.

"No, curse all," he muttered, "I'll not go sniffing after the wench like a dog after a bitch. If I have need of a woman, one of these other younger ones will serve."

But, although the group of women chosen by Pemispan to prove the Roanokes' hospitality included several girls prettier than Rycko, girls who smiled at him, spoke to him softly and shamelessly in their native tongue and brushed against him provocatively, Dion had not picked one for his companion when night fell. As the women had found their partners, one by one, and disappeared until there was none left, Dion had kept shaking his head, turning aside murmured invitations—and swearing all the time that he was not looking for Rycko.

It was a night such as Dion remembered from the summer before, with a star-studded sky of purple velvet, a wind made thick and heady by the perfume of honeysuckle, the lisping of the timid waves on the white sand, the eerie, somehow fitting, cry of a loon. And the log he and Rycko had used for a classroom—was that still there or had the winter storms washed it away? He walked down the beach toward where it had been—what else had he to do, and a stroll would be welcome after the cramped confines of the bark.

The log had been washed away or covered by sand but the

girl was there. She sat quietly until his quickened step brought him to within five paces of her; then she rose, swiftly, lithely, her shoulders touched by the faint gleam of starlight, her head thrown back, her hands held out, her full lips parted to reveal her white teeth.

She was more lovely, he realized, than he remembered her—and the dreams that had tormented him into summoning Margery Hollis had made Rycko achingly desirable. Her breasts were higher, more pointed, more demanding than Margery's, her thighs were slenderer, more sinuous than the Englishwoman's. Where the Lime Street girl let her passions mount in time with the fervor of her caresses, Rycko burned with desperate abandon from the start.

As now—she was upon him in a catlike motion, her long fingers plucking at his clothes.

"Ah, quick—I must see you—white—white—O, all the gods made you, Dion!"

"Rycko! Rycko!"

She bore him to the sand, a writhing, moaning bacchante, enfevered by the aphrodisiac of his touch. She wailed a cry once, twice, three times—unutterably plaintive, inexpressibly joyous—to break the choked babble she murmured in his ear. Her hands sought, clutched and fell away, her mouth kissed and nibbled and then her teeth sank into his shoulder.

It was woman-hunger and that alone that cast Dion into delirium within the Roanoke girl's arms. It was the flesh, not the heart, that rejoiced in this envelopment by Rycko's sweet-scented warmth. It was the satisfaction of a base appetite, no worthier emotion, that wrenched the final wild cry from both of them as the leaping flame of their joining volcanoed and hurled them into ecstatic agony.

Oh yes, it must have been a brutish coupling, nothing more. For he was Dion Harvie, fourth son of Sir Clement Harvie, Lord Avronbeck, and she was a copper-skinned savage girl whose duty, as prescribed by her chief, was to make the white man welcome.

Dion's voice was drowsy when he spoke again. "And why did you hide? Why were you not with the others when we came ashore?"

"I had to know that you still wanted me. I dared believe you'd seek me in this place."

Her arms tightened about him and she pressed her face to his. "As you did," she said, contentedly.

Dion Harvie said gruffly, "I was but taking a stroll and chanced to come this way."

She leaned back to look up at him and her tears of just-spent rapture glistened on her long lashes as her mouth curved in a slow smile.

"I know," she said demurely. "It was but chance that brought you here."

5

THE FORT, of course, was built first. It was almost identical with the fort put up at Mosquito Bay, shaped like a four-pointed star around a square, with the bastions raised on the sides of the square instead of at the corners. The stronghold, which was named Fort Raleigh, did not have a gate on its water side as the fort on St. Johns Island had; instead Lane cut a narrow opening on that side, wide enough to permit the passage of only one man at a time.

Two ten-foot-long cannon, culverins which threw an eighteen-pound ball, four smaller demi-culverins and four little sakers (which got their name from the Saker hawk) were mounted on the parapets of the fort. In the center of the square was built a magazine, with walls and roof of logs thickly plastered with clay to protect it from fire-arrows, as suggested by Simon Ferdinando.

With the fort finished, the Cross of Saint George raised above it, Lane turned his attention to the dwellings and storehouses. Because the fort was too small to enclose these buildings, they were arranged in a cluster some two hundred yards south of the stronghold, close enough so that the people in them could run to the fort in case of attack but not close enough to give an assaulting force any cover.

The houses were story-and-a-half or two-story affairs with brick foundations. Lane had intended to use stone both in the fort and in the houses but Philip Amadas' "rich deposits of marble, granite and other divers rocks of excellent quality" proved to be located miles in the interior of the mainland, so Lane set a portion of his force to brick-making. The clay of Roanoke Island proved ideal for the purpose and the Indians had, during the past years or centuries, piled great heaps of oyster shells close to their hunting camp, shells that provided plenty of lime; within a couple of days the kilns of Roanoke Island were turning out brickbats at a surprising rate.

The sides and roofs of the dwellings were of rough boards, fastened by nails made at the forge that had seen duty at St. Johns Island. The roofs were thatched and all the homes and storehouses were excellently built, as Philip Amadas' journal (still doggedly kept by the round little captain in spite of all Grenville's and Lane's rebuffs) testified.

Now, he wrote, *I am proved right in what I told Master Richard Hakluyt, the geographer at Oxford, of what Sir Walter Raleigh would need in Virginia, even though Master Hakluyt did not credit me with these advices. For I told him to tell Sir Walter that these would be needed—men expert in the art of fortification, millwrights for corn mills, sawyers, brickmakers, carpenters, thatchers, masons and lathmakers. And all these are busy so we will have a brave town close to Fort Raleigh.*

The "brave town" was just starting to rise in the forest when Sir Richard Grenville sailed back to England for supplies, chiefly horses and cattle—and married couples or even unmarried women who might be eager enough for a fresh start to brave the fearsome mysteries of the New World. For Grenville had finally agreed with Raleigh that what was needed most were families to take the settlement of Virginia out of the class of a military expedition and give it permanence as a colony.

"And I'll return posthaste," Grenville promised Lane just before boarding his flagship at Port Ferdinando, "with all you need and more. Whilst I'm gone, I leave Virginia in your capable hands, Captain Lane, and look forward to seeing vast steps of advancement here when I come back."

"And that ye'll see Sir Richard," Lane nodded. "That, I'll promise ye."

Grenville said, "Though the dogs irk ye at times bend every effort to stay friendly with the Indians." He stepped aboard the smallboat that was to carry him to the *Tyger* and turned back before he seated himself on the stern thwart. "By that," he added, "I do not mean you should suffer insult or injury from these savages, Captain, without demur."

"And that I won't!" the captain said fervently. "Never the Queen's honor, or mine, shall be soiled by these animals."

Simon Ferdinando, standing beside Dion Harvie, dug an elbow into the younger man's side.

"I wish you well," he muttered in a low voice, "but I do not envy you, living under that fire-eater's command whilst we're gone. Would'st you could come with us—I'd rather see you under my wing than Lane's."

"So you could claim the Queen's reward?" Dion asked with a grin. "For know ye, friend Simon, I still think ye'd hand me over to the hangman, given the chance."

The big Portuguese wrinkled his broad face in the hurt frown of a man close to tears.

"Mistrustful boy," he said reproachfully. "Must you always meet my friendship with y'r damned suspicions? Here I love you as I've loved no other Englishman and you stand convinced I'd play the traitor for the Queen's gold and deliver your head to the noose!"

"Why I believe you're my friend," Harvie said lightly, "but I'd rather test my belief at a time when there's no rich reward to—"

"A pox on rich rewards!" Ferdinando broke in "If I were so hot for this reward you speak of, why didn't I grab you that night near Queenhithe and shout for the Queen's men? Y'think y'r pretty toy of a sword stopped me, mayhap? Ah, friend Dion, there were a dozen chances for me to overpower you, even though you stepped about like a cat on hot bricks, and yet I held my hand."

"And once you swore you never met me near Queenhithe," Dion reminded the Portuguese.

"I did?" the pilot asked blandly. "Ah well, I have a stinking memory for such things. But Sir Richard's fair snorting to be off, so farewell, Dion, and I'll make sure Captain Amadas delivers those letters to your people that you'd not entrust to me."

"Farewell, Simon," Harvie nodded, "and—and a good voyage to you, you puzzle I can't fathom."

He stood on the shore of the outer sandbank, watching the sails diminish in the distance. As he watched, he sped Grenville's flotilla on its way with an airing of his whole store of curses, enhanced by some new Roanoke invective, on Captain Guy Groven and Queen Elizabeth's stubbornness that made her support the handsome scoundrel against all her courtiers, even her favorites, Essex and Leicester, Sidney and Raleigh.

And would Gloriana ever change? Would she ever tire of Groven and throw him out of court—or to the hangman—or was he, Dion, doomed to spend the rest of his life in hiding or in exile? And if in exile, why couldn't it be some civilized place, like Italy or even Germany? Oh, this Virginia was pleasant enough in some ways; there was room for a man to stretch here and once away from the Indian village all the smells were sweet. Here, a gentleman was not bothered by the sight of beggars with their running sores or by the skinny children of the Lime Streets of London eating swill to stay alive, or by the corpses that littered the city with each plague (and it must be time for another soon). In Virginia, there were no ravaged, raddled faces of high-born boys and girls, scarcely out of childhood, who had tasted every vice and now cast about frantically for new sensations. Missing in this New World were the great gentlemen and ladies who posed and preened and puffed in their assumption that they had been chosen by God to rule, though the heart of the best of them was blacker than the soul of the least worthy Roanoke—

And how now, Dion Harvie?

He must be careful, he told himself; he must guard against these mad thoughts that broke into his mind and urged him to be a traitor to his England, his class. True, the simple Roanokes had a primitive honesty, an openness that was refreshing after the deceit that was the rule in London, a childish joy of life, a humility that made them stare in astonishment at Manteo's conceited blathering. But all these were really only things that could be found in an idiot, a fool too feeble-witted to explore the more involved emotions life had to offer.

"And now," he heard Captain Ralph Lane say, "we'll return to the town and get back to work! You all heard Sir Richard—there's much to be done to prepare the settlement for his return and not too much time to do it in."

But there was time—plenty of it.

The days passed into weeks and the weeks into months, and, once the dwellings outside Fort Raleigh had been finished, the Englishmen found time hanging heavy on their hands. They could have planted crops but they were either gentlemen, soldiers or craftsmen; of all the people Hakluyt had told Raleigh the colony would need he had not included a farmer. Nor, Captain Lane reasoned, was there really any need for farmers; the Indians had plenty of maize in their storehouses, both at Roanoke and at Dasamonquepeuc, and they were glad to share their grain with their white guests. They could have hunted and fished but here again was no need to fish or hunt except for pleasure. The Roanokes were so expert at those tasks and so pleased to hand over half of what they caught that it seemed silly for the Englishmen to bother with hunting or fishing for food. They could have explored the mainland and some of them did, but when the first parties returned from their explorations with neither gold nor the discovery of a passage to the Southern Sea the others gave up their plans to survey the land to the west and spent their days lolling about their village, experimenting in making mead from wild honey, experiments that produced a drink "warranted to make a man sob, swear or swound." With idleness came stark boredom and with that came frazzled nerves, snappish voices, petty annoyances blown up into unbearable ordeals, until a smile was rare at Fort Raleigh, a friendly word was hard to hear above the grumbling.

A gentleman, Robert Wellman, and Captain George Stafford, Lane's aide, became involved in an argument over the location of a certain house in Westminster, outside London, and ended by drawing on each other. That fight was stopped by Lane's roared command, but there were others between the craftsmen that were not broken up until one or both of the embattled pair had been punched, kicked, clubbed, gouged or even carved.

"Your friends seem sad," Rycko told Harvie one night as they lay on the beach, still wet from their swim in the moonlight. "Why is it that they shout at each other and wave their hands and even fight? They are not hungry and they are not cold—why are they so unhappy?"

"They're sick of each other's faces," Dion explained, using the Roanoke tongue, "and sick of this island."

"Why don't they go some other place, then? Oh, not you, Dion, but the others? Why don't they live apart from each other if the other's sight sickens them so?"

"Because, my sweetling," Dion laughed, "then they would be lonely. Besides, Captain Lane wouldn't allow it. No, he must keep us all here at Fort Raleigh or if we leave we must go where he sends us, do what he tells us, and come back here when he summons us."

"But if he sees his men so discontent," Rycko said, "he must know it would be better to have them separate before they start a war among themselves."

"Not Lane," Dion grunted. "He sees no further than his nose and that's all snotted up with military rubbish. Icod, my friend Walt made his biggest mistake when he chose Ralph Lane to govern this colony whilst Grenville's gone!"

Harvie did not know it, but Ralph Lane was bothered by the same doubts of his qualifications as governor of Virginia, although he would not admit them even to himself. The captain was discovering that to try to control a small group of men, each one a highly temperamental individualist, was a far different job than commanding a company of soldiers who had been trained to obey orders. He knew the gentlemen all looked down on him because he lacked a proud background and while his natural instinct was to bow to these social superiors he forced himself to be crudely brusque with them, as though to prove that name or wealth meant less than nothing to him, the plain man with no ambition except to serve his Queen.

The gentlemen despised the captain as a nobody cloaked in authority by some awful error made in London and did everything they could to hamstring Lane's rule. They refused to "hale and draw" with the craftsmen or the soldiers and they were always complaining about the fact that they were given the same rations as the commoners and no better quarters, nor could they hire less favored "Virginians" to wait on them.

As for the craftsmen, Lane had found them even harder to deal with than the gentlemen, if that were possible. The millwrights and coopers, the brickmakers and carpenters, seemed to think that to be told to do anything besides saw timber or make barrels, bake bricks or do carpentry, was an insult to their craft. They were as proud of their guilds as the gentlemen were of their escutcheons; they were all citizens of London and, as such, deserved respectful treatment—and Lane's commands could hardly be called respectful. The soldiers they despised as serfs, the gentlemen they mocked as popinjays who could not hammer a nail straight or tell one end of a mason's trowel from the other.

Even the soldiers were becoming unruly. They had been recruited with the promise of plunder and they had come to Virginia with visions of grand sackings such as had made the Spanish *conquistadores* rich; now the soldiers found themselves with nothing more valuable to loot than a clay pot or a copper trinket. Moreover, the privilege of brewing mead was not extended them by Lane's orders; the captain insisted on sobriety in the ranks and the soldier who stole a flagon of the powerful stuff from a gentleman or a craftsman was dealt with harshly. Even the comeliest wenches—or so they insisted—were monopolized by the gentry and those damned guildsmen.

So Captain Ralph Lane found his administration going to pieces in his hands in spite of the stricter rules he made, the louder he bawled his commands. His nights were tormented by dreams of mutiny; his days were clouded by his colonists' near-overt contempt.

He knew only one way to regain the authority, the obedience, that was slipping away from him. It was a way that had been used by other soldiers before him and would be used again long after he had been forgotten—that was to start a war. Clever, tactful, able administrator he might not be but he was an experienced soldier; let the arquebus and the culverin bang and boom and he would show them all, gentleman and craftsman and soldier, that they needed him, Ralph Lane, if they would live.

Captain Lane turned his brush-browed eyes on the Roanokes. Poor stuff, he admitted to himself, but they would have to serve.

6

DION HARVIE WAS the messenger who provided Ralph Lane with an excuse to start a fight. Dion had not tried for the position, he was not certain he even wanted the honor, but he found himself the Roanokes' only confidant among the white men.

He won this place because, of all Lane's company, he was the only man who got to know the Indians and, knowing them, grew to admire much of what they did, how they lived, the principles on which they based right and wrong.

Boredom and the other Englishmen's suspicion of him as a man under Queen Elizabeth's frown more or less forced the young son of Lord Avronbeck to spend his time with the Roanokes, especially Rycko and Wanchese. The lithe, copper-skinned girl with the doe's eyes and the catamount's fire gave him her woman's obeisant devotion; Wanchese gave him a man's companionship. Rycko's were the nights; the days were spent with Wanchese, following the old hunting trails, fishing together, making talk.

It was with Wanchese that Dion crouched beside a salt lick, deep in the forest, and brought down a tender yearling buck with one arrow, thudded into the tawny hide behind the forequarter so that the flint reached the heart and dropped the deer in his tracks. It was Wanchese who showed Dion how to cast a one-handed net and draw in the mesh with an encircling sweep that did not permit a single mullet or sea trout to escape. Wanchese's teaching gave Dion Harvie such adroitness with the fishing spear that the young Englishman was nearly able to match the Roanoke's skill in gilling the tough-skinned, sharp-snouted sturgeon that grew to prodigious size in the rivers that fed the sound. Wanchese's hand fashioned bucktail hair snares for rabbits and quail and Harvie's fingers imitated, blunderingly at the start but skillfully after the first mistakes.

The Roanoke taught Dion many things: how to start fire by spinning an oak wand between the palms, the rod's point set in a hollowed block and the hole filled with punk; how to tell tomorrow's weather by the wind, the sunset, the way the songbirds fed, the movement of the fishes; which berries were delicious and which were deadly; what were mushrooms and what were poisonous toadstools; how the curiosity of geese and swan would force them to paddle in toward shore to investigate a foxtail waved at the end of a long pole from a hiding place in the reeds; how a skunk could be rendered impotent (and this was a dangerous game) by jerking it into the air by its tail before it could set itself to fire; how to read trail signs made by animals and birds that gave exact directions to the practiced eye and were invisible to the white man.

Wanchese proved to be far different from the stolid brave he had first seemed. Dion learned that the Roanoke possessed a keen sense of humor that found laughter where an Englishman's blunter risibilities could not. Dion's friend also revealed a deep pride in his people, their ancestry, their religion, their values. And Harvie, developing an open mind despite himself, discovered that Wanchese had reason for his pride.

Thomas Hariot, the Raleigh expedition's scientist, might fill his notebooks with facts and fancies about the natives but it was Dion who came to know them, young Harvie who learned the tribal ways that Hariot never dreamed existed. And as the weeks passed, as Dion grew closer and closer to Wanchese and Rycko, the name of "savage" for an Indian became more and more a grimly absurd title.

In late August, Wanchese had come to Dion with the proposal that Harvie become his brother.

"You have been good for me," the sub-chief had explained, "as I have been good for you. You are not like these other white men who think our ways are wrong because they are not their ways. I have asked Pemispan and he has nodded his head to my plea that you be made a brother, though we have never made a white man or even a brave of another tribe a brother, before this."

Dion had said, dubiously, "I must ask my chief, the Captain Lane. And if he says no I must bow my head. But even if he does say no, I thank you for the chance to be your brother."

At first, Lane had said no, sharply, contemptuously.

"Now here's a pretty thing!" he had sneered when Harvie had gone to him with his request. "Here we have an Englishman, and with a high-born name, at that, asking permission to join in some savage rite that would seal a bond with these mangy dogs! I've told ye all a thousand times we must ever keep ourselves a league above these natives, never lowering ourselves to their heathenish ways. Nay, Master Harvie, y'r mad idea's an insult to us all."

Harvie had protested, "But it would be to our advantage to have a spokesman and a listener at their councils. As Wanchese's brother, I'd be admitted to their gatherings and so learn what was on their minds."

"A spy ye'd be? Well—"

"No, Captain Lane, by y'r leave. I'd be a friend who'd mayhap smoothe out differences before they got too weighty."

"I need no envoy to their camp," Lane had bristled. "Let 'em raise their differences if they be so minded—my soldiers and my guns will speak for me, no faint-hearted lad who blanched at what was done at Aquascogok. And, for that matter, Manteo has full entree to all their stupid parliaments."

"Manteo," Dion had said stubbornly, "is almost an outcast from his own tribe. He's strutted himself out of Pemispan's regard complete, so Wanchese tells me, and—"

"So Wanchese tells ye, eh? That thick-skulled, sour-faced bastard is but envious of Manteo's successes that he had not the wit to share! Nay, I say again, ye'll join no idolatrous rites to become Wanchese's brother. Brother! God's bones, next ye'll be askin' leave to make that smooth-skinned wench of yours y'r wife!"

Dion's lips had flattened into a tight line and his voice had roughened when he spoke.

"Captain Lane, I know ye've been named governor of this settlement by my friend, Sir Walter, and as such I'll give ye the respect y'r position affords. But I am not used to insults from any man, governor or knave, and I don't intend to swallow them, even from you, sir!"

Lane had hesitated, his little eyes peering at Harvie, and then had forced a smile to his red face. His next words had attempted jocularity.

"Y'r pardon, Master Harvie. If I spake hastily, it was because I was upset by y'r request. You are of great value to this colony by y'r interpreting and y'r friendship with the Roanokes but I feared the tedium of our days here had unsettled you so you'd make a grave mistake by this thing you asked to do. But if ye have y'r heart set on it, why go to! Aye on second thought, we c'ld use the information ye'd bring from the Indian councils to prepare ourselves for treachery."

So, although he never meant to act as spy for Lane, Dion had gone through the blood brother ceremony with Wanchese. The rites were simple; the two men, one straight, tall and copper-skinned, the other an inch taller, wider of shoulder, with his sun-baked torso only a shade lighter than the Indian's, and with the beginnings of a beard fringing his face, stood before Pemispan and swore a solemn oath to help the other in time of need and never to betray the other's trust in him. A shallow cut was made in the forearms of both Harvie and Wanchese, and the arms were bound together so that the blood intermingled. That done, Dion was given the Roanoke name of Pemecolemanmeo, White Gull From The Sun's Dwelling. The name, blessedly, was shortened to Pemec for common usage.

In the councils he attended after becoming Wanchese's brother,

Dion found that Manteo had been all but expelled from his own tribe. The bulky brave, still clad in his ridiculous court finery (spotted, ripped and threadbare now) was relegated to the fringes of every gathering and when he raised his voice in his arrogant boasting of what he had done and been in England he was not given the courtesy of a listener—Pemispan, Granganimeo, Wanchese and the other men talked through him and around him as though he were a cawing crow or a wailing child.

As for Harvie, he squatted with the others and kept his ears open, his mouth shut, speaking only when he was asked a question by the Roanoke chief. Did the white men plan to stay on the island much longer? Yes, it was the intention of the Great Chief, Raleigh, that they stay through the cold moons and longer. How much longer? It was hard to say, Dion squirmed, but it might be for many, many moons; it might be that the white men would never leave the island.

Pemispan nodded equably. In that case, he said, it would be best to make certain preparations to make sure there would be enough food for all. The maize was not growing as well as it should; first, the rain God had been too generous and later he had turned his face away from the island and the fields around Dasamonquepuec.

"When we thought you were to stay with us only a little while and then go back over the sea, to come again in the next hot moons," the chief explained, "we opened our storehouses, as we should. But now our harvest will be small and we must save what we can for the cold moons, when nothing grows and many fish swim to the bottom of the sea and sleep."

"You mean you will refuse the white men more maize, O Pemispan?" Dion asked.

"Nay, that would not be friendly," the chief replied. "But we must all eat one kernel where we have eaten three. We must leave our bellies two parts empty and one part full lest we run out of food and have nothing at all to put in them. We must not waste what we have—as I have seen your white brothers waste the meat and the fish and the meal before this."

Dion had seen the waste, too, and had been repelled by it; deer slaughtered for their livers and the rest left to rot, wildfowl killed for sport and let float away. Only the sweetest fish were taken from the nets the whites occasionally set to relieve their ennui, the more common species being cast up on the beach to stink there until the Indians carried them away to bury in their fields. Corn meal had been thrown away because the Englishmen tired of the stuff.

"I will tell the Captain Lane this," he promised Pemispan now. "He will be strict with his orders."

Lane listened, tugging at his moustache, as Harvie delivered his message. A frown deepened into a scowl as Dion explained Pemispan's concern for the foodstocks and when Harvie finished the captain brought his doubled fist down on a table with a crash.

"That savage dog has the insolence to tell me this?" he roared. "By the Book, I'll show him who decides how much food we are to get!"

"But sir," Dion protested, "Pemispan's caution makes sense! Ye've seen the Indians' fields; ye know this year's crop is poor! And if we do not tighten our belts now, we'll face starvation in the winter."

"Starvation—nonsense! These swine have crammed storehouses that we know naught of—hid somewhere on the mainland. Nay, 'tis plain they mean to force us to leave here by cutting off our supplies, being afraid to take more direct steps! And I'll not be pushed out, I tell ye, by this scheme or any other!"

"Captain Lane," Harvie argued, "I've explored the mainland with Wanchese and before that with Captain Amadas and Captain Barlowe as far back to the west as the Roanokes claim for their own land and we saw no storehouses or even fields beyond Dasamonquepeuc, save one small plantation at a camp they call Weapemeoc."

"Then ye were blind!" Lane grunted. "I have good word that Pemispan has enough stored grain to feed a multitude, cleverly hid in caves and such."

"And who gave you this word?"

"What does it matter who told me this? 'Tis enough to know it's there! These Roanokes may hoodwink you but not me! No, by God's gullet, 'twill be them that'll suffer by this brave swindle!" He tramped to the doorway of his headquarters hut and shouted, "Captain Stafford—turn out the troop!"

"What d'ye mean to do?" Harvie asked.

"Do? I mean to steal a march on Pemispan and make sure we get what's rightfully ours before he has a chance to hide it! I mean to take over that Indian whoreson's storehouses in the name of the Queen!"

"Captain Lane, I swear 'twould be a grievous mistake to—"

"Silence! I'm in command here! I've dealt too softly with these treacherous villains and now I see what must be done to remedy my error. A show of strength will cow these weak-spined mongrels once and for aye!"

"I tell you—"

"Master Harvie," Lane rapped out, "ye'll go to y'r house and stay there, by my order! I'll take no chance on word of my plan being slipped to Pemispan and ruining all!"

"Ye think I'd inform 'gainst my own people?" Dion asked in a frigid voice.

"I do not know," Lane barked, "but I do know I must not take the chance. Captain Stafford"—this to the dark-faced officer who appeared in the doorway—"escort Master Harvie to his house and take steps to see that he stays there."

"I'll not forget this insult," Harvie said steadily.

Lane made a derisive gesture, then grinned suddenly and leaned forward over the rude table that served as his desk, his sanguine face upthrust at Harvie.

"Insult?" he drawled. "Now, Master Harvie, ye'd call it an insult to help ye keep y'r own trust?"

"What d'ye mean?"

"Why, 'tis simple," the captain smiled. "Ye're a blood brother to Wanchese, no? And ye've even got y'rself an Indian name, ye've made y'rself all but a man of their tribe, right? So how can ye be included in the troop that raids y'r friends' storehouses without standin' as a traitor in their eyes?"

"I might settle this without need for a raid! Seizing their stores could start a war, unless I'm there to mayhap soften the blow, Captain!"

"A war—ah well, I doubt the savages w'ld dare go so far but if they do they'll end it, and on my terms. But with you held here, the Indians c'ld never blame you for going 'gainst y'r blood brother oath, c'ld they? Nay, I'm holding you to help you, Master Harvie." He turned to Captain Stafford. "Take Master Harvie to his house."

Cursing, Harvie permitted himself to be escorted back to the house he shared with three other gentlemen, Wellman, Thomas Dutton and Michael Wyles, and the artist, John White. He sulked in a corner of the main room, refusing to be drawn into conversation by White, while a stone mason named Henry Lorton, drafted into Lane's service in this new "emergency", paced back and forth in front of the door, a musket over his shoulder and the beak of an oversized burgonet constantly down to his nose. He watched with bleak eyes as Lane and Stafford lined up their men and marched them off toward the Indian village, the Cross of Saint George banner at the head of the file, the sunlight gleaming on the helmets and breastplates, the swords and arquebus barrels.

"A brave array," White said thoughtfully. "I'd sketch them but I've a hundred sketches of the soldiers and my drawing materials grow scarce."

"Oh aye, a brave array indeed," Dion muttered bitterly. "A proud troop that marches out to betray a friendship by a rifling of the Roanokes' stores. A fine report Lane will give to Raleigh and Grenville, I don't doubt—aye, our doughty captain will have it that the savages swooped down upon us and were driven off only after a great fight."

"Don't blame Captain Lane too much, friend Dion," White said mildly. "He's only looking out for our welfare in this thing. Mayhap he'll come to terms with Pemispan without needing to seize the corn."

"That man?" Dion grunted. "He'd feel cheated if the question was settled without some sword-waving. Why Walt chose him as governor is beyond me—better Stafford or Arundell or even you."

"And that," White smiled, "is a compliment come by in a roundabout way. But if 'twill soothe y'r feelings, Master Harvie, I'll tell you something I'd not like repeated. Sir Richard carried letters from me to Raleigh in which I said I admired Ralph Lane as a soldier but doubted his excellence as a governor. Ah no"—he raised a hand as Harvie's head swung around in surprise—"I did not lodge complaint of Lane on my own. Y'see, Raleigh pledged me to report to him everything I saw—he trusts my eye, being a dauber of paints—and pass judgment on the rights and wrongs of this expedition."

"I hope ye made Lane out a headstrong spitfire," Harvie said.

"Nay, I did not draw quite so damning a picture. I tried to be fair to our captain, even though I'm human enough to aspire to the position he holds now."

Harvie stared at the quiet-voiced White.

"Y'mean ye'd be governor of this place?" he asked. The artist nodded. "And y'think Sir Walter'd entertain the idea, friend John?"

"I flatter myself he would," White said, "and does already. Know ye that before we left England he asked me would I be governor of Virginia. I told him that as I was foreign to this New World and a painter first, no administrator, he'd best name another to fill Grenville's boots while Sir Richard was away. I said I would send word if I found I could handle the office, after examining the situation. That word has reached him by now and I trust Grenville will bring Raleigh's commission to me when he returns."

"Good!" Harvie exulted. "Excellent! With a sensible man as governor, we can patch this break with Pemispan and his braves and right a pack of wrongs, to Roanoke and—yes, to Pasquiwoc, as well. May God speed Sir Richard's return and the commission that'll send Lane back to bluster and stamp about in England, where he belongs!"

"Now, Dion," White said, uneasily, "because I'm no soldier you'll not expect me to shun firmness where it's required, will ye? For I must warn you that I have been called a hard man by those who've run against my stubborn will. And I hold with Lane in this—the Indians must be kept in their places till they're civilized enough to deserve a gentler treatment."

"Well—yes," Dion said reluctantly. "I suppose that's required. As Englishmen we have a position to hold that they can't understand but—ah well, mayhap Lane is partly right in saying I've come to be too friendly with the Roanokes. Still, I can't help but think these Indians would take kindlier to being civilized if we taught them civilized ways with a softer touch than the torch and this plunder of the storehouses they've shared with us."

"Methinks you credit them with too much intellect," White said. "These Roanokes have many good things that could be said of them—their cleanliness, their generosity and such—but we must never forget they are but high-scale animals, after all. Their minds can't grasp a fact unless it's forcefully lodged. They needs must be impressed firmly, even harshly, lest they forget what we teach them for their own good."

He leaned forward to put a hand on Dion's arm.

"For look you, these savages are less than children, and you know how sternly children must be dealt with to bring them up correctly."

Oh Christ, Dion groaned inwardly, *here's another who holds that Indians are animals and must be whipped to make behave! Well, I don't, call me turncoat, Indian-coddler though they may! Nay, Wanchese is no animal, nor Pemispan, and who could be more human in his vanity than that bastard Manteo? And as for Rycko—*

Now hold; 'twas but a short time back when you told Captain Amadas that you felt for Rycko as you felt for your father's greyhound bitches, nothing more—you named her animal then; why do you protest now?

"Aye, friend John," he said slowly. "You must be right in this."

Ralph Lane's little army was gone all day and dusk was spreading over Fort Raleigh when the *tump* of a drum marked the return of the column. Dion went to the doorway, his eyes bitter as he watched the men come into camp, carrying sacks of shelled corn, greasy bundles of smoked venison strips, racks of smoked fish and heaped baskets of potatoes. At the head of the parade marched Captain Lane, with Stafford beside him, grim triumph reflected in the governor's face.

It had, quite obviously, been a bloodless victory; Dion had heard no shots and there was no sign of a fight having taken place in any of these returning warriors. Indeed, most of the men were plainly disgruntled; it was apparent that they resented having been called out for porter's duty without even the excitement of a battle to lighten the chore.

"It was as I thought," Lane said later, at the heaped supper table. "The cowardly wretches made no move to stop us. Oh, Pemispan babbled something about a breach of trust, according to Manteo who served as our interpreter, but when I told him that the Roanokes had already broken faith with us by scheming to starve us, he backed down like a scared cur. Nor did his braves do aught but scowl as we took our fill of their goods, then went across to Dasamonquepeuc—and in their canoes, mind—and did the same thing there."

He looked down the table at the silent Dion and boomed a laugh.

"Did ye say they'd wage war, Master Harvie? Ye do not know the rascals half so well as ye think, f'r all y'r blood brother nonsense and y'r Roanoke name!"

Harvie glowered back without replying. The young man was disappointed by the Roanokes' failure to fight this outrage. Oh, he did not want any Englishmen killed nor did he want a war, but by their refusal to meet villainy with anything but a few empty words the Indians had proved that all the arguments he had advanced in their behalf had been wrong; they were a spineless lot, after all, and he a fool for having thought them brave and honorable men.

Manteo, he noticed, was in his element. The turncoat Roanoke sat at the first table with the gentlemen, treated as a sort of pet by the people he admired and aped, mimicking the foppish manners of such popinjays as Wellman and Dutton. Harvie told himself that Manteo could never return to his tribe now; he had come over to the English boot, blade and burgonet, and there would be no going back. The Roanokes might cringe and whine before Captain Lane and his troop, as Lane had said they did, but they would deal with Manteo far differently if they could lay their hands on him.

And, he asked himself, what was his own position in the eyes of the Indians? Had Wanchese damned him for a faithless blood brother? Had Pemispan and Granganimeo taken back the tribal name they had given him and branded him a traitor?

Well, what did he care if they had? He was an Englishman, no Roanoke—for him to act otherwise was to be as contemptible as Manteo.

But his heart was lightened, nevertheless, by what Rycko told him when she met him that night in the cove where they had always met.

"All the men are angry," the girl said, "and some at you, but not Pemispan or Wanchese. Wanchese bade me to tell you that he knows his brother, Pemec, tried to keep the white men from doing this evil thing. And he says that what befalls those who are to blame will not touch Pemec—unless—unless his brother denies the blood bond and declares himself an enemy of the Roanokes."

"And I do not," Dion said slowly. "Mayhap I should be a loyal Englishman in this but I cannot. I—what befalls the ones to blame? What did Wanchese mean, Rycko?"

"I do not know, Dion. The women are never told of the men's plans. But I saw all the men were very angry and tobacco was burned to the war gods."

7

And so the war broke out, although Captain Lane refused to dignify the conflict by that name and called it knavery instead. Lane had expected—hoped for—a pitched battle, with the Indians drawn up in close-packed ranks, fine targets for his cannon and his muskets. He found out, as more able English generals than he would discover in the future, that Indians did not fight their wars that way.

The Roanokes made their first strike four nights after the raid on their barns and in a few wild minutes evened the score with the Englishmen. The whites had robbed them of their food? Then the Roanokes would empty the Englishmen's barns, but by fire instead of plunder. The watch had just cried the hour of midnight when the five storehouses behind the dwellings simultaneously blossomed into flame.

Panicky confusion seized Fort Raleigh. Lane had made what he really thought were airtight plans of defense but he never had accepted Simon Ferdinando's warning that fire was the Indians' best weapon, he never had considered the possibility of the Roanokes using the torch although he had used it himself against the Pasquiwocs. When the alarm sounded, then, the captain ordered all the men into the fort and slammed shut the heavy gate that barred the one entrance; the soldiers, gentlemen and craftsmen scurried to their posts on the parapets—and watched helplessly as the fire roared through the storehouses.

Lane then rushed his men outside the walls of the fort and tried to form them into bucket brigades to fight the flames. The attempt was hopeless from the start. There were not enough buckets to go around and the barns were crackling, hissing infernos before the first pitifully inadequate splash of water was tossed in their direction.

The storehouses gone, the captain directed his efforts to prevent the flames from spreading to the dwellings and in this he was fairly successful. Men mounted to the thatched roofs and beat out sparks and embers that whirled up from the burning barns and drifted over the tiny town. One house was burned to the ground and another lost its roof before the flames were checked, but the village was saved.

Dawn brought a scene of desolation and the Englishmen's hollowed eyes were despairing as they looked at the smouldering ashes of what was to have been their food supply for the winter. Not one kernel of corn, one single potato, one slab of meat or dried fish, had survived the fire—and the Indians who had previously supplied the white men with these things were enemies now.

"By the Book," Ralph Lane stormed, "we'll wring the secret of their hiding places for their stores if we have to use torture! Captain Stafford, line up your men!"

Dion Harvie was with the column that tramped out of Fort Raleigh, an arquebus grooving his shoulder. He had no clear idea of why he had joined the troops. Perhaps he thought he could in some way act as a last-minute peacemaker; perhaps he reasoned that now, in a time of real danger, his place was with his own kind; at any rate, he marched with the others to the Indian hunting camp down the shore.

The place was deserted. The council fire was a mound of grey, sodden ashes, the huts had been stripped of their lousy furnishings, the canoes were gone, even the totems, logs topped by crudely carved heads and stuck upright in a circle where the ceremonial dances were performed, had been uprooted and taken away. Not a bird sang from the brush about the clearing, not even a buzzard specked the sky over the village.

"They've left us their fine fields," Lane said, "and so we are in no trouble, after all. When last I saw their maize 'twas about to tassle. Aye, we'll keep our bellies full in spite o' their damned sneaking outrage on our barns."

The Roanokes had left their fields, as Lane had said, but only their fields. Before they had abandoned their camp, the Indians had cut every stalk, green ears and all, and bundled them away. The armored, helmeted captain stood on a rise, surveying the ruined cornpatches, and Harvie saw rage give way to fear in the Governor's red face.

"The devils," Harvie heard him mutter. "They'd starve themselves, they would, to defeat us! What manner of madness is this?"

He straightened his shoulders with obvious effort and turned to his aide, Stafford.

"To Dasamonquepeuc!" he ordered. "We'll take their village before the swine have time to do the same thing there as they've done here. At once, Captain Stafford—to Dasamonquepeuc!"

The need was for all haste but the crossing to Dasamonquepeuc was not made until five days later and then, of course, it was too late. For when the Englishmen hurried back to the shore below Fort Raleigh they found every one of their smallboats stove in, the few canoes they had commandeered gone. Raging now, Lane ordered the craftsmen to build new boats and kept them at their tasks until the men muttered, then yelled their protests and finally threw down their tools and said they'd be damned if they'd work like slaves without a bite to eat.

All work on the boats stopped while a party led by Dion Harvie was sent out to net some fish. Because no one but Dion had bothered to learn the art of spearing or seining, the Englishmen sweated through hours of clumsy effort before they were able to return to Fort Raleigh with a beggarly boatload of trash fish that, in other days, the "Virginians" had scorned. Another group, dispatched to hunt for oysters, diligently searched every sandbar within wading distance and came back with the report that the oysters had been bewitched—there was not one to be picked up.

"Nor has there ever been one to be found on a sandbar," Dion told Lane with a wry laugh. "We must have boats to reach the oyster beds offshore and then, because we have no long rakes such as the Roanokes used, we'll have to dive for them."

"Curse this condemned country!" the captain raged. "Why aren't the oysters cast up on the shore like the grapes? Ah, the grapes!"

The grapes were sweet and plentiful but half-cooked fish without salt (all the salt had been destroyed in the fire) and grapes made a miserable meal for men accustomed to great chunks of venison and bear steaks. Work on the boats was resumed, but half-heartedly; it was only after Dion tracked down and shot a big buck and a smaller doe that were divided among the carpenters and shipwrights—to the accompaniment of squalled curses from the gentlemen and soldiers—that the jobs were speeded up.

When the makeshift flotilla finally reached Dasamonquepeuc even the most optimistic Englishman expected to find no more than was there. Here again there was no sign of the Roanokes or a morsel of food, stored or growing. The cornfields had been sheared as completely as the fields on the island;

the main village of the Roanokes had been emptied of every scrap that could possibly have been of use to the white men.

"Burn the town!" Lane bellowed. "Burn every stinking hut to the ground!"

"By y'r leave, Captain," Dion put in, "would it not be better to leave these poor huts unharmed? That way, the Roanokes might come back to this place and we c'ld come to terms with them. These savages are a people of strange whims, as ye know; it could well be that having scored a—er—setback on us before they fled, they're satisfied and anxious to make peace. If we leave their village standing they'll come back here, I think, and —and mayhap with stores we could deal for."

"Hm," Lane murmured, "perchance you have something there, Master Harvie. If they come back with stores—I see y'r point. We c'ld wait till they'd settled down again and stage another raid—and then make sure they'd not burn us out a second time! Good, good—we'll not put this smelly town to fire, then."

The thought of offering the Roanokes a false security that would lure them back to be raided again had not been Dion Harvie's idea at all but the tall, wide-shouldered young man shrugged off Lane's interpretation of his advice without a protest. Enough, he reasoned, that he had saved Dasamonquepeuc from the torch; perhaps Wanchese and the others would know he had tried his feeble best to make amends for what his countrymen had done.

If the men of Fort Raleigh had been idle before, they made up for it now. Hunger proved a more biting pain than hurt pride and gentlemen who would never have dreamed of the thought a few short days before now found themselves weaving fish nets, hoisting timbers into place on the new barns, scrambling through the thick, mosquito-infested brush after game, diving for oysters which they tore from their beds with shell-gashed hands, hunting seabirds' eggs, searching for bee trees, wading through swamp muck after frogs, rigging snares for rabbits and water rats.

Before a month was finished, Captain Ralph Lane's company was a bedraggled, fly-bitten, thorn-scratched, mud-stained, gaunt-faced, droop-mouthed crew. Some few toughened under the demands of this new life and proved themselves men of courage and forebearance, most of them slogged through each day in bitter hatred for everything and everybody they must endure.

And the perpetual whining cry was: *Where is Grenville?*

The Fall gave way to Winter and cold winds whooped down out of the northeast, the Sound became a churning sea, the grape vines rattled under the stinging whiplash of the sleet that swept the island. The game on Roanoke Island was exhausted and, for days at a stretch, the water between the island and the mainland was too wild to permit a crossing in Lane's small-boats so the meat supply failed. There was plenty of wildfowl aloft but the ducks and geese and swan whirled by on gale-quickened wings and never landed within gunshot. The oysters were still there but what man could dive into that icy water to get them, even if a boat could reach the beds? The fish traps were wrecked by pounding waves and when they were not wrecked they were empty more often than not. Pemispan had told Dion that many fish went to the bottom of the sea and slept during the cold moons; now Harvie believed it. The great schools of bluefish and mackerel and sea trout and herring that had made the waters of the Sound froth that summer vanished. Even that reviled animal, the water rat, grew scarce and the rabbits on the island were completely wiped out before Christmas, a day of howling winds and spitting snow. Cranes, gulls and cormorants were filling but rank in taste and tough in texture. The clams and mussels were small and bitter. Even the spring water took on a brackish taste that left the drinker thirsty.

And where was Grenville and his supply ships?

"We've been abandoned," was the muttered growl. "Raleigh and Grenville have forgotten us."

"Not so," cried John White when the doleful murmuring reached him. "The supply ships will be back in the Spring, when these winter storms die down."

"Aye, Spring," Ralph Lane gloomed, "but can we last till then? Half the troop is sick and the rest, save but a handful, are close to rebellion. By God's teeth, I ne'er commanded such a hapless company."

"And had you not angered the Indians," White dared counter, "we'd never have found ourselves in this position."

"Now, damn me!" Lane blared. "Look you at who dares criticize my command! His Majesty John White, a fancy dauber of pretty pictures! Mayhap in my place ye'd ha' coaxed the savage bastards to deal kindlier with us by doing their portraits to hang in their halls?"

"I'd have had more good sense than to cut off my own supplies by making enemies of the people who furnished them, dauber or no!"

"And I suppose this is what ye'll tell Raleigh—if ye live to meet him, hey?" Chin jutted, eyes bulging, fists doubled, Lane spat the question into John White's face. The painter did not flinch; instead his eyelids drooped with unspoken contempt.

"And I know full well ye've plotted behind my back, John White!" the captain went on. "Oh aye, I know ye plan to discredit me before Raleigh, twisting the facts to fit the picture ye'll splash with y'r tongue! Well, I'm ready for all ye scheme to do to my reputation—I have my friends in England, sir, and they'll see I'm not mistreated in any accounts to Raleigh."

"And I have the word of every man on this island," White said coldly, "that ye've handled all our affairs in the worst way, risking the success of this colony—aye, our very lives—to give yourself a chance to rattle y'r sword."

"Rattle a sword, ye call it, when I swept the heathen savages off this island and the mainland coast, back into the deep forest to the west?"

"Oh aye, ye conquered them," White said, his lip curling, "and scored a mighty victory." His eyes swept the little village, paused to scan a knot of hungry, ragged settlers and moved back to Lane. "The rewards of which," he added drily, "are most munificent."

Lane tried to speak, choked, whirled and stamped off, his swagger a mere shadow of what it once had been. White looked after him thoughtfully and Dion Harvie, a witness to this clash, heard him murmur: "Speed Grenville's return with my commission from Raleigh as governor of this place."

January and February and March passed and Grenville's relief ships did not come back to Virginia.

But the Roanokes came back—and lost no time in letting the Englishmen know that their "strange whims" had not made them forget there was a war on.

8

THROUGHOUT THAT LONG, dreary winter, Dion had more time to think than was good for his peace of mind. There was no Rycko or Wanchese to fill his days and nights and when he had finished tending his deadfall traps and snares (which caught less and less game until setting them became almost an empty ritual) he had nothing to do unless he joined the others in their perpetual haranguing about the injustices of their existence. He passed up these futile conclaves, not because he was less bitter at the fate that had cast him into this wretched situation but because his ears ached at the monotonous repetition of threadbare woes. More, his scorn was fired by the others' ludicrous attempts to impress their fellow colonists with what they had been back in England.

So, gradually, Harvie slipped further and further away from the other English gentlemen at Fort Raleigh. Because his whole upbringing forbade overstepping the caste lines that separated him from the craftsmen and the soldiers, even if he would, he found himself a lonely man with only his own thoughts to offer him release from the deadly emptiness.

He still lived in a crowded house with White, Wellman, Wyles and Dutton and still ate at the first table—for the order of rank at mealtime had not been discarded, regardless of how menial the gentlemen's tasks might be between breakfast and dinner—and sat in on Lane's frustrated councils, but it had become increasingly hard for him to consider himself as a comrade of these people.

He might recognize their table talk, the dog-eared stories of old duels, old intrigues, old adulteries, old villainies, old triumphs, as desperate attempts to cling to dear memories and so ward off despair that would lead to madness; he might know that the petty bickering was needed to fend off the deadly lethargy of complete melancholy, but he could not join the others in either.

Instead, he stood apart and viewed his countrymen, these members of his own class, detachedly, analytically, clinically, comparing what they were now with what they had posed as being before they met harsh reality. That man, for instance, was still blatantly proud of his conquests among the ladies of Elizabeth's court, he had been acknowledged as the champion seducer of his circle—and here he had earned himself a new reputation as a malingerer on even the easiest jobs. That other gentleman bore one of the oldest, proudest names in all England—and yet a man had to watch his tiny store of food carefully when this high-nosed courtier was on the prowl. Over there was a titled bravo who had matched Lane in his fire-breathing—yet more than once that winter he had dissolved into sobs in his fear that he would never see London again. The gaunt, grey spectres of starvation, loneliness and ennui had stripped away the trappings of fine manners, haughty lordliness, monied superiority—and left what? Strangely shriveled without their fine cloaks of inherited importance, this high-born group stood revealed as a collection of selfish, vain, dishonest, fearful, jealous, lying—yes, *stupid*—men who needed the dazzling glitter of Elizabeth's court to blind others and themselves to their shabby insufficiencies. They did not have—had never had—a scrap of true greatness in them.

True greatness—would England, Dion asked himself, ever give honor again to the true greatness she had known in the old days? Would there return the spirit that was England's when there was a Harold or an Alfred or an Edward the Confessor, when knights knew humility and bent their efforts for the common good, not for the fattening of their purses, the bolstering of their own positions, the cuckolding of men they smiled upon as dearest friends?

And how would the coming years treat the reign of the virgin, Elizabeth? How could her rule escape shame in history's appraisal if these small-souled men at Fort Raleigh were examples of the courtiers on whom Gloriana must depend? What would the world say a hundred years hence of Englishmen who betrayed the generous friendship of a simple, trusting people like the Roanokes and, when their treachery brought them just retribution, cursed the Indians and plotted more treachery to avenge their own wrongdoing?

If it was true, as the old seers held, that a man's real worth was tested in adversity, then these men of Fort Raleigh had proved themselves of base metal when touched by the acid of misfortune. Not one, with the possible exception of John White, had been big enough to admit his miseries were the consequence of the white men's misdeeds; each sought to fix the blame on the Indians' perfidy, his companions' shortcomings, the delays of Raleigh and Grenville, the unreasonable blows of an unjust fate. The guilt was always someone's else, never theirs.

They had robbed the Roanokes of their supplies and had laughed at the betrayal of their friends; when the Indians had hit back, Pemispan and his tribe had become a pack of ravening wolves. They had strutted and posed as superior beings, ordained by birth and God to rule, and when their superiority had been put to the proof it had collapsed like a gale-swept house built of rotten wood. So Dion Harvie saw his old beliefs crumble and in their place grew a respect for human qualities he would have scorned a year before. Truth, honesty, self-searching, humility, compassion—where did any of these fit in the nature of an Elizabethan courtier? And if these were among the new principles toward which Dion reached an uncertain hand that winter, what magic ruled Roanoke Island to make him turn away from what he had so jealously guarded, the gilded splendor of the name of English *gentleman?*

9

WARM WEATHER BROUGHT relief to the infant Colony of Virginia, that Spring of 1586. The fish returned to the Sound and even the inexpert fish traps set by the Englishmen yielded fair catches. The water lost its chill enough for the oyster-gatherers to dive; the storms whirled off to the other side of the equator and hunting parties were able to paddle across to the mainland in search of meat. Best of all, the marrow-numbing cold gave way to balmy breezes, bright sunshine, warm rains that laved skinny shoulders instead of stinging them, as the sleet had.

Hunting parties returning from the mainland said that Dasamonquepeuc was still deserted; there were no signs of the Roanokes.

"They've slunk out of this region for good and all," Ralph Lane predicted. "Now we can root out the other tribes, the Secotans and the Croatoans and the Pasquiwocs and the Hatorasks and we can truly claim this whole land for Her Majesty. We must plan an expedition 'gainst these other dogs, and soon."

"But don't ye think 'twould be better to keep these others' friendship?" Dion asked. "We need seed corn if we're to plant our own fields, and seed potatoes, too. As for tobacco, which we're charged with raising by Sir Walter's orders, we can't produce a stalk unless the Croatoans or the Secotans give us some plantings—God wot the Pasquiwocs wouldn't give us a grain of sand or a drop of salt water, not after Aquascogok."

"We'll seize these things in our expeditions," Lane explained, "and, Master Harvie, I'd thank you to keep y'r counsel to y'rself—as ye've kept y'r proud highness apart from all of us durin' the hardships when we needed all comradeship to survive. Now that we've weathered the grim winter, don't think ye can worm y'r way back into our favor, sir. Nay, we'll long remember that you counted y'rself too good to join the common band when danger was afoot."

"And that," Harvie blazed, "is crooked thinking! Name me

one time when I did not do my share and more! Because I didn't see fit to spend my days weeping at our lot and reviling Sir Walter for not sending relief ships doesn't mean I didn't do all I could to help this company endure!"

"Ye didn't weep at our lot—nay, ye were too concerned about the lot of the dirty savages to heed our woes!"

"If you think I was concerned," Harvie cried, "think ye what Sir Walter will be when he hears of the cowardly way you dealt with our friends! I swear he'll—"

"And *I* swear I'll have ye shot f'r mutiny if ye—what is it, Stafford?"

The eyes of the men at the council table swung toward the doorway where Captain Stafford stood, his dark face wearing a worried frown.

"There's a hunting party back from the mainland, Captain Lane," the aide said in a grave voice. "They bring bad news, sir."

"What news?" Lane barked.

"They had killed three fine deer, they say," Stafford went on, "and were carrying the meat to their boats when they were fallen upon by Indians."

"*Indians!*" There was the squeal of bench legs scraping on the rough floor, the clump of boots as the men sprang to their feet. Stafford nodded.

"Aye, Roanokes," he said quietly. "Led by Pemispan himself, they were, and daubed with the colored clay Master Harvie has told us they smear themselves with when they go to war."

"Our men—" Lane began.

"Made their escape," Stafford finished, "with no worse than slight arrow scratches suffered by three of their number. They had to abandon the meat and they left one of their boats in their retreat."

"They ran?" Lane cried, disbelievingly. "Now, by God's eyeballs, what coward sounded the retreat? A volley would've—"

"Y'r pardon, Captain," Stafford broke in "I asked the same thing, of course, and was told there was no target to shoot at—the arrows came out of the forest from all sides and there was a whooping and yelling that my serjeant says would have unnerved a stone statue. They caught only a peek here, another there, of Pemispan and the rest. Ours was a hunting party, sir, not led by an officer and scantily armed. The men can't be too harshly blamed for retiring to this island."

"They can't, eh?" Lane growled. "Well, by God, I have a different mind on that! Half rations for five days for every man-jack in that party. And we'll go to the mainland instanter, Captain, in full force. We'll teach these heathens a lesson to repay their insolence."

But there were no heathens to be taught a lesson when Lane led his troop ashore near Dasamonquepeuc. Footprints showed there had been at least a hundred Roanokes in the area a few minutes before but even though the red-faced captain pushed his search far inland, nothing was found except the footprints and even these were lost less than a mile from the beach. The small-boat that had been abandoned by the hunting party had disappeared, rowed away or sunk in deep water, and there was no trace of the three deer carcasses.

"A stab in the back, a scurvy trick!" Ralph Lane raged. "If they'd but come out to battle, I'd teach 'em a lesson! Burn the village, Stafford, and this time"—he cast a black look at Dion Harvie—"I do not mean to be dissuaded by any turncoat's weeping."

"Now, by the Book—" Dion began. He stopped at a touch of a hand on his arm and murmur in his ear.

"Quiet, lad," John White said, "before Lane finds the excuse he seeks to string you up for mutiny. Endure this fool's raving till Sir Richard returns and then we both will have our day."

"And what's that ye're mumbling, White?" Lane demanded. "More trickery, I'll be bound!"

"Why, Captain," White protested smoothly, "I only counselled Master Harvie to remember his proper station as your subordinate."

"Ah—well—mayhap ye did, though I doubt it," Lane said gruffly. He turned back to Stafford. "Burn the village, I say, Captain!"

If he gained any satisfaction by sweeping the deserted, storm-tilted huts of Dasamonquepeuc with fire, Lane's face did not reflect it when he returned to Fort Raleigh. The governor was in a black mood that was not lightened by his order to deal five lashes each to members of the hunting party who had "let these swine escape my heavy hand." Captain Stafford tried to protest the whippings and found himself the target of a tirade that accused him of siding with Harvie and White and which set the aide's face in rigid lines of contemptuous anger.

"By y'r leave, Governor," he said stiffly, when his superior had finished, "I'll resign my commission in y'r troop as soon as Sir Richard returns to Fort Raleigh."

"Resign and be damned," Lane snorted. "And as f'r Sir Richard —I have my doubts he'll ever come back here, as he promised. Nay, the high-and-mighty Grenville's so caught up in his infernal politics that he's forgotten us, as have all the rest of the great gentlemen in England."

"And that," White muttered to Harvie, "Grenville will be happy to hear about when I tell him, I doubt not."

Two nights after the Roanoke ambush of the hunting party, all the settlers' fish traps were wrecked. Another expedition to the mainland failed to find a trace of the Indians and Lane raved, yelling his demand at the silent forest that Pemispan come out and fight like a man.

The night after the destruction of the fish traps, the boats beached under the very eyes of the fort were holed beyond repair. Lane, fairly frothing, had the sentries dealt ten lashes. The following night, the patched fish nets were wrecked again. That time, Lane turned on Manteo.

"I think ye're in league with 'em!" he stormed. "How is it that ye didn't give warning when y'r foul-flavored kinsmen slipped up on us? Ye've boasted enough of how ye were the best scout in the whole tribe—did'st brag y'rself blind that ye didn't see them at their evil work last night?"

Manteo whined that it was not his fault that the nets were wrecked; he could not be on guard twenty-four hours a day and the Roanokes had picked a time when he was not on watch to do their work. Lane countered with the reminder that Manteo had been found asleep on watch four separate times. The turncoat Roanoke came back with the complaint that while he might have dozed four times, Lane's other soldiers could have been found asleep on post forty times if they had been watched as closely as he had been.

"The Great Queen," Manteo lamented, "gave orders I was to be treated as a brother but you have never dealt with me as an equal, though I've lost my own people in your behalf."

It was a whimper Dion Harvie was glad to translate to Ralph Lane, nor was the captain's rejoinder hard to give back to Manteo.

"Ah, God's sake, I'm weary of y'r grumbling! Her Majesty might have bade Sir Richard Grenville to show you favors but that was only 'cause you amused her, like a court fool might. She did not intend that you puff up like a toad and lord it over y'r betters as ye've tried to."

Thus, in the days that saw a stepping-up of the Indian harassment of Fort Raleigh, Ralph Lane's anger plunged the camp into acrimony even worse than the unrest of the past winter. Lane was at odds with his own aide, his Roanoke guide, most of the gentlemen, a great majority of the craftsmen and all his soldiers, who did not seem to fall into step any better because of the lashings, the cut rations, the other punishments with which the captain tried to deal with the growing revolt.

While the blustering captain struck out wildly in all directions, Pemispan and his braves carried on what amounted to a siege of Roanoke Island. Fish traps could not be set out overnight without a strong guard and even then the Indians kept the fish away by thrashing the waters about the traps, out of sight and gunshot, turning back the schools that rode in on the tide. Hunting parties that ventured to the mainland found no game; the Roanokes kept far enough ahead of the hunters to make sure that no deer or bears or even rabbits were seen. Wildfowl that would have racked up in the coves and marshes of the island were frightened away by the natives; even the muskrats were scattered.

With the white men's food supply cut down to the previous winter's dangerous levels, the Indians began a new phase of their curious war. A sentry pacing the parapet at night might hear the hiss of an arrow past his ear, close enough to chill his blood but apparently never meant to kill. Parties gathering wood or hauling a seine or digging clams or working on a new boat saw painted Roanokes rise out of nowhere to stand whooping at a distance, shaking their war clubs and spears, before they disappeared, leaving the whites to try to gulp down their panic while they blasted away at shadows that never turned out to be Indians.

An outbuilding went up in roaring flames one night, another the next and a third the next. Lane had all hands stand to for six nights running and on the seventh gave in to the demands of his sleep-starved troops and cut back his duty roster to the usual number of guards. The fourth barn was fired that night.

Lane had wanted a war and he had one. Despite the fact that only three of the men in the first hunting party attacked had suffered even a scratch, the captain found himself losing battles he could not fight, as helplessly as though the enemy had weapons while he had none. When he had planned to bolster his authority by a war, he found himself losing the little he had before he raided Pemispan's storehouses. If he got a salute now, it was a grudging one, given in poorly-veiled contempt. For the most part, nobody bothered to raise a hand or even give him a "sir" and his orders were carried out reluctantly and belatedly—or ignored.

The Roanokes called him Wastomug, a name freely translated as "Buzzard's Carrion." The depth of the insult could be appreciated when it was realized that the Indians left only the most loathsome offal to the feathered scavengers.

Dion Harvie learned of Lane's new title from Rycko.

Yes, the girl returned to Roanoke Island and to Dion Harvie, braving the guns of Fort Raleigh that, considering the tattered state of the white men's nerves, certainly would have filled the air with shot if she had been seen. Rycko crept to the cove that had been her and Dion's love chamber and there she crouched for hours before Harvie came within reach of a tossed pebble, a hissed hail.

"Rycko!" he gasped when she peeped from behind a yaupon

bush. He looked about him and saw that the other members of the party sent out to search for berries were beyond earshot. "Great God, Rycko, what do ye here?"

"Come back when the others are gone," she whispered.

"Aye. Wait."

Dion hurried back to the berry-hunters, pointing toward a rise to the west. "The last time I came this way," he said, "I think I remember seeing some laden bushes, the fruit nearly ripe, over there. Let's look in that direction—there's nothing further up the beach."

The hillock he had pointed out was bare of berries, but the search had been successfully detoured from Rycko's hiding place and, by a stroke of fortune, there was a carpet of wild strawberries coating a glen just beyond. It was nearly three hours later when Dion could get away from the fort and make his way to the cove by a roundabout trail.

His meeting with the girl was wordlessly eager, frantic. His hands roamed over her smoothness, his mouth fastened on hers with fierce hunger, whether he was brutal or tender in taking her was never remembered by either.

And Rycko met his devouring onslaught with a rapacity that matched his. She was sleek where he was gaunt but the urgency of her demanding embrace proved that she had starved for this feverish ecstasy as achingly as he. Her cry was a muted scream, his an exultant groan, as their joined craving wrenched assuagement, each from the other.

"And now," he murmured when he struggled out of the half-swoon, "why do you risk coming here, Princess? You must know Captain Lane is so hot for a Roanoke head he'd not hesitate to stick yours on a pole, could he snatch it from your pretty shoulders."

"Ha, Big Wastomug," Rycko scoffed, and explained the name as Harvie grinned. "We Roanokes can come and go as we will without him seeing us. I was here twice some time ago and did not know you at once because of the hair on your face—it was so smooth when I last saw you. There are many of us on this island now and we have been here for two moons—the Englishmen have walked around us and even over us and never seen a sign to tell them we were here. Aye, if he would, Pemispan could have killed them every one, without being seen."

"And why hasn't he?" Dion asked curiously. "God's sake, I'm glad he hasn't but he has a name as a fierce warrior and yet he hasn't slain a single one of us."

"That is Wanchese," Rycko explained. "Pemispan holds Wanchese's counsel highest of all and your brother has made him believe that by keeping food from the white men he will make them sail away from here."

She looked up at him, her dark eyes searching anxiously.

"But when the others sail, Pemec," she went on, "you will not go with them, will you? You're blood brother to Wanchese, one of us; we all know you have been made ill at what the other white men have done to us. Pemispan wants no harm to come to you—he bade me tell you this. You will stay with us when the others sail away, Pemec?"

He bent to place a kiss on her forehead.

"How can you ask me to do that, Rycko?" he said gently. "These people are my own people, as the Roanokes are your people. If I were a Pasquiwoc or a Secotan and I asked you to come with me away from your own people, what would you say?"

"I'd say yes, with great gladness," Rycko said fiercely. "If you would ask me to walk to the bottom of the sea with you, I'd say yes!"

"Well—er—well, you talk of something that will not happen, Rycko," Harvie stumbled. "These white men will not sail away. Instead, great canoes will come soon with more white men and more guns and plenty of food and we will have a new chief who will not do the things that the Captain Lane, Wastomug, has done. The man who paints, John White, will be our new chief and he is a good man. When he is chief we will make peace with Pemispan, so I will not have to sail away at all."

While he told the girl this, Dion Harvie felt the digging jab of something he had not admitted until recently, his conscience. He was telling the girl he would stay here in Virginia when all his plans were to go back to England the moment Raleigh's word told him the Queen had forgotten or forgiven him.

"And, besides," he hastened to say, "we are different kinds, as the sun is different from the moon. We can join for a little time, as the night and the day can join at dawn and dusk, but when you take your man for all time, he must be as you are, an Indian and a Roanoke."

"But you are a brother to Wanchese," she argued stubbornly. "I saw you from a hiding place when you mixed your blood with ours and took the name of Pemecolemanmeo and became one of us. So there is no difference as of night and day between us."

Her deep eyes sought his again.

"Is there a woman you care more for than Rycko?" she asked slowly.

Dion Harvie had the swift vision of Margery Hollis as he had last seen her. He had lied to her in saying there was another woman whom he loved—why hesitate in lying now?

"Yes," he said, "there is a woman. She is named—Margery and she has my promise to return to her."

Rycko's head bowed and her long forefinger traced meaningless patterns in the sand at her side. Her ripe breasts lifted in a deep sigh and she raised her face again.

"I feared this," she said calmly. "I feared the gods would do this to me. Is this woman finer than Rycko in all things? In this—and this—and this?"

"Ah, no, Rycko," Dion panted. "Never—never!"

And his phantom betrothed was whirled back into the limbo she had been summoned from as the wildness descended on the long-limbed Englishman and the tawny Roanoke girl.

Again, and yet again, they feasted on each other, with searching mouth and hands and hearts, until surcease from their hunger, but never satiation, came and they talked in hushed murmurs as the moon climbed the sky.

Rycko's realization that Pemec would never be hers beyond these brief encounters did not sour her; she endured her grief with a stoicism that was her birthright; if her gods had arranged things other than she would have them they had at least given her these moments of happiness which she would not mar with overt sadness. As for Dion, he had changed in more ways than he realized during the past winter. His new convictions included one that brought him guilt at the thought that Rycko really deserved more than the consideration of just another luscious mistress. And these twinges of conscience, these new disturbing scruples, would not be stilled.

"You say more white men are coming in great canoes?" Rycko asked drowsily. "Are they the ships that are far south, Pemec?"

"Ships? To the south? Ye've seen ships, then?"

"Not we Roanokes, but word has come from far-off lands that great ships have been in the sea south of here, making war on the Waspaines that you call Spaniards."

Dion's brow wrinkled in puzzlement.

"War on the Spaniards?" he mused. "Does that mean Grenville's delayed relieving us to raid the Spanish Main? Or does it mean that Philip has at last wearied of Elizabeth's diddling and has started a war?"

"I don't know of such things, Pemec, but the word was that the Waspaines' enemies won great victories, with the taking of much of the gold you white men love. And these white men are led by a chief who wears a beard as red as the setting sun, so it is said."

"A red beard? Then it's not Grenville—his beard is black. It could be—*aye it must be Drake!* And if it's Drake, pray God he sails this way and finds us!" His face fell and he shook his head gloomily. "But he won't," he added. "Why should he? Sir Francis Drake's after Spanish treasures and there's none to be found in these parts. Nay, he'll follow the course of Philip's plate ships and miss us by a hundred leagues."

She slid her eyes at him and looked away.

"And would that grieve you so, Pemec?" she asked quietly.

He said, bitterly, " 'Twould probably mean my finish. I don't know how much longer I can stand Lane's insults without drawing on the mouthy dog and so give him the excuse to hang me or have me shot for mutiny."

"He would do that?"

"With great pleasure," Harvie nodded. "I've been stopped at the very threshold of a sudden end before this, responding to his baiting, and the time will come when I'll not be stopped."

"Then—then this Drake will be told you're here," the Roanoke girl said slowly. "If his coming means your safety, he will be called to this place, Pemec."

"But how can you tell him we need his help?" Dion asked. "He's God knows where and probably does not realize we're alive —or if he does, how can he find our island?"

"There are ways," Rycko said simply. "Drake will come. And now, before I leave, Pemec. . . ."

Dion kept Rycko's news of Drake's whereabouts (for he was sure it was that stubby, flame-bearded wizard of the high seas) to himself. He convinced himself there was no point in telling Lane; the captain would ask him how he knew these things and if he found out that Dion had spent a night with Rycko he would be sure to accuse him of spying for the enemy. He considered telling John White but saw no reason to share his secret. Even if the whole fort knew Drake's fleet was close nothing could be done to insure his coming to Virginia's aid; there was not a vessel big enough or seaworthy enough to go out to meet Drake's galleons and an expedition down the coast would be sure to run afoul of the Pasquiwocs.

He kept silent, then, and found reasons almost every daylight hour to mount the spindly watch tower and strain his eyes to the east. And every evening he slipped away from the others to meet Rycko in the cove where, the first demands satisfied, at least temporarily, he plied her with questions about Drake's fleet.

Yes, the word had been dispatched to the man the Waspaines called *El Draque*—The Dragon—and, no, there had been no reply. And yes, it had been made sure that the red-bearded one could find Port Ferdinando; he would be guided there by the Indians all along the coast, with the exception of the Pasquiwocs who had refused to lend any aid to the white man. And no, there was no telling when the fleet might reach Roanoke.

"Are you this impatient?" the girl murmured. "Are you so eager to escape all these things we have here—and now?" The vision of

Sir Francis Drake's vessels standing in to Trinity Inlet faded in the red haze of the next moment but it returned, sharp, clear, wonderful beyond description.

May moved into June and on June sixth, 1586, Captain Ralph Lane scored his great victory.

10

He laid his plans well, did Captain Lane. He had no way of knowing that Pemispan, anticipating the arrival of Drake's fleet and the departure of the Englishmen, had called off his guerilla war against the white men and, therefore, he saw the end of the siege as a sign of a Roanoke "change of whim".

If Pemispan was tired of war and wanted peace, Lane told his council, so much the better for the success of his scheme.

"You'll note," the captain said, "I've sent that worthless Manteo out with the fishermen. I could not have him hear what I plan and I charge ye to keep it from him. My plan is this: 'Tis a fact that the Roanoke dogs want to get their hands on Manteo more than all else—true, Master Harvie?"

Dion nodded grudgingly. He had no love for Manteo and yet to hand the turncoat over to Pemispan would be little short of murder.

"So we will send word to Pemispan that we'd treat with him about Manteo," Lane went on. "I'm certain he'll agree to a parley on those terms."

"But Captain Lane," White objected, "ye know full well Raleigh would be most concerned if the Queen's pet were tossed back to the people he betrayed—why, they'd tear him apart like wolves, sir, and what could we tell Sir Walter then?"

"Ah," Lane said with an impatient gesture, "we'll guard Manteo, never fear. What I'll use him for is to get Pemispan and his subchiefs out of hiding for a parley, nothing more. Ye have my word on this, if Manteo's safety worries you."

"And at the parley?" White asked slowly.

Lane twisted an end of his moustache between thick thumb and forefinger.

"I'll treat with the savages in a way they'll understand," he said curtly. "Leave all that to me. Master Harvie, ye'll go to the mainland and find Pemispan—you'll be safe enough, I trow, because you wear an Indian name. Or are you queazy about this?"

"Nay, captain," Dion said. "I welcome the chance to stop this war between us and the Indians. I'll go instanter—if you truly intend a peace parley."

"I do," the governor nodded. "So go to them and say I'd speak with Pemispan about Manteo and what they want to have done with him. Fix a time and place where we can meet in council."

Harvie studied the captain carefully. Had he somehow gotten word of the approach of Drake's fleet and so wished to smooth the situation at Fort Raleigh to make a better showing in Drake's eyes when the sea rover visited this place? Or was some other scheme hiding in that bullet head?

"Captain Lane," he said, "I'll need your word, sir, that this bid for a parley is an honest one. I mean, I'd not lead the Roanokes into any kind of a trap."

Lane's eyebrows shot up in pained ingenuousness.

"How now, Master Harvie?" he rumbled. "God knows ye've blamed me enough for what ye've called mistreatment of the Indians—now would ye suspicion me when I say mayhap I have been to rude to them and would make amends to bring peace to this colony?"

Dion considered. To take Lane at his word was a tough task and yet it was a fact that Lane had suffered enough setbacks to throttle his pride and beg an armistice with the Indians. A parley was what he had been hoping for, asking for; how could he let his mistrust block it now?

"Y'r pardon, Governor Lane," he forced himself to say, "but this change in y'r way of thinking is surprising, ye must admit. I'll go to the mainland at once."

He wondered if he were watched by Roanoke eyes as he went to the beach to board a skiff and set sail for the mainland, where lay the charred ruins of Dasamonquepeuc. Rycko had told him that there had been plenty of spies on the island but that Pemispan had found other duties for them when the Roanoke chief had eased his seige. Still, he told himself later, there must have been at least one scout to pass the word, for when he beached his little boat and stepped ashore he was met by Pemispan, Wanchese and a dozen braves.

The Indians' greeting was grave, reserved, but not hostile. Wanchese stepped up to him and touched his shoulder with a brief "Ho", and Harvie responded in kind. Wordlessly, the Roanoke chief and his men squatted in a circle, Harvie among them.

"The Captain Lane," Dion said without preliminaries, "whom you call Wastomug sends me to ask Pemispan for a council."

"A council?" the chief asked. "Does an eagle hold a council with the starving buzzard? What need is there for this?"

"The Captain Lane says he seeks peace between the Chief Pemispan and the white men, that they may live as friends," Dion offered.

"We do not want his friendship," Pemispan said bluntly. "We know what kind of friendship he gives others, No, a few days will pass and the ships of *El Draque* will be here to take Wastomug and the others away from here. We want you to stay but Rycko says you must go."

"Yes," Dion nodded. "I must go with the others. And you ask what need there is of a council—what of Manteo?"

"That dropping from a spotted toad!" Granganimeo spat. A ripple of hissed curses ran about the circle.

"He is a false Roanoke," Dion agreed, "but the Captain Lane says he wants to talk to Pemispan about Manteo. Perhaps the Captain Lane sees now he has been wrong in many things and among them is the way he has listened to Manteo. Perhaps the Captain Lane wants to make things right before—before he goes away."

But Lane does not know of Drake's approach! Still, there will be other Englishmen coming here; if I can help bring peace between them and the Roanokes I will be doing a service for my country.

"Wastomug would turn traitor against his own traitor?" Pemispan asked, contemptuously.

"I do not know, O Chief," Harvie said. "I only know that he bade me ask you to meet him in council and speak of Manteo."

Pemispan sucked at the clay pipe from which curled a bluish thread of rank tobacco smoke.

"What is your thought on this, Pemec?" he asked, at last.

"I—I do not know," Dion said again, uneasily. "Lane swore he was honest in this but—but if there is a council I bid you to be careful. Lane is a man of many tricks. He says one thing and he may mean another. What I have told you is what he said to tell you—only that."

"You mean he would violate a council?" Pemispan asked. "Never have I heard of such a thing! Could a white man do that? Has an Englishman no truth in him at all?"

Dion flushed under the old Indian's demanding gaze.

"We have truth in us, O Pemispan," he replied, "as much as any people."

"Say yes or no, Pemec," Wanchese said bluntly, "to whether we should make talk with Wastomug."

"Tell us," Pemispan nodded. "You are one of us."

Dion shook his head slowly. He replied, "I ask you to make your own decision."

"Huh!" Granganimeo grunted. "We do not fear this Captain Lane, this Wastomug! Let us have this council with him, O Pemispan. Let him come to an appointed place and there we'll treat with him as he would treat with us if he caught us all unprepared."

"No," the Roanoke chief said. "No, we will not be as evil as he has been. I say this. Pemec, tell Wastomug we will be at this spot when the sun next rises out of the sea." He lifted a hand as Granganimeo began a protest. "And if you find that Wastomug plots treachery, then you will warn us so we will be ready. That is your duty as our brother. If we do not get a warning from you we will know the Captain Lane really speaks truth when he says he wants peace. That is what I say to you, Pemecolemanmeo."

"Excellent," Lane grinned, when Dion Harvie brought Pemispan's word of a parley place. "Ye did well, Harvie, and now we can settle this war once and for all. Stafford, I bid ye come with me to my headquarters."

He hurried away, gesticulating with his blunt hands, bobbing his helmeted head as he talked to his aide. Dion looked after the governor and Stafford and then turned away, his heart sickened. Lane was too obviously gleeful, too open in licking his lips over what was to happen on the morrow. Lane planned a lot more than a parley with the Roanokes; he had another scheme up his sleeve and he had intended to use him, Dion Harvie, as the bellwether to lead the Indians into disaster.

Well, by God, he would not do this! Pemispan had been wise enough to prepare for this trickery; he had bade Pemecolemanmeo to bring him word of a trap and, call him turncoat though they would, he would give that warning! Walt would not want him to do otherwise than warn the Roanokes—Raleigh would approve heartily of his going back to the mainland and spoiling Lane's plan. In a few days, Drake would arrive and even if Lane did rave and curse over his failure, his authority as governor would soon be over. Now to warn the Roanokes!

He started for the skiff he had just used. He had covered half the distance to the boats when there was the scuff of sand behind him and a hand on his shoulder.

"Master Harvie," said Captain George Stafford, "I'll take your sword, by y'r leave. On Captain Lane's orders you're under arrest."

Dion whirled. Behind Stafford was a squad of Lane's soldiers in breastplates and helmets, carrying pikes.

"Now what's this?" Harvie cried. "Under arrest—and I've just finished an important mission for the captain? Is the man mad?"

Stafford shook his head, a thin, wry smile on his lips.

"Not so mad," he said, "that when he saw you heading for the boats he didn't suspect you might be planning to—er—disarrange things, Master Harvie. No, he bade me tell you that for your own safety 'tis best you be guarded in your house until—until tomorrow at noon when this parley will be finished."

"Now, by the Book!" Harvie raged. "This is a wondrous thing, treating me like a felon after I've carried out his orders to the minute! Take me to him, Stafford, and I'll tell him what that polecat needs to be told! I'll—"

"Ye'll come with us to your house, Master Harvie," Stafford said, sharply. "That's Governor Lane's order and he must be obeyed."

"You—you know what he plans to do tomorrow?" Harvie asked.

"Yes, I know," Stafford said impassively. "And I will follow my orders, just as you must now."

"But—but, I'll give my oath not to leave the island," young Harvie said desperately.

"Not good enough, I fear," Stafford replied. "Captain Lane thinks you could find some means to get word to the Indians unless you were kept in your house. Of course we know that's impossible—eh, Master Harvie?—but we must abide by his curious safeguards."

And there, Dion groaned silently, *goes the chance to have Rycko carry the word to Wanchese!*

Dragging himself along on leaden feet, Dion permitted himself to be led to the house he shared with John White and the other three men. That Lane was determined there would be no leaks to the Roanokes was proved when he ordered the four men who lived with Harvie to move to another house for the night; Dion was a lone prisoner in his home, guarded by two of Lane's pikemen.

He spent the night pacing the floor of the downstairs common room, listening to the bustle and stir of the fort, the clank of armor, the tramp of marching feet, the preparations for the morrow. He hoped desperately that there were still some Roanokes hidden on the island to be warned by the commotion but the hope lacked conviction; Pemispan had said he would parley with Lane honestly and Dion had learned enough about Roanoke principles to be fairly certain that the chief's stand would ban pre-parley spying.

The pale light of the false dawn found Fort Raleigh almost

deserted. Dion, peering out a window, saw that most of the soldiers were gone, doubtless shipped over to the mainland under cover of darkness. His eyes bitter, he watched Lane, White, Stafford and three others board a barge to be rowed to the meeting place. He growled a savage curse when he saw Ralph Lane pause just before getting aboard and raise a hand in a mocking salute to the house where Harvie was held prisoner. The gleam of the captain's teeth shone in the uncertain light and Dion heard, or thought he heard, Lane's derisive laugh.

"Oh, the whoreson!" Harvie rasped. "The scum! By all the gods, Walt will hear about this—aye, and Drake, too, for they say he's no heartless butcher in his dealings with the natives. If I could but break free of this place I'd—I'd—"

He would what? There was one half-finished smallboat left on shore when Lane's barge had gone; could he somehow float that to the mainland to warn Pemispan? There was the watch tower that could be seen from the spot where the council was to be held but how could he stretch his lungs in a shout loud enough to be heard a half a dozen miles away? How could he signal Wanchese and the others to be aware?

Time hurtled by and still there was no answer, until—

The cannon at the fort! If he could escape his makeshift prison, he might make his way to the fort and set off a gun—the boom would carry to the mainland—Pemispan would know something had gone wrong—perhaps Lane would turn back, thinking the cannon signalled a Spanish attack or Grenville's arrival at last! It might work—if he could get free.

He went to a front window and studied the sentry who leaned on his pikestaff outside. The man was half asleep on his feet, bowed by the weariness of near-starvation; he would not be hard to overpower. The other guard was out of sight if he was still posted at the house. He would have to depend on the second sentry's being as drowsy as the man at the front door. If he wasn't and if Lane had given orders to cut him down if he tried to escape—and he was sure Lane had—well, he would have at least tried to warn Wanchese away from the deadfall he had helped build.

He inched open the door, holding his breath lest the hinges

squeal a warning. There was one squeak and his heart froze but the sentry dozed on. Another inch, another—Harvie squirmed through the opening and leaped on the soldier.

The sentry squawked one hoarse cry before Harvie's hand clamped over his mouth. The pike went spinning as Dion wrenched it out of the guard's hand. The helmet was jammed down over the struggling man's eyes, his arms flailed the air wildly. He exploded a loud *"oof!"* as Harvie wrestled him off his feet and slammed him to the ground, then jumped on him.

"God's sake," the soldier gasped, "don't deal so rough wi' me, sir! I done nothin' to you, sir, to have ye kill me!"

"Quiet!" Harvie hissed. "Keep still or I'll slit y'r gullet!"

"God's sake, I—"

"Quiet, I tell ye! Or do ye want to die?"

"Not me, sir! Not Henry Lorton! I but stood the guard Cap'n Stafford posted me on, no more. I didn't harm ye, Master Harvie—ye mind I didn't! Picked me, Cap'n Stafford did, where there's a dozen men that had more sleep than me and more to eat, too. He has it in f'r me, he does, and I get all the nasty work whilst the others sail over to the mainland, they do, to fill their bellies and bounce the Indian wenches. I tell ye, Master Harvie—"

"Tell me nothing, fool! You're the only sentry?"

"Oh aye. There was one other, Peter Hollingsworth, but the hound slipped away, I trow, to catch a nap somewhere, soon as Cap'n Lane was out of sight."

"And who's at the fort?" Dion demanded.

"Three or four cannoneers, no more. And they're all on the watch tower, every one, lookin' at what's goin' on on the mainland, I'll be bound. I don't even have the fun of that, I don't, 'cause Cap'n Stafford has it in f'r me and I—"

"Stay here," Dion said grimly, "and ye'll not be hurt. Give the alarm and I'll carve you up like a goose. You understand?"

"Oh, aye, sir. Ye'll not hear a peep out of me, Master Harvie. I'll tell 'em ye must've climbed the chimney or summat to get away. Aye, that's what I'll say. Go to it, Master Harvie, with whatever ye want to do—ye'll get no objection from me, I swear."

Dion hesitated, then turned and ran for the fort. There was no outcry raised behind him; Henry Lorton was as good as his word. He cast a glance at the watch tower that spiked the sky above the fort and saw what Lorton had told him was true—the tower's platform was crowded with men. No sentry guarded the gate.

He scurried down the narrow passageway leading into the ramparted square, scrambled up a ladder to the gun platform. A smoldering brazier provided him with a glowing linstock and he headed for the fuse of the nearest cannon, a small saker but it would have to do.

"Hi!" yelled a frantic voice from the tower. "You there! Hold!"

"Devil take you!" Harvie shouted. He pressed the match against the fuse, watched the taper spark and splutter, jumped aside as the little brass gun thumped, jarring back a foot on its heavy stand. Through the black smoke that vomited from the muzzle, Dion could see the small ball arch out and down to hit the empty waters of the Sound with a splash.

There was the rattle of feet on the watch tower ladder, a chorus of shouts, and the guard was upon him, led by a serjeant. Dion vaguely recalled the man's name as Thomas, a gloomy, stringy fellow with a long nose and a tremendous adam's apple.

"So 'tis you, Master Harvie," the serjeant panted. "Now, why did'st shoot off the saker, for God's sake? There's naught going on out there—all the action is on the mainland, that way!"

"I mean to warn the Roanokes," Harvie explained defiantly. "That gun will scare them off from Lane's trap. Ah, you can tell him I spoiled his scheme—I'll face the worst he—"

"But Master Harvie," Thomas broke in, "the thing's been done. The saker, even if 'twas heard, couldn't warn the savages."

"Been done?" Dion asked. "I was too late?"

"Oh aye," the serjeant nodded. "Cap'n Lane and the others are on their way back here already. Oh, 'twas a neat ambush, I vow!"

"Pemispan—did he—"

"He caught it in the first volley," Thomas enthused. "Y'see, Cap'n Lane moved his arquebusiers and pikemen to the mainland durin' the night and hid 'em. When the dirty savages came out of the forest to meet the governor and his party, all unsuspectin', why, the cap'n lifted his blade and—bango!—the Indians went down in a heap. 'Twas a fine sight, I tell ye! You can see what we left on that shore if ye'll climb to the tower and look."

Slowly, the bile of loathing for all civilized white men, hatred for himself, choking him, Dion Harvie climbed the rickety tower and stared toward the mainland.

The plume-crowned body of Pemispan lay sprawled on the sand and around him were scattered the riddled corpses of four other Roanokes. They lay face-down and Dion at that distance could not tell which one must be Granganimeo, which one his tribal brother, Wanchese. It was enough to know that he had helped lure them to their death, enough to know that his honor had been blackened by the perfidy of Captain Ralph Lane.

He was swallowing his nausea when a hoarse shout sounded behind him.

"There, beyond the banks—sail—*sail!*"

He turned to look toward the sea. Yes, there they were, the twenty-three ships of Sir Francis Drake's fleet, arrived a few minutes too late to save the lives of the Roanokes who had trusted the white men enough to meet them on the promise of a peaceful parley.

Part 5

1

IT WAS suffocatingly hot that July twenty-seventh, 1586, when Sir Francis Drake's flagship, the six hundred ton *Bonaventure,* dropped anchor in Plymouth harbor and Drake summoned Dion Harvie to his cabin.

The stubby, barrel-chested, bowlegged, flame-bearded Drake was in a touchy mood. He hated heat and had good reason to; he had been caught more than once in the Southern Sea doldrums and had watched his provisions rot, his water casks run dry, his men sicken and die while his sails hung limply under the brazen sky. Moreover, because he refused to bow to the weather by wearing something more comfortable than his stifling corselet, his wide ruff, his padded breeches and long boots, even in the hottest season, he was beset by a sweaty, itching torment that made him quick to flare up in anger. Drake's officers and men walked lightly when the temperatures were high; they almost tiptoed when they brought Dion to the spacious, tapestry-hung cabin of the sea rover, Spanish harrier, pirate made honest admiral by the Queen's cynical "writs of reprisal," Sir Francis Drake.

The man the Spaniards feared and hated as "El Draque" sat in a carved chair, scowling at the open window through which no breeze stirred, his fingers drumming impatiently on the table that had been set before him. As Dion entered the cabin, Drake cast him one sharp, unfriendly glance and then returned his blue eyes to a study of the window.

Dion waited, shifting from one foot to the other. It was a

relief to be out of the *Bonaventure's* stifling hold at last (and when would there be an end to his languishing in ships' holds?) but the frown on Sir Francis' round, short-bearded face did not promise much in the way of respite from the trials that seemed to trail Dion Harvie.

"Sit down, sir," Drake said with a brief wave of his hand. "There are certain things we must get straight, Master Harvie, before I know which way to move in your case."

"Thank you," Dion said and crossed the cabin to a bench opposite Drake's table. He knew he cut a shabby picture in comparison with the splendor that was the Admiral's. His newly-grown beard was a wild furze, his hair was long and ragged and the months on Roanoke Island had not been kind to his clothes. He had not been one of the "Virginians" whose wardrobes had been replenished by the sea chests of Drake's fleet; in fact, none of the succor Drake had handed out to Ralph Lane's little band had been given Dion beyond enough food to fill out his big frame and a pallet in the *Bonaventure's* forecastle among the hard-bitten seamen who bunked there. . . .

Dion Harvie, who had fled England to escape the Queen's wrath was coming back as a renegade mutineer. He had been spared an offhanded yardarm hanging only because Francis Drake was suspicious of some of Ralph Lane's accusations and, furthermore, because *El Draque* was notoriously careful to get all the facts before he ordered a man hanged. In this, the red-whiskered adventurer was unique among the Queen's admirals.

There were, Dion reflected, some things that might temper Drake's anger now. Granted that the heat and the admiral's discomfort worked against his case, it was still true that Drake's fleet was heavily laden with treasure taken at Cartagena and other Spanish strongholds in the West Indies before the ships had rounded up to Trinity Inlet. It was also true that the fleet had made the eastward crossing from Hatorask to Plymouth in the almost unbelievably fast time of thirty-eight days with no help from the Trade Winds. On the other side of the ledger, though, there were—

"And first, Master Harvie," Drake said to break in on Dion's thoughts, "there is this charge that you tried to kill Captain Lane. The charge, I might say, is endorsed by a dozen gentlemen who witnessed the outrage."

"I called Lane out," Dion admitted proudly. "I bade him draw so I could carve up his liver to throw to the crabs."

"Um—yes," Drake said heavily, his eyebrows lowered. "You know, of course, that this was outright mutiny."

"Nay, Sir Francis," Harvie protested. "By y'r leave I'll call it an attempt to deal justice to a skunk who tricked me into calling my friends to a cowardly ambush."

"Your friends? You mean the Roanokes?"

"Yes," Dion nodded, "and good friends, though they were savages. Lane dealt basely with them from the start, sir, and when they showed generous friendship to us they were first robbed of their stores, then their villages were burned and, finally, Pemispan, their chief, and his aides were called to a peace parley and shot down without a chance."

Drake leaned back in his chair and tented his fingers under the red beard.

"Captain Lane," he said, "tells me the savages waged fierce war on him in spite of all his efforts to make friends with them."

"Hah!" Harvie snorted. "And did John White say the same, may I ask?"

"Master White," Drake said slowly, "supports you in this affair, as you know. But—well, Captain Lane *was* governor of your settlement, Master Harvie; 'twas your duty to follow his orders, odious though they might be. Many a time I've ordered men to duty that almost surely spelled their death and never did one of them blink an eye at it."

"But did you once order one to trap his good friends in ambush? I know ye didn't, Sir Francis! It's not empty flattery, sir, when I say you're honored and loved by all your men because you've been as honest with your foes as ye've been with your crews—no treachery can be found in anything ye've ever done."

Drake brushed at his moustache with a knuckle and looked up at the window again. Dion followed his eyes and repressed an exclamation of delight; the edge of the tapestry by the opening was stirring faintly—thank God a cooling breeze was blowing up!

"Well then," the thickset admiral said as he turned his blue eyes back to Dion, "let's say that Captain Lane dealt unwisely with the savages. White says so and there are others, but that doesn't change the fact that you drew your sword on your commander. Your place, Master Harvie, was to hold your peace till you could lodge a proper complaint with Sir Walter Raleigh or Sir Richard Grenville."

"My rage at seeing the murdered bodies of my friends," Harvie explained in a low voice, "forbade me holding my peace, sir. I felt I'd be betraying their friendship if I didn't at least try to spike the villain."

Drake pushed back his chair and rose. Clasping his hands behind his back, he began pacing up and down behind the table.

"You put me in a bad position," he complained. "If you'd but said you were crazed by all your hardships on Roanoke Island—if you'd excused your headstrong action by saying the sun had touched your wits or that you'd been bewitched by some savage wizard, you'd furnish me with an excuse to pardon you. But did you? No, you raved and cursed and struggled to get at Lane, swearing you'd carve him up at your first chance—and so forced me to make you a prisoner aboard my vessel. Even if the other colonists had not seen fit to sail with us as they did, I'd still have brought you back to England to meet whatever fate awaits you here."

He shook his head, wiped the back of his hand across his sweaty forehead.

"And that can't be too pretty," he added, "from what I've been told. Her Majesty—"

"Her Majesty was angered because I pinked her favorite, Captain Guy Groven," Harvie supplied. "Dost know him, Sir Francis?"

"Er—I've met him," Drake said. "Indeed, who couldn't help but meet the hound—but enough of Groven! It still stands that Her Majesty has put a price on y'r head. Raleigh saw fit to befriend you, and at great risk to him, but I have no claims on me to do the same."

"Except," Dion said boldly, "that my father is Sir Clement Harvie, Lord Avronbeck, who has befriended many a gentleman in his day."

It was a waterline shot, this reference to Lord Avronbeck with the unspoken reminder that Sir Clement had always been friendly to Drake while other noblemen still sneered at him as an upstart with a home-made coat of arms. It was a jog to Drake's memory that recalled the fact that Lord Avronbeck had helped him over thin ice in a touchy situation with the Queen that might have cut short the admiral's career before it had fairly begun. That had been back in the days when the man who was to become Elizabeth's top naval hero had been just a few years beyond the status of a penniless son of a penniless refugee from Bloody Mary. It was a shot Harvie would have preferred not to fire but in this crisis all his guns had to be brought to bear.

Drake had stopped his bandy-legged pacing and was nodding reflectively when Dion dared to look at him again. The fiery-bearded admiral was nothing if not grateful to the men who had helped him in his struggle to the top and in this again he was unique in Elizabethan England.

"Aye, Sir Clement's son deserves a hand from me, I trow," Drake murmured, "and God knows I owe Groven nothing, nor Lane, for that matter. The way the governor—" He broke off short and looked up at the window where the tapestry was waving deliciously now.

"An end to this damned heat!" Drake exclaimed. "And none too soon, else I'd be a puddle of sweat on the deck here." He turned his piercing eyes back to Harvie. "I'll promise you this, then, Dion Harvie. I'll get word to Raleigh in London before Lane reaches him and I'll be bound by what Sir Walter counsels me. Of course, when Lane spreads his story that young Master Harvie, wanted by the Queen, is back in England, all Her Majesty's greyhounds will be after you—and barking at those who might have sheltered you, I know. Ah well—time enough to deal with that when it comes—perchance you might overpower y'r guard and escape again, for aught I know."

"Aye, Sir Francis," Dion nodded, "and I thank you."

The stubby admiral waved a hand.

"No thanks yet, Master Harvie," he said. "Mayhap Raleigh's temper has changed in this past year and he'll bid me hand you over to the hangman or the axe. And I've no time to spend pleading your case, sir, Avronbeck's son though you may be. With all the hullabaloo there'll be over Lane's desertion of Virginia, on top of Burghley's cries at my actions against the Spaniards, I'll be up to my ears in debates, accusations, bickering and slander, you'll see. My enemies at court might turn pale at the sight of surf along the shore but they all can use their tongues far better than I ever could hope to. So now, back to the fo'scle, sir, and—but wait. I guess ye've had enough of that hole for a time, eh? Instead, ye'll use Jenkins' cabin—he's gone ashore to see his people—and have the ship's storekeeper give ye some clothes to take the place of those rags."

In the cabin of Drake's third officer, William Jenkins, and clad in a respectable outfit of plum-colored galligaskins, hose and doublet, his ragged beard trimmed to a clipped point, Dion Harvie passed the long hours of waiting by laboriously writing his own report of the Roanoke Island affair. Because he had neglected his writing since the day he had left Balliol College, he sweated gallons over the task, cursed his quill for not finding words, blotted his pages disgracefully, resorted to an eerie spelling which outraged even the haphazard rhetoric of the day.

But he got it all down, every bit of it. He told of the "stolen cup" incident at Pasquiwoc, the mismanagement of Fort Raleigh, the rifling of the Indians' storehouses and their retaliation, the ambush of Pemispan and, finally, the abandonment of the Colony of Virginia in the face of all Sir Francis Drake's efforts to keep the outpost manned.

Dion had a flair for description, a talent for narration, that overcame even its miserably untidy presentation and when Sir Walter Raleigh read his report, days later, it was as though the man who had spent his fortune to set up the Virginia colony had been there to see and hear what happened. . . .

2

Captain Ralph Lane had returned to Fort Raleigh with all the lordly air of one great conqueror prepared to meet another, Drake.

"Well," Dion heard him bellow when the news of Drake's arrival was yelled to his barge nearing the shore of Roanoke Island, " 'tis good he's come but we do not really need him now—I've crushed the savage dogs! Stafford, did ye ever see a neater plan? White, what do ye think now of my worth at dealing with enemies, eh?"

Neither John White nor Captain Stafford replied. Harvie saw that both men, painter and soldier, wore faces that screamed their disgust at the treachery on the beach at Dasamonquepeuc. Ralph Lane was oblivious of their bleak silence.

"Now, when we've been provisioned by Sir Francis," he went on in a voice that carried over the water to where Harvie waited, "We'll carry on expeditions 'gainst the Secotans and the Pasquiwocs and the others. That is, we'll do that if those other tribes can be found—all the Indian swine probably will take to their heels when they hear what happened to Pemispan."

Beyond Lane's returning flotilla, Dion Harvie could see three pinnaces from Drake's fleet clearing Trinity Inlet and bearing down on Roanoke Island. If he gave Lane what was due him, then, it must be done before Drake interfered. Wanchese must be avenged, the wrong dealt Pemispan paid for, and now. He hefted his rapier, taken from him when he was arrested and retrieved from the armory in the confusion, and edged closer to the place where Lane would land.

The bull-voiced governor was the first to leap from the leading barge and wade ashore, looking back over his shoulder at the approach of Drake's pinnaces.

"And I hope," he roared in a voice that had all its old bluster, "that Sir Francis brings plenty of good food for a feast of welcome. God knows we've little to offer him from our stores except stinking fish."

"Mayhap," Dion Harvie said quietly, "we can serve Sir Francis a double portion of stinking lies and perfidy, Captain Lane. For God knows, too, we have enough of that in you to feed an army."

Lane whirled, his hand going to the hilt of his heavy sword, and then fell back a pace.

"What's this?" he roared. "Why are you free, Harvie, when I gave orders—"

"I broke free," Dion cut in, "so I could see your triumph from the watch tower. You must be a proud man, truly!"

"Now hold, you puppy! I'd have ye know—"

"Draw, damn you!" Dion grated. "Draw y'r blade and see if ye're so brave 'gainst a man who's not been tricked by y'r black heart!"

Lane's face went white with fury as his hand swept back to the sword's hilt. Dion's rapier came up and he began a lunge when a pair of arms encircled him, pinioning him from behind.

"Hold, hold!" John White panted. "Hold, Captain Lane! For God's sake, let's not have a brawl here now, with the relief we've been praying for so long right at hand! Give over, Dion—hold y'r blade, Lane!"

"Let me loose, damn you!" Dion cried, struggling. "Let me at that whoreson who killed my friends! I'll avenge Wanchese and—"

"Hold, Dion!" White yelled again. "Stafford, give me a hand, for God's sake!" Lane's aide fastened himself to Harvie's sword arm and clung there.

"Mutiny!" Lane roared. "Black mutiny, by God's teeth! I knew ye'd overstep y'r bounds one day, Harvie, and now it's come! I'll have ye hanged f'r this and now! Serjeant—fling a noose over—"

"What's this?" asked a cold, hard voice from the shore. The men on the beach turned to see Sir Francis Drake, impressive in high doeskin boots, slashed and diapered yellow satin breeches, gleaming corselet and burnished helmet, step out of a smallboat and stalk toward them.

"What's this I find?" the red-bearded admiral asked gravely. "The word I got was that a group of honest Englishmen were in need of help—I changed my course to come here to give aid —and I find a brawl going on, instead of a welcome. What does this mean?

Lane rammed his sword back into its sheath and made an attempt to bow.

"Sir Francis," he said, "I bid ye welcome now and most heartily. It's to our shame that one of our number, a renegade who'd—"

"A pox on your foul mouth!" Dion shouted. "Call me a renegade, would you, when you're the bastard—"

"Silence!" Drake barked. His eyes flamed briefly into the struggling Harvie's and turned back to Lane.

"You, I take it," he said in a clipped voice, "are Captain Lane, the governor of this place?"

"Aye, Sir Francis," the captain said. "Governor of Virginia by Sir Walter Raleigh's commission and bound to deal with this mutineer out of hand. I'd not spoil y'r welcome with a hanging but this scurvy knave must be strung up instanter for the common good."

"Not so, Sir Francis," John White protested. "This lad's well meant, sir, though headstrong, as you see. He has a grievance, sir, that deserves reckoning—aye, Captain Lane has dealt harshly with him from the first and has just shot down young Harvie's friend, Chief Pemispan."

"And Wanchese!" Dion cried. "My brother in the tribe and the one—"

"Quiet, Dion," White said. "Wanchese was not killed. He and two others escaped, though Granganimeo was slain."

Dion slackened his struggle abruptly. He could never condone Pemispan's murder but the news that Wanchese had escaped was a relief that tempered his rage. He looked up to see Drake's eyes resting on him again. The wide-chested, bowlegged sea rover was regarding him speculatively, fingering the tip of his short beard.

"You mean," he asked finally, "you'd draw your blade against a countryman in behalf of a savage? God's right hand, methinks Captain Lane has a right to call you renegade, young sir."

"Call me that, then," Dion rapped back defiantly. "If it's to be a renegade to find honesty in a Roanoke friend where there's been nothing but vile treachery in Lane, then I'm one!"

"He doesn't mean that, sir," White said desperately. "He's all unstrung—and I confess I'm not too easy myself at the way Pemispan was dealt with by Captain Lane's scheming."

"Another whining milksop who'd have us buss the Indians' buttocks," Lane sneered. "Oh yes, I've known he was against me for these many months." He turned to the long-nosed serjeant, Thomas. "Fetch the noose," he said, "so we can deal with this traitor now."

Sir Francis Drake held up a gloved hand.

"A moment," he said. "I bid ye realize, Captain, that I'm in command here, as an admiral in the Queen's service."

"And I am governor of this place," Lane returned, caustically, "and as such give the orders here."

The men behind Drake, the officers and seamen who had accompanied the admiral aboard the two pinnaces, gasped. They knew, as Lane was to discover, that Sir Francis Drake was never one to have his authority questioned, even by Elizabeth's right-hand councilors, much less by a blustering army man.

"You think so?" Drake asked after a choked pause. "You think your tiffety-taffety commission as governor of this hole in the sand gives you rank over me?" Drake's neck was swelling now, and his eyes bulged. "Well, let me set you right on that, by God! I came a hundred leagues off my course when word reached me by the natives that you were in trouble here—'twas said that if I didn't come with help you'd all perish."

"Pooh," Lane snorted. "I have the Indians cowed and—"

"Silence! I say I came to your rescue and from the looks of you 'twas not too soon. So if by no other right than salvage I claim authority over you. If you'd dispute my claim, why then we'd best put it to Her Majesty and let her rule on it!"

Lane's bravado vanished as he swept a low bow.

"By no means, Sir Francis," he said. "By no means! Nay, I'm more than content to yield any poor authority I hold to Her Majesty's greatest admiral."

"Hmph," Drake grunted. "My thanks for y'r compliment.

And so I'll decide on what's to be done with this cockerel, this Harvie."

"Beyond his mutiny, Sir Francis," Lane explained, "he's wanted by the Queen for some dastardly crime in England. Aye, Sir Richard Grenville bade me keep close watch over this fine young cutthroat so he might be handed over to the Queen when the time was ripe."

"And so ye'd string him up?" Drake asked curtly. "Ye intended to hand over his skeleton to Her Majesty, perhaps?"

"No, but I—"

"Enough," Drake said bluntly. "He's in my keeping now." His eyes moved back to Harvie. "I'll take your pledge, young sir, that ye'll behave if you're let loose."

"And I can't give you that, Sir Francis," Dion Harvie replied. "No, I'd be tempted to slice that bastard's gullet every time he got within sword's reach of me."

Drake's scowl was thunderous. "So then, by Christ, ye'll go into chains, Sir Bravo!" he whipcracked. He turned to his second-in-command, a slender young man Dion later came to know was Captain Christopher Carleill, Lord Walsingham's stepson and Walsingham's son-in-law, as well. "Take this man under guard, Captain Carleill," the red-bearded admiral said, "and hold him till I consider what should be done with him."

Dion was marched to a skiff that was rowed out to a pinnace that, late in the evening, sailed back to the big *Bonaventure* with Drake aboard. It was on the trip out through Trinity Inlet to the fleet lying offshore that Harvie overheard Drake's complaints to Carleill about Ralph Lane's behavior.

"God's sake, Chris," the stubby sea rover grumbled, "the man's all if's and but's. You heard my offer to him and the way he received it—I said I'd give them a stout vessel, the bark *Francis,* and smallboats, with a most excellent master and crew, together with enough supplies to stand them a full month's stay, to wait for Grenville. And how did he take that? Though with one breath he claims he has the savages all cowed, in the next he says he doesn't dare wait here another month for Grenville for fear the people of that chief he slew—what was his name?—Pemispan, will massacre them all."

"I think," said Carleill quietly, "our Lane is hot to go back to England and still afraid that when he gets there he'll have to dance to some lively music."

"I wish they'd stay on their island," Drake said, "at least until Grenville returns with some gutsome settlers. 'Twould be a sin to abandon the settlement after Raleigh's put so much into it—'twould annoy Gloriana, too, to have the place that was named for her deserted after only a year."

"And what about Sir Richard?" Harvie heard Carleill ask. "Why hasn't he relieved the colony as Lane said he promised?"

"Ah, you know Grenville," Drake snorted. "The man is always deep in one intrigue or the other—he eats and sleeps plans to make his name the greatest in the world and forgets to take care of the things at hand. I don't doubt that he's forgot there was a pressing need for supplying Virginia. No, in my dealings with Dick I've heard him cry a thousand times: 'I was delayed!' "

"And what do you propose to do with Lane and the others?" the younger man asked.

"Why, try to coax them to stay here another month, then use the ship I'll furnish them to sail home if they will," Drake said. "That John White is all for staying—I think he has his eye on Lane's office and expects Raleigh's commission as governor when Grenville returns. We can only try to convince them they'd serve the Queen best by staying here—but I confess I haven't any high hopes of talking them into it."

He turned from his conversation with Carleill to speak to Harvie.

"And you, Master Harvie," he called, "doubtless would be overjoyed to stay here with your savages?"

"The question is, Sir Francis," Dion replied coolly, "just which man you call savage, the honest Roanoke or the treacherous Englishman."

"Pah!" Drake spat, his face darkening. "What manner of Englishman are you to be such a turncoat?"

"A worthy Englishman, I hope," Dion retorted. "An Englishman who was taught to try to bring honor to his Queen by what he did, not stain England's name by foul dealings. At least that was what my father taught me."

"Well—hmph—Lord Avronbeck's a good man, a lusty friend of mine," Drake said. "But I've heard a bit about you, Master Dion, and know you're wanted by the Queen. So, as it stands—ah, damn all, why must I have these problems to vex me, on top of everything else? No, into chains you go, Harvie or no Harvie, when we reach my flagship."

It had not been chains for Dion, after all. By Drake's relenting order he was kept free of shackles but he was placed under guard in the noisome forecastle which was almost as bad. While Drake conferred with Lane, trying to convince the Virginia governor that his duty was to stay at Fort Raleigh as long as possible and while Lane balked and hedged and offered arguments against the idea, Dion Harvie stewed and sulked in the dark, smelly confines of the idly swaying vessel. He was there on the thirteenth of June when a raging storm struck the coast.

The lurching of the *Bonaventure,* the scramble of feet on the decks above, the hoarse cry of orders and the rattle of lines in their blocks told Dion that this was no ordinary blow. The six hundred ton warship wallowed heavily in the tremendous seas, swinging close to her beam's end a dozen times before Drake and his crew took the *Bonaventure* out to sea, away from the dangerous inshore waters.

Harvie was not allowed above decks that day nor the next, when the storm subsided and Drake rounded up his scattered fleet and returned his ships to the roads off Trinity Inlet. He was above, gulping a few grateful lungfuls of fresh air under the eye of his guard when a grim-faced Drake, Carleill and half a dozen other officers boarded the flagship and went to the poopdeck for a council. It was less than two hours later when barges and skiffs from Roanoke Island began arriving with Lane, White, Arundell, Stafford—all the gentlemen, craftsmen and soldiers who had been at Fort Raleigh. And with them was the Roanoke, Manteo.

"Oh aye," chuckled Dion's guard, a one-eyed sailor known as

Peeper, "they come arunnin' once they saw how another storm might leave 'em without no ships to get home in. Y'see, the *Francis,* what the admiral was goin' to let 'em have, was swept away in the storm and them fine heroes be'ant takin' no more chance on another blow, even though the admiral offered 'em another vessel, bigger than the *Francis.*"

So, on June nineteenth, 1586, Drake's flagship fluttered "weigh anchor" pennants from her masthead and the fleet moved out of Port Ferdinando. Behind them, the Englishmen left a deserted Fort Raleigh, where Ralph Lane had said he would build "a city the likes of which has ne'er been seen in this New World."

3

It is a hundred and eighty miles, as the crow flies, from London to Plymouth and Sir Walter Raleigh made the journey in three days and nights and dared slip away from court without Elizabeth's permission to do it.

He reached the seaport in the midst of a windy downpour and, soaked to the skin and reeling with weariness, had himself rowed out to the *Bonaventure* a scant hour before Drake's flagship and the vessels of his fleet which carried Spanish treasure moved out of Plymouth harbor and set sail for the Thames and London. Once aboard, Raleigh's first request of Drake was that Dion Harvie be summoned to the admiral's cabin.

"And if ye'd been half a day later, friend Walt," Dion heard Sir Francis tell Raleigh as he entered the luxurious cabin, "I couldn't have waited for you. I've been whistling up this wind for what seems a century and now it's here it's ideal for my purpose, to run up to London close to our coast and as far as possible from any of Philip's carracks that might be—but here's your lad, Walt, and I'll be leaving you two to—"

"No, please stay, Sir Francis," Raleigh insisted. He laboriously heaved himself out of the chair he was slumped in and made his way to Dion to embrace the younger, taller man.

"Ah, Dion, Dion," he said, "it's good to see you! You've lost the fuzz-faced boy somewhere in Virginia and found the bearded man, I trow."

"And nearly lost him too," Dion grinned. "I'd be a bundle of bones rattling at the end of a rope if it hadn't been for Sir Francis's interference. That bastard Lane—but how are my family, Walt, my father and my mother, my sisters?"

"We'll speak of them later, by y'r leave," Raleigh said. He staggered with a lift of the deck and put out a hand to steady himself.

"Sit down, sit down!" Drake commanded. "God's sake, ye're worn to the bone, Walt! Page—*page!* Where's that fiendish boy? Ah, there you are! Food and drink for Sir Walter, and quick!" The young page scuttled out of the door as Dion lent an arm to Raleigh to help him back to his chair. The haggard, mud-splattered knight leaned back and exhaled gustily.

"I'm getting old," he grimaced. "There was a time when a ride like that would have been nothing and now—but Dion, before all else, I want you to tell me what was the trouble in Virginia."

"And what wasn't?" Dion asked sourly. "I have a full report I've scribbled out in my cabin. I'll get it and—"

"I'll send for it," Drake broke in. "Page!" A second boy popped into the cabin, then popped out again at the admiral's order to fetch Harvie's papers.

"And whilst we wait," Dion said, "let me ask what happened to Sir Richard? Why didn't he come back with the supplies he promised to bring?"

"Ah, Dick," Raleigh sighed. "Though he's my cousin, I must say he's uncommon hard to tear loose from new involvements to take care of the old ones. For weeks I kept at him to stock his ships and sail and for weeks Dick found excuses to delay. Then the money ran out and I had to arrange new loans and—but he finally sailed and time enough ago to have reached Virginia two months since unless he's gone off chasing Spanish treasure ships, as he most likely has. And I take it my own relief ship I sent out after Dick's fleet sailed didn't reach you before you left with Sir Francis?"

"You sent your own vessel?" Harvie asked.

"Aye," Raleigh said wryly, "and it took my last groat to outfit her, I'll be bound. But knowing my cousin, I couldn't rest easy until I'd sent at least one bark to Virginia that I knew would go straight there instead of hoicking all over the Spanish Main in search of plate ships."

"But why," Drake asked, "did you entrust the relief of your colony to Sir Richard? I don't mean to speak against him but you must admit he's—er—forgetful of urgencies at times."

"Because," Raleigh explained, "Dick came to my rescue with money I needed—he's in this venture pounds and pence." He sighed again. "If Her Majesty would loose the pursestrings just once to take this whole affair out of the hands of investors and speculators I'd be a happy man."

The page with the tray of food and wine arrived simultaneously with the boy carrying Dion's notes. Raleigh, with a murmured apology, fell upon the meal ravenously, eyeing the blot-sprinkled top page of Harvie's report as he ate.

"God's little finger," he laughed, after he swallowed, "I'll need an interpreter for this, Dion—though I thank you for it. Cans't tell me in a few words what it says? Or better yet, both of you explain why Lane abandoned Virginia."

Drake, with Dion offering comments, told Raleigh of his efforts to have the colonists stay on Roanoke Island and of Lane's reluctance to risk it.

"I don't know the man well enough to damn him, Walt," the red-bearded admiral ended, "but to me he seemed a poor choice for governor of your colony, all full of his own importance and yet quick to knuckle under when his authority was challenged."

"And a mean, treacherous hound," Dion said. "I tell you, Walt, he's to blame for all our troubles at Fort Raleigh. The Roanokes were more than kind to us—oh yes, I'm called a renegade for my stand!—and Lane repaid them with the worst villainy."

"Now Dion," Raleigh protested, "you wouldn't have me side

with the savages against an English soldier, no matter how faulty the Englishman, would you?"

Harvie started to speak, gulped and fell silent. He stared at the man who had been his friend for so many years, his protector against the Queen's hangman, the man who had been closer to him than any other except his own father. Raleigh was the finest example of what Dion thought an English gentleman should be and yet he, too, had no place in his whole thinking for a conception of an Indian as anything but some kind of high-grade animal.

It was a despairing thought. It meant that he, Dion, could not find a single Englishman to stand beside him in this strange new way of thinking he had developed at Roanoke Island, this philosophy that maintained that although another man might have a darker skin and worship different gods he still could possess qualities which would make these things mere differences, not inferiorities.

He must be a true renegade then. He considered Wanchese as a much better man than Ralph Lane. He had thrown aside all the armor of family and national pride that had been fitted to him since birth to place himself, naked and unarmed, against the ranks of civilized society. And this he had done with reckless disregard of the fact that he would find no allies in his forlorn cause.

"But of Captain Lane," Raleigh was saying, "I agree he made a poor showing in Virginia. He'll have no place in my new settlement, I pledge you."

"New settlement?" Drake asked. "You mean you've plans to set up another colony besides the one you started at Roanoke Island?"

Raleigh pierced a chunk of beef, dripping with rich sauce, on the point of his knife and carried it to his mouth, sluiced it down with a gulp of wine. The two other men waited until he could speak again.

"Yes," he said, "I'm minded to establish a colony further north, on the Bay of Chesapeake. From what I've heard, the country there is better suited to a settlement and they say pearls abound in those waters. My new investors demand either gold or pearls or at the very least a new trade route to the Southern Seas and some charts I've laid hands on—oh, guaranteed authentic, gentlemen!—show there's a great river flowing into the Bay of Chesapeake that has its source in the Southern Seas itself. I'm convinced that none of the rivers around Hatorask go that far and with the savages stirred up against us at Roanoke, that land seems barred to us for the time being."

"They'd not be stirred up, I vow," Dion said earnestly, "if John White were governor and he made amends to the Indians for what Lane did to them."

"Amends, Dion?" Raleigh asked with rising eyebrows. "Since when have the subjects of the Queen paid tribute to savages?"

"Not tribute, justice," Harvie argued. "God knows it's no dishonor to—ah, I waste my breath!"

"No, no, Dion," Raleigh smiled. "You know I'm always ready to hear your advices. When I've taken care of other details and rested a bit we'll have a long talk and you can tell me your views and I'll tell you mine. Meanwhile, pray forgive me whilst I go over some things with Sir Francis that must be cared for."

"Of course," Dion said, rising, "but before I leave, tell me how my family fares—my father and mother and my sisters."

Raleigh's smile faded abruptly and his eyes dropped to the plate in front of him. A chill struck at Dion's belly as he saw his friend hesitate, seek words and then force himself to meet his stare.

"Things do not go—too well, Dion," Sir Walter said in a low voice. "Misfortune's struck at Sir Clement since you left England."

"Misfortune? What kind? Why didn't you tell me instanter, Walt, instead of holding me with all this prattle about your damned colonies?"

Raleigh's face stiffened, the corners of his mouth drooped.

"Prattle? Damned colonies?" he asked. "That's what you think of—"

"Have done!" Harvie said with a fierce gesture. "Prattle or learned discourse, why waste time talking about Virginia when ye knew my father's met misfortune? What happened, for Christ's sake?"

Sir Walter pushed back his bench and sprang to his feet, his scowl black.

"Now by God's gullet," he barked, "I'll not be spoken to this way by any man, Dion Harvie! I've taken enough from you, I'll be bound—I've hid you at the risk of my career and my life, I've befriended you when nobody else in all England dared, and now you yell at me as though I were a peasant!"

"Gentlemen, gentlemen," Drake said soothingly, "let's halter our tempers, eh? Friend Walt, you must know the boy's anxious to hear about his family and you, Young Harvie, admit you spoke rudely."

"What happened to my father?" Dion blared.

"Why, naught you didn't bring to him!" Raleigh grated. "Did you think Elizabeth would twiddle her thumbs forever, letting you and yours go unpunished for what you did? Nay, you know better than that! Three months ago your father clashed with Walsingham in some matter of the Dutch War and so angered the Queen that she dragged up your crime and ended by naming the House of Avronbeck disloyal."

"Disloyal?" Dion cried. "My father and his father before him have always been the throne's most loyal supporters, as she well knows! That red-haired witch would call our house disloyal because one of her male doxies, a skunk named Groven, picked a fight with me and got himself stabbed? Why, she's—"

"Hold, Master Harvie!" Drake barked. "Hold, I say!"

Sir Walter Raleigh put out a hand as he dropped back into his chair.

"Aye, Dion," he said in a quiet voice, "for the love of God hold y'r tongue! And I beg y'r pardon for the words I used when you angered me. I should have told you about your father at once, I know, but I was anxious to hear your story of Virginia and knew you'd be all undone by what has happened to your family so I put it off."

"So tell me now!" Dion said harshly. "What did the Queen do?"

"Sir Clement was lodged in the Tower but I think he's comfortable there and in no danger of the axe—probably he'll be pardoned in time."

"You've seen him lately?"

"Nay," Raleigh said. "I've tried, and at some risk, but he's not to be visited, by the Queen's orders."

"Ah, Walt, Walt!" Dion exclaimed. "Why wasn't I caught by the Queen's men the moment my blade sliced Groven? Why didn't those men who ambushed me that night I visited my family kill me then? Or, at the start of all this, why didn't Charles wait in some dark hallway for me and deal me a knife between my ribs?"

He turned as he felt a hand on his shoulder and found Sir Francis Drake looking up at him earnestly.

"Courage, young sir," the admiral said quietly. "This thing may not be so black as it looks. When I get the Queen's ear perhaps I can—"

"No good," Raleigh broke in, dolefully, "at least not now. The Spanish gold you bring her may lighten Gloriana's heart but I doubt it'll raise her mercy in Avronbeck's case enough to win her pardon now. Nay, she needs time."

"My mother?" Dion asked.

"Gone to Scotland to her father's with your sisters," Raleigh said, "and at Sir Clement's bidding. I saw her, Dion, before she left and she was very forbearing, as you must be. She bade me tell you when I saw you that you must do nothing rash—that your only wise course, for her sake and for your father's, is to curb your rage so Elizabeth will not be more inflamed."

"Curb this, curb that!" Harvie cried. "By the Book, it seems it's time to have done with all this meekness! Nay, I'll—"

"Ye'll bring the axe down on your father's neck!" Drake thundered. "Ye'll send y'r mother and y'r sisters into everlasting exile, or worse! God's sake, young sir, Elizabeth is the *Queen!* Would you give her the fleabite y'r pride demands and so plunge all y'r loved ones into disaster? Ye're selfish enough to do that?"

"They'll think I'm cowardly to stand silent while Her Majesty the Red Bitch—"

"I'll have no more of that talk, sir!" Drake's eyes blazed as he pounded the table with a doubled fist.

Dion turned toward the cabin door, his eyes blurred by tears of frustrated grief. His hand was on the latch when he turned back to Raleigh and Drake.

"My half-brothers?" he asked. "Did they stand by my father in his trouble?"

"Only Adam," Raleigh replied gravely. "Charles and Blount didn't. Adam went to Scotland with Milady Avronbeck and your sisters. Charles and Blount stayed at Avronbeck Hall."

"But how did the Queen allow that, if she was wrought up enough to throw my father into the tower?"

Sir Walter looked down at the table again, cleared his throat, and spoke to the dishes in front of him.

"Charles," he said in a low voice, "renounced his father and even testified that Sir Clement had plotted against the Queen's best interests."

"The dog!"

"Aye," Raleigh nodded, "all England knows him for that, and worse. He even involved Lord Avronbeck with Edmund Campion, the seditious Jesuit who was beheaded back in 'Eighty and—"

"Elizabeth believed that?"

Raleigh shrugged, spreading his long-fingered hands.

"Her Majesty believes what suits her needs," he said abruptly. "Whether she actually swallowed the great lie or not, she let Charles and Blount stay at Avronbeck Hall—after seizing more than half the estates as a penalty for Sir Clement's trumped-up crimes."

"Then there's one cur I can use my sword on, at least," Dion grated. "Even the Queen must know how we two have always hated each other—if I deal Charles what's coming to him it couldn't hurt my father's cause."

"It could and will," Raleigh said. He got up again and walked to Dion's side. He put out both hands to grasp Harvie's arms, his gaze steady.

"Consider, my dear friend," he said, "how what you'd do to Charles would spoil everything. Even Gloriana can't forever stomach the lies your half-brother's told her—the Queen really has as much disgust for human animals who'd betray their own father as the rest of us. Now she uses the treacherous son's evilness to feed her own anger 'gainst Avronbeck but in time, and unless you do something to ruin it all, the wormy stuff will sour her palate and she'll turn on Charles.

"But if you kill him—ah, then the Queen will feel her acceptance of the hound's perjury is vindicated, else why should Charles be murdered if not because he exposed a plot?"

Raleigh's hands clenched tightly on Harvie's arms.

"You must hold still, Dion, though that'll take more courage than the boldest stroke against your half-brother. Believe me when I tell you this; I swear it's not for any thought of my ventures that I bid you heed my advice and Sir Francis's—and your mother's—and hold still!"

Dion's head drooped, his shoulders sagged, as he stared at the rich carpet that covered the cabin deck.

"And this, I suppose," he said dully, "means I'm to go back into hiding." He chuckled mirthlessly. "Aye, write it down in history that Dion Harvie spent his life in some hidden hole, sitting on his hands instead of raising them to deal justice to villains, holding still instead of fighting for the ones he loves."

4

Dion Harvie was not to know it until much later, but the single supply ship Sir Walter Raleigh had dispatched for the relief of Virginia reached Trinity Inlet just four days after Fort Raleigh was abandoned. Lacking orders to deal with the discovery that Lane had deserted the fort, the skipper of the bark hoisted sails the first time an arrow hissed out of the underbrush and plunked into a bulwark.

Two weeks later, Sir Richard Grenville's three ships finally arrived at Roanoke Island. Raleigh's cousin searched the island without being attacked by the Indians, decided that Lane and his company had quit the place and then turned back to England himself. However, Grenville, as he wrote in his journal, was "unwilling to lose possession of the country which Englishmen had so long held." Therefore, he ordered fifteen of his men to stay on the island and left them enough provisions to last two years before he raised sail for the homeward voyage.

Sir Richard had no way of knowing that Ralph Lane had not followed his advice to "bend every effort to stay friendly with the Indians;" he could not know that he was setting down a handful of whites in a country where every white man save one—Dion Harvie—Pemecolemanmeo—was hated as a thing so low that he would violate a peace parley with murder.

5

Dion went back to Lime Street—and Margery Hollis.

He did not protest too much against this move. After he accepted Raleigh's word that to raise his hand against Charles would be to send his father to the block, Dion was almost listless as to what Sir Walter did with him. He cursed the situation, certainly, but he did what Raleigh wanted done and only grumbled.

"Burnie's the best place for you—the only place," Raleigh said.

"A murrain on Burnie's place," Dion muttered. "A murrain on London. God's teeth, my life goes 'round in circles—to Roanoke and back to Burnie's, to Roanoke and back to Burnie's."

"And is that so bad?" Raleigh asked exasperatedly. "Thank God, instead, there is a Burnie's—I don't know where else I could hide you. Ungrateful man, you vex me with your surliness, when I gamble so heavily to protect you!"

"I know you do, friend Walt," Dion nodded, "and I'm not really ungrateful. It's only that my life seems wasting away with nothing done except saving my own skin."

"There's time enough to avenge your wrongs," Sir Walter said. "Patience, Dion—again I counsel patience. And don't look so downcast. Directly Drake's message reached me that you were back, I got in touch with Burnie and arranged for your rooms—and for that woman who entertained you when you were here last and you found so pleasing."

"Mag?" Dion gave a clipped laugh. "When I last left her I said I could not come back to her because I loved another, yet here I am."

"But for a little time, mayhap. Things may change tomorrow in spite of all my doubts and you'll be able to forget the Queen's men."

"And till then, you're sure I'm not gamey enough by this time to be sniffed out by the Queen's men even at Burnie's?" Dion asked. "You know that misbegotten Lane will doubtless belch my name all over England, as much as he hates me. What will you say when Gloriana asks how it is that I've been sheltered at Fort Raleigh?"

Raleigh grimaced, shrugging.

" 'Twill take some doing," he admitted, "but between Drake and White and me—aye, and Grenville, too—I think we can convince Her Majesty that Lane is belching empty air. Nobody among the gentlemen who were at Fort Raleigh has any love for Ralph Lane, neither has he any standing at court. He's to be discredited as governor and all the blame for the abandonment of the colony will be laid to him. Any complaint he makes about a certain Dion Harvie being a member of the colony can be called the slander of an inefficient fool. We'll all deny his story and make a spiteful liar out of him."

"But Sir Richard—John Arundell—there are some gentlemen who have even less love for me than they have for Lane," Dion pointed out. "They think me a turncoat and they'd welcome a chance to throw me to the headsman."

"Dick," Raleigh explained patiently, "has invested in my American adventure and so would not like to see the Queen angered to the point of recalling my patents. John Arundell is a relative and can be convinced. Sir Francis wants an English supply post near Spanish Florida and is ready to stretch the truth a bit to help me as much as he can. The other gentlemen can be—er—induced by one way or another to believe it wasn't Dion Harvie they knew in Virginia. The soldiers and the workmen don't count."

"And how about Simon Ferdinando?" Harvie asked. Raleigh snorted.

"Ferdinando again!" he exclaimed. "Before God, ye'll make him a villain yet, won't we? Ye'll never believe that Simon is y'r friend—mayhap one of the best ye have."

"I'd like to believe it," Dion said grudgingly, "but the believing comes hard."

"Then let me vouch for Ferdinando's saying nothing about you being in Virginia. When he came back here with Grenville he reproached me for having kept you hidden that whole winter and out of touch with him. I vow he feels like some burly brother to you, Dion."

"You didn't tell him where I hid, did you?"

"No. I wouldn't trust Simon that far or many men I know, to share the secret of Burnie's cuckoo's nest."

Drake's treasure ships anchored in the Thames on August seventh, 1586, and the wild jubilation of his welcome so completely overshadowed the return of Raleigh's settlers from Virginia that only a handful knew that Lane and his company were back and these few did not bother to question why they were.

Even Elizabeth, usually too sharp-eyed, long-nosed, querulous, when it came to the idea of anyone acting without her royal permission, was so rabid to count the Spanish gold that Drake had brought her that she paid scant heed to Lane's return. Another time she would have been outraged by the abandonment of a land she had named in tribute to her sanctified virginity; now, she only sniffed and said she had had her doubts about the success of the venture from the start—and complimented her sagacity in refusing to use her own money to finance it.

It was a simple matter to smuggle Dion Harvie ashore in the

midst of Drake's welcoming celebration; he made his familiar way to Lime Street with his face boldly bared.

If he had been seen by any of the Queen's men it is doubtful if they would have recognized this stub-bearded man as the Dion Harvie, soft-skinned young gentleman of fashion, they had been ordered to seize three years before. Dion was twenty-one years old now but the change in him was more than had been brought by his step over the threshold of maturity.

Dion Harvie had been a gay, laughing youngster who had enlivened every social gathering he was part of; he had been sought after as a walking, talking, romancing guarantee that every party, every ball, every banquet, every rout he attended would be a success. He had had a hard head for wine-bibbing, a properly insouciant hand at cards or dice, a light amusing touch in love-making, a good voice for a song, a good foot for a pavane, a nimble tongue for conversation, a nice taste for dress, when he was eighteen. All his indiscretions had been entertaining—up to the affair of Helen Harvie, Charles' wife, and the clash with Groven. Dion had been the blithe, handsome epitome of the young Elizabethan gentleman.

And now his smile was more rarely seen and too often twisted cynically when it came. His eyes did not dance as they had; they seemed to look inwardly as much as they scanned what lay before them. His exquisite taste in dress had suffered; he did not much care what covered his big frame, so long as it was warm in winter and cool in summer; a glaring wrinkle in his hose or even a hole was not the shocking thing it had been. Because he had been so much alone on Roanoke Island, a near-outcast, his tongue was less ready to come up with a remark and never with one of the quick and flippant words that had been so diverting in other days; he was more prone to study what was to be said and often swallow it unspoken. His temper was still volatile but roused by different things than it had been; now he forgot to be touchy on his own account but turned his hot anger against what he considered injustices to others.

An amazing change? Granted, but it must be remembered that Dion Harvie's whole life had been altered in a series of violent contortions that would have changed far more solid characters than his. Men matured early in the Sixteenth Century but not so early that a boy of eighteen could be expected to have established his own philosophy firmly enough to resist the battering ram of stark disillusion. Dion's eyes had been too young, still too clear of the veil of egotistic ignorance, for him to have missed recognizing the truth when he had met it on Roanoke Island among the Indians. Pemispan, Wanchese, even Tolepuec, had proved themselves to him more noble than haughty Sir Richard Grenville and certainly Ralph Lane. Charles Harvie had proved himself more contemptible than even Manteo for, opportunist turncoat that Manteo might be he still would have suffered himself to be burned at the stake rather than falsely accuse his father. Dion's Queen, to whom he was bound to bow in allegiance or bear the name of traitor, threw her most loyal courtier, Lord Avronbeck, into the Tower. And why? Because of a fit of anger that had had its birth years before when a "lover" who somehow could titillate Elizabeth's leathery sensuality had been hurt.

All his ideals: pride in Queen and country, esteem of the position he had been born to, arrogant superiority over creatures whom civilization had spurned as unworthy, belief that wealth and family excused him from all humility, had crumbled or were crumbling. And in their stead had grown untended—even unwanted—principles which were frightening in their absolute contradiction to his world's tenets.

Yes, Dion had changed, and the humpbacked Burnie marked the change the first time he peered up at the blue-eyed, wide-shouldered young lodger who returned to Lime Street.

"I bid ye welcome, Master Harvie," the little man chuckled, "new beard and all. Ye look as though all that time spent in the New World did ye no harm. Ye're well?"

"Well enough," Dion nodded. "Better than some others who deserve to be far easier."

"Aye," Burnie said, "I heard about y'r father, of course. 'Tis a stinkin' shame but what can we do save wait for Her Majesty to head off in another direction? Sir Walter didn't come wi' ye?"

"No, he went to the court with Drake. He trusted me to find my way here and God knows I should be able."

"And so ye should, so ye should. Ye'll find it just the same as when ye were here last, though there's been a parade of fine gentlemen in and out these past few months, takin' their ease here till Gloriana looked the other way. Things are exceeding touchy at Hampton these times, I vow! The Queen's backside aches, it seems, from straddling the fence twixt war and peace with His Catholic Majesty, Philip, the scurvy knave. Then there's a whole bushel of rumors of a revolt in Scotland, in Ireland, in England itself, to spoil her temper when she forgets Philip for a moment. Ye've heard of Ballard's plot?"

"I've heard of a hundred plots," Dion said wearily. "Which was Ballard's?"

" 'Tis but recently uncovered," Burnie said, "and not finished yet, I trow. All I know is that this priest, John Ballard, was seized and confessed on the rack that he and others schemed to free Mary of Scotland and murder Elizabeth. They say he's named his companions and if they're caught and confess 'tis sure to mean Mary's head on the block, poor foolish sweetling."

"Murder and more murder," Dion said, "and for a throne on which no man or woman has ever found a second's peace."

"Nay, never peace, perhaps," Burnie chuckled, "but ah, the power that's there! And who'd rather have peace than power, pray? But here I hold you on y'r feet whilst I prattle away. Come, young sir—to y'r rooms. There's somebody waitin' there who's eager to bid ye welcome."

Dion hesitated, his face clouding.

"Oh—ah—Margery?" he asked. "Walt told me Mag had been arranged for. I hope the price wasn't too high—Sir Walter tells me his Virginia venture has all but emptied his purse."

"It has, it has," Burnie nodded, "but Mag did not come high this time, Master Harvie. Nay, she'd have paid for the chance to be with you again, I vow, if that was the only way it could be fixed."

"Paid for—you're joking, of course."

"And am I?" Burnie asked, peering up at Dion. "I tell the truth, sir. And I'd have ye know that since you left here, that demented woman—but la, is this Burnie who gossips?"

"Look here, what's this you try to tell me?"

"Nothing—nothing at all, Master Harvie." The hunchback grinned and bobbed and headed for the stairway, holding his taper high. "Mind the steps."

"Margery—"

"Now, now," Burnie chuckled. "She's but a few steps above—let her do her own talking, eh?"

They reached the third floor and turned down the hallway to the door of the rooms that had confined Dion for so many weeks two years before. Burnie flung it open and stood aside, bowing Harvie in. Dion stepped onto the thick rug that stretched from the threshold and walked into the room, his eyes fixed on the brown-haired woman who sat near the window. At his approach she rose and sank in a graceful curtsey.

"Milord," she murmured in the soft, easy voice Dion remembered well. "I bid ye welcome back to London Town."

"And glad I am to be back," Dion replied mechanically, "because it means seeing you again, Mag."

His eyes searched her quiet beauty and found it unchanged from what it had been eighteen months before; she was as clear-skinned, as slim and supple as she had been then and she still exuded the fragrance of clean womanflesh. Her teeth, when she smiled slowly, were still white and even, her hands—there was a change there, certainly! Margery's hands had been soft and smooth, with immaculately tended nails; now they were red-knuckled and the nails were broken. They looked like a serving wench's hands! And why was that, when Mag certainly could demand the highest price for what she had to offer?

She saw him staring at her hands and moved them behind her back, her face flushing.

"Don't be ashamed of 'em, Sweet Mag," Burnie sniggered harshly. "Icod, they're y'r proud banners—they're all ye've won f'r y'r loftiness, I trow!"

Frowning, Dion turned to the little landlord.

"What's this?" he demanded.

"She'll tell ye," Burnie laughed. "Or mayhap she won't. 'Tis hard to figure what Sweet Mag will do or won't do these times, Master Harvie. Aye, she's zanier than a moonstruck maid, is Mag." He raised a hand as Dion's scowl deepened. "Ah, but she's within her rights," he added quickly. "I've always been one to hold that a man or woman could cut off their own ears if their heart told them it was the right thing to do, and no business of mine would it be."

He chuckled again and moved out into the hall.

"I've things to look after," he said, "and so, I guess, do the pair of ye. I'll leave you."

As the door closed behind Burnie, Dion turned back to Margery, then took a step closer to her and drew her hands from behind her back. He examined the travesties of what they had been, turning them to look at the calloused palms, the scraped knuckles, the inflamed cuts. Her dark eyes were pleading when he looked up at them.

"They'll heal, milord," she said hurriedly, almost frantically, "and till they do I'll keep them out of sight. Had I known the day you were coming back I'd have—fixed them so they'd not be so ugly. I'd have left—I'd have found means."

"What is all this?" Dion asked gently. "Why have you mistreated these poor fingers of yours so cruelly?"

"I—I have been working, milord—working as a kitchen wench in a great house at Westminster." Her voice was low, shamed. "I meant to keep it secret from you—but your return caught me unawares; I had no time to quit my place and mend my hands before I saw you."

"A kitchen wench?" he asked. "God's teeth, Margery—why?"

She searched for words and failed to find them.

"Didn't I leave you well furnished for money to keep you till you found another protector?" he asked. "And why didn't some gentleman take you up instanter? Couldn't Burnie arrange a situation easier for you than ruining your hands as a common slavey?"

"I—I am a fool, I know, milord," Margery faltered, "but since you left I've let no man touch me." She raised her head and set her mouth in a wry curve. "A virtuous stand for a whore to take, eh?" she asked. "As if it mattered one whit whether I slept alone or offered myself to all comers! But I said I was a fool, milord—humor me in my delusions."

Dion kept his hands on the girl's forearms, his eyes searching hers.

"You're no fool, Mag," he said at length, "but I confess I don't understand. I mean—God's sake—a woman as sweet and comely as you, with all your talents, should never have aught but the easiest life. And to choose a kitchen over the other—"

"Was an idiot's idea, I know," Margery broke in. "Have done with it."

"Was it that you—" Dion began and then broke off, biting his lip.

"I know what it was you were about to say," Margery said, smiling faintly, "and it was no pox, milord."

"I did not think that!" Harvie said stoutly. "That never entered my mind, I vow!"

"And who could blame you for the thought?" she asked. "I'll tell you that I spread the story that I was infected so's to keep men's hands off me—ah, it works wonders with the hottest rogue—but it was never true, I swear it!"

"Then why—"

"Because, Dion," she said, her mouth still twisted, "I seem to have forgot who I was and what I was and fell in love! Aye, I'll be honest with you, though you're insulted by the idea! I've sworn I'd always be honest with you, no matter what, and here's my first chance to test this honesty."

"In love, Mag, and with me?" he asked dazedly.

"Aye, isn't that mad enough to convince you I'm a fool?"

"But I—I never—"

"No, I never tried to cozen myself into believing you ever hinted at love. I don't expect it now. Keep on thinking of me as a pleasant doxy, if I still please you, and forget my foolish whims, milord."

Dion dropped his hands and turned to walk past Margery to the window, staring across the rooftops and chimneypots at the peaks of the houses that lined London Bridge. As Margery watched him, he shook his head violently and brought a fist down on the sill.

"Now here's a pretty thing!" he jerked out. "My life's not tangled enough but what a strumpet must protest her love for me! Icod, I knew I'd lost favor in eyes a-plenty but have I brought the name of Harvie so low that Lord Avronbeck's son is sighed over by a whore?"

"Milord—I beg you forget what I said!" Margery cried.

He wheeled for the window, his eyes accusing.

"Forget your honesty?" he demanded. "You greet me with your hands all ruined in a servitude you did for the sake of this strange constancy you fastened on—and now you bid me forget it? You've toiled in a stinking kitchen when you could have taken your ease on silken sheets and drunk your wine from silver cups and now you tell me to wipe my thoughts clear of all that?"

"I lied—I truly had the pox, Dion—I was broke out in sores and—"

"You lie now, Mag, and I'll not have it! No, let me face it—the great Dion Harvie who fancied himself the cleverest fellow in all England has made a conquest that suits him! Oh, he has landed his father in the Tower, handed Avronbeck over to his foul half-brother, banished his mother and his sisters to Scotland, fixed things so a friend who trusted him was murdered—but he was a savage Indian and of no account, of course—and now at last he's done a noble thing! He's raised a strumpet from her bed of easy venery to scrub pots in a kitchen so she might be worthy of his love!"

He barked a hard laugh.

"Aye, he's done a worthy thing, finally," he jeered. "Let his father rejoice, let his mother and sisters take comfort, let Pemispan's bones smile!"

He turned from the window and made a cold, cruel bow.

"I'd not besmirch this new chastity of yours, milady," he said caustically. " 'Twould be like violating a pure maid, I vow! So get ye hence and tell Burnie to send me a proper harlot—one who'll count the cash and never dream of love!"

"Dion—your pity, for the love of God!"

"Pity, madame?" he asked, his eyebrows arching. "Now it's pity you ask for—I thought 'twas my whole heart—mayhap my name as your husband."

"No, Dion—you know I never hoped—"

"You hadn't reached that wish?" he broke in. "Ah well, 'twill come, Mag, do you persist! Aye, if ye stay, I can expect to waken some morning to see you weeping in y'r misery over my betrayal. Too bad you'd lost y'r maidenhead a thousand times before I set eyes on you or else—"

"Dion, Dion!"

"—you could accuse me of base seduction and perhaps hire an avenging brother who'd see I did right by you."

Margery was weeping now, quietly, letting the tears run down her cheeks as she kept her brimming eyes fixed on him. He turned back to the window and stared out over the town's roofs.

"How is it you've brought no bastard with you from your retreat?" he asked, over his shoulder. "With a child, you could implore me to give it a name, Margery, and I'd likely be enough a fool to—ahh, God!"

He bent his head, raised a fist to his mouth to bite his knuckles. There was a silence and then Margery spoke in a voice that was little more than a whisper.

"What troubles you, Dion," she asked, "beyond what I said?"

He wheeled from the window and she caught her breath at sight of the anguish written on his face.

"What troubles me?" he asked in a white voice. "And what does not? My father—but it's more than that, even! It's worthless me, I guess! What am I good for, Margery? And if there's something I'm meant for, what is it—which way do I turn to find it?"

"Worthless, Dion?" the girl asked. "Nay, you're not worthless. Even if there was naught else you did, you gave me something real to live for."

"Oh aye," he rasped, "you chose a worthy sponsor for your change if it was me! I've failed in everything I tried to do and so I strike out where I can and that's at you, poor Mag. Out of the muddle that's my brain I still can find the pride to curse you as insulting because you spoke honestly of love."

"It was not my place, milord, to—"

"Not your place? What is your place—what's mine? I once thought I knew but not now. Now I know only that I know nothing. And why am I cursed?"

He flung a backward gesture toward the window.

"Out there," he cried, "there are a thousand young men like me who live the gay and happy lives that were set out for them. They drink, they dance, they laugh, they love as gentlemen should and never torture themselves with doubts about what's right and what's not. They have a Queen; let her say what to do and they do it as good Englishmen—didn't God give her the right to speak for him? Or if not listen to Her Majesty, they hear what the Church says—let the priests give the orders in God's name. Between the Throne and the Church surely this world must be as right as it ever can be—why must I think different? Why must I listen to commands that name me renegade among my own kind?"

"Mayhap," Margery said, "a man hears words that don't come from the Throne or the Church and still are meant to be obeyed."

"And mayhap they're the Devil's words," Dion said, "and Beelzebub's picked me to work for him. For what archbishop would say other than that the Indians of the New World are at best damned souls, put there by God to be converted or be killed?"

"And you think different, Dion?"

"So different that if what I thought were known I'd be burned at the stake for heresy," Harvie replied bitterly. "I think Pemispan and Wanchese better men *in all ways* than any Christian gentleman on Roanoke Island—nay, better than nine out of ten here in England! I think we could learn from them, not they from us, and I include all priests of the Church and counselors of the Queen—Her Majesty herself!"

"Hush, Dion."

"Oh aye, I'll hush, lest my ranting plunge my family deeper into disaster."

She moved toward him and put a hand on his arm.

"You're weary, Dion," she said softly. "Rest—you need plenty of rest. The hardships you went through in the New World—"

"There were no hardships save a few missed meals," he protested. "Nay, I've suffered nothing compared to what the Indians went through. And what complaint do I have, matched against my father's and my mother's and my sisters'? I took no blow or cut—why, I even had my own woman in the New World to ease me."

"Your own wo—ah, still you're weary, Dion," Margery said. "Come, rest. Sleep. Tomorrow we can talk and you can tell me more about the time you've been away and—"

"How now?" he asked with a rueful twist of his mouth. "Ye've no questions about this Indian woman of mine and yet ye say ye love me? There's no jealousy in you?"

"No, milord," Margery Hollis said. "If this woman eased you, as you said, how could I hate her?"

"By God," Dion Harvie grumbled, "the world's gone topsy-turvy when women are not jealous." He lowered himself to the bed and patted the counterpane beside him. "Lie here, Mag, and use your sweet self to make me forget all my worries."

But later, in his sleep, his face darkened and he cried out as Margery watched him and used her unbound hair to wipe his sweat-slicked forehead.

6

It was as Sir Walter Raleigh had predicted; Ralph's Lane's eager disclosures to the Queen bounced back to label him a spiteful liar.

It may have been that Lord Avronbeck's enemies in court, satisfied that they had trapped the lion and did not need the cub, helped Raleigh in making Lane's squeals sound like ridiculous slander. Certainly Grenville helped, either out of his concern for his Virginia investment or because Lane's miserable failures on Roanoke Island had been due to orders partly his, and helped to such an extent that the tormented Lane turned his vilification on Sir Richard.

"I am accused," he wrote Elizabeth in a hot-headed letter better left unwritten, "while Grenville, that man of intolerable pride and insatiable ambition, is hailed as a hero. I plead Your Majesty, that if this man who now heaps contumely on my head had done aught but scheme against the success of the colony and had filled his promise to relieve Fort Raleigh I would have won through beyond all expectations."

Because he did not have the wit to see that a plot had been arranged against him, he butted his thick head against the wall of court intrigue until a sharp word from Elizabeth sent him back to the army with even his poor title of Captain stripped from him.

"And so," Raleigh told Dion, "that's the end of Captain Ralph Lane, poor clod, and we're well rid of him, I trow." He frowned and pulled at his sharp beard. "But there's another in his place—God's teeth, and what another! Gloriana says this new bravo must go on my next expedition to Virginia or there'll be no next expedition."

"And what lusty blockhead has she picked to bedevil you this time?" Dion asked idly.

"Blockhead? No!" Raleigh said with a shake of his head. "No dolt like Lane, this fellow, but twice as unhappy a pick, as you should know when you hear his name. Guy Groven, no less."

"*Groven!* That swine? You'd take him to Virginia?"

"It's not what I'd do but what the Queen bids me do. Aye, she could tell me to take the Foul Fiend and I'd have to try to summon him up. A swipe of her pen and I'd have no patent, remember. And with my limp purse I've had to gather a syndicate of subpatentees to finance this latest endeavor; if my patent's withdrawn, and me in debt to the subpatentees, it'll mean disgrace and ruin for me, sure."

"But Groven—"

"Well, console yourself that this shows Groven must be losing favor in the Queen's eyes, else she'd not be parted from him. And with him gone from her side, your father's friends in court can work better to get the name of Avronbeck back under her smile."

"And in Virginia," Dion nodded, "many things could happen to Guy Groven—or even on the way there."

"I heard naught of what you said," Raleigh smiled tranquilly, "but just the same I'll have to see that you sail on another ship than Groven's."

"Another ship?" Dion asked. "Y'think I'm going back to Roanoke, Walt?"

"If things are as they are now when sailing times comes, ye'll sail with us, certainly," Raleigh said. "If your father's freed, if the Queen forgives you, you can stay here and God be with you, but till then you're under my orders.

"Besides," he went on with a quizzical grin, "I thought you'd rather be in Virginia than in wicked England. Or have you changed your mind about how much more wondrous are the Indians than we poor benighted Englishmen?"

He held up a hand as Dion's face flushed and the younger man started to speak.

"Nay, I'm not taunting you, Dion," he said, seriously. "I really thought you'd found things in the New World you missed here."

"And so I did," Harvie said acidly, "but they'll not survive there long under a rule like Ralph Lane's. Great God, what Groven would do there!"

"All the more reason," Raleigh nodded, "that you go back to Virginia with us to keep him from making mischief."

"You think he'd listen to me—if I didn't cut him down on sight? You think anybody would listen to me this next time any more than they did the last time I was there? Nay, they'll cry *renegade,* as Lane did."

"I'll be in command this time, remember," Raleigh said, "and what's done will be done on my orders. I think you're too harsh in damning all the men who were with you at Fort Raleigh but I admit, too, that the Indians were dealt many an injustice by Lane."

"Aquascogok was burned on Grenville's order, not Lane's."

"Oh aye, Dick was overzealous there, I confess. But he did tell Lane to keep friendly with the Roanokes when he left, didn't he? And Dick's a haughty man compared to me—you'll see that I treat fairly with the natives. And, in line with that, I have a plan, Dion, to get Lord Avronbeck out of the Tower, out from under Elizabeth's capricious hand."

"Why, then I'm for it!" Dion cried. "Whatever the risk, it'll be worth it! What is your plan, Walt?"

Raleigh, a gleaming figure in blue silk, paced across the room to a chair and lowered himself into its upholstered depths, his rapier slung across his lap as he crossed his knees.

"What would you think," he asked, "if your family went to Virginia with us?"

"My father in Virginia?" Harvie asked. "Why—why I can't imagine it, Walt. He's no explorer, no adventurer like you—he's a courtier, Walt, and does his work for England in the Queen's councils. And he's not young, though he doesn't look half his age. I can't dream of him wanting to go to the New World."

"Again," Raleigh said, half petulantly, " 'tis not a question of what certain people want in this case, but what suits Her Majesty. And I have a good idea that with persuasion by some others—Leicester, Grenville, Drake—Elizabeth will agree to Avronbeck's exile in my custody."

"Exile—for my father?"

Raleigh grimaced and shrugged.

"So terrible a fate?" he asked. "From what you've told me, Virginia's no dungeon, certainly, and fairer in many ways than England herself."

"A hundred ways, Walt! But my father—why, 'twould grieve him to his death to be exiled from his England at this age. And my mother and sisters—"

"Mayhap can accompany him or join him later," Raleigh broke in. "As for breaking his heart for lack of England, Sir Clement always has been one to serve the Crown wholly in whatever capacity's been ordered. I said exile because, bluntly, 'twould amount to that, but if 'twere masked under the title of Commissioner of Plantations would he not be happy to return to England's service, though across the Western Sea from London?"

Dion rubbed at his lip with the knuckle of his forefinger.

"Aye, he might be," he said grudgingly, "but—but—"

"And what better influence," Raleigh pursued, "could affect the treatment of the Indians than Avronbeck's honesty and merciful heart? You, he and I working together—we'd be more than a match for a dozen Grovens and a hundred Lanes!"

Harvie walked to a table to spill wine into a goblet, raised the silver cup and looked over its rim at Sir Walter.

"But what of Avronbeck Hall?" he asked. "What of my father's estates?"

"Now there," Raleigh replied slowly, "we'd have to give in and bear the pinch. I know Elizabeth will agree to Avronbeck's exile to Virginia only if she's assured she'll get the Avronbeck holdings Charles hasn't already ceded to her. It would have to be worked this way; Sir Clement will have to agree not to sue for redress but, instead, leave the Avronbeck holdings in Charles' unworthy hands. Believe me, Her Majesty will take care of that Judas in good time —but you will have to leave his fate to her. You'll have to let your personal honor go unsatisfied there."

Dion Harvie drained his cup and set the goblet down on the table. He wondered at himself; he should be outraged that he had been robbed of his chance to deal with Charles' perfidy by the same plan that would free his father, and yet there was no more than a dull resentment at the prospects. His honor would go unsatisfied—and was this honor so precious a thing that it should be even considered against a chance to get his father out of prison?

He had seen Ralph Lane satisfy his honor at Roanoke Island; the bristling captain must have thought that in his slaughter of Pemispan he was merely keeping his pledge to Grenville that "never the Queen's honor, or mine, shall be soiled by these animals." And he, Dion, had tried to satisfy *his* honor, stained by Lane's murder of Pemispan, and had been balked. He had been furious then because he had not buried his sword in Lane and yet—yet Lane was now scoffed at in a disgrace that must be torture to a man like the ambitious soldier.

So—was it possible that the words he had heard so long ago, something about God, not man, dealing vengeance, could be the truth? Did he actually interest Himself so closely in the lives of puny humans that He righted wrongs in His way without man needing to deal his own fallible justice?

No. No, this could not be—it was a dream. For if God did take

His own vengeance why didn't He take it so it could be witnessed and thus give humans proof of the right to hope? There was Bloody Mary, for example. During the cruel years of her reign a million prayers had gone up that Mary be stopped, stricken in her inhuman arrogance. And Bloody Mary had stayed powerful, relentless, and. . . .

And two children she had felt within her were never born; she had died of a broken heart, deserted by her husband, afraid to show her face to her subjects, betrayed by her closest followers and even rejected by the Church for which she had plunged her England into a blood bath. Then was this not God's vengeance for all to realize?

Dion shook his head to clear his brain of questions he could not fully grasp, answers he could not bring himself to believe. He was no philosopher, he told himself; he was a bewildered fool beset by thoughts that named him renegade to the established order. As far as vengeance on Charles was concerned—he must be going mad but Charles's death seemed no primary personal duty. The need to satisfy his honor there suddenly had lost its bite.

"If these things can be arranged for my father's safety," he told Raleigh slowly, "I'll leave Charles's future to the Queen—or whoever deals with him."

Silence weighted the room as Sir Walter Raleigh stared at his friend, his mouth agape. The nobleman had expected at least an echo of the wild outburst that would have come from the Dion Harvie of three years before at the suggestion that he quiet the demands of his honor. Raleigh realized that Dion had changed in the past year spent on Roanoke Island. Still, for the stripling who had been the touchiest young man in all England, as a gentleman of the code to accept the proposal that he leave revenge on Charles to others was impossible! Raleigh started to speak, closed his mouth, repressed a shake of his head.

What strange magic, he asked himself, *does my Virginia possess to change this man so?*

7

DION HARVIE HEARD only fragments of the story of Anthony Babington. He was too bound up in Raleigh's plan to free Lord Avronbeck to have much patience with Burnie's stories of other plots, other intrigues, other successes, other disappointments.

The hours between Raleigh's visits he spent with Margery, even though he knew she loved him with a love that was more than fleshly and although he knew, too, that he did wrong by accepting her love. Margery might say she did not expect his love in return for this astonishing devotion she offered but Dion must have realized that with each kiss, each gentle word, he gave her another bit of hope, another part of a dream that some day would have to be smashed and the girl left to bleed to death of tears.

At times, he was stabbed by remorse and cursed the girl for her infatuation, cursed himself for his weakness in not sending her away. There were other times when he determined to rid his life of Margery for her own good—and the bellowing denunciations he had rehearsed turned into ineffectual spluttering, his grim-jawed determination melted, his resolve faded, as she used every wile of soft skin and warm flesh, wanton abandonment and quiet comfort, to beat him.

Margery had been taught and had taught herself to be irresistible in love-making; she had used her talents calculatingly as a harlot to gain mere money and security—how could she be less than a thousand times more seductive when she was striving to hold the only man she ever had loved? To keep Dion the girl resorted to allures that would have made a bacchante gasp—and a breath before the stark brutishness of shameless lust revolted Dion she transformed herself from the burning, arching, undulating high priestess of Astarte to the lenitive, soft-voiced, serene mother-wife whose touch was cool and whose kiss was gentle.

If these were coils she wound around him, he did not recognize their haltering; he thought only that he would be a fool to throw aside a mistress so perfectly versed in so many things, no matter how ridiculous her feeling for him might be. He thought himself convinced that when the time came to leave Margery he could do it as he had once, with a goodby kiss and a gift—just that and it would be over.

So the days passed with Margery seldom out of reach of Dion's hand, days spent reading the plays of Christopher Marlowe and Thomas Nashe, chuckling over Richard Tarleton's *The Seven Deadly Sins,* even (in Dion's case) exercising rusty Latin to plough through Joseph Justus Scaliger's *Catalecta.* Or in tinkling a clavichord or playing the flute or talking nonsense or what seemed weighty discourse—or in love play that Margery made sure was never satiating. . . .

8

"NAY, NAY, MILORD, ah, now have done, I beg you! God's sake, will you never let a poor girl rest? You'll wear me to a rattling bag of bones, I vow!"

"Stop squirming, artful witch! Y'know you teased me into this."

"My gown—you'll tear—now see what you have done! In shreds, I'll be bound, with hardly enough left to cover me."

"And who wants you covered, Mag? You're better thus, with this peeping through here and this—"

"Ow, milord, this be rape! I'll cry the house down, I swear!"

"Scream, then, and prove to everybody that I can still wring cries of delight from you! Roar your enjoyment and I'll—*who's there?"*

Dion raised his head from the curve of Margery's neck and swung his face toward the door. The knock sounded again and with a muttered curse Harvie disengaged himself from Margery's embrace and slid off the bed. The girl fumbled with her disordered brown hair, pulled her clothes back into place and slipped across the floor to the closet that led off the room as Dion moved toward the door.

"Who's there?" he asked again.

" 'Tis Raleigh, Dion," said a low voice beyond the door.

"Walt? It does not sound like you."

"But it is, Dion. I—I have a message for you that brought me here at this odd hour. I'm straight from the court and she—but open."

Dion slid the bolt and peered through the opening. He saw his friend, heavily cloaked for that time of year, his wide-brimmed hat pulled low over his eyes, standing in the gloomy hallway.

"From court, you say?" he asked. "There's news of my father, then? The Queen's agreed that—what troubles you, Walt?"

Raleigh turned to shut the door behind him, bolted it and then walked to the bed Dion and Margery had just left and seated himself on its edge. He looked strangely weary, his handsome face lined, his shoulders drooping. Slowly, he pulled one gauntlet glove from his hand, as slowly he stripped the other. Deliberately, he placed them on the rumpled coverlet beside him.

"What is it, Walt? Has something gone amiss with y'r plans? Has Gloriana dealt you another blow?"

Raleigh raised his haggard face to meet Dion's anxious stare. Harvie had seen his friend downcast before, when Elizabeth had made her last-minute refusal to let him join the second expedition to Roanoke Island, when his half-brother, Sir Humphrey Gilbert, had perished at sea, but he never had seen him so completely desolated, so heartsick that his misery made of him an old, enfeebled man.

"Walt—f'r God's sake!"

Raleigh raised a hand to pass it over his forehead in a tired swipe that shoved the hat back on his head. His long fingers dropped to the jeweled hilt of his rapier, then fell lax and impotent, to the bed. His voice was hoarse, strained, when he spoke.

"I never thought to bring you such a report, Dion," he croaked. "I confess I'd rather have another tell you what I have to say. Your father—Dion, you've lost your father."

The words tolled through the room and seemed to echo jarringly before they were silenced. Dion stiffened, his face gone grey under his tan, his blue eyes wide, his lips drawn back with his gasp, his hands hooked into claws at his sides.

"Lost—my—father? What d'ye mean?"

"I mean—I mean—ah, God, how can I tell you?" Raleigh said. "He's dead, Dion, and by foul conspiracy! I did not know—none of us knew—the Queen planned this calamity."

Dion's long strides carried him to the bed, his hands grasped Raleigh's silken shoulders and shook him fiercely.

"Out with it, man!" he cried. "What befell my father? He's dead, you say, and by whose hand? Quick, tell me!"

"By the axeman's," Raleigh said tonelessly. "And by Walsingham's, I think, and other enemies at court."

"My father sent to the block?" Dion grated. "By Christ, there'll be a reckoning of this! Hold my hand 'gainst Charles, you said, and I agreed—was it to let these stinking plotters have free way 'gainst my father that you bade me hold still?"

"Nay, Dion, you know—"

"I know my father's dead and that's all I need to know now! Ah, I thought I did right by leaving vengeance against Charles to the Queen and to God! I was fool enough to think my half-brother's crimes would be repaid by other than my sword! Aye, I was hoodwinked properly by your sensible words, Raleigh! What did the Queen promise you to make me stay my blade?"

"I did not know," Raleigh said lifelessly. "I was kept in the dark about all of it. I can't blame you for charging me with treachery, Dion—God knows I'm guilty of a blindness that is almost as bad as betrayal. But they worked in darkness—believe me! I was dealt smiles and false words while all the time his enemies arranged your father's death."

"Then they will answer to me—all of them! And Elizabeth, too, can I get within a sword's length of that red-haired dyke!"

"Dion—"

"Nor bid me hold again, Raleigh!" Dion barked. "I've listened to you once too often, with y'r specious arguments! Nay, this time I'll do what I should have done at the start and would have, had you not stopped me! First Charles, who started all of this, then Walsingham and finally, pray God, the bitch who ruins England, Elizabeth!"

"Dion, Dion," Raleigh implored, "I know you're half crazed by this but guard against a madness that would kill you, with y'r father! There's naught to be done now except—"

Dion grunted a hard laugh.

"Naught to be done?" he cried. "Oh, hear the noble Raleigh now! Hear the Queen's pet whimper and whine whilst he lifts his leg 'gainst all honesty, all decent need for swift revenge!"

Raleigh's pain-stricken brown eyes gazed into Dion's hard blue glare and fell.

"No, Dion," he murmured, "I'll not be roused against you. I loathe myself for standing by, my hands idle, whilst the villains worked behind my back, so what can you say to sting me? If a sword would remedy the least part of this, mine would be out and striking ere now."

"Your sword, sir?" Dion asked scornfully. "You know it's but a pretty blade, worn to complete your dress. You daren't bare it for fear its shine might annoy the Queen's eyes and bring disfavor on your damned ventures."

Raleigh's head came up, his lips thinning.

"My sword," he rapped back, "was bloody when you were a boy and—"

"Ah," Dion broke in sardonically, "but that was before you made y'rself a puppet to dance to every string Gloriana might pull. That was before you came to fear that any honest move might turn the Queen's frown on your precious Virginia. Aye, let Avronbeck die on the block, let his son, Dion Harvie, be lied to—all worthy people mean nothing to Raleigh, 'gainst his love for that sand patch, Roanoke Island!"

"Now, by God—" Raleigh growled as he flung himself to his feet.

"Sir Walter! Dion!"

Margery Hollis flung herself between the two men as Raleigh's hand flashed to the hilt of his rapier.

"Aside, wench!" Dion grated.

"No, Dion, you must listen! This is madness, to accuse—"

Harvie's hand reached out to grab Margery's shoulder and send her spinning to one side.

"Begone, whore, strumpet!" he yelled. "Whilst my father was being murdered I wallowed in you! I could not hear the cries for help he sounded because I was too concerned with pretty dalliance! If there are ghosts he'll visit me to curse me and what can I say? 'Y'r pardon, Father, but I was too busy with my doxy to be y'r true and faithful son.' And he—and he—"

His voice broke in a sob and he stood shuddering, his hands at his face, while the horror of his failures crowded in on him. There was the whisper of Raleigh's blade being returned to its sheath, the pad of a footstep on the carpeted floor, and Dion felt a hand on his shoulder.

"Your sorrow is mine," Raleigh said quietly. "Forgive me for the grief I've brought you. Believe me when I tell you I thought I did what was right."

"You thought—oh Walt, what have we not thought wrong, the two of us?" Dion asked brokenly. "And the blame's not yours. It's mine—all of it. Had I not speared Groven—"

"Nay, Dion," Sir Walter interrupted gravely, "don't damn yourself too heavily with that thought. For Avronbeck had enemies at court who worked always to bring about his downfall and if it had not been the Groven affair they would have found another to use. You know y'r mother's family has been suspect since her brother fought for Mary at Carberry Hill 'gainst the people Elizabeth supported. Then, although we know it's damnable, slanderers linked y'r mother with the Campion plot and—"

"A scurvy lie!" Dion burst out. "My mother never—"

"We know, we know," Raleigh said wearily, "and so did those who whispered their slanders but the Queen's suspicious ear heard the whispers. All this began when that young idolizer of Mary of Scotland, Anthony Babington, was named by the Jesuit priest, John Ballard, as ringleader of a plot to assassinate Elizabeth and place Mary on the English throne, with Spain's help."

His hand went up to tug at his sharp beard.

"They say Ballard confessed only after weeks of racking but Babington babbled volumes where Ballard spoke syllables. He —Babington—admitted he plotted with Philip to land a Spanish army under the Prince of Parma when Elizabeth was killed. Yes, he said, Mary of Scotland knew everything about the plot; he even gave his judges the cipher used in letters Mary sent Philip by him."

His voice sank to a mutter.

"And now—too late—I learned when he was tortured to disclose his accomplices, somebody—who was it, Walsingham?—forced him to name your father, Sir Clement, as the leader."

"Oh God," Dion groaned, "could such a hellish thing happen in England?"

"It has happened," Raleigh said stonily. "Three days ago Babington, Ballard and three others were publicly executed at Lincoln's Inn Fields. And today, September twenty-third, 1586 —ah, mark the black date well!—the most loyal man in England, Sir Clement Harvie, Third Lord Avronbeck, was beheaded at Tower Green, here in London."

Dion buried his face in his hands.

"So we were helpless, Dion," Raleigh went on, with an effort. "Your father's trial was secret and, besides, when y'r half-brother lost all right to call himself a man and accused Sir Clement of joining the Campion conspiracy and when Babington lied to win the mercy he never got, Sir Clement was doomed. And not, dear Dion, by a word or deed of yours."

Dion stood in the center of the disordered room, staring at his unslippered feet, tracing the design in the carpet with unseeing eyes, his dark hair fallen forward on each side of his wrenched face, his shoulders sagging, his arms limp. Despair had emptied him of his hot fury; now in the coldness that gripped him grew a steady resolve. No more would he be misled by any vapid thoughts of divine vengeance superseding man's; no longer would he ponder questions of what was really right or wrong; now he would come back to sanity and see this world about him as it really was, not as the weak-kneed philosophy born on Roanoke Island would have it seem. Treachery, villainy, deceit, murder were the necessities of life today? He could be treacherous, he could be villainous, he could lie, he could kill, with the most accomplished of his enemies. Did the power of retribution lie in the hands of a woman whose withered ear demanded false flattery? Then he could spill guile that would delight her—until the time came to stab her through her black heart. Elizabeth had killed his father because of a plot Avronbeck had wrongly been linked with? Those plotters had been bungling fools; he'd plot so as the Queen would never discover it until it was too late to help herself.

Spanish Philip, Mary of the Scots, you who followed Lady Jane Grey and the Duke of Norfolk, Ridolphi and Campion and the others who hate Elizabeth, you have a new champion now! Take Dion Harvie as a man dedicated to avenge the wrongs against his father and his house with sword and perfidy, to match the murder and villainy of those who rule England!

Dion raised his head and looked into the worried face of his friend, Sir Walter Raleigh.

"I see the truth in what you say," he lied, "and you need not fear. I'm past my spasm of anger now, Walt. I know it would be madness, indeed, to do aught but accept this sad disaster in silence, praying to God that He find means to bring justice to those who killed my father."

Raleigh eyed him narrowly, then relaxed as his hand touched Dion's shoulder again.

"You're wise beyond your years, Dion," he said. "I feared you'd be driven to rash deeds that would be running yourself through with your own blade. Before I came here, I checked with Charles' situation, thinking you'd dash at him instanter. Know you that Charles, quaking so long as you're abroad, has surrounded himself at Avronbeck Hall with a troop of soldiers lent him by the Queen. He does not stir without an escort fit for a prince in a hostile land and he lives in terror, so 'tis said, of assassination."

Dion clucked his tongue.

"Poor Charles," he said gently. "I would there were ways to

let him know he has naught to fear from the Dion Harvie who puts all his enemies' fate in God's hands."

Raleigh nodded slowly, still eyeing Harvie. From a corner of the room, Margery Hollis watched, her dark eyes wide and knowing, her heart clutched by the chill realization that the man she looked at was the cold-hearted, conscienceless apparition of the man she had held within her arms when the knock had sounded at the door.

9

WHERE HE HAD avoided Burnie, Dion Harvie now sought the humpbacked little landlord, the misshapen font of information, at every opportunity. Through the gnomelike enigma whose interwoven spy channels the Queen herself could have envied, Avronbeck's son kept watch on every move made by his half-brother, Charles.

Sir Clement's eldest son, Dion learned, was as terrified as Raleigh had reported him to be. He seldom ventured out of Avronbeck Hall and then only under heavy guard, he kept the place an armed camp. He suspected his closest intimates, especially Helen, the wife who had cuckholded him with Dion, and Blount, his partner in his father's betrayal, of plotting to kill him.

"He's even employed a taster, like a king," Burnie chuckled. "Aye, some poor thrall must take a bite from every dish and sup a mouthful from every cup before Charles Harvie will touch it."

"And the Queen's not moved to seize the rest of my father's lands?" Dion asked.

"Not yet," Burnie answered. "They say Walsingham needs must wait a proper time before putting Charles out into the cold bare-arsed, seeing that 'twas Charles' lies that whetted the axe for Sir Clement."

"And what of my mother and sisters?" Dion asked.

"Well, my poor information is that Milady and y'r sisters have been taken to Lochlaven, where poor Mary was once held. They say it's a fine castle and they're not specially guarded, the place being on an island.

"Adam, you probably know, was killed out of hand as Milord's chief aide. They say the Queen offered him a pardon if he'd sign affidavits that Sir Clement conspired to assassinate Elizabeth and he spat on the envoy who offered it."

God rest Adam's soul then, Dion thought bitterly, and give surcease to the poor fool who could not understand that treachery was in the mode.

Mary, Queen of Scots, went on trial for her life at Fotheringhay Castle and although she argued her case bravely and well and although her judges all fell in love with her, the evidence was too overwhelming that she not only had conspired to kill Elizabeth but also had murdered her husband, Henry, Lord Darnley. Her death sentence was sent to the Queen for signature.

And Charles stayed in his makeshift fortress.

Spain edged closer to outright war with England after the Spanish ambassador to Elizabeth's court, Mendoza, was expelled. Christmas came and went as did Dion's birthday. Raleigh and his subpatentees recruited more settlers—now called "planters"—for the third expedition to the New World.

"We'll have more than a hundred men and women," Raleigh told an unhearing Dion, "to found a permanent settlement this time."

The year 1587 dawned and still Burnie reported that Charles had not dared dismiss his guard.

"And I have my old friend Ferdinando back to act as pilot," said Raleigh. "Y'know he's been with Frobisher for a time, hunting Spanish ships, but with little luck. And now I've got his pledge to guide our expedition again."

"And Guy Groven still sails with you?" Dion asked.

"Oh yes," Raleigh sighed. "It can't be helped. Already, he's beginning to strut about as though the whole venture's his doing. He's to be named a governor, no less."

"A governor? I thought you and John White—"

"Oh, with these subpatentees, I needs must hand out titles like a monarch at a levee," Raleigh grimaced. "Nearly everybody not a laborer will bear a name and 'governor' is the common one. I'll be governor-general and John White will be captain-governor or some such thing. You—what would you have for your name, Dion?"

"I have a title now on Roanoke," Dion said unsmilingly. "It's Pemecolemanmeo. I once thought it fine—I doubt I'd have the right to wear it again."

"A savage name," Sir Walter scoffed. "I'll think ye up one that'll be fitting to an Englishman."

Then name me lying traitor, Raleigh, or smirking falseface.

"I spoke of Ferdinando," the nobleman was saying. "He asked after you and bade me give you his friendliest wishes. Of course I denied knowing where you were but he only laughed at me there."

"Simon?" Dion asked. "So he sent his friendliest wishes, eh?" He ran a hand over his long hair, then chuckled. "Y'know," he went on, "I've come to believe you're right and Ferdinando *is* my friend, as you have always said. I'd like to see him if it could be arranged."

"See Ferdinando? And for what reason, pray?"

"Reason?" Dion waved a casual hand. "For company in my exile, that's all. He tells a marvelous tale and can make me laugh; I'd fain hear how many great ladies swooned in his clutch whilst he was with Frobisher and how he tweaked King Philip's beard a new way on this voyage. Aye, Walt, I'm hungering for company and who could blame me? Why not have Ferdinando come here? You've always held that he's the loyalest of loyal to you."

Raleigh frowned at the floor.

"He is," he said, too tardily, "but—well, mayhap Burnie would object. He's touchy about who sees this place, you know."

"And he'd agree to anything you told him," Dion countered.

"Aye, but—you'd trust Ferdinando seeing you here, after all your doubts about him?"

"Trust, trust? What's trust but risk these days?" Dion asked.

"And if I risk all with you, why not with Simon Ferdinando?"

Raleigh's eyes were puzzled as he looked at Dion's even smile.

"You think you run a risk with me?" he asked slowly. "You mean there's doubt of me in your heart?"

"Not the smallest speck," Dion said warmly. "I know that what you do is all in my interest. And I've been armed with a faith that all the evils that befall me and mine will be cared for by a higher power than me."

Again Raleigh's calculating look struck Harvie and glanced away.

"Methinks I hear a bitter echo in your words," the knight said in a low voice. "Ye'd not bandy words of God, would you, Dion—speak sacrilege?"

"I'm most devout," Harvie protested earnestly. "And with this new faith, what have I to fear from Ferdinando, even if he is not the true friend he says he is?"

" 'Tis good to have a faith," Raleigh said uneasily, "but foolhardy to test it too recklessly."

Dion's hand dealt Raleigh's shoulder an affectionate slap as the tall young man laughed, his blue eyes dancing.

"Come, Walt," he jibed, "you're disputing your own arguments. You said Ferdinando could be trusted, that he was my friend, when I doubted it—now that I feel you spoke truth, you balk like a nervy nag. Fetch him here—I'd like to see that black-bearded rogue again and enjoy a laugh or two. God knows I've not had my share of chuckles these past twelve months—certainly I deserve this much."

"Well—all right, then. I'll bring him tomorrow, but Burnie—"

"If you're worried about Burnie, why not bring Simon to a tavern where I can meet him, then? Think you I'd be recognized as Dion Harvie after all this time?"

Raleigh's brown eyes swept the broad-shouldered figure before him and a hand went up to the knight's beard in a thoughtful tug.

"No," he said slowly. "No, I vow you'd be safe to walk into Hampton Palace Court now and not be known with that beard. There is a tavern near here, the Boar and the Plume—"

"I've heard of it," Dion broke in. "I'fackin's, Ferdinando himself sent word to meet him there when I first lodged here. And I passed it when I walked here last August, just off the *Bonaventure*."

"Be there at eight o'clock tomorrow night," Raleigh said. "I'll have the Portuguese there to see you—and I hope it's right to do."

"Oh aye," Dion nodded. "It's the right thing to do, friend Walt, never fear."

When Raleigh had left and as Dion was sipping wine, staring out the window at the London rooftops, Margery came into the room from the closet where she had stayed during Sir Walter's visit.

"I could not help but overhear, milord," the girl said in a low voice, "and I'm concerned that you asked to see Ferdinando. You've named him treacherous enough to me—when I was in your confidence. Why do you trust him now?"

"And that," Dion said brusquely, "is my affair."

"That's true," she nodded, "but let me guess, to pass the time. I remember that Burnie once told me this big Spaniard or Portuguese or whatever he is was Walsingham's man. Now you hate Walsingham, I know, though you talk of leaving revenge to God."

"You think I lie when I say that?" Dion asked harshly, his eyebrows up.

"I know you do, milord," Margery said evenly, dispassionately.

"Now, by Christ, I'll not take that from you!" he raged. The wine slopped over the goblet's brim as he slammed it down on a table. "Who are you to—"

"The one who knows you best, Dion," Margery broke in, her chin held high. "You hide no secrets from me, nowhere in all of you."

He stared at her, brow thunderous, and then snorted before he leaned back his head and laughed at the ceiling.

"Ha, Mag the sibyl, Mag the seeress!" he crowed. "Go on, sweet sorceress, and tell me more of what I really am!"

"A heartsick wretch," Margery said softly. "A man whose sadness hurts me cruelly."

Dion barked a grating laugh and made a mocking bow.

"My thanks, great lady, for y'r sympathy. 'Tis meet, I suppose, that Dion of the House of Harvie be pitied by a common whore."

The girl's face tightened for an instant and then smoothed. Her lips that had thinned momentarily curved in the suggestion of a wistful smile.

"Why do you flog me so with that name, Dion?" she asked gently. "Are you still striking out where you can and I'm the only target, as you once said? If it eases you, milord, strike hard!"

He moved toward her, his face black, his fists clenched.

"I'm done with your martyr's ways, your sad forgiveness! Aye, I'll strike hard—'tis past the time I should have done it!"

His hand lashed out. There was the crack of his knuckles against the woman's face, the bleat of pain that escaped her lips before she bit down to shut it off. She stood there in front of him, chin still high, unmindful of the trickle of blood that came from the cut where his ring had gashed her cheek. The smile was still in place, though wrenched ajar before she brought it back to what it had been. Quiet. Unreproachful.

His blue eyes bored into hers, the harsh twist of his mouth grew grimmer, the set of his taut body stiffened.

"Get out," he said tonelessly. "Ye've brought me to this—ye've goaded me into striking a woman. Ye've dragged Harvie down this far, now leave him be."

He turned back to the window, nauseated by shame, revolted by the sight of the serene, bruised face that still looked up at him although he had put it behind him. His brain spat a hundred curses on the meddling woman who dared say she knew him, who told him he could hide nothing from her. The foul invectives failed to sting even his own guilt; they were empty, meaningless, the rantings of an idiot mind, hollow in their viciousness.

He hated her, then, but he could not satisfy his hate by hurting her by his words or by his blows or even by his thoughts. She was armored against his bitterness so that no word of his could wound her. He could smash that lovely face, stamp on her gentleness, revile her forbearance and she stayed untouched. She was—

He whirled to face her again.

"Who are you?" he asked gravenly. The question was not an idle one; it needed answering.

Her eyes were wide, wondering, as she stared at him.

"Who am I, Dion?" she asked, in turn. "I'm Mag, who loves you."

His hand swept aside her answer impatiently.

"You're not the complaisant wench I used to know," he said. "Who are you that you know of Walsingham and what I hope to do with Ferdinando?"

She hesitated, biting at her full lower lip, then spoke slowly, thoughtfully.

"It's true I've changed," she said, "and know things now I never would have begun to guess a year ago. I don't know why, milord, but—but I spoke truth, though it angered you, when I said you could never hide a thing from me. I know, for instance, that you think that because Ferdinando is Walsingham's man you can work with the Portuguese to get close to Walsingham's toy, your half-brother, Charles. You think Walsingham is eager to rid himself of the foul weakling who betrayed his own father so Avronbeck's estates might be gobbled for the Queen. You think the First Minister, then, would even let you be Charles' executioner to rid himself of the need for having your half-brother killed himself."

"Aye, he'll agree," Dion jerked out. "Treachery's his god."

"And now is yours?"

"What else? Honesty? Trust in other traitors? Brotherhood mayhap? Nay, Mag, I've seen the Indians worship those gods and seen the result. If I ever thought to bend a knee to prettier idols I've been cured of my foolishness—they're shams, Mag, to stun dupes for the real god's knife."

"No, Dion," the girl said, in a voice that was barely more than a whisper. "No, you're wrong."

"You say this," he sniggered, "after all the bright and shining deities treated you so prettily? You were but eight years old, as I remember, when these gentle powers made you sell your maidenhead to keep from starving."

"And still I say you're wrong. I speak of you, not of Mag Hollis."

"*I* speak for Dion Harvie! And I say that no matter how you've guessed my course, I still intend to follow it, right or wrong. Or will you play the informer and ruin all my plans?"

Slowly she shook her head, her eyes still placid.

"No," she said. "You know I'd never do that. I can but beg you not to do this—and why should you listen to me?"

"Why indeed?" he asked, his voice brassy. "I'll listen to you when you ask the questions you're intended for, such as those that deal with this—and this—"

"Yes, Dion," she said resignedly. "Here, or there, or on the bed?"

He knew then how he could hurt her—by his loveless act of love.

10

"HE'S FINALLY dropped his guard, then?" Dion asked.

"Aye, complete," Ferdinando rumbled. The spade-bearded Portuguese drained his tankard and raised it over his head, beckoning to a blowsy serving wench. The slattern made her way through the noisy crowd, oblivious to the hands that pinched and pawed, and came to the rough-hewn table where Harvie and the pilot sat.

"Two more," Simon ordered. "And pray don't keep us waiting whilst ye serve some customer other than ale in the back room."

"That was not y'r order the other night when you were so randy," the wench giggled. "Then, I had to keep a dozen thirsty men waiting f'r close onto—"

"Enough!" Ferdinando grinned. "Fetch the ale!" He turned back to Dion, his big hand going to the pearl pendant that dangled from his ear. "Aye, the soldiers who were at Avronbeck Hall have been withdrawn; Charles thinks enough time has passed to prove you're not about—you're dead, he hopes—and while he's still uneasy about Blount and his own wife, he fears no attack from outside."

"And Walsingham—" Dion began. The Portuguese cut him off with a warning gesture.

"Friend Dion," Ferdinando said, his voice lowered, "must I be forever cautioning you to shun names like the plague? God's sake, you blat about like a skewered sheep and every word a ravelling of the hangman's rope."

"Well then, *your friend*—is he agreed to my plan?"

"My friend, Dion?" Ferdinando asked blandly. "I have no friends, save you. What plan, pray? I know nothing nor will I ever save that you're thinking of a visit to y'r old home and asked me to sound out the prospects of y'r welcome. And I tell you that y'r half-brother's dropped his misguided suspicions and can be reached with no bother any night you choose to make y'r visit."

"And Wa—*your friend* can be trusted to keep hands off?"

"Ah, ah, more talk of my mysterious friend! I tell you—that's a good girl, Polly. Here—for you." The wench caught the spinning coin, bobbed a thank-you and wedged her way back through the crowd that jammed the Boar and the Plume.

Ferdinando drank deeply from his tankard and set it down on the scarred table in front of him. He wiped his mouth with the back of his hand and hunched closer to Dion.

"I can say this: If you're concerned about the Queen's men spoiling your reunion with your dear half-brother, you needn't be. I have it that certain people have decided 'twould be a waste of soldiers' pay to use them to hunt Charles' ghosts and phantoms. Nay, there'll be no hands in this meeting but yours and Charles'—and mine."

Dion raised his head abruptly, peering at Ferdinando over the tankard's rim.

"Yours?"

"Of course," Ferdinando smiled. "Whose else, Raleigh's? You

know what he would say to all of this—he is uncommon touchy about reunions, it seems. Who better at y'r side than Simon Ferdinando? And you needs must have somebody with you."

"I can do this alone," Harvie growled. "'Tis my duty."

"And 'tis *my* duty to go with you," Ferdinando added equably, "for was it not my doing that you can go?

"And," he added, raising the tankard again, "if I was offended couldn't it be my doing that you didn't go?"

Dion's cup slammed down on the tabletop as his short-clipped beard bristled.

"Now by God's gullet!" he began. "I'll tell ye now—"

"Nay, friend Dion," Ferdinando broke in smoothly, "let me tell you, instead. Y'see, I have my price for—er—arranging things such as this and now it is the right to go with you to Avronbeck. And why? Because 'tis always best for a man in my calling to look ahead, far ahead. Suppose the men I trust in certain actions decide the time has come to turn out Simon Ferdinando or even suppose that gentle Simon has need for a—let's say—loan against future labors and my employers are stricken stingy? Then it's invaluable to have at hand certain memories of certain events that *I have been part of* to coax money out of the stingy ones or warn those ingrates who'd cast me adrift that I'd better be retained."

He leaned back on his bench, his smile wide and warm, his hands spread palm up at shoulder level.

"You see?" he asked. "'Tis simply explained why I must go with you to call on brother Charles."

"I see," Dion growled, "that the day will come when one of these ingrates or stingy ones will have y'r throat cut."

"And that," Ferdinando grinned, "has been tried before but I'm still here. When do *we* ride to Avronbeck, Dion?"

"Tomorrow night—you can get horses?"

"Oh aye," the Portuguese nodded, and then groaned. "But no matter how fine an animal I'll get for me he'll be bound to have a cutlass for a backbone that'll split me in half before we're outside the city walls." His black eyes narrowed. "Who knows of this but me?" he asked. "That dwarf, Burnie?"

"No, nor Raleigh, nor any man."

"Or woman? What of Milady Mag?"

"You know about her?"

"What don't I know about?" Simon asked calmly. "Oh, I'll confess Raleigh hid you well that first winter but I've known of Lime Street and Burnie and the beautiful Margery since you came back with Drake. And did not intrude on you, ye'll mind, till you sent Raleigh to me with the word you'd see me. Which sh'ld prove I'm y'r true friend, if you still need convincing."

"Or prove," Dion amended, "that the Queen's taken back her reward for me since she's had my father murdered and you hoped times would change so she'd renew it."

Ferdinando scowled, then recaptured his grin.

"Dear Dion," he sighed, "when will you learn to trust me? You haven't answered me about Margery—does she know your plan?"

"Aye," Dion said grudgingly, "but she'll be no danger. The woman thinks she loves me and she'd never blab."

Ferdinando's blunt fingers drummed on the tabletop as he looked at his tankard, his thick brows down over his eyes. Finally he shrugged his heavy shoulders and returned his gaze to Dion.

"You may be right," he acknowledged. "Women in love are more to be trusted than priests and noblemen—till they're cast off. And you have a way of making women love you, Dion. There was Rycko, remember? God's sake, she would've cut off her hand for you, and she a savage wench who shouldn't be civilized enough to know faithful love." He emptied his tankard with enormous gulps and shoved back his bench. "But I must be about the things I have to do. Tomorrow night, then, I'll meet you—where?"

"At Queenhithe, where we met that night I was waylaid."

"Waylaid? I never heard of that." The big Portuguese wrapped his heavy cloak about him and turned away from the table. "I'll be there at sundown. Till then."

11

AVRONBECK HALL loomed menacingly under a starless sky, enormous, cloaked in shadows that the lighted windows did no more than pinpoint. The month was March and the oaks that bordered the sweeping lawn twisted their just-budded limbs in sleepy welcome to the first Spring winds; the ground was spongy under the feet of the two men who tethered their horses in the trees and moved toward the great house.

Simon Ferdinando's sword hissed against the cloak that covered it; Don Harvie's rapier swung free, the younger man's cape flung back to clear it. They walked rapidly, silently, toward the rear door that Dion had entered two years before to be greeted by his father, his mother and his sisters.

"You're sure the kitchen's open to us?" Dion hissed. Ferdinando hunched his shoulders.

"As sure as I can be about anything," he whispered. "A slavey's been paid to unbar it—though I was told the servants who loved y'r father would have gladly prepared your way without pay."

"And Charles and Blount are home?"

"Less talk, for God's sake! Ye'll put the house on guard. Yes, both our pigeons are cooped. Now, careful with the door."

A hinge squeaked, but with only one rasping grunt before it quieted. The two men stepped into the kitchen, half lit by the sleeping fireplace, and shut the door behind them. Now Ferdinando drew his sword, Dion his rapier. Their footsteps whispered over the flagged floor of the kitchen toward the door to the hallway that led to the front of the house.

Dion's heart thudded, his throat tightened, as he pushed open the door and peered down the arched hallway. Far ahead, at the furthest part of the corridor, lay a rectangle of light that marked the opening to the great hall where Charles should be. There was a muted voice, another, from the room and then the clink of metal as of a flagon touching a cup. The two men drifted down the hallway.

Dion's blood froze, his nape prickled, his breath stopped, as there was the click of claws on the floor just inside the door and the sleek head of a greyhound poked around the corner, three feet from him. The animal's ears shot up. It uttered a low growl as its short ruff rose.

"The dog, Charles!" That was Helen.

"Huh? Dog? Dog?" That was the man to be killed, Charles.

"Look at him! What is it, Rip?" So Blount was there, too. A convenience.

"See what it is," Charles ordered thickly—that had been a flagon and a cup, all right. "Don't stand there, fool—see what it is!"

"And why not you?" Blount asked. "You're as near as me."

"God's teeth, what a coward I have for a brother," Charles snarled. "Afraid of the wind that makes a stupid dog nervy."

"No more a coward than the man who sends him to see what's up 'stead of seeing himself." So Caroline, Blount's wife, was in the room, as well. "I'll tend to it."

Ferdinando's elbow nudged Dion and the two men stepped into the doorway, the snarling greyhound retreating before them.

Dion found himself face to face with Caroline, the mousy sister-in-law he never had bothered to bed. Beyond her and close to the fire, Charles and Blount sat at a table, tall goblets in their hands. Helen was to the right, a piece of embroidery in her lap, her round eyes fixed on the doorway.

The hound was the only thing that moved for the space of ten seconds. Caroline's mouth hung ajar as she stared up at Dion. Charles' head, turned toward the door, stayed drooping over the cup he held. Blount kept his hand suspended above the flagon's handle. The needle in Helen's motionless hand twinkled in the light from a sconce above her head.

"Muh-muh men!" Caroline stammered to break the stark silence. "Blount!"

Charles' goblet toppled as he shoved himself away from the table. He lurched to his feet, his blade rasping as he drew. Helen squealed. The greyhound barked. Blount quavered a curse.

Dion stepped into the room, brushing Caroline aside as he

stalked toward his half-brothers. It was a precious moment; it was sweet to look into Charles' puffed and raddled face and see recognition dawn in the eyes of the man who had condemned his father. It was worth all Dion had cast aside to watch the terror flow into Charles' desperate stare, to see the disbelieving horror drain the blood from his half-brother's pouched cheeks.

"Yuh-you've got a beard," Charles stuttered, senselessly.

"You've got a throat," Dion smiled.

Charles thrust out his left hand in a desperate gesture.

"No, no!" he cried. "No! They said you'd not come here! They said you were dead! They *promised* me!"

"Mayhap I am dead, dear Charles," Dion said, quietly. "Mayhap I truly died when I heard my father'd been axed and now I am a ghost. They say ghosts can walk and you'll be sure if they're right or wrong in a minute, when I kill you."

"No, Dion!" Blount found his voice and shrilled his plea. "You can't kill us, your brothers!"

"I can't?" Dion turned speculative eyes on the younger half-brother. "I vow I can. I can kill a score of such brothers and find it most—"

"Have done!" Ferdinando barked harshly. "No time for pretty speeches now! Take the older, Dion—he's your meat. I'll handle Blount."

"I'll take both and—"

"Behind you!"

He ducked instinctively at Ferdinando's blared warning, half turning, his sword held low. He was enveloped by a clawing, panting whirlwind, that scratched, bit, kicked, as it uttered half-human cries.

His first thought, after the surprise passed, was that Caroline had masked her spirit well. He had always thought of her as a pale-faced cipher who had not dared take the direct action Helen had, but had contented her dissatisfaction with Blount in provocative glances and slope-hipped allure—yet here she was, the only one in the room who sprang to the fight.

He flung her off, sending her spinning up against the wall with a crash that brought an explosive grunt from the woman. He turned back in time to meet Charles' savage charge. Ferdinando was ahead, to one side; apparently Blount had leapt first and the Portuguese had sprung to block him.

Charles' first slash scored. Dion was still off balance when the parricide's vicious stroke whistled through the air; he had time only to raise his blade to deflect Charles' cut so that the steel bit into his shoulder instead of his neck. There was a blaze of pain that staggered Dion. He reeled backward, his vision hazing, then steadied enough to parry Charles' second thrust. That done, his wounded shoulder ceased to be; he surged forward as full of strength and confidence as though Charles had never touched him.

His oldest half-brother's face, agleam a second before with the triumph he had seen in a killing stroke, sagged and greyed as Dion came at him. Always the coward, he fought now with a determination born of hopelessness; if there had been a chance to escape what was coming to him he would have dropped to his knees, begged cravenly or fled ingloriously; he knew there was no hope of deliverance from the doom he had feared and from which he had tried to hide and in his despair he fought better than he knew how.

Dion pressed forward, his rapier searching high, probing low, reaching for the hole in Charles' frantic guard. The cold hate that had let him smile at Charles' burbled remark about his beard served now to keep the half-brother in merciless focus; it was as though Charles' moves were labored, turgid, ridiculously easy to foresee. A grim elation rose within Dion as Charles went back toward the wall, toward his death. This was the fullest reward of life that had ever been given Dion; this led to the ultimate ecstasy. With the stroke that killed Charles would come a sheer delight incomparable to any earthly rapture. Love—laugh at love as the provender of bliss! Love was a shabby substitute for hate when it came to gratification, the realization of all desire.

Cut, slash, parry, lunge. Smile at Charles and add to his agony by withholding the final stroke a moment longer! Let him live another heartbeat, yet another, so he may fully savour the absolute hopelessness! Let him gasp another lungful of precious air, swallow again the vomit of despair, wheeze another groan from between his locked teeth! Let him look a second longer at Death before Death swept him off to Hell!

Across the room, Blount screamed and there was the thud of a falling body. Ferdinando's sword had done its work, then, and now was the time for Dion's rapier to go deep.

He sent Charles' blade high with an upward press, recovered and sent his sword in.

And held his lunge!

This was not vengeance—this was murder! The man before him was as helpless—had been as helpless from the start—as though he had no sword. Fear born of awful guilt had doomed Charles before Dion had even stepped into the room; his oldest half-brother had been tortured past any pain Dion's rapier could inflict by the cancer of his own thoughts, his dreams, the memory that shrieked the damning indictment of parricide.

Kill Charles? Charles was already worse than dead.

Dion dropped his sword, stepped back.

"Not on my hands," he said, dispassionately. "I leave you to—"

Lightning blinded him, a thunderclap clashed in his ear and he pitched down down down into blackness. . . .

Part 6

1

THE MISTS BOILED and swirled and thickened and cleared. There was pain, a swamping, enveloping pain that streaked and stabbed, swaddled and burdened; it was endless and it had always been and then it was gone and not remembered. There was ebon night everlasting and bright light that revealed nothing. But always, in darkness and in blazing noon, in pain and with pain fled if it had ever been there, there was a vagueness, a confusedness, a reaching out for something solid, something to be clung to no matter if it held him in the deepest well of agony.

There was a struggling, too, to wrench himself out of these places floored with the footless sands of the Hatorask dunes, these halls of vaporous walls, these forests in which he toiled through impenetrable, ethereal thickets. And there were his cries for help echoing always through the corridors and the forests.

He was alone, terribly alone, although there were faces, voices, always with him. His father smiled at him over his silvery beard and murmured something in a voice too low to be heard and in a language never to be understood if it were heard. Elizabeth, red wig towering, bared her horse teeth at him in a lewd grin and was Margery Hollis, a great bruise spreading on her cheek. Wanchese stared at him stonily, unforgiving, his eyes lit by the fire that had belonged to Pemispan, Wingina. Rycko held him tightly and muttered brokenly. Raleigh's face was close, his voice was clear.

"Lie back, Dion," he said—or was it Simon Ferdinando? "And hush, man, hush!"

Hush the wild weeping, then, 'cause Raleigh bade it hushed. And weep for whom or what? Weep for the world and Dion Harvie and Pemispan and the seaman who pitched into the bilge-water of the old *Tyger*, his neck broken by a pump bar. And Sir Clement, Lord Avronbeck, and his son, Charles, who betrayed him. Weep for them all and laugh at Simon Ferdinando's tale of the husband who was cuckolded and cozened and who thanked the man who tricked him.

Yes laugh, 'twas always friendlier than weeping. Laugh at the heathen savages who did not know Truth but thought they did, and Ralph Lane with his silver cup and the soldier, Henry Lorton, who had squawked like a hen when he, Dion, had jumped him, on his way to save his friends, the Roanokes. And Rycko who dared love him as though she were a civilized woman—ah, he knew she did, he knew she did—and Mag Hollis who was—what? No matter what, laugh at her or weep or use her like this—aye, this was one real thing amidst confusion.

"Sweet Mag," he shouted, for he knew there was no one to hear, "you are a lovely thing and gentle and so close. If I could love a single thing, a woman or a friend or my father's head upon the block or the sun or a white gull, Pemecolemanmeo, a lengthy name but good, good—or was—I would love you! For your juice as sweet as the grapes and your exceeding wisdom and your heat and even your tears. But laugh, don't weep, sweet Margery."

She answered him but she was gone before she spoke and the pain dug deep, then shimmered just above him like heat waves trembling over a white sand shore and he was lost, alone and jostled by a throng.

Captain Guy Groven was a pitiful thing, blind, misshapen and limping, smeared with reeking dung. Sir Francis Walsingham was a benign saint, exuding an aura of mystic light. Charles was a greyhound with raised ruff. 'Od's blood, these were things he had not known; this was most interesting! But shut the door against the rain—he could not stay with these people in this downpour.

"Three days," Ferdinando said, "and we'll be away. Three days. And how did he stand the journey?"

('Twas a rough voyage—aye, now I recall—with the vessel

pitched from wave to wave like a chip in a brook but 'twas not Amadas' bark at all, it was a horse, I vow. D'ye hear me? It was a horse, not Amadas' bark! Listen, curse you, when I speak!)

"Better than I thought he could," Margery said. "Sir Walter's friends were kind to us."

(Raleigh has no friends, only subpatentees. I must think up a proper name for myself in Virginia where there are governors and captain-governors and governor-generals. Some great name. What is the Indian word for treachery?)

"He never found his senses in this past month?"

(Who is this *he*?)

"I—I dared think he did three or four times. In the house where we first stayed, where Sir Walter had me brought when he could not rest for crying for me, he seemed to know me when—at certain times."

(Know you? Could I help knowing your voice, Margery?)

"And since?"

(Peek and pry, damn you! You always have been the nosy bastard!)

"When we reached Plymouth Town, here, he saw the ships in the harbor and knew this one and asked me if you were to be pilot —he would not sail without you."

(I've opened my eyes. I see you two talking there across the room, the cabin. I see you as plainly as I hear you. Margery, you wear a gown of rusty red, with a cape tied about your shoulders and that's blue. And you look weary, Mag, with your eyes all shadowed and your mouth drooped like your back. Wine for Margery, Ferdinando, and make her smile and sparkle once again!)

"I never thought I'd see him here."

(See me, eh? Then why do you not hear me?)

"Nor did I. When I first saw him after his wound I did not think he'd last the night. Else I'd not—"

(Not what? Speak up! Why look down at the deck and twist your hands? And you, Ferdinando, why y'r smirk?)

He watched the black-bearded Portuguese tug at his ear pendant, his dark eyes fixed on the girl who stood before him, his wide mouth curved in a grin. He saw Margery raise her face to the big man's smile, her shoulders back, her hands clenched.

"You think I tricked him, sir?" she cried. "How could I know he'd live? The physician said he'd not. And he was in torment, as you saw, and after—after, he was quiet, wasn't he?"

"Aye, he was," Ferdinando nodded. His grin died slowly. "And I don't think you tricked him, milady—ah, I did not mean to sneer, believe me! I say that I don't think you tricked him into what happened, nor does Raleigh. We heard him scream for you and beg that you do what you did, and did only after all your own protests."

The tall Portuguese pulled harder at the pearl.

"Mayhap," he said slowly, almost embarrassedly, as though admitting some great error, "there's more to this than we can see. I was with him when he cried for you and ordered what he did and I thought it madness from his wound. So did Sir Walter when I first told him but the physician said unless we did what Dion bade, he'd die. And later—when 'twas done—all of us saw what happened to him. We watched him sleep for the first time and we saw him smile and—" He shook his shoulders as though shrugging off a question too heavy to ponder. "God's teeth, I'm no man to recite priest's words and yet—and yet—I've seen strange things and why couldn't there be stranger things still that I couldn't see happen before this? Why couldn't a man near dead get wisdom that he'd laugh at when he was well and act on this wisdom and by it save his life? And if it was madness, as Raleigh says, well then, the Indians believe their madmen talk with their gods so why not Dion for that once? He'd skewer me if he heard me say this but I'm fool enough to half believe something —*something* beyond delusion spoke through him and so kept him from dying."

"And so," Margery Hollis said in a low voice, "made me his wife."

(That's it then. I've made Mag my wife. *My wife!* Those two speak of madness but this is no part of some mad dream. Margery Hollis, Lime Street doxy; Margery Harvie, wife of Dion Harvie, fourth son of Sir Clement Harvie, Lord Avronbeck.

(This is no jest, I know that by the way they speak, their eyes. They are not mocking me, though they pretend they don't hear me when I shout at them. No, this thing happened and Ferdinando and Walt watched me marry her.)

The mists rolled into the ship's cabin, blotting out the two people who stood across the room. Dion spent a century, a breath, wandering through shadowy moors and veiled halls and came back to the low-ceilinged cabin. Margery was alone with him; Ferdinando had left. Timbers creaked, the deck tilted one way and then another, a salty breeze curled in through the window opposite the bed, there was the *slush* of water outside.

Margery sat on a stool, her eyes on her hands folded in her lap, her face in a repose that smoothed the lines Dion had seen when he had watched her talk with Ferdinando. She was tranquil, at peace, resigned. She was beautiful, with a luster she had never possessed even in her most artful moments. Her serenity flowed from her, enveloping Dion, stilling the harsh exclamation that leapt to his lips, pressing back the outrage that stirred within him.

She felt his staring eyes on her and slowly turned, her long lashes lifting from her cream-smooth cheek. She looked at him and smiled, gently, wanly, and then dropped her eyes back to her hands. *She does not think I see her!*

He wet his lips and found the voice that came back to serve him once again.

"Margery?" It was a husky whisper but she heard.

She stiffened, still staring at her hands, and slowly, slowly, brought her brown eyes around to meet his.

"Yes, Dion?" she said and her voice was only a shade stronger than his.

"Margery—Mag—I heard you and Ferdinando talking—when was it?—and you said—"

The effort to speak, more than a physical endeavor, forbade him saying more. Margery's eyes were clouded where they had been calm when she had first looked at him; the tension that had been absent from her face was back again. She parted her lips to answer him and closed them again with her words unspoken.

"What did it mean, Margery?" he gasped. "I'm all bewildered—it seems I have been dreaming for a year, ten. Was it madness, all of it? And did I truly make you wife?"

Her eyes closed for a brief moment and then she opened them to meet his beseeching stare. She nodded and her hand came out to push back a lock of his hair from his forehead, lingered against his face as though this were some parting gesture and returned to her lap.

"Aye, Dion," she said in a low voice. "Aye, we were married. 'Twas no trick, I swear it!"

"But how—why?"

She addressed her hands, tightly locked now on her knees, as though their grip was needed to stop their trembling. She spoke rapidly, with no inflection except a troubled undertone.

"It was seven days after you—were wounded, milord," she said, "and Sir Walter came to me at Burnie's where I waited. I was all undone because I knew naught of what had happened to you after you flung out of the house that day with only a word that your revenge was at hand. Raleigh—"

"My half-brother Charles?" Dion interrupted. "I remember that I had him—" He fell silent, seeing Charles goggling at Death again.

"Ferdinando killed him, milord, after you were struck down."

"So? Then 'twas Simon who killed him, eh, not me? But how was I struck down?"

"Ferdinando said a woman, your brother Blount's wife, cracked your skull with a heavy candlestick from behind."

Dion found the strength to attempt a grin.

"Dear Caroline," he murmured. "I was so wholly wrong about her—of all of them she was the only one with spirit. So after I was wounded?"

"You were bad hurt, Dion," Margery said, watching her interlaced fingers. "Ferdinando took you to the hut of one of the Avronbeck peasants, more dead than alive, then rode for London to get Raleigh and a physician. You stayed there for two days and then they moved you to a cousin of Sir Walter. Then—then Raleigh came for me."

She looked at him and then back at her lap.

"You—you were exceeding low, milord," she went on, "and they could not quiet you, for all they did. You—you cried out for me—ah, you were dying, so they thought, all of them."

There was a silence as Margery's voice caught in her throat, tears trembled in her eyes. Heavy footsteps crossed the deck overhead. There was the cry of a shipmaster and the rattle and clack of gear on deck.

"Go on, Margery," Dion said.

"I found you drained of everything but your mad conviction, milord," the girl said. Her face came around to him again, her chin lifted. "And I did try to coax you out of y'r humor—Ferdinando and Raleigh will not gainsay me! But you must marry me—aye, marry me or die! And—and the physician—a nobleman himself, Dion—said that it was true. Raleigh—yes, and Ferdinando—would hear none of it until the physician said 'twould make no difference save y'r last hours would be quiet, ye'd be freed from y'r torment. And so they nodded, finally, and—and a rector was summoned and read the words."

She talked on and Dion saw it all, as though he were looking down on the scene from some perch high in the room. How could he know it was late afternoon, with the sun slanting through tall windows and dust motes swimming through the light? How did he see the group around the bed in more detail than he would have remembered them if he had been possessed of all his faculties? Raleigh stood at the foot of the bed; Ferdinando sprawled in a chair, his booted feet stretched out in front of him, looking down into a cup. Margery, in a dark gown and with a travelling cape about her shoulders, reached down to hold his hand—Great God, but he was white and wasted!—and the frocked rector, an old, white-haired man, leaned over both of them. Against the further wall were two men he did not know, the physician and his host, Raleigh's cousin, watching the ceremony that changed Margery's name to Harvie.

If this scene were part of his mad delusion it was a sharply-etched fragment of it; a cunningly daubed painting of vivid colors, a memory with even the feel of the sunlight on him and the smell of the place, rank with its sickbed stink.

Now, as he closed his eyes to shut out this vision, he felt a curious peace, a relaxation which was more strange than the phenomenon itself. He should have been aghast that his delirium had made him marry a strumpet; he should have been outraged that Raleigh would permit it, even to quiet his last hours, but there was no anger, no shame, no remorse, only a quiet acceptance as though this thing that had happened was right.

"And when the physician said you'd live, though the odds were you'd never regain your senses," Margery was saying, "Sir Walter —Sir Walter bade me to keep our marriage silent and leave you till a divorce could be arranged. And I said no."

Her hand clasped his and he felt his own fingers tighten.

"It was not right," she burst out, "but I could not help it! I thought—I thought—God help me I thought you meant it when you wept for me with your last breath! I thought I would be faithless—faithless, *me!*—to leave you then.

"Besides," and her voice grew stronger, "you needed me, Dion, as a nurse if nothing else. Raleigh's cousin had a wife but—but she only wanted you out of the house—all feared the Queen's wrath at what had been done. So I went with you to another house in Wiltshire—ah, that journey was a nightmare!—and stayed with you while your hurts mended, but not your mind till now. We lived in a rude cottage and you grew able to walk about, though you *would* get lost sometimes and I would have to hunt for you. But I always found you 'cause when you lost the way you'd shout for me."

"I shouted, true enough," Dion said grimly. "It seems I've spent a lifetime shouting in the darkness. But go on."

"There is not much more to tell you. Word came from Raleigh that we were to ride to Devon and board Ferdinando's ship at Plymouth. By then you could ride, with me on the pillion and directing you. The journey tired you and—and your strange ways frightened off inkeepers so we slept in hedges and once we met two highwaymen but God put pity in their hearts—or mayhap they were frightened at you, too—at any rate they did not harm us and we reached Plymouth three days before the expedition sailed."

"And are now bound for Virginia," Dion said.

"With your mind mended," Margery said softly.

"And with a wife."

There was a silence and then the girl spoke slowly.

"A few words spoken by a rector needn't change what we have always been, Dion," she said carefully, "and it would ease my position with the other women in this Virginia we sail to. None save Ferdinando know I'm aught but a wife so—"

"Raleigh knows," Dion broke in.

"But Sir Walter did not sail with us."

"Did not sail—you mean the Queen again refused to let him leave?" As she nodded, he asked anxiously: "Was it because of what happened to Charles and Blount? Did Elizabeth—"

"No, Dion. Leastwise Ferdinando says Raleigh was held back at the last minute again when Her Majesty decided she needed him to stay in England to help guard against the Spaniards. He can tell you the story better than I can but from what I overheard and what was told me, the Queen was well content with Blount's and Charles' death and wanted only that you be gotten out of the country lest you plot further."

"As I would—and will when I return," Dion said tonelessly. "My father is still only half avenged and my mother and sisters—"

"Are returned to Avronbeck," Margery put in. "Don't ask me why—put it down to the Queen's whim or something I know naught of. But Elizabeth called your mother back to her court, and your older sister, in spite of Walsingham's protests. Or so did Sir Walter tell Ferdinando and he tell me. Your family thinks you dead of a fever in Virginia and have thought so ever since Drake came back."

"Raleigh told them this? Ah, he is a master at fixing things! But mayhap it is best they think me dead; they'll not worry over a corpse and their joy will be all the greater when I go back."

He turned toward Margery and smiled.

"And so, milady, we are a most respectable pair, eh, to help

Raleigh settle his new colony? God's teeth, to do this thing right, mayhap we'd best produce a dozen brats betwixt us!"

His eyes widened as the girl's face went white. Agape, he watched her as she slowly stood up and turned to show herself in profile.

"Mag! No!"

Her head bowed, she murmured a prayerful whisper.

"Yes, Dion," she said, "and I'm guilty to the fullest. I—I could not stand the thought of your leaving me and so—and so I prayed to have your child to keep a part of you when you were gone. I truly meant to go away before I swelled so much that you would see but then—"

She turned back to him, her entreaty stark upon her face.

" 'Tis not too late, Dion, if you'd have me—rid myself of the child. God forgive me but I'd do even that if it would make you happier!"

The silence that followed was broken by the racheting screech of a tern that wheeled past the window. The vessel heeled gently and levelled. A wave thumped the side softly and sluiced past.

"No, Margery," Dion said at last. "No, I'd not murder your child—our child."

She wept then, her face buried in Dion's shoulder so that the pain of the wound he had taken from Charles throbbed through him. Unmindful of the ache, Dion put his arm about his wife, Margery, and held her close, looking up at the timbers above him and wondering.

2

Sir Walter Raleigh's third expedition to the New World left Plymouth on May eighth, 1587, and its size marked the dwindling of Raleigh's fortunes. Whereas the second expedition had been comprised of seven ships, the 1587 company sailed in only three and the biggest of these was the old *Admiral,* which Arthur Barlowe had commanded in 1584.

There was no proud Sir Richard Grenville to lead this expedition. John White was top man among the colonists with the title of Governor. None of the other "governors" whom Raleigh had given titles as subpatentees risked the journey to Virginia; with Spain growing more bellicose by the day, they decided that they would be safer in England than in a far country, out of reach of Elizabeth's naval protection. But Captain Guy Groven sailed with the expedition and so did Manteo, although he would have preferred to stay in England.

The third expedition was smaller, shabbier, than its predecessor but it was vastly more important in one thing: whereas the voyages of 1584 and 1585 had been exploratory and military ventures, the 1587 expedition was launched for the sole purpose of colonization, the realization of Raleigh's old dream. Now the men who signed up for the trip were noted on the books as "planters" and each was promised five hundred acres of land in Virginia. And, most important of all, there were women and children aboard the three vessels that headed for the New World in 1587.

There were ten married couples besides Dion and Margery Harvie; Eleanor and Ananias Dare, John White's daughter and son-in-law; Thomas and Joan Warner, Thomas and Jane Colman, Arnold and Joyce Archard, John and Alice Chapman, Ambrose and Elizabeth Viccars, Thomas and Audrey Topan, Edward and Winifred Powell, Griffin and Jane Jones and Henry and Rose Payne. The Archards and the Viccars brought their sons, Thomas and Ambrose; John Sampson brought his son, John; Roger Pratt brought his son, also John. Included in the company were five apprenticed boys, Robert Ellis, William Wythers, Thomas Smart, George Howe and Thomas Humphrey.

And two of the women, Eleanor Dare and Margery Harvie, were pregnant.

The tiny fleet took the course followed by the other two expeditions, past the Azores and then to the West Indies where the three ships paused at the same "Mosquito Bay" where Ralph Lane had built his fort and seized the Spanish frigates two years before. After refilling the water casks and taking on salt, the three ships headed north.

Raleigh had given Ferdinando instructions to go to the Chesapeake Bay where better anchorage and more fertile land was supposed to be found and the Portuguese had promised to take the expedition there but as the *Admiral* neared Hatorask, Ferdinando grumbled and shook his head. He was enigmatic in his answers to White's questions but he spoke more openly to Dion Harvie.

"I don't like the idea," he said, "and never have, though Raleigh pressed it on me till I agreed. I say you all should be landed at Roanoke Island, where you at least have been before and know what to expect."

"Aye," Dion said, "but we know, too, our welcome by the Roanokes will not be happy."

Ferdinando grunted and reached for his goblet, drank deeply and wiped his mouth before he went on.

"I say," he told Dion, "that no matter how sorely wounded the Roanokes were by Pemispan's murder they'll deal better with you than the savages further north, once you've made amends. Look you; you know the humors of these people, you know they can be cozened with no trouble at all. As I've heard it, Wingina—or Pemispan to call him by his later name—walked into Lane's ambush like a babe, and after he had been given every reason to mistrust the captain. So I say John White and you can make your peace with Wanchese and your life there will be far smoother than in a strange place like the Chesapeake country."

He sipped again and reached for the jug, looking across the table at Dion.

"Or mayhap," he added, "you don't want to make amends to the Roanokes."

Dion fingered his beard, looking down into his half-filled cup.

"I'd rather do that than anything I know," he said slowly, "to show Wanchese I took no part in Lane's villainy. But I doubt Wanchese would listen to me—he'd sooner spit on me, I trow. Besides, what have I to say about it? John White is governor and Guy Groven is his captain; betwixt the two they'll order you where they will."

"No man orders me about," Ferdinando growled. Wine splashed from the jug into the cup. "And as for trying to make me take them to the Chesapeake, what would they do if I confessed to them I know naught of sandbars or channels or rocks or currents north of Hatorask? Think ye they'd risk their skins to be shipwrecked in the Chesapeake? Never those two!"

Dion's eyebrows arched as he raised his cup.

"And truly don't you know those waters?" he asked quizzically.

Ferdinando shrugged expansively. "Between we two," he said, "even if I didn't, I could smell 'em out for the danger that might be there."

"Then why refuse to go there? I know it's for more reason than that you think Raleigh's people would be safer on Roanoke Island."

Ferdinando finished his drink slowly, pensively. When he looked back at Harvie, the big bearded Portuguese seemed embarrassed by what he had to say.

"Look you, Dion," he said, "you know I've always held you a friend—aye, ever since that first day when you drew your blade on me for calling you a pink-hosed popinjay, remember? And at the first, I confess, I called you friend to talk down your suspicions—at least for the main part. I knew there was a reward for you and—ah well, that's been a deal of weeks ago. But as time went on and when you made that second voyage with me, when Grenville tilted his nose and Lane let wind through his mouth, I came to really be your friend. I truly don't know why I did, God knows you made no offer to meet me halfway. 'Twas something—something—mayhap it was your goodness."

"Goodness!" Dion exploded.

"Aye, goodness," Ferdinando nodded calmly. "I told you I could sniff out dangers in a sea—it's true. And so can I sniff out the goodness in a man, and his evil, no matter what a face he tries to turn to me."

"But God's bones, Simon!" Harvie protested. "You cannot know me half as well as you think! There's not a man less worthy to be called good than me!"

"Ah well," the Portuguese smiled, "I'm wrong, then. We'll not argue the point. It's enough to say I got to be your friend and still am, more than ever since—since the night at Avronbeck Hall."

"You proved my good friend there, certainly."

"And now I'd land you in the Chesapeake, a sea apart from where I'll be and amongst y'r enemies and with never a friend save your wife?" Ferdinando asked. "Never!"

"But neither have I friends on Roanoke Island," Dion said. "Wanchese must hate me more than he hates Lane, for I was a brother to him, I was given a tribal name. I vow Wanchese would use his axe on me at the first chance. Wanchese a friend? Hah!"

Ferdinando pushed back his stool, arose and stalked brace-legged against the ship's motion, to the window and stared out at the sea. He spoke without turning, his words borne back into the room by the warm wind.

"I am a thick-skulled mariner," he said, "and so my thoughts must be all nonsense. But I feel Wanchese must know how you fared on the island those last weeks and months when Lane and the others turned against you. He was not wholly in the dark that you were treated as an outcast because you counselled softer treatment of the Roanokes."

"Pemispan had his spies on the island," Dion acknowledged. "Rycko told me that."

"Then Wanchese heard," Ferdinando nodded, "if he was not one of those spies and saw, himself. And think you then he does not know you played no part in Lane's murder of Pemispan? Dost think Wanchese so faithless that he believes you were a traitor to him and the tribe?"

Dion looked at Ferdinando's broad back and felt a weight lifted from his heart, a weight that had been there for a full year and only by its removal showed how it had burdened him. Not until now had Harvie fully realized that the thought that Wanchese remembered him as a traitor, his guilt over his failure to prevent the ambush, had churned within him, never quiet, always embittering, since the day he had peered at murder from the watch tower at Fort Raleigh.

Now he knew what Ferdinando said must be true. Rycko had told him the Roanokes came and went on the island almost at will for weeks and months before Pemispan was killed; how could they have helped but see that he was treated as a renegade and known why he was an outcast? So he was not a villain in Wanchese's memory!

"God grant you're right in this," he said soberly, "and I think you are."

"I know I am," the Portuguese said brusquely, "and so I know Wanchese and the other Roanokes will be your friends when you need friends—as who would be in the Chesapeake country?"

"John White," Dion pointed out, "is governor and he was most kindly of all the company to me at Fort Raleigh."

"White!" Ferdinando snorted. "A painter and an ambitious politician! Think you White will be better than Lane was, now that he's governor? He befriended you before because he needed to discredit Lane and used your treatment to that end. Now he's got the position he sought, ye'll find him no friend of yours. Already he's complained to me that Raleigh burdened the company, as he says, with you and milady."

"He said that?" Dion asked, his voice stunned.

"That and more. Friend John White has grown a nose with a high bridge of late—he complains always that he's forced to share quarters with those he calls his inferiors while you have a cabin to yourself and swears that when we reach land he'll set unseemly insolence to rights. I vow, he'll establish a nobility in Virginia before he's through, with himself as king and his son-in-law, Ananias Dare, as crown prince.

"Although," he added, "that man Groven might dispute the throne, the bragging bastard!"

"What of Groven?" Dion asked. "Of course I've been penned in this cabin like a prisoner—I haven't seen anyone but you and Margery—but my wife told me she heard some hints that Groven had been left behind, or delayed, or some such thing."

The spade-bearded pilot sent a laugh ringing through the cabin as he turned from the window and came back to the table, reaching for the jug.

"Your darling Groven?" he asked. "He's on the flyboat astern and still frothing, I'll warrant, over what happened in the Bay of Portugal, calling me a scoundrel ten times over but doing naught but call names."

"And what happened?"

"Ah, 'twas a simple mistake," Ferdinando chuckled. "Y'see, in London and in Plymouth whenever I talked with Groven the fellow boasted enough to sicken a sow about what a great mariner he was. Though how a soldier could come to know more than Cabot himself I never found out. Anyway, a few days out of Plymouth and with a tiffety-taffety rain squall off our starboard bow, the flyboat, *Swiftspeed,* signalled us in great alarm. We hove to and when *Swiftspeed* came alongside, there was Groven bellowing demands that we put into the Bay of Portugal instanter; there was a hurricane coming, by God, that would sink us all if it struck us. I laughed at him but White was fearful—he said his daughter could bear no storm in her condition, much less a hurricane."

The wine splashed into the cup and his blunt-fingered hand raised it to his lips as Dion waited.

"So," he went on, "I put into the bay, cursing Groven in four languages for the fool he was. The squall hit us and—poof!—it was over. So we set sail again."

He grinned at Dion over the lip of the cup.

"But I forgot," he added, "that night had fallen with the squall and that I'd ordered no stern light for the others to follow us by. The pinnace, *Mercury,* came out all right—I knew she would with Purseman her master—but *Swiftspeed* had trouble, for all she carried Groven, the greatest navigator since Magellan."

He laughed again and downed his drink.

"Of course I could've put about to collect the lost sheep," he said, "but cursed if I would. Groven knew so much about the sea—let him find his own way and be damned to him. Then John White was about my ears, accusin' me of everything down to murder most foul. Oh aye, I'd abandoned the flyboat and I was in Spanish pay and I meant all aboard *Swiftspeed* to perish and—God's sake, I had broke all the Ten Commandments and a few besides!"

He shrugged and set down his cup, shaking his head.

"It would be sweet," he went on, "to say *Swiftspeed* turned back to England—'twould make your own course so much easier, Dion. But fortune—or the Devil—favored the noddy and the flyboat caught up with us two days later, showing every reproachful signal pennant in the locker, I'll be bound."

"You—you'd abandon a vessel in your charge to make things easier for me, friend Simon?" Dion asked in a low voice. The pilot's face flushed and he scowled blackly.

"Now, by God's toenails, what a thought!" he blared. "I tell you 'twas a mistake, at first, and then a trick to play on the braggart! I did not even think of you and how you and milady would be better off without Groven! And as for abandoning the flyboat, those aboard her were in no danger, ever! Why, I never gave your position the least concern, Dion! You believe that, don't you?"

His blunt stare faltered and fell away before Dion spoke quietly, and with a smile.

"Of course I do, friend Simon," he said. "Why, of course."

3

THE THREE VESSELS anchored off Hatorask on July twenty-second, 1587, and Dion Harvie left the cabin he shared with Margery for the first time when John White summoned him to the poopdeck of the *Admiral* for a council.

Dion was reminded of the change in his appearance when White's mouth dropped frankly at first sight of him. He still wore the rough woolens he had worn during his month of madness, in hiding in the Wiltshire cottage; his hair was long and raggedly trimmed, although Margery had tried to barber it; his beard was shaggy enough to prove that scissors in inexpert hands brought whimsical results when used on a pitching, rolling ship.

A bit of looking glass had told him that even with fine clothes and a barber's attentions he still would seem a stranger to John White after these long months. His madness had marked him indelibly with lines that creased his cheeks and ran deep between his nostrils and his mouth; the anguish of his father's beheading and the bitter gall of hate that had followed it had stained his blue eyes; the bewilderment at all the questions that still remained unanswered showed in the uncertainty that had banished his cocksuredness.

John White had known two Dion Harvies; now he met the third. The first had been the brash youth he had first seen at "Mosquito Bay," jutting his chin at Sir Richard Grenville, treating Ralph Lane with lofty contempt. The second had been the Dion Harvie who had matured during the grim winter of 1585 and 1586 and who had grown still older too quickly with Pemispan's murder. Now this was the third Dion, whose voice was quiet, even gentle, when he spoke.

"You sent for me, friend John?"

"Aye, friend Di—aye, Master Harvie!" White's tone changed to a bristle. "Aye, and mark you're well enough to come on deck at last—now that the work is done."

"He has been very sick, Master White," Ferdinando rumbled, "else he'd have been on deck and out-drawing every man-jack of you, as he always has before this."

He stood behind White, who was seated at a table, and smiled over the artist's head at Dion as if to say: *You see how your friend White has changed?*

"Besides," the Portuguese went on, "his lady has more than made up for his absence with her work aboard the *Admiral.*"

"His lady?" sniggered a voice from behind Dion. "Icod, this Virginia air does wonders for a man's manners. I'd say his—"

"And best not say it, Captain Groven!" Ferdinando whipcracked. "Ye've already tasted certain steel—don't tempt it again!"

Dion Harvie turned slowly and confronted Captain Guy

Groven's sneering elegance. The captain wore a burnished corselet and helmet that gleamed in the sun. At his side hung a heavy sword, the duplicate of the one that had served him so poorly at Wenrick's gambling house; his well-turned legs were encased in fawn-colored hose that rose to slashed breeches of black and gold. He made a pretty figure and he knew it.

He was a bold and arrogant man until his slate-grey eyes tried to hold Dion's bleak stare. There was a brief and silent struggle and then Groven's glance shifted to Ferdinando, he coughed a laugh and sauntered around Harvie to take a place at the end of the table.

"This is no place," he said, "to discuss things best settled in other, more direct ways. I'll take up this question at a better time."

"Not so," White said, bitingly. "We'll keep our own tempers guarded, sir, whilst I'm governor of the colony! I mean to make this place an orderly settlement, not the madhouse that Lane's was at times. No brawling, by my head, or both the brawlers will be thrown in chains, I vow!"

Dion saw Groven grimace behind the hand he raised to stroke his brief moustache. He sighed inwardly; he had been here before. Nothing had changed except names and faces; White was Lane now, and Groven was White; as John White had set out from the start to undermine Lane in his position as governor, Guy Groven now barely masked the same intent to climb over White, by any means available. There was this great difference, though; where White had at least masqueraded as a friend to Dion, Captain Guy Groven would always be an enemy, in face as well as fact.

"Harvie," White was saying, "I called you to this Council because you were closer to the Roanokes than any of the rest of us last year—too close, I trow, for my liking. But mayhap you curried confidence from them to aid Lane as a spy in some arrangement I knew naught of."

"No," said Dion with a slow shake of his head. "No, I was no spy for Lane or any of you."

"I see," the artist nodded. "Then you favored the Roanokes

because you truly loved them more than Englishmen, eh?" There was a ripple of scornful snickering among the men gathered on the poopdeck, a muttered remark from Groven that brought a guffaw from the men around him. Dion's lips thinned but his voice was easy, calm, when he spoke.

"Aye," he said. "That's true."

"And still hold to this unnatural stand?" Groven asked from the end of the table. Dion turned his eyes to the man who had been Elizabeth's favorite.

"It's been a year," he said simply, "and nothing that's happened to me in that time has changed my stand."

Groven's white teeth showed in a thin smile.

"A twisted mind," he drawled, "baffles the wisest men. You prefer savages to civilized men; some other strange ones prefer mares to women. Has't tried that yet, Master Harvie?"

Dion's body tensed; he felt his heart drained to an icy lump as fury swept him. And yet—and yet—where was the spat curse, where was the leap at Groven? What held him where he was, a spiritless lump that took this insult without moving?

"Enough!" White crashed out. "I tell ye, Captain Groven, we'll have no baiting of this man, for all we abhor his philosophy! Ye'll obey my orders, sir, whilst I am governor!"

"Oh aye," Groven smiled smoothly. "Y'r pardon, Master White."

The artist-governor scowled at the man at the end of table, then turned his frown back to Dion.

"Now then," he said, gruffly, "no matter that you'd be a turncoat 'gainst y'r kind, we do have need of y'r services."

"And he'd be only right to bid you swallow y'r demands and choke on 'em," Ferdinando rumbled. "God's teeth, I knew my friend could expect little from this company but even I did not expect him to be plagued in such a way!"

His black brows lowered as he swung his inquiring gaze at Dion—*why didn't you at least curse Groven, Dion?*—and spoke again to White.

"This man's just recovered from a wound that should've killed him," he said, "and now he's treated like a bear in a pit with all of you playing the mastiff. What heroes have we here! Well and able, he'd clean this deck of all of ye and—"

"Hold, Simon," Dion said quietly. "By y'r leave, I'll manage this my own way." He looked squarely at White, ignoring Groven's mirthless laugh. "What services do ye need of me?" he asked.

"Why—why we must seek out the fifteen men Sir Richard says he left here last year when he relieved Fort Raleigh far too late," the governor said. "We'd hoped they'd sight our sails from the watch tower but they've not appeared and so we must delay till we go to the island and gather them up."

"And I—"

"You're known as a friend by Wanchese and the other Indians —you'd be safe to go ashore in case the devils still make war on us."

"Come, come, Master White," Ferdinando boomed, "ye don't mean a parcel of ignorant savages who own neither harquebus or culverin could frighten a troop led by Captain Groven! To hear the way he routed the Irish rebels, a man would think our brave captain would insist on landing on the island alone, that he might show the Roanokes how a hero can surmount all odds."

White twisted on his bench and gave Ferdinando a cold stare. "And you, sir," he said, "had best keep silent, lest my report to Sir Walter of the abandoning of the flyboat be too severe."

"I'll help ye write it," the Portuguese returned promptly, "and laugh at you when Raleigh tears it up."

The governor choked on what he was about to say and turned back to Dion.

"If you'd show yourself willing to make amends f'r past mistakes," he said, "ye'll go ashore and bring Grenville's men to us. If ye don't, we'll know ye're still bound to play the malcontent and will treat you in keeping with y'r stand. Which shall it be?"

"Oh, I'll go to the island," Dion shrugged, "but not to prove I'm any different than what I was. No, I've not changed, friend John, and I wonder that you have so much. Make amends for past mistakes? I mind it was not a hundred years ago that you told Drake I had a grievance 'gainst Ralph Lane that deserved a reckoning—was that one of my mistakes? Or was it my mistake that your report to Raleigh echoed everything I said was wrong with Lane's treatment of the Roanokes?" He raised a hand as White's lips shaped his reply. "But we waste time, Governor. Give me a smallboat and some rowers and I'll go to the island instanter—and signal you from the watch tower if all's well."

He deliberately turned his back on the table and walked to the ladder leading to the waist. Ferdinando's boots clumped behind him and the Portuguese pilot's hand steadied him at his elbow as he stepped down onto the lower deck.

"God's sake, Simon, stop treating me like a child," he fretted. "I'm strong enough save in my head—why didn't I throttle that damned Groven when he insulted me?"

"Ah, ye're still sicker than ye know," Ferdinando grumbled, "but I will say I was astonished when you spoke not a word to curse Groven for the hound he is."

"My tongue was nailed down as fast as my feet," Dion grimaced. "'Twas as though—you know, Simon, it was as though Groven was some blind beggarman who spat at me only because I could see and he could not—aye, I dreamed of Groven as such a wretch when I was mad."

"Blind beggarman, eh?" the Portuguese snorted. "Would to God he was! I tell you, Dion, he means harm to you."

"And neither am I blind, friend Simon," Harvie smiled. "So I can see whatever move he makes to harm me."

The two men entered the cabin where Dion had stayed during the westward crossing. Margery sat on the edge of the low bed, mending a shirt that was not Harvie's; since she had come aboard the *Admiral* she had spent all the time she could spare away from Dion in cooking, sewing, cleaning for people aboard until now her hands were as rough and calloused as they had been when Dion had come back to her at Burnie's. The woman, round-faced now and thick-middled, raised her eyes with an instinctive smile as Dion walked in, and lifted her cheek to Harvie's brief kiss before she turned her eyes to Ferdinando.

"Welcome, Simon," she said. "How did'st my husband fare

before the governor? I've sat here imagining all manner of things good and bad—which way did it go?"

"Neither way that was important," Dion replied. "I'm to go to the island and seek out the men Grenville left here last year, that's all."

Her eyes were fearful as she glanced quickly first at Dion and then at Ferdinando.

"There's danger?" she asked.

"None at all," Dion said before the Portuguese could speak.

"There isn't, truly, friend Simon?"

"Naah, naah, milady," Ferdinando growled. "I go with him, so what danger could there be? Oh aye, Dion, before you joined the council it was decided that I go with you to keep you from getting lost on the island."

"I do not need you to—"

"And so I go along to satisfy my own curiosity, then! Come, come, get y'r cloak and strap on y'r blade and let's be at it!"

Dion cast the big man a level glance, shrugged and turned to drop another light kiss on Margery's cheek. Her hand came up to grasp his sleeve and she murmured: "Do take care!"

"With you and the child waiting for me here, how could I not?" he smiled. He pressed her shoulder before he walked across the cabin to take down the cloak and belted rapier that hung on a peg. As he strapped on the blade he sensed Ferdinando's gaze shifting from him to Margery, felt the big pilot's wonderment.

"By the Book," the Portuguese said when they were crossing the deck to the ladder that dropped to the smallboat, "I cannot understand it! To see you two together, 'twould seem you'd been married for years, not weeks. And more than that, she has the manner of some lady gently reared and betrothed in proper style and so you treat her, instead of—" He glanced sideways as Dion. "But I offend you," he apologized. "Curse this tongue of mine."

"No need to ask pardon," Dion said. "I feel the same as you —I cannot understand it either. Something—the buffet fair Caroline dealt me—makes me think that all this is right though we both know—or should—it's all the making of my madness. Someday, mayhap, my mind will clear and then I'll have the senses back to treat this as it is, a droll comedy."

"Uh—aye," Ferdinando said, and sighed. "Aye, no doubt that's what it is."

The smallboat, rowed by two sailors who obviously did not relish their duty, shot through Trinity Inlet on an incoming tide and crossed the Sound to the north side of Roanoke Island and the outlet of the creek where Ralph Lane had built Fort Raleigh. As they neared the island, Ferdinando scanned the shore and the Portuguese jerked terse comments over his shoulder at Dion.

"The fort's still standing, at any rate, and seems in good repair," he said. "I see no smoke from any chimney but the day's hot and there's no need for fires. Still, you'd think they'd have made a sign by now, eh?"

"There's no one there," Dion said soberly, and added: "Alive."

Ferdinando looked back at Harvie, then ahead at the island, and nodded.

"I guess we knew we'd not find anyone," he muttered. "Fifteen men left here by Grenville where a hundred fled in fear of the Indians. How could they live?"

The smallboat's prow grated on the sand and the Portuguese splashed over the side and up onto the beach, Dion behind him. Without waiting for an order, the seamen at the oars backed water and sent the little craft scurrying out from the shore to wait at a safe distance. Dion looked up at the ramparts of the fort, the sagging watch tower, the embrasures from which Lane's useless cannon had stared.

The place was blanketed by the emptiness of desolation, the silence of death. The narrow entrance to the fort was choked with weeds, the paths that had led to it were barely traceable. A faint wind stirred a strip of bark that dangled from an upright of the watch tower; it must have whispered but both men went rigid at the thunderous sound. Something, a bird, a rabbit, clattered through the brush to one side and Ferdinando's hand clutched the hilt of his sword.

"God's bones," he grumbled with an attempted laugh, "I'm nervy as a fainting maid over nothing."

"There's no one here," Dion said, "nor has been for many a day. Let's try the town."

Ralph Lane's "great city" duplicated the melancholy of the fort. The winter that had passed since Dion had last seen the place had dealt harshly with the town; here a roof had fallen in, there a toppling tree had crushed a warehouse; windows were hollowed eyes looking hopelessly at ruin. The house where Dion had been kept prisoner while Lane ambushed Pemispan lacked most of one whole wall; its front door sagged on one rusted hinge. The open sheds where the shipwrights had labored to keep ahead of the Roanokes' depredations were all slanted at an angle from the prod of some fierce storm. Dried seaweed caught in the bushes showed where a great tide had reached its high water mark.

"Halloo!" Ferdinando bellowed. "Halloo, you Englishmen!"

There was a thumping, snorting flurry behind the caved-in warehouse and both men's blades flashed free in the sunlight. The bushes waved and tossed—and spilled out a fine buck that bounded off, its white flag arching with his leaps.

"And that settles it," Dion laughed shakily. "There's no man close to where a deer's been sleeping away the noon heat. Mayhap Grenville's men went to the mainland, Dasamonquepeuc, or—"

"There's one that didn't," Ferdinando grunted, and pointed.

The skeleton lay under a grapevine, still encased in rusty corselet, an eroded helmet glimmering dully a yard away. The man's arms were flung forward, the whitened fingerbones even now seeming to clutch at the space he must have grabbed as he fell. As Dion and Ferdinando walked over to the remains, a tiny wren flitted past, just touched the skull with its feet and then whirled off again, chirping shrilly.

"A club," Dion said softly, "and from behind. He was running, this one, when they caught him."

The hole in the skull was almost perfectly round and with the diameter of a fair-sized orange. Whoever he might have been, Dion told himself, this wretch had not suffered a moment beyond the terror of the chase. And had he known he died because a fool named Ralph Lane must nurture his self-importance?

"This is enough," Ferdinando said. "Now we can tell White there's none of Grenville's party left here."

"And that will mean he'll be straightway for the Chesapeake," Dion pointed out.

"He can be straightway for Hell, f'r all I care," grinned the Portuguese, "but he needs must get there with another pilot. Nay, I'll tell friend John I'll go no further than here and let him squall and scream—it'll get him nowhere."

"I'd not change Raleigh's plan to—"

"And I would," Ferdinando broke in brusquely. "I say again that I'll not leave you with no friends to help you when you need it and when I sail back east there'll be none to even speak a word for you if your Roanokes are not there."

"But I have no proof the Indians won't deal with me as with this poor wretch," Dion protested. "There's no way to know how Wanchese feels toward me. Mayhap he spits on my memory as a—"

"Behind you," Simon Ferdinando murmured.

He knew before he turned that he would find Wanchese standing there and yet the sight of his tribal brother spiked Dion with a pikepoint of doubting fear. It was not fear that Wanchese might kill him; it was a dread that hate might glare at him from the Indian's eyes. Why should Wanchese not hate him? The Roanoke had met nothing but treachery in white men; how could he have clung to any trust he might have placed in one of them, and he too weak to prevent what had befallen Pemispan or even avenge it?

He wet his lips, tried to raise his hand in the Indian greeting. His voice stayed dumb; his hand stayed at his side. The two men stared at each other, the Englishman haggard, his eyes haunted, his wide shoulders trying to brace against what would come; the Indian crag-faced, impossible to read, arms folded across his broad bronzed chest. It seemed a long time that neither stirred or spoke, while Ferdinando watched silently, his hand on his cutlass, and then Wanchese slowly raised his right hand.

"Ho, Pemecolemanmeo," he said. "I am happy to see my brother."

Dion's knees weakened at the joy that swept him but he forced his shoulders back, raised his scraggily-bearded chin and smiled his answer.

"Ho, Wanchese. Your happiness is mine."

There was no embrace, no handclasp, only those few words and yet the Portuguese who watched knew the feeling that flowed between these two men, the son of the English lord and the tall Roanoke, was deeper than any he had seen between two men before. He would never understand this but he recognized it then, and accepted it; there were many things that had befallen Simon Ferdinando of late that he would never understand.

Wanchese's eyes lingered only briefly on Dion's face and then dropped to the skeleton that sprawled under the grapevine.

"That," he said, "is not our work. No, when Pemispan was killed we went back to the west where we have a village, Ocanahowan.

"We did this because the gods told us to and we did not come back here for more than three moons. When we came back, we found these white men killed and whatever they had brought with them taken for they were without food or clothes or anything they would need. We were much ashamed that we had not been here to kill these men ourselves to answer the cries of Pemispan's ghost but had let others avenge him. And for this we gave Tolepuec's tribe, the Pasquiwocs, much meat and furs and tobacco."

"The Pasquiwocs killed these men, you say?"

"Yes, though the Croatoans say they helped, so they could get gifts. But the Croatoans never had made war before, even when their food was stolen from them by the Pasquiwocs, so who could believe they would do this? But we gave them certain small gifts to make them content."

Dion looked about him, at the houses that were falling down, the dilapidated fort, the overgrown trails. He remembered the deer that had been flushed from behind the storehouse, the small game that had scurried out from underfoot as they had walked up from the beach.

"You do not hunt here any more, Wanchese," he said, "and why is that?"

"This island is taboo," Wanchese explained. "Here we Roanokes gave our love to other men and were repaid in violence and murder. So this island must be cursed; demons must rule this place. No man is wicked enough by himself to do what the man Lane, Wastomug, did unless the demons counselled him. So must the meat on this island be tainted by wickedness and the berries and even the fish along the shore. Till now we have not been on this island since we returned and found the dead white men, many moons ago. But when word was brought that white men came again to the island, I had to see if it was my brother, Pemecolemanmeo, and it is you."

He turned his dark eyes on Ferdinando.

"And the big Bright-Ear," he said. "Ho, Ferdinando. You are welcome." He turned back to Dion. "Who comes with you?" he asked. "We want it to be Wastomug so we can deal with him."

"No, Wanchese. Lane is not with us but the man John White is governor. And there is a Captain Groven and—and there is no other of the company save White who was here last year."

"And do you mean to live here once again?"

"I do not know. Raleigh told us to go to the Chesapeake country and settle there."

Wanchese shook his head emphatically.

"No good," he said. "Powhatan is chief there and always thirsty for war and very strong. You would not live long there, Pemec. Why do you not stay on this island again, as you did?"

"You mean you'd have white men live in your country after what they did to Pemispan and Granganimeo, Wanchese?" Dion asked.

"That was the treachery of one man, Lane, who led the rest," Wanchese said quietly. "Lane is not with you this time, you say, else we'd find him and kill him if we had to board your great canoes and hunt him like a snake. This man White is governor

—I remember him and he did not talk like Lane. He made marks on something once and it was me, legs, arms, head, eyes —all of me. A man who can do that can't do what Lane did, can he?"

"I don't—think so," Harvie answered, slowly, reluctantly.

"Of course this is the place for you," Ferdinando broke in. "Here, ye've got the start of y'r town by what's left of the old one. Food—you saw the animal we roused. Wanchese and his tribe are friendly—what would you more? And this Powhatan, Wanchese warns you, would murder all of you, the women and the children and—"

"Women?" Wanchese interrupted in his guttural Roanoke. "I caught the white man's word. You bring women with you this time, Pemec?"

"Aye," Dion nodded. "And one of them's my wife, Wanchese, my woman. I have been"—he sought the Roanoke word for marriage and could not find it—"I have been mated to this woman since I left here."

The Indian's face was impassive as he digested this information and then he smiled.

"She must be more beautiful than any woman I have ever seen," he said, "if you take her for your wife instead of Rycko."

"Ooh-ah," Ferdinando groaned. "I had forgotten Rycko!"

"And so had I," Dion said. "Or almost."

4

So IT WAS back to Roanoke Island instead of venturing further north to the Chesapeake country for the people of Sir Walter Raleigh's third expedition. Simon Ferdinando refused bluntly to carry the settlers further and after several heated conferences he carried the debate.

John White was to say later that Ferdinando proved a villain, first by trying to lose the flyboat in the Bay of Portugal so the

Spaniards could seize her and next by stranding the expedition at Roanoke Island in the hopes that all would perish at the hands of the Indians there. Actually, though, White seemed to Dion Harvie to secretly welcome the idea of ending the journey at the island instead of wandering northward. For one thing, White's daughter, Eleanor Dare, was nearing her time; she had not stood the crossing well and the father dreaded the child being born at sea amidst—as his imagination put it—a raging storm. Then, too, White must have been convinced he saw in detail every wrong step Ralph Lane had taken at Roanoke Island; he must have been sure he could make a success of what Lane had failed at here, whereas in a strange country there would be bound to be new problems that he would have to face without benefit of experience gained at Lane's expense.

Furthermore, the warning of Powhatan's savagery chilled White. At Roanoke Island, he had seen the Indians wage a strange war that might cripple the colony's food supply but never killed a man—why, these Roanokes even left the revenge for their chief's murder to another tribe, the Pasquiwocs! He could believe that Wanchese had no hidden motive in asking Dion to bring the settlers back to the island; the new governor knew that whatever their faults, the Roanokes did not list deceit among them.

What John White might say and write later, then, would be far different from what he thought and acted upon in July, 1587. He protested every move made by Ferdinando, true, but that—to Dion, at least—was obviously because he despised the Portuguese who scoffed at his authority and newborn prosperity. Simon Ferdinando had antagonized far bigger men than John White; the spade-bearded man with the pearl ear pendant had a faculty for bringing otherwise cool-headed people close to apoplectic rage with his manner, his utter disregard of the dignity of his superiors.

When Captain Guy Groven wrecked a raft in Trinity Inlet by ignoring Ferdinando's warning that the raft was overloaded and the trip should not be attempted on an ebbing tide, White promptly blamed the pilot for the accident.

"It was not enough to tell Captain Groven the time was not right to float the raft," the governor said pettishly, "you should have impressed it on him more weightily."

"A thing like telling an ass to walk this way, not that," Ferdinando grunted. "Nobody tells that man what to do."

"Y'should have come to me and let me advise the captain," White persisted. "He'll listen to me."

"Ah, will he?" Ferdinando grinned. "Methinks I recall some tilt at words yesterday when you'd have him start building a dock close to the fort."

"Well, that—in that Captain Groven was right," the governor said lamely.

"And in the search for gold before the new land is cleared for fields to grow maize and potatoes and tobacco—was he right there, too?"

"That question's not yet settled and I'm sure I can convince him—and what concern is it of yours, Sir Pilot? The administration of this place is my duty. Yours is to discharge the cargo from the vessels and prepare for the voyage back to England for supplies."

"Then give me the authority I need over His Majesty and Highmost Lordship Groven in the matter," the Portuguese blared back. "God's sake, this place is full of captains and no two agree! You'll come to grief, I vow, like Ralph Lane did unless you portion out the command and make sure no man steps over into another's territory."

"I did not mind," John White said acidly, "that you were engaged by Sir Walter as chief counsellor to this venture."

"Ah, no! I'm but a thick-skulled mariner, milord!" He made a sweeping bow. "And I'll be safe home, back in England, when your fine hodgepodge comes down about your ears."

He stalked off, leaving a fuming governor behind him, and walked down to the beach where Dion Harvie toiled at trundling the casks and crates discharged from the smallboats up to the warehouses and the fort. Ferdinando frowned as he saw Harvie straighten with an effort and wipe a weary forearm across his forehead; the young man who had been the brightest figure of the Amadas-Barlowe expedition of but three years before looked old and worn now.

"Leave off y'r labors for a time," he told Dion as he crunched his way through the sand up to Harvie. "Ye've been doing the work of three of these others, and you just out of a sickbed."

Dion summoned a tired smile and shook his head.

"This is good for me," he told the Portuguese. "My muscles need stretching after all their laziness. That's proved, right enough, by my puffing and groaning over a task I ought to be able to do with one hand."

"And when were you a giant? To do what you've been doing would make me puff and groan and there never was a day when I couldn't pick you up between my thumb and forefinger." Ferdinando seated himself on a keg and looked up at the fort where Groven's workmen were repairing parts of the parapet that had caved in. From the town came the sound of hammers and saws; smoke rose from the chimney of the rebuilt brick kiln. Axes rang in the forest behind the clearings and there was the whooshing crash of a felled tree.

"A busy place," Ferdinando said, "in spite of all the crossed orders of the leaders."

"Aye," Dion nodded. "I believe John White will really be a good governor for this place. That hard face he's put on may be a mask against his fears he'll not succeed."

"Mayhap," the Portuguese said sourly, "but I doubt it. How's your goodwife today, Dion?"

"Uncomfortable," Harvie said, "but the women say that's nothing odd. Dame Lawrence is kindly tendering whilst I'm at work."

"I'm glad," said Simon acidly, "that one of the old women can tear herself away from dancing attendance on Goodwife Dare, the Governor's daughter. Ye'd think a princess was about to be born, the way those biddies cluck and clack about the fair Eleanor—and never give a thought to your wife."

"Well, Mistress Dare is a frail sort, Simon, where Margery—"

"Is a great robust wench?" the Portuguese broke in. "God's sake, your Margery has as much need of attention as John White's daughter if not more. The fair Eleanor was coddled and cushioned on the voyage over here whilst Margery worked night and day to care for you and for anybody else aboard who needed what she could help at. And so when she has need of help herself, she's left alone and—"

"Not left alone, Simon," Dion smiled. He brushed a strand of black hair back from his lean face. "When Dame Lawrence leaves Margery and I'm not home, an Indian woman, Munipeo, walks in the door as if by magic and does for my wife. She comes from the mainland each day by a canoe that she says she hides by the tree on the west shore, where the eagles nest."

Ferdinando chuckled as he nodded approvingly.

"I ought to have known that Wanchese would look after you and yours. And this Roanoke woman—she's not Rycko, by any chance?"

Dion's smile faded.

"Nay, 'tis one of Wanchese's own wives, I think," he said. "Rycko—I've not seen Rycko yet and from what Wanchese hinted, I won't unless I seek her out on the mainland, where she's staying. She—she must not want to see me now I have a wife."

"I don't know why not," Ferdinando shrugged. "God knows the laws that rule such things are loose enough among the Indians. Didn't old Wingina offer his prime wives as partners to us when we first came here? And don't the Roanokes look at a toss as something no more important than a sneeze? Wives, concubines—I never have found out just which was which in this place."

"But Rycko," Dion said slowly, "is different than the others, I think. I know once, when it seemed the right thing to say, I lied to her and told her I was pledged to a woman in England and she seemed saddened by the thought, not unbothered as another Indian wench would have been. You said yourself you wondered that an Indian could know faithful love as you said Rycko had for me."

"Aye," Ferdinando said, with pursed lips, "and I pray Rycko's strange love do you and your wife no harm, now."

"It won't," Dion said earnestly. "I don't know how I know that, but I do."

"Then ye've naught to—ho, the striped skunk's finally left his hiding hole, eh?"

Dion followed Ferdinando's eyes to where a smallboat, just landed, was discharging its passengers. Last to leave the boat was Manteo, his head twisting ceaselessly, his eyes furtive as he looked here, looked there. The Roanoke who had cast his lot with the white men was far from the gorgeous figure he had presented when he had come back to Roanoke Island the year before. He still wore Englishmen's clothes, but they were ill-fitting cast-offs where they had been beautiful.

The Roanoke had changed in other ways. He had been a handsome man the first day Dion had seen him, when he and Wanchese had paddled Granganimeo close to the old *Tyger* while Ferdinando and Harvie and Amadas had waited for the Indians to make the initial move. Then, he had been a hawk-visaged, proud-eyed man and fearless in his meeting with these white men and their great ships, their gleaming armor, the guns that had disturbed the flocks of cranes. Now, he was not fearless; his turning head, the hunch of his shoulders, his slinking walk, all shouted that he was deathly afraid. And, Harvie told himself, well he might be; Wanchese might forgive all the other whites save Ralph Lane for what they had done but neither he nor any other Roanoke would ever forgive Manteo for what he had done.

Dion watched him who had been an ambitious Indian hurry up the path to the fort and turned back to the curl-lipped Ferdinando.

"And where has he been hiding?" he asked. "Strange, I should have forgot all about Manteo this long time. The last time I saw him, he was scrambling aboard Drake's ship, panicky as a chased rabbit. Icod, I didn't even ask Raleigh, back in London, what had happened to the renegade." His mouth twisted in a grimace. "And here I am naming Manteo a renegade for turning against his people when I've earned the name myself for turning against mine."

"Not in Manteo's way," Ferdinando grunted. "That swine did what he did to supply his selfishness, from what I've heard, and you've gained nothing, God knows, by your stand. As for Manteo, he found himself no hero when he went back to London. The novelty of his first visit had worn off, you see, and all his new-found friends were sick to death of his strutting. He knocked about here and there, deep in wine most of the time, and finally was given passage back here by Raleigh, who was glad to get rid of him."

"But how dared he come back?" Dion asked. "I'd think he'd shun this place like the Pit."

"Oh, he balked at first, a-plenty," Ferdinando explained, "but Groven filled him with fine stories about how he'd be made king of the Indians once that fine gentleman subdued the savages. These stories were so splendid and the wine that went with them so free-flowing that Manteo braved the return. He sailed with Groven on *Swiftspeed* and has not dared come ashore till now—I guess he's reassured by the others' welcome."

"Best bid him stay out of sight," Dion said. "An arrow out of the forest is hard to guard against."

"Bid him y'rself," Ferdinando grinned. "Besides, I vow 'twill be no simple thing like an arrow that ends Manteo's days."

"But if Manteo is killed," Dion pointed out, "then White and Groven will have an excuse to call it war again and we'll be back where we were a year ago. 'Twill be the same sorry tale over again, save this time we have women and young children to consider—in time, at least two babes."

"Well, your child will be safe enough," the Portuguese shrugged, "so why worry of the others? And, by-the-bye, when's your son to be born?"

"Son?" Dion asked. "You know this, too, that it will be a boy?"

"Of course! As I know Eleanor Dare's child will be a girl."

"Simon the Seer," Harvie laughed. "Well then, my son should be born within a fortnight, Dame Lawrence and the Indian woman say."

"By God," Ferdinando said, and slapped his thigh, "I'd give a sackful of rubies to have your son happen before John White's grand-daughter! 'Twould be a happy thing to see the first white child born in Virginia be Dion Harvie's. White puts such haughty pride in his daughter's condition 'twould be—"

"Now, now, Simon, have done. What grandfather wouldn't beam? And—"

"Did you have my leave to loll about this way?"

The question whip-cracked from behind Dion and Ferdinando. The two men turned to see Guy Groven scowling down at them, his hands on his hips, his booted feet spread wide apart.

"Ye did not work on your way here, Harvie," the captain snarled, "but now ye're here, by Christ, ye'll work or get an empty plate at mealtime!"

Ferdinando leapt to his feet with an oath, his big hand sweeping toward his cutlass.

"You dare say that?" he thundered. "You have the gall to say Dion's not worked, when he's close to fainting by the labor I bade him quit a moment? He's done more in an hour than you've done in all the time we've been here and—"

"And Harvie's under my command, not yours!" Groven shot back. "Tend to y'r sailors, Pilot Ferdinando, and let me tend to my men!"

"He's White's man, then, if he's not mine—he's never yours! 'Twas the governor who ordered him to risk his neck to find the temper of the Roanokes, wasn't it? So let John White tell Dion what he must do now, not you."

"Governor White," Groven said, smirking, "has turned Harvie over to my troop. The governor agrees with me that Harvie's safest in a soldier's place, where he can be guarded 'gainst the temptation to betray us to the Indians."

The cutlass screeped as it came out of its ring.

"Now, by God's gullet," Ferdinando raged, "that is too much! Accuse him of treachery, will ye, when he's the one who's made it easy for you by being Wanchese's blood brother?"

Dion's hands caught the Portuguese's sword arm as Harvie threw himself between the two men.

"Hold, Simon," he said. "No brawling, if ye'd be my friend. You know my position here—would'st make it worse, and Margery's, by branding me a trouble-maker? Put up y'r blade, I beg you." He looked over his shoulder at Groven. "I'm back to work instanter, Captain," he said, "and I'll try to keep at it more intently."

Simon Ferdinando slowly replaced his cutlass, scowling at Dion.

"God's blood," he muttered, "but ye've turned out to be a gutless one! Where's your spirit gone, man; where's your old fire?" He swung his black stare away from Dion's whitened face to confront Groven again. "I'll hold," he growled, "but I warn ye now—if my friend's mistreated and he does not find the mettle he once had and deal with you himself, I'll spit you like a capon, captain, general, governor or king!"

He whirled and tramped away, still muttering, shaking his head. Dion heard Groven's contemptuous snort as he bent to hoist a box to his shoulder and headed for the storehouse.

God's blood but ye've turned out to be a gutless one! Yes, he had that, and how, and why? It was not fear that made him hold his hand; of that he was certain. Indeed, he had felt more fear when his hand had been quick to his blade than he did now, when this strange reluctance to anger haltered him.

Where was his spirit, his old fire? Gone, and in its stead a serenity that filled the place where fire and spirit had been with peace of mind that endured in spite of all, past understanding.

Whence had come this serenity, then? God-given, or had it been spawned by madness? And how could he dare to think it had come from Heaven? What kind of God would bestow it on a man such as Dion Harvie? What Almighty would consider a gift to a man who hated as he had, who killed as he had, who failed as he had in all places where he should have won through, who could find truth and beauty in the heathen beliefs of the Roanokes, who could look with love and almost reverence on a whore he had married in delirium, a strumpet who carried his child?

So then, if it was impossible that God had given him this peace of mind, it followed that it had come out of madness, that he still was mad.

5

GEORGE HOWE was killed on July twenty-eighth. An undersized, inoffensive man, he was wading in the shallow water at the southern end of Roanoke Island, clad only in short drawers and armed only with the forked stick he used to catch the indolent crabs sloughing their shells in the weeds along the shore, when he was murdered.

It was outright murder; there was no question of that. Since their arrival, the whites had done nothing to offend the Indians; they had been too busy rebuilding the fallen-down houses and barns of Fort Raleigh to even begin to think of any disciplining of the Roanokes. When Howe failed to return home—he had wandered far from the fort to a place where the crabs were thicker and was not missed until past dark—a search party was organized and scattered through the island. It was not until the first light of dawn that he was found, his head bashed in and sixteen arrow wounds in his dead body.

The arrows had been wrenched out of the corpse except one, a long shaft with feathers dyed deep red, that jutted from Howe's throat just under the sagged chin.

"And that," Dion Harvie said as soon as he saw it, "is no Roanoke arrow!"

"What d'ye mean?" John White blazed. "How's one arrow told apart from another? Of course this man was killed by y'r dear friends, the Roanokes!"

"And I say he wasn't," Dion said, stubbornly. "I know enough of Wanchese's tribe to tell they never use a shaft that long and none of their arrows carry red feathers, only black. This is a foreign arrow and George Howe was slain by Indians from another tribe!"

"Now by God's bones," Guy Groven sneered, "we have our Master Harvie defending his lousy heathens even in murder!"

"Ask Manteo," Dion said in a flat voice. "Ask y'r pet if this is his tribe's arrow! If he's honest, he'll say it was fashioned by another tribe and then, mayhap, ye'll believe him if you won't me."

"Have Manteo brought here," White ordered.

The turncoat Roanoke was summoned to the governor's headquarters. He cast one look at Dion and when Harvie saw his stare he knew he had made a mistake. Manteo knew him for Wanchese's tribal brother; Manteo had been at Fort Raleigh when Dion had been taken into the Roanoke tribe and could not help but know that Harvie despised him for what he was. Manteo hated Wanchese; Groven had promised Manteo kingship over the Roanokes when Wanchese was deposed—how could Dion have expected Manteo to tell the truth?

"Have him swear by his gods," he told White before the governor put the question, but even then he knew what the answer would be.

Manteo swore readily by his gods that the red-feathered arrow was a Roanoke shaft. Yes, it was a war arrow, made to kill men and not deer. Of course George Howe had been foully ambushed.

"You see?" Groven asked White. "You see this renegade's the complete liar. I say in chains with him lest he do what you say he tried to do before—warn the savages that we're out to avenge this crime!"

No, not again, Dion's brain shouted. *I'll not be stopped a second time!*

His rapier still swung at his side, more out of habit than for any use until now. It slipped free with all its oldtime fluidity and flickered in front of Groven's handsome face. The captain crossed his arms over his head and cowered against the wall.

"Halt!" he squealed. "Take him, somebody! Jesus!"

Dion's leap carried him to the door of the house White used as his headquarters. A pikeman brought his weapon down, then howled as Harvie's blade spiked his forearm. The pike clattered to the floor while the soldier clutched his arm, whimpering his pain.

Outside, another soldier swung blindly at Dion with his heavy sword. Dion parried the swipe instinctively, thrilling to the jar of his rapier against the heavier steel. He started a *riposte,* then checked it as the other man dropped the point of his blade in suicidal panic. Behind him, Harvie heard the yell and thump of confusion. He plunged into the nearest thicket, brambles tearing at his clothes, and headed west.

The chase was noisy, easily tracked. Dion drifted just ahead of it, moving as quietly as all the half-forgotten training he had gotten while hunting with Wanchese permitted, hiding under the searchers' very eyes when they closed in. And slowly, cautiously, he made his way to the western shore, close to the huge dead oak where the eagles had built their aerie.

The canoe which brought Margery's Indian nurse was hidden cunningly but not invisible to Harvie's eyes, gifted again when they needed to be with Indian sight. He pulled the light, one-man craft to the water, launched it.

The hue and cry of the search was far to the south, close to the place where George Howe had met his death. Dion climbed into the dugout and pushed off.

He was a quarter way to the mainland before the thud of a gun, a harquebus, told him that he had been seen. There was a scattering of shots but Dion did not pause to turn his head; he was far out of range of a harquebus, he knew, and all the boats in which Groven and the others could give chase were on the other side of Roanoke Island. By the time the searchers made their way back to the fort, launched their boats and circled the island after him he would be landed at Dasamonquepeuc.

Wanchese was awaiting him when he beached the canoe. The big Roanoke listened, stony-faced, as Harvie babbled his story.

"—and so they plan to start a war again," Dion panted. "You must take your people back to the west, to Ocanahowan, before they come here."

"We are not cowards to run like Croatoans," Wanchese said, with dignity.

"It is not cowardice to save y'r women and y'r young from being slaughtered," Harvie cried. "I tell you I know this man Groven—given the chance he'll be worse than Lane."

"We did not kill the man Howe," Wanchese said. "That was the work of Pasquiwocs. That was not our arrow."

"Manteo says it was," Dion protested, "and they'll believe

Manteo—they believed him over me and would they be more just to a Roanoke they've already named a murderer? Take your tribe away, I tell you! Take them to the west before the soldiers come!"

Wanchese considered, staring toward the east. Finally, he nodded solemnly, then laid a hand on Dion's shoulder.

"You come with us?" he asked quietly.

"I? I cannot come with you, Wanchese."

"But they"—nodding toward Roanoke Island—"will make you suffer for warning us. Come with us and be safe. You are more one of us than one of them. Be one of us in body as in heart, Pemecolemanmeo. Take Rycko for your wife and—"

He broke off, his deep eyes fixed on Dion. Slowly, reluctantly, he shook his head.

"No," he said, "you cannot do that. You have a wife on the island and she is with child. No, you cannot leave her. I know that."

He stared at the island again, then looked at Harvie, frowning.

"I would go with you to try to get your wife," he said slowly, "but I would do nothing more than be killed and leave my people without a wise chief. The young men who follow me are not ready to be chiefs; they have yet to learn many things. The tribe suffered much when Pemispan and Granganimeo were killed. If I was dead that dog Manteo might get to be chief and that must never happen. No, I cannot go with you to try to get your wife."

He put his hand again on Harvie's shoulder.

"I am sick in my heart about this, Pemec," he said. "I am sick to leave you to go back to them."

"I know, Wanchese. But—but Margery needs me and I can do nothing else."

"Farewell, then, Pemec. We will be watching you."

"Farewell, Wanchese."

The Indian held up his hand, gave Dion Harvie a last, long look, turned and walked up the trail toward the village of Dasamonquepeuc. Harvie started back to the canoe.

"Pemec?"

It was Rycko's quiet voice and as he stopped, still facing the water, there was the whisper of her moccasins on the sand behind him. Her fragrance came to him before there was her soft touch on his arm. He looked down into her wide dark eyes, her face as lovely as it had always been, her red mouth tremulous in an attempted smile.

"Ho, Rycko," he said. "I—I have hoped to see you."

"I had waited for you to come," she said softly. "The island is *taboo* or I would have waited where I did before, in the cove. But I thought—no, I did not expect you, in my heart. Wanchese told me about—the wife you brought back here. And Munipeo, the woman who cares for her, says she is good and kind and beautiful and fitted to be your wife, Pemec. She will give you many sons, Munipeo says."

"She—she is all things fine," Dion faltered. "As you are, Rycko."

Her eyes flashed up to him and dropped again, the long lashes fanning her cheeks.

"I have given you no sons, Pemec," she murmured, "though I have prayed to the gods I would. Aye, even at the very moment my soul kissed yours I remembered to pray. But the gods did not listen."

"Mayhap they did and knew that such a son would never see happiness. For we are of two people still, Rycko, no matter how close we have been together."

The girl considered this. After awhile she nodded.

"It may be so," she said. "Yes, I think the gods did listen and were wiser than I was in saying no." Her eyes came up again. "And now you go back to her, your wife, and those who will hurt you?"

"Yes, Rycko," he said. "I go back."

"And I will never see you again if they kill you."

"They will not kill me."

"Wastomug would have killed you, Pemec, if the red-bearded one, *El Draque,* had not come to save you. He would have hung you by the neck for—the word?—mutiny."

"But John White's no Ralph Lane, Rycko," Dion said with forced cheerfulness, "and he'll not hang me. And Simon Ferdinando's there to stop him somehow if he would. Don't concern yourself over me, Rycko, but keep yourself safe, out of the white men's hands, until this thing is finished and we can meet again."

The Roanoke girl placed both hands on Dion's chest as she moved close to him.

"Put your mouth on mine, Pemec," she breathed, "before you go away. No more than that because it would not be right, but that, I beg you."

Her kiss still burned his lips as Dion pushed the canoe off for the trip back to Roanoke Island.

All things fine, he told himself, *aye, she has been that. She gave me everything and asked nothing in return save a son by me. And if she had had a child what would I think now? Why, I would be proud and think it right, somehow. And it would not mean I'd think any less of Margery or her child. What I feel for Margery is not what I feel for Rycko; they are things wholly apart, yet each is strangely right and therefore like the other.*

Perhaps the people of Fort Raleigh had not expected him to return; perhaps there was confusion back at the fort that slowed the pursuit; perhaps Ferdinando had thrown blocks in the path of the chase; at any rate, Dion made the trip back to the island without seeing another craft and hid the canoe beside the tree with the eagle's nest without a challenge. He slipped through the dense cedars back to the town and crept along a path that brought him to the back of the small house, no more than a hut, that had been given Margery and him. He crouched there, listening. There was a babble coming from the part of town nearest the fort but no danger signs close by.

A wraithlike figure, Dion edged around the side of the house to the door and stepped inside. Margery lay on the low bed under the window; beside her squatted the impassive figure of the Roanoke woman, Munipeo. The squaw turned her flat eyes toward him and arose from her haunches.

"She sleeps," she said quietly in Roanoke. "She does not know of your trouble."

"My thanks a thousand times over," Dion whispered to the Indian, "and get you to your canoe and to Dasamonquepeuc.

Wanchese leads the tribe to Ocanahowan. Hurry, lest they find you here."

"I go," the woman said. Moving noiselessly, she was out the door and away.

Dion tiptoed to the side of the bed and looked down at his wife, Margery Hollis, Lime Street strumpet, gentle-faced Magdalene who would be the mother of his child before many more hours had ticked past. He knelt beside the bed and brushed a kiss across her forehead, a caress so light it barely touched her dream and made her smile.

He sat back on his heels and looked at her, his blue eyes deep. Now, before he handed himself over to whatever White and Groven would do to him, was the time to look at Margery and try to answer all the questions that he had put aside before. If they ever could be answered.

Why, for instance, was Margery so—so *pure* to him? There was nothing he did not know of her life before Burnie had brought her to him; she had neither hidden nor tried to hide anything from him. Their first winter together he had learned and had revelled in all the accomplishments of the flesh with which she had entertained him; there never had been an earthier relationship between a man and a woman. There had never been anything between them then except a mutual lust that had demanded serving.

And during this past winter, although she had changed in her love for him, he had still treated her as the whore she had been, more grossly, in fact, than he had before she avowed her love. His change had come in an insane desire to hurt her and in this he had succeeded only when he mocked her love by sneering at it while he tasted the fruits of it. He had hated her that winter and never known the reason for his hate—maybe it had been because he wanted to destroy all things except hate and had despised her love because it refused to wither under his black mood.

After the ride to Avronbeck Hall, since the blank period of his madness, there had been no hate, no lust, only a wondering respect, amounting to obeisance, in his regard for her. Love, in the real meaning of the word? How could he tell? Affection, certainly, and gratitude for what she had done while he had been helpless in the grip of insanity. Respect for the finer being she had made herself somehow. Admiration for her unselfishness. Homage as the mother of his child. But love—well, was love not all these things; affection, gratitude, respect, admiration, homage?

No. Love was what he had for the Indian girl, Rycko; he knew that now. He had told Ferdinando that he had almost forgotten Rycko but he knew now that he never had, that he never could. The thought of Rycko had kept coming back to him in England, as the memory of Margery had never come to him when he had been in Virginia that winter of 1585 and 1586.

Come with us and be safe, Wanchese had said. *You are more one of us than one of them. Be one of us in body as in heart. Take Rycko for your wife.* And then had stopped because it was impossible. But would to God it had been possible, for Wanchese had been right; he was more a Roanoke at heart than an Englishman.

Still, he did not reproach Margery or the need to come back to Fort Raleigh and face White and Groven's punishment; he accepted the duty with all his newfound serenity. Though the hangman's rope might dangle before him he knew no fear, he found no resentment in the fate that had brought him to this place.

Where was the fire and the spirit Ferdinando had missed? Where was the fierce will gone that had prodded him so relentlessly before? He did not know nor did he expect ever to know where they had vanished; it was enough that all those things had been replaced by an acceptance that somehow was more satisfying than any triumph fire and spirit and fierce will ever had scored, call it gutless or call it godly.

Margery's eyes opened and she gazed at him in utter peace a moment as her smile widened. Pregnancy had treated her well, her unborn child had given her a tranquil loveliness that blended perfectly with the beauty she always had had, softening it, making it more real.

"I've been sleeping," she said peacefully, "and would I could say I've been dreaming of you but I haven't—I don't think I dreamt at all." Her eyes shifted to the patch of sunlight that showed her it was mid-morning and returned to her husband. "Why aren't you at work?" she asked. "Or have they finished the unloading?"

"Something happened," he said. He leaned forward to take her hands in his. "I'll tell you," he went on, "rather than have you hear it from somebody else—I'm in trouble again."

"Trouble? Why then—"

"No, no; lie still, Margery. I'd bid you not worry but I know 'twill be impossible for you not to, but I can ask you to remember the child and keep yourself from fretting overmuch for his sake."

"Dion, what happened?"

Quietly, directly, he told the story of George Howe's murder and of Manteo's lie that the arrow was a Roanoke's, of his escape from White's headquarters and his race to Wanchese with the warning.

"And now I'm come back," he said, "and must leave you to surrender myself to the governor."

"But you—you could have fled with the Indians," she said slowly.

"How could I?" he asked with a light laugh. "First, Wanchese would not be burdened by my going—the Roanokes travel fast and I'd be a drag on them if I went. Next, I've wagered all I own 'gainst Ferdinando that our child will be a girl—he says a boy—and I must be here to collect my fortune when the babe is born."

He bent forward to kiss her again.

"And John White will deal fairly with me," he said. "He's no Ralph Lane, remember. And when I tried to warn Pemispan, White said I did the right thing, so how can he deny that what I've done now is just as right?"

"But what of Guy Groven?" Margery asked. "You know he hates you. He's waited three years for this time, Dion, and—"

"And White's still governor and Groven's under him," Dion

interrupted gently. "And our good friend, Ferdinando, stands by us so it cannot be too bad. I go now, Margery, before they come to get me. You'll be all right alone for a minute, till I send Dame Lawrence to you? I had to tell Munipeo to flee whilst she could."

"Of course I'll be all right," Margery said, her chin raised and her mouth struggling to smile. "And come you back soon and tell me what happened."

"I will," he promised, "or send Simon with a report, if I'm detained."

Her arms were tight about him and he could feel the fear that possessed Margery as he held her for what might be the last time. This, he told himself, was no proper parting if he was to be hanged; there should be tears and wild avowals of undying love instead of this quiet farewell, made under the mask of a confidence that was not there. But this was better, vastly better.

He straightened up from the embrace, bent forward again to kiss her forehead and then turned and walked out the door, not daring to look back. He strode unswervingly down the path to the clearing that marked the town square; he walked toward a crowd of armored men assembled there, Groven in their midst.

A head swung to look at him, eyes stared, somebody yelped an exclamation.

"It's the traitor!" Groven bawled. "Seize him!"

6

"And so," Simon Ferdinando boomed, "I prove I'm right again in all my prophecies. A fine boy, Dion, and born at seven o'clock this morning! Mark the date, August the twentieth, so ye'll not forget the lad's birthday. And Margery's well and hearty; she sends all love and says she will bring the babe to see you when she's up and about. I asked her to let me carry it here but 'twas as though I'd proposed throwing the brat into the fireplace, she was that wrought up to think I'd take an hour-old baby on a short journey."

"Best that the boy sees his father for the first time in some place other than a prison," Dion said wryly. " 'Twould be bound to give him a mighty poor opinion of his sire."

"Bah, he's clever enough to know you shouldn't be here," the Portuguese scowled. "And won't be long—John White's weakening every hour."

"And is Groven?"

"Nay, but who cares about him? He's still raving for the rope but White won't listen. Nay, John White still hears the buzz of the bug I put in his ear—that if you're harmed past this outrage that's put you in gaol, the Roanokes will hear of it and come down with terrible vengeance. Every time White seems to listen to that bastard Groven I find a chance to remind him of what might happen to his new granddaughter if the Roanokes avenge your wrongs. And there again I was right, friend Dion; Ananias Dare's wife birthed a girl-child as I said she would and they've already christened the baby Virginia."

His face fell as he added: "Virginia Dare did beat young Harvie in arriving by two days, curse it! But"—his face brightening again—"ours is the first boy born here! What will you christen him, Dion?"

"Clement, Margery said, if it was a boy."

"A good name, Clement Harvie. God grant that some day, when times change, he'll be a Sir Clement Harvie, eldest son of the fourth Lord Avronbeck."

"God's gullet," Dion laughed, "don't tell me your prophecies extend that far!"

"You think it impossible?" the Portuguese demanded. "Naught's impossible in the matter of titles, I say, when that skunk Manteo can be given one. Lord of Roanoke and Dasamonquepeuc, icod! I tell you, I fair vomited when John White went through the rigamarole of that ceremony a week ago today! A mighty lord is Manteo! Throughout the service he kept peeping over his shoulder as though expectin' Wanchese's axe to comb his hair.

No sooner was the thing done than Lord Manteo went scuttling for the hole he's hiding in."

"And still no word of Wanchese, eh?" Dion asked. He raised a hand to brush a fly from his cheek and chains clanked.

"No," Ferdinando gloomed. "No, but he must be laughing at White, somewhere in the forests, for White's great raid on Dasamonquepeuc. I told you about that, didn't I? You would have enjoyed seeing Groven's face when it happened, Dion. He was so full of mouthy boasting when word came that there were Indians back in Dasamonquepeuc; he waved his sword enough to start a hurricane—and saw to it that his soldiers were well ahead of him when they stormed the village. Oh, he stabbed a few Indians, but not until somebody else had shot them down. And then—oh, 'twas a merry jest!"

"But not for the Croatoans," Dion said soberly.

"No, not for them. But Groven—he was fair stunned when Manteo had to tell him that the Indians he'd conquered were not Roanokes or Pasquiwocs but mere Croatoans, come to Dasamonquepeuc to scavenge the leavings of the Roanokes. Oh, the hurly-burly that came then! John White needs must send a load of presents—that he could not afford, by any means—to the Croatoans with Manteo and humbly beg their pardon for the slight mistake. White was sorely vexed, truly, that Groven's blunder made him spend stores he needed grievously and all to soothe the hurts of the mangy Croatoans."

"He needs stores grievously?"

"Aye, he does," the pilot nodded somberly. " 'Tis the old story of what you've told me happened under Lane—waste of what was here and fatal delay in getting crops into the ground—ah no, Groven would rather hunt for gold. Now the harvest won't come till too late if, indeed, the plantings are not killed by frost. And, of course, there's no trade with the savages, not even with the Croatoans now."

"Then Margery—"

"Is well supplied," Ferdinando said. "I made sure of that, you may be certain. She eats better than John White, though the governor does not know it, and will all winter even if another speck of food is not found in the colony. She protested 'gainst taking the hoard I hid for her but a woman is easily convinced against her will when her child's welfare is mentioned. Aye, Margery's well fixed but—" He frowned thunderously and tugged at the pearl pendant.

"But what?"

"Well," the big Portuguese went on reluctantly, "there's something afoot that I don't like. Groven and some others have started a move to get White to return to England with me, the better to plead with Raleigh for more supplies than Raleigh intends. You know Groven lost that raftload of goods in Trinity Inlet and you know, too, that it was Groven who convinced White that there was too great a risk in the Indies to try to deal with the Spaniards for necessaries. Hence, we came here short of goods and the presents to the Croatoans and all the rest means Raleigh must double the amount of his relief. Groven holds that White's own voice is needed to insure ample returns—and I think Groven but wants White out of the way so he can govern."

Dion looked down at the iron cuffs at his wrists.

"And if White goes—" he started, his voice measured.

"But he won't!" Ferdinando blared. "I'll see to it that he don't. Have no fears there!"

But later, when the pilot had gone, Dion recalled the hint of uncertainty that lay behind Simon's stout declaration. If John White left Virginia before he finally decided Dion's fate, whether he would be kept as a useless prisoner or freed to do menial work under guard, Guy Groven would not hesitate to settle the question.

With a rope.

A week passed in which Dion stayed in chains, visited often by Ferdinando but never by Margery.

"That old woman White," the Portuguese raged, "still dilly-dallies like a granny. Whenever he's at the point of letting you go free, Groven gains his ear again and he says no—not yet. And as for Margery, he says 'tis not fitting that you be given the comforts of a visit from your wife and child—not yet. Not yet, not yet! And though Margery's pining to see you and show you y'r son, she holds on my advice lest some slip-up in a secret visit vex White right into Groven's camp. 'Tis hard but she has strength, that woman!"

Then, on August twenty-seventh, Ferdinando came to the makeshift jail, bowed in defeated gloom. Before he spoke, Dion knew what he had to say.

"'Tis no use, friend Dion," the big Portuguese sighed. "I've used my best arguments and threats to no avail. White sails on the morrow for England and in my vessel. And I—I needs must go or name myself a mutineer in Raleigh's opinion. I have thought of seizing the ship—the seamen will do my bidding quick enough, but—"

"Ye'll not do that, Simon," Harvie said quickly. "No, I'll not have it, come what may."

"Oh well," Ferdinando grimaced, "I may as well be honest with you and say I cast aside the idea at once. I—you did not know it, but Raleigh saved my neck one time and I owe most everything I've made of myself to him. I couldn't serve him that falsely, even for you, Dion."

"Nor would I let you," Harvie added. "Then Groven will take command when White sails?"

Ferdinando nodded heavily.

"Aye," he said, "and White and I have made him promise on stern oaths that you'll not be harmed beyond being kept in chains a bit longer, to 'teach you discipline', as Groven puts it. But—ah, I do not trust the man, even when he swears on his mother's honor."

"Margery—will she be let bring the babe here for me to see?"

"Groven swears that, too, on the same oaths. White wants it done instanter but—well, the governor's in a rush to prepare his leave-taking and there are a thousand things to be done at this last moment so he can't look after your case himself. And when I put in a word he flies off in such a temper, worried as he is about leaving his daughter, Eleanor, and her child, that I thought it best to tiptoe lest he drag poor George Howe's body up out of the grave again and spoil everything."

Dion nodded dully. With White and Ferdinando gone he would

be robbed of two barriers, one weak, one strong, that had stood between him and Guy Groven's revenge for a sword wound suffered more than three years before. He had no illusions about Groven holding to any pledge he gave now; he had slim hope that he would live long past the time the *Admiral's* sails were out of sight beyond Hatorask.

So why had he come back to Fort Raleigh from Dasamonquepeuc, after all? To see Margery for a few brief minutes and to kiss her what could well have been a last goodby? To be on hand to know that his child was born a son? Or was it some silent command from some unseen director that had told him that by coming back to face his fate he could spare wife and son the evil Groven might turn on them in his absence? Yes, that had been the reason, plainly seen now, and instead of applauding himself for having done a worthy thing, Dion felt that he had, at last, been *privileged* to make amends, this way, for a small bit of the unworthy things he had been guilty of in other days.

A saint, y'think y'rself, you smug fool, he grunted inwardly, *when truly ye've fouled every life ye've touched!*

The blackness of the despair he had fended off till now crashed past his guard and swamped him. It was not right, it was not just —he had never meant to deal wickedly with any man or woman he had ever known; he had not done a hundredth part of what other men had done and they walked free and honored and content while he sat in a hole of a prison, reviled and chained as a damned renegade, husband of a strumpet, father of a son conceived in a spiteful embrace.

Gutless—yes, he had been that. A man worthy of holding up his head would have made sure, somehow, that Groven never lived long after the two of them were remet. Or, failing that, he would have joined Wanchese and gone west with the Roanokes, not meekly put his head in the noose and tell Groven to kick away the barrel he stood on. Or at least he might have stood aside and nodded when Manteo mouthed the lie about the Pasquiwoc arrow in Howe's neck. What did it really mean to him whether Manteo or Wanchese led the Roanokes? The Indians were savages as all sane men knew and it did not matter whether one dog or the next ruled the pack. But no, he had to sob and moan and beat his breast about injustice to the Indians and so wind up kicking at the end of Groven's hemp.

To hell with noble principles that led to ruin! Too late to mend things now but there was a satisfaction in denying all the lofty ideals that had brought him here! If there was another chance he'd—

His head dropped to his hands as Ferdinando's touch warmed his shoulder.

"Hold hard, Dion," the Portuguese said huskily. "You own something now I've never seen another man possess—don't let Groven steal it from you."

So that was it. He owned a peace of mind that all Groven planned to do could not destroy and he had come close to throwing it away in the last minute. He raised his eyes to Ferdinando's and nodded.

"I thank you, Simon," he said quietly. His voice firmed. "And when do you sail?"

"Tomorrow, on the tide," the Portuguese said. "I—I'll be back at the first chance, Dion. I vow I'll make the crossing in a fortnight when I come back to Virginia; I'll put wings on my vessel to return."

"I know you will," Harvie nodded. "And—and when you're back, we'll have a—a christening feast for little Clement, I'll be bound."

"I'll bring him presents that'll make his blue eyes bulge."

"And so his eyes are blue?" Dion asked.

"Like yours," the pilot enthused, "and so is his dark hair. He's you in every part of him—but ye'll be seeing him yourself 'ere long and see."

His grin wide and gleaming and the effort that it cost him showed in his dark eyes. His hand came out and Dion grasped it in a hard grip.

"Farewell, Dion Harvie," Ferdinando said, his voice husking again. "Keep your heart high, my dear friend, and know always that I've loved you like a brother—more—for this long time."

He jerked out a laugh. "Icod, I'm solemn as a priest," he laughed, "when this is parting for but a little while. I have to go now—farewell."

He started for the door, then turned.

"I don't know why I must," he said, sheepishly, "but I'd tell ye that—that night you were ambushed near Avronbeck Hall—those were my men, Dion. I hired them to waylay you in hope of the Queen's reward—and kept myself hidden in the plot so Raleigh wouldn't know. I cursed those dolts to hell then but now I thank Christ that they were such bunglers. Forgive me, Dion, for my treachery."

"I do," Harvie nodded, "and thank you for answering that old question in my mind."

"I think I really hoped the plot would fail from the start," Ferdinando offered. "I truly do." He shook his heavy head and grimaced at the floor. "But that was a tidy lot of gold, that reward," he reminisced. He looked at Dion again. "And of course you know that what I said of Raleigh, that he was a false friend of yours, was a lie. Y'see, I thought mayhap ye'd turn y'r trust from Raleigh to me, could I convince ye, and then—"

"But I didn't and the plot didn't win through, so no harm done," Harvie said. "Farewell, Simon Ferdinando."

7

". . . By order of the Governor of the colony of Virginia, *pro tempore,* Captain Guy Groven," the serjeant finished and looked up from the paper he had read. Dion remembered seeing the man before—where was it?—ah yes, he was one of the soldiers who had seized him when he had come back to Fort Raleigh after bidding Margery goodbye; he marked the wart that dotted the man's cheek beside the left nostril.

"And so," the serjeant grunted, "there's need for hurry. The sun's minutes away and Captain Groven wants this done before the town's awake."

"You know it's murder, don't you?" Dion asked evenly. "You know you're hanging a man who's had no trial, who—"

"I care naught for that," the serjeant said hastily. "I but carry out the orders given me."

"And doom an unshriven man," Harvie said, his voice steely. "Even cutthroats are allowed a priest before they don the Tyburn necklace. And they're not smuggled to the gallows in the dark before dawn."

"Y'want an audience?" the wart-marked man asked, his lip curling. "Mayhap you have a speech to give about how the worthy savages were right in killing George Howe."

"I was promised that I'd see my wife and baby," Dion said. "Guy Groven swore on his holiest pledge and now—" He was stricken by a cold dread and his manacled hands came out to clutch the soldier's coat. "My son!" he cried. "Has Groven dealt with him as he's dealing with me?"

"Nay," the soldier said, backing away from Harvie's grasp. "They're well enough. God knows your wife has stirred up enough trouble since White sailed, demanding to be let see you. 'Twas decided necessary to put a guard on y'r house to keep her in, as the public peace requires. And some say—" He fell silent.

"Say what?" Dion demanded. "Tell me, man!"

"Well, there's been wondering how her child, son of a renegade villain such as you, c'ld wax so healthy while Dame Dare's daughter grows pale and listless, though she's had all proper care and prayers beyond the counting. And there is talk of witchcraft that—"

"*Witchcraft!* So that's Groven's next move! May God damn him everlastingly if he harms Margery and my boy! I vow I'll return to—"

"Enough! Take him to the place, men!"

Hands seized Harvie and shoved him out of the windowless hut that had been his prison. Outside, some senseless fury seemed to seize his guards. The length of chain between his ankles let him hobble but no more than that and when jerking hands pulled him along the dark path to the gallows, he sprawled and fell time after time, to be hauled to his feet with a curse and a hammering of blows and kicks. Hands shackled, he could not protect himself against the punches or break his falls; his brain hazed with pain, agony flamed through him, he licked away the blood that trickled from his split lips and smashed nose, he peered ahead through eyes pounded to bleared slits.

In the approach of death, in his suffering, his torment focussed solely on Margery and their son. What was to be dealt him meant nothing; his fear of what Groven would do to his child and Margery wrenched him in agony. Christ had only had all mankind to mourn for on His way to the Cross; Dion had the realization that a just-born child, a woman who had been visited with a strange grace through him, would suffer and die because he had failed them both in all things.

"My God," he groaned, "do You not forsake them!"

The gallows fingered the lightening sky in a clearing close to the creek, west of the settlement. It was a relic of Ralph Lane's Fort Raleigh, never used during that first grim and fruitless winter but still stout enough to hold a kicking wretch until he quieted. It had been raised soon after the fort was finished, a symbol of the white man's Roanoke Island; first, the cannon had been placed to deal properly with the Catholic Spaniard and the heathen Indian, and then the gallows had been built to take care of such of God's anointed who might displease authority.

At the base of the gallows stood Guy Groven, his teeth shining as he smiled at Dion Harvie's misery. As Harvie looked at this man who faced him he wondered dimly at the hate that motivated Groven. There had been the fight at Wenrick's, but was that the sole basis of Groven's bitterness, had that sword thrust served as nourishment to Groven's spleen all these years? Or was there some force beyond that which had cast Groven in this role of implacable malevolence? Did Evil choose its champions as the priests said God chose His saints? And, if so, had Groven been appointed to bring final failure to Dion Harvie?

"And so, Master Harvie," the captain grated through his grin, "I save Her Majesty the trouble of stretching y'r neck and prove myself a most earnest soldier. Ye've hidden from her men a long long time but not from Groven, in the end."

"My wife—my son—" Dion gasped.

"Will get the treatment they both deserve," the captain said mockingly. "Oh aye, they'll get fair justice from me, I vow."

"Fair justice such as you have given me?"

"And what does a renegade deserve?" the captain sneered. "Who'll plead mercy for a man who plots with the Indian dogs to massacre the colony?"

"Plot? Does warning Wanchese to flee sound like a plot to call a massacre?"

Groven thrust his face closer, his lips curled back over his vulpine teeth.

"Y'think we've not discovered what ye've managed to do, even in prison?" he grated. "Oh aye, ye're clever enough in y'r villainy —'twas but by a stroke of good fortune that our sentry stumbled on that Roanoke spy of yours!"

"Spy?"

"Oh, admit y'r plan—it's spoiled, in any case! Admit that the bitch was called here to the island to hide and spy us out for a ripe time for Wanchese to attack! Y'r spy is dead, shot down after she confessed to Manteo why she was here."

"Manteo—I take it that you found a Roanoke hiding on the island and—"

"And dragged her before Manteo who's the only one who talks the gibberish. And Manteo said this woman was y'r spy and—"

"Manteo lied! I swear I know of no plan—"

"Enough! Serjeant! The rope!"

"But I tell ye—"

The noose rasped at his throat and was pulled tight, choking off his words, strangling him. He struggled instinctively and uselessly against the hands that lifted him to the barrelhead where he stood teetering, fighting for breath. Flame seared his lungs, his belly knotted in an agonizing gripe, thunder boomed through his skull, spirals of dazzling colors never seen by man whirled through his eyes into his brain.

Delirium claimed him—or *was* it fantasy? Was that chorused scream an echo from the Pit or was it a Roanoke warcry? Were those shots, those yells, real or fragments of a dream? The hands that gripped him—the fingers that tore loose the rope—were these the hands of a demon of madness or was it truly Wanchese who held him?

Groven—was that really Groven who lay there with the arrow —a *black* feather and not crimson—jutting from his eye?

The whoops, the screams, the smell of burnt corn powder, the despairing wail from the direction of the town, the glare of leaping flames—all these were *real!* And so—

"They are safe, Pemec," Wanchese said, and Dion Harvie nodded before he crumpled into oblivion.

Part 7

1

JOHN WHITE came back to Roanoke Island in 1590. Three years had passed in which England's war with Spain, the battle against Philip's Invincible Armada, had balked every attempt to relieve the colony at Fort Raleigh. Sir Walter himself had finally been forced to abandon his great dream and had sold out his interests in Virginia. White had met a thousand reverses in his efforts to launch an expedition to go to the rescue of his daughter and the other settlers—not knowing that the colony had not survived as such a week beyond his departure from Roanoke Island.

As for Simon Ferdinando, if he tried to raise his own expedition he left no account of his endeavors when he dropped out of sight. White's stern indictment of the Portuguese pilot as a Spanish agent must have stripped Simon of Raleigh's trust finally because the burly, spade-bearded man with the pearl ear pendant never held another position in any project with which Sir Walter was connected.

Raleigh himself, his pinnacle as court favorite won from him by Essex, went into eclipse. He went to Ireland, serving under Sir Richard Grenville and thereafter never regained the honors he had risked for Dion Harvie, though he tried ceaselessly until his days were ended on the block, to which Essex had preceded him.

Finally, and with little hope still alive, White sailed on March twentieth, 1590, with a fleet captained by a John Wattes. The governor of Virginia was little more than a passenger aboard

Wattes' flagship and the flotilla carried no supplies for Fort Raleigh; John White's one hope was that Eleanor Dare and her daughter, Virginia, had somehow survived and could be brought back to England.

Wattes was in no hurry to get to Roanoke Island; his vessels operated in the West Indies, raiding minor Spanish ports, for months before, on August twelfth, they anchored off the northeast end of Croatoan Island. Nobody was put ashore here; for what reason a landing was not made was never known.

On August fifteenth, Wattes's fleet anchored at Hatorask and John White saw a single column of smoke threading its way skyward from the woods that crowned Roanoke Island. It was an encouraging sign and the governor of Virginia fell to his knees in thankful prayer.

Stormy weather prevented a trip from Hatorask to the island for two days and on August seventeenth, when the first attempt was made to run Trinity Inlet, a boat capsized and seven of Wattes's men were drowned. In spite of this accident, White prevailed on Wattes to launch two more smallboats which reached the island after dark and overshot Fort Raleigh by almost a mile.

Dion Harvie, Pemecolemanmeo, saw the Englishmen miss their landing and used flint and steel to light a fire to guide them in.

Dion had been at Onacahowan, far inland, when word was sent him by Wanchese that sails had been sighted approaching Hatorask. The Englishman-turned-Roanoke had loped the trail with effortless ease to Dasamonquepeuc and thence had paddled to Roanoke Island where, by climbing a tree, he saw the Cross of St. George, not the Spanish flag that he had seen before from this same vantage point, flying from the masthead of Wattes's flagship.

So they had returned, the men who meant to civilize this country and make it another England, the champions of a gracious, all-wise Queen and a beneficent, humble Church, the Lanes and the Grovens and Whites and Charles Harvies, the Grenvilles and Walsinghams and Norfolks and Burghleys.

But also, Pemec reasoned, Simon Ferdinando might have returned and if the bull-voiced pilot was part of this expedition he, Dion, wanted to see him and tell him what had happened to Raleigh's colony.

Yes, if Ferdinando had come back he must be told of Wanchese's last-minute rescue, of the savage raid that had cut down every white man except six, himself and five others who somehow had escaped the Indian axe and arrow and had been made prisoners. Ferdinando must know that he, Dion, had saved these men and all the women and children from massacre; he had convinced Wanchese that his revenge did not demand their death. Instead, he would tell Ferdinando, Eleanor Dare and the others had been spared but as captives, which actually meant slaves.

And because the Roanokes abhorred the idea of humans being kept in bondage, believing death a far more merciful fate, these whites had all been handed over to the lowly Croatoans. To have given them to the Pasquiwocs would have meant their immediate torture and death and to have turned them loose to fend for themselves would have meant their slaughter by either the Pasquiwocs or the Chesapeake Bay Indians who, under bloodthirsty Powhatan, were ranging along the northern borders of Roanoke country. So the whites' fate as Croatoan slaves, although never enviable, was the best that could be arranged.

Dion would tell Simon Ferdinando further that he had heard that the Croatoans in turn had traded some of these white slaves to tribes living to the south and west of their island—Wanchese had told him that the shiftless Croatoans had hardly a white man or woman left to trade off. But by starting with the Croatoans the trail of these survivors of the Roanoke massacre could easily be picked up and the Englishmen and women ransomed without too much difficulty.

During the stormy two days while Wattes' ships had tossed at anchor, Dion had taken steps to point the way to Croatoan in the event Simon Ferdinando was not a member of this expedition. For Dion had no intention of showing himself unless Ferdinando—or possibly Raleigh—was there to greet him; he would never make his presence known to John White or any other Englishman. There was no fear of the rope in this; Dion Harvie was now Pemec and Margery was Tettem and their son, Clement, was Granolemanmeo and their people were the Roanoke people and would be for the rest of their days, and their son's days and his son's sons. As a Roanoke, with all his old life put behind him as completely as his madness once had blotted out actuality, Dion Harvie had found happiness and knew that Margery had found as much, and more, than he.

No, he would never go back to "civilization" though he were offered Elizabeth's throne but at the same time he realized he owed his erstwhile countrymen and countrywomen a chance to escape the existence they must regard as torture. And so, on a great oak close to the ruins of Fort Raleigh, he carved the word CROATOAN, to tell the men in the ships off Hatorask where to look, in case this expedition did not include Simon Ferdinando whom he could tell what had happened to Walter Raleigh's lost colony.

One thing he would not be able to tell Ferdinando or any other man would be what happened to Manteo. Even his blood brother, Wanchese, refused to tell him that and Manteo's name was *taboo* among the Indians. Dion could only guess what had befallen the renegade Indian and he did not like to dwell long on the guessing.

He could tell Ferdinando, though, that Rycko was dead, shot down by Groven's men as a spy and by her death bringing Wanchese and his tribe to the island to save Dion. But he would not tell Ferdinando that he still mourned her in the dark, velvety nights when he sat on the white sands of the cove where they used to meet.

Just before dusk on the day that John White embarked in a smallboat for Roanoke Island, Dion began carving a second CROATOAN on a tree nearer the beach where it could not be missed, even if the searchers were too timid to make a landing. Night fell before he had finished more than the letters C R O A and so he put aside the task until the morning. It was during that night that the smallboats reached Roanoke Island and missed their landing and Dion struck a light to guide them.

The boats stood offshore all night, their occupants blowing trumpets and singing English hymns, calling for an answer. Dion did not hear Ferdinando's bellow among the voices and knew the Portuguese was not among the new arrivals—trust Simon to make himself known at the first chance.

To make sure Ferdinando or Raleigh were not there, Pemecolemanmeo stayed on the island until dawn. Then, when he could scan the two boatloads and see only John White to recognize, he edged back into the underbrush and made his way to his canoe on the western shore of the island and paddled back to Dasamonquepeuc.

The carved tree, he told himself, would lead White to the Croatoans and to his daughter and his grandchild. There was no more he had to do. He could go back to his wife and his son and his people now. His other life was finally finished.

L'ENVOI

Dion Harvie was never to know that John White did not go to Croatoan Island although he saw the markings on the trees. History was never to explain why this father and grandfather who had spent three years frantically trying to get back to Virginia would neglect to travel the handful of miles to Croatoan Island to investigate the meaning of Dion's carvings and yet that is what happened.

Some blamed John Wattes for refusing to risk more of his men in a landing on Croatoan. Others said White, unnerved by the desolate scene of Raleigh's lost colony, broke down completely and raved in delirium for days while Wattes set sail for England. Some accounts had it that the fleet actually tried for Croatoan Island and was blown eastward by a gale until it had to make for Plymouth.

Whatever the reason, nether White nor any other Englishman ever found out what happened at Roanoke Island. And although reports of blue-eyed, fair-haired, English-speaking Indians in that part of the New World persisted until as late as 1715, the "civilized" world refused to believe them; they were lies—although what purpose such lies would serve never was explained.

Still, if civilization has officially decreed that the word CROATOAN, carved on a tree on Roanoke Island, meant nothing and all Raleigh's colonists were slain and there really were no blue-eyed Indians and that the speech of the inhabitants of North Carolina's Outer Banks is not almost pure Elizabethan, then it must be so. And the story of Dion Harvie and his Margery and their happiness, therefore, must also be an idle tale.